PRAISE FOR *STILLHOUSE LAKE*

"In this rapid-fire thriller . . . Caine spins a powerful story of maternal love and individual self-realization."

—*Publishers Weekly*

"Amazing."

—*Night Owl Reviews* (Top Pick)

"A chilling thriller . . . *Stillhouse Lake* is a great summer read."

—*Criminal Element*

"*Stillhouse Lake* is a true nail-biter right up to the end."

—*Fresh Fiction*

"Highly entertaining and super intense!"

—*Novel Gossip*

"What a fantastic book!"

—*Seattle Book Review*

T0025827

HEARTBREAK
BAY

OTHER TITLES BY RACHEL CAINE

Stillhouse Lake Series

Bitter Falls
Wolfhunter River
Killman Creek
Stillhouse Lake

The Great Library

Paper and Fire
Ink and Bone
Ash and Quill
Smoke and Iron
Sword and Pen

Weather Warden

Ill Wind
Heat Stroke
Chill Factor
Windfall
Firestorm
Thin Air
Gale Force
Cape Storm
Total Eclipse

Outcast Season

Undone
Unknown

The Honors (with Ann Aguirre)

Honor Among Thieves

Honor Bound

Honor Lost

Stand-Alone Titles

Prince of Shadows

Dead Air (with Gwenda Bond and Carrie Ryan)

HEARTBREAK
BAY

RACHEL
CAINE

THOMAS & MERCER

Text copyright © 2021 by Rachel Caine, LLC
All rights reserved.

Published by Thomas & Mercer, Seattle

www.apub.com

Amazon, the Amazon logo, and Thomas & Mercer are trademarks of Amazon.com, Inc., or its affiliates.

ISBN-13: 9781542093675
ISBN-10: 1542093678

Cover design by Shasti O'Leary Soudant

Printed in the United States of America

*To the amazing Dr. Reese, Dr. Lamont, Dr. Potter, and
especially miracle workers Gracie Rosenberry
and Faith Newsome.
Much love to the amazing Mary Crowley Cancer
Research Center's work into rare cancer.
To Sarah, Lucienne, Tez, and Gemma—always first to
cheer.*

*This book would not be possible without the kind
support of Liz Pearsons, who has always understood
Stillhouse Lake and all its players, and believed in the
impossible.*

*Finally, to my beloved husband, Cat: Thank you.
Always.*

PROLOGUE

There was something eerily hypnotic about driving at night. The wheel felt warm and almost alive under her hands. *She* felt alive, for the first time in a long time. Energy jittered through her veins, anticipation like metal pressing on her tongue—so sharp she could taste it. The night was dark, but in the morning everything, *everything* would be new and wonderful. She could imagine the sunrise washing everything pink and yellow and perfect.

She just had to make it through to the other side. And she could. Morning was within reach, and she was ready.

Thinking of that gave her real peace, for the first time in a long while.

Peace cracked in half when she heard a rustle from the back seat, then a fretful cough, then an intake of breath. She felt a surge of raw, tired fury.

Don't cry, don't you dare cry . . .

The first wail was loud enough to shatter glass, and just an instant later came the out-of-tune chorus of the second child. She felt her whole chest collapse under the weight of sheer, brutal frustration. Her eyes blurred with tears, and she wiped them away as she thought, *It's okay, it's okay, it will all be okay, you know what to do.* She reached out with a trembling hand and switched on the radio, turned it up, and forced herself to keep breathing, breathing as the children shrieked. *Hush, sweeties,* she mouthed, but didn't say because she couldn't be heard anyway, and they wouldn't understand.

Morning was on the way. She tried to imagine the dawn glowing on that black horizon, guiding her into the future. The music would help. It had to help.

She drove into the long, cold tunnel of the night, listening to screams until screams turned to hiccups, then slowly died to fretful, mewling cries, and finally back to silence. She turned the music down and took a left turn from the narrow, lightless road onto another, watching the GPS on her cell phone; it was the only way to navigate out here in the wilderness. Rural Tennessee was as black as the bottom of a well this time of night. No communities to speak of anywhere close; she could just make out a faint glow on her left that would be Norton, most likely. She was up in the sparsely populated foothills—some paranoid compound types hoarding guns, maybe a few old family cabins that hung on by hunting their own food. Nobody to note her passing by.

She'd made this drive a solid, patient routine. Nights and nights and nights like this, always the same schedule. Plenty of rural roads, less-traveled paths. She didn't mind. The girls were always so difficult to settle, all her neighbors knew that. She'd seen them giving her that look, that *can't you keep them kids quiet* look, so many times.

She stared in the rearview mirror at the babies, and felt tears come. Hopeless, helpless, angry tears. *I love my kids. I do. This is for the best.* Tomorrow would be different. Tomorrow, everything would be *right.* She just had to hang on to that.

She coasted the car to a gentle stop and rolled the window down. The sound of frogs hit her first: a chorus so loud it felt like a drill in her ear. The road she was on was paved, but only just, and fraying at the edges into sediment and mud. No way to turn around.

It stank out here, in the pit of the night. Murky water and rot. Not clean, like the lakes. This place was pitted with old, stagnant ponds, rank with algae.

Folks stayed away for a reason.

She sat and hummed tunelessly to herself and listened to the night chorus for the longest time. The girls were quiet, and when she looked in the rearview mirror, she saw their angelic little faces relaxed and calm in sleep.

I should just turn around and forget, she thought. But the truth was, if she did, if she drove on home, she'd be out here again—tomorrow, next week, next month. She knew herself too well to think she was going to change that much. The flutter in her stomach, the itch to move on . . . that was so strong now it was just unbearable. Only the driving had helped these past few weeks.

It wouldn't help much longer.

The flash of headlights in the distance caught her by surprise, and she almost gasped. Then she sighed in relief, because it meant the waiting was done. Now she felt an upswell of excitement, of promise, of morning on the horizon.

"It's going to be all right," she sang to her babies. They barely shifted in their sleep. "Momma's going to take care of everything."

She just had to choose to be strong.

1

GWEN

It all starts so sweetly, because on Friday night, the adoption papers come through.

Sam Cade, my lover, my partner, is now officially the father of my two children, Lanny and Connor Proctor. And when the court documents arrive, we sit down with the kids, and we all eat cake and cry and hug, and there is so much love, *so much*, that it fills me to bursting. And the whole weekend seems wonderful. Better than ever.

But I wake up in the dark predawn hours of Monday with a pounding heart and the instant, heavy conviction that something is wrong. There's a faint, bloody taste in the back of my throat, the residue of a nightmare that slips into fog before I can remember it.

Except for the whisper, the last soft word. *Gina.* My old name, dead to me now because Gina Royal, the ex of a serial killer, is a memory, a ghost. And I know that dream voice so well that I feel a rush of adrenaline flood my veins. I have to tell myself that it isn't real, can't be real, that my ex-husband, Melvin Royal, is dead and gone and rotting in the ground. But my body doesn't care about logic. It just reacts to him in ways that I can't control . . . even if he's just a product of my haunted imagination.

I know why he's haunting me. He doesn't like being replaced in the lives of his children. But Melvin Royal, monster, doesn't deserve to be remembered at all.

Burn in hell, Melvin.

I breathe until my pulse slows, the taste goes away, the adrenaline shakes subside.

Finally, I glance at the clock. It's 4:00 a.m. I turn slightly and feel Sam's warmth next to me; my lover isn't getting up yet, and he's gently snoring. Undisturbed. I try curling into him, our bodies fitting together like puzzle pieces. It ought to bring me some kind of peace, take me back to dreamland.

But I feel a restless prickle of hair at the back of my neck. The nightmare is gone, but something's still not right. I've learned to pay attention to primal instincts. They've saved my life more than once.

I slide out of bed without waking him—or so I think, until I'm reaching for the closed bedroom door. Sam's voice, when it comes, is completely alert. "Is it the kids?"

"I don't know," I tell him. "I'm just checking. Probably nothing." I don't want to tell him about the dream. Melvin's a shadow that always lies between us, for good reason. And the dream has nothing to do with my current anxiety.

"Well, I probably could use a glass of water anyway," he says in a no-big-deal tone. He's already up, shoving feet into shoes. I've done it, too—reflex, always ready to run. It's spring, but early morning's still chilly; I feel the cool air on my bare legs as I swing open the bedroom door.

I'm instantly disoriented. This isn't my hallway. It's too wide, and the carpet's the wrong color. I feel wildly out of time and place, and then it all steadies around me. I'm remembering the old house, the one on Stillhouse Lake. We've moved. The lake house, currently rented out, is on the market but hopefully will sell in the next couple of months.

We're in Knoxville now. A new house. New, friendly neighbors. Good schools. Everything is fine.

Except the insistent pull at the back of my neck tells me it's not.

Gina, Melvin's whisper says from the back of my mind. *You can run all you want. But you can never run far enough.*

You're dead, I tell him. *That's far enough.*

The hallway's dark, just night-lights along the baseboard to illuminate the way. Connor's room is first on the right from ours; I ease his door open a crack and see that my son is not asleep. He's sitting up, staring into the darkness. He turns, and his face is pale. "Did you hear it?" he asks me in a low whisper. He's not my little boy anymore, except in moments like this; he's got the growth of fifteen. I still want to take him in my arms and rock him, but I don't. I'm starting to realize how difficult it is that even my youngest isn't a baby anymore. That I have to let him grow up.

"It's okay," I tell him. Sam's behind me in the doorway. "We've got this. You know the plan?"

He nods. He does. Everybody in this house knows the plan.

I close his door, and I hear him get up and throw the interior deadbolt I installed for safety. *Good.* Step one: delay an intruder from getting into his room. Step two: if the all clear doesn't come within a few minutes, hit the silent-alarm button that signals an alert straight to the Knoxville police. Step three: Get out through his bedroom window, run for help. Don't stop for anyone or anything.

We all know the plan because there's always a chance we'll have to use it.

I go to the bathroom. It's dark, but I check the window anyway. Firmly closed and locked and too small for most intruders to slip through. Then I continue to my daughter's bedroom. It's also dark, but when I open it up, I catch a whiff of fresh, damp outside air. Her window's closed, but it hasn't been for long.

Dammit.

I flip on the light, and Lanny—Atlanta, but no one except teachers uses her full name—groans and turns over to glare at me. She's still wearing club makeup—dark glitter around her striking eyes, painted silver stars on her cheeks. She's dyed her hair into a shimmering rainbow of colors. "What?" she snaps, and groans into her pillow. *"Mom!"*

I have to swallow a volcanic explosion of frustration and anger and fear. "Where were you?"

"Nowhere."

"Lanny. You obviously just came in. You left your window out of the alarm circuit, *again.* Do you know what kind of danger you're exposing your little brother to when you do that?" Sometimes, that appeal works.

Not tonight. She rolls up in her covers and throws the pillow over her head. "Would you just leave me alone? It was a good day, why do you have to ruin everything?"

My daughter is seventeen-going-on-thirty, and there's not a lot I can do about it. She knows it's not safe out there. She's determined not to care, or to prove that she can handle whatever comes at her. It terrifies me. It also exhilarates me that my child is so *strong*, when fear of losing her isn't tearing me apart. But she's not an adult yet, and I know I have to find a way to keep her in line for another year until she can freely make her own choices. Her own ghastly mistakes that I can't prevent, and consequences I can't save her from. That's the hell of being who we are: the normal stumbles of most girls her age are different for the child of Melvin Royal. Stakes are always, always higher.

I want to roll my children in Bubble Wrap and set them safely on a shelf and never, *never* let the world chip and crack them. But they're not made of porcelain, and no matter how strong that protective desire might be, I have to fight it. I have to relax my grip, not tighten it.

I can yell at her, but I've tried that before. Lanny, like me, is stubborn. I'll have to be smarter, not louder. I'm acutely afraid that my independent, brave, smart, sometimes reckless daughter might just . . . leave. Run away. And on her own, she'll be unprotected.

I need to find a way to keep her with us just a little while longer. I know I have to face losing her to the world, whatever danger that brings.

But not yet.

"We'll talk later," I say. She groans again, this time in rejection of the whole idea. I shut the door and leave her without another word. When I turn, Sam's watching me with level, calm intensity, and when I sigh, he just shakes his head. He understands. Better than I have any right to expect.

"Do you think she was out with Vee?" he asks me.

"Probably," I tell him. Vee—Vera Crockett, late of the rotten little town of Wolfhunter, Tennessee—became our responsibility not long ago, but Vee has never let anyone rule her for long. After just a few weeks living with us here in Knoxville, she pushed for emancipated-minor status; thing is, she had it anyway because she's never obeyed anyone's rules, and if I hadn't helped her get it legally, she'd have just taken off and lived rough. Again. So we helped, and at least it ensured that Legally Emancipated Vee stayed relatively close in case of trouble.

Vee's a girl with a lot of damage, but I do have faith in her. She's not broken. At least not any more than the rest of us. And it's exactly right for Vee—the same age as my daughter—to have talked Lanny into sneaking out and clubbing, against strict house rules.

"Maybe I should take it out on Vee," I say. "Without her, Lanny wouldn't be taking these kinds of risks."

"Look in the mirror and tell me where she gets her risk-taking gene again?"

"Well, Vee's enabling her."

"I'm not saying what they get up to is safe, but at least we know that Vee's a survivor. She'll fight like hell to protect Lanny. You know that. And you're going to have to let Lanny live her life, eventually."

I do. That's the hell of it.

I knock the all clear on Connor's door, and Sam and I settle on the couch in the living room. I feel rather than hear his long sigh. "Girls," he says. "God, I love them, and at the same time I have no idea what to do at times like this. Is that stupid?"

"Normal," I say, and lean into his embrace. "Girls are tough at this age. Regretting signing those papers already?"

"Never. Not for a second." He moves hair back from my forehead, a gentle touch I would have flinched away from a few years ago. But now, it soothes something inside me. "Were you that tough at her age?"

I have to laugh a little. Bitterly. "I was a good little rule-follower with strict churchgoing parents. I didn't even own a pair of blue jeans. No drinking, no drugs, no boyfriend, no clubs." I'd hit eighteen—or more accurately, eighteen had hit me—like a runaway bus. I'd been utterly unprepared for the charm onslaught of a controlling older man who targeted me the way a lion targets a slow gazelle. Melvin Royal had been the ideal suitor, according to my parents. He'd played the role to perfection because he knew exactly what he wanted: a captive child-wife he could isolate and train as he wanted her to be.

And that's who I became. I'd worked so hard to lose any semblance of who I was, who I could be, and became exactly what Melvin Royal required. I'd thought that was happiness.

Until it all collapsed in such horror. Then I had to find out who I really was. What I could really do.

Sam kisses my temple, and I blindly turn toward him until our lips meet. I don't like thinking about my earlier life. Melvin's whisper is always there, far too close. The kiss turns deeper, sweeter, and I focus on it to try to push away the memories.

Until he breaks it with a regretful sigh and leans his forehead against mine. "I need sleep," he tells me. "Sorry. Early lesson in a few hours."

"I know," I say. He's working currently as a flight instructor, teaching private clients on small aircraft, but he's also taking classes of his own and getting recertified on commercial jets. Busy man, but he's here, against all the odds. And I'm no longer afraid to say that I love him.

Like everyone in our house, the two of us are damaged. He's the brother of a serial killer's victim. I was a serial killer's wife. Our traumas hit head-on the day a drunk driver crashed into the house I shared with Melvin Royal, and that accident uncovered not just Sam's sister's body but a path of horror that stretched out for years.

That crash made wreckage of both our lives, but in very different ways.

We've come to terms with the legacy of Melvin Royal from both sides, and built a relationship over that dark, angry scar. It still bleeds, sometimes. And it always, always aches.

"Go back to sleep," I tell him, and kiss him again. It's regretful, but sweetened with the promise of a future. He hugs me and slips back to bed.

I'm too restless to try to rest, tempting as it is; I'd only toss and turn and disturb him. I head quietly back to our office. Benefit of a new house: more room. Sam's got his desk, I have mine, and as I shut the door and turn on the lights, it's another déjà vu moment: my battered old desk, my old filing cabinets, a clean and different room wrapped around them.

I've mounted pictures on the walls. Some are of places, some are of people. My kids and Sam, surely. My very select group of friends in happy times when Sam and I barbecued a couple of years back. All normal, at first glance.

Second glance, every picture means more. The east wall is my favorite. That beautiful, striking piece of art is the handiwork of a terrified young woman named Arden Miller we came across while hunting my ex. She's now safe and living under a new identity; I check on her from time to time as her artist's star rises. Like Sam, she came out of a dark place and is finding her light.

Next to that picture is a photo of two young women dressed in casual shorts and T-shirts with their arms around each other—normal as can be. When I first saw them, they'd been captives in a locked basement in Wolfhunter, broken and terrified—a mystery I never should have taken on, but that had launched me into the idea of finding missing people as a private investigator. The two women sent me that snapshot, no note, no location, but it reminds me that they've found their own safety now.

I keep only pictures of successes on this wall. Good memories. Even Vee has a place there on the end, arm around my daughter while they both flip off the camera. Vee is a success too. She survived Wolfhunter.

Not everyone did. The west wall, the one I keep in shadow, has other photos. That view of Stillhouse Lake reminds me that people died there as part of my ex-husband's plot. The apparently peaceful photo of a cemetery is really a photo of Melvin Royal's cheap, anonymously numbered tombstone in the far distance; it reminds me he's dead and gone. I need to remember my failures as much as my successes; they teach me to think harder about the risks I'm taking. Because not all those risks are mine.

I know it's wrong to keep score but it's the only way I can make sense of things these days.

Out of habit, the first thing I do at my desk is check on my ever-present internet trolls. I have a list, and I run the searches to see what they're posting. Lately things have died down a little—other outrages for them to scream about, other people for them to torment, guilty or not. But as the ex-wife of serial killer Melvin Royal, I will never be off that list of easy targets to hit, and sure enough, I see one of my most persistent trolls is back agitating for a reinvestigation of my "involvement" in Melvin's crimes.

Being married to a serial killer is, in a lot of people's eyes, proof enough that there must be something very wrong with me. But this guy isn't about justice. He just likes hurting people . . . but at a distance, from safely behind his computer. Nothing new here.

I check work emails. I have a few boring background checks to do, but that can wait until later. The investigative company I work for—mostly remotely—does a fair amount of standard corporate busywork, vetting potential executives for high-profile positions. It's still surprising to me how many of those turn out bad in the end. It's almost like rising to the highest levels of power comes with a side order of sociopathy—who could have seen *that* coming? And if they have enough money and power, they rarely have to face any meaningful retribution for the lives they've ruined.

I'm not neutral on the subject.

When my phone buzzes ten minutes later, it sends my pulse racing so fast I feel it in my temples. Immediate panic reaction, just like waking up from the dream earlier. I immediately think of the people I love, and who could be calling at this hour . . . and why.

Caller ID shows it's my best friend from Stillhouse Lake, Kezia Claremont. She's a police detective, one of just two that the tiny town of Norton employs. "Kez?" I blurt out the second I have the phone to my ear. "What's wrong? Is it your dad?"

"Nothing like that," she says. "Sorry. Did I wake you?"

I swallow the panic and manage a hollow laugh. "Not remotely. I've been up the better part of an hour already. Bad dreams and a kid who doesn't believe in curfew."

"I had a feeling you'd be awake," she says. There's no humor in her voice; I don't think I've heard her this grim in quite a while. "I caught a case. Now I'm out here in the middle of goddamn nowhere in the dark and it's just . . . it's bad."

Kez has rarely shown me soft spots or vulnerabilities. It worries me to hear a tremble in her voice.

"What's going on?" I lean my elbows on the desk, lean into the conversation. I hear her take in a deep breath on the other end.

"First glance, it seemed nothing much. Accident, most likely. But not anymore." She doesn't want to tell me. I feel that tug on the hair at the back of my neck again, and a cold chill comes with it.

"Prester isn't there?" Detective Prester is her partner, a good man, steady, with the eternal eyes of a cop who's seen it all. Twenty-five years her senior at least.

"No," she says. "I'm trying to let him rest; the old man hasn't been looking too well lately. It's just me and a coroner out here. And a pretty useless sheriff's deputy."

"You need some company?"

"I can't ask you to do that."

"You didn't ask," I tell her. "But I'm on the way."

2

GWEN

Eerie. It's the first word that comes to me as I top the rise on the no-name back road and see mist coming off the pond, curling and twisting like a living thing. The whole scene is painted in the red-and-blue light bars of the vehicles assembled: a county sheriff's cruiser, Kezia's unmarked car, and a coroner's van that looks as if it might date back to the 1970s, at least. I roll to a stop behind Kezia's car. This place is narrow, a barely passable road into the dark, and it occurs to me that the more cars are here, the harder it will be for any of us to get out. But the important thing right now is the haunted quality in Kez's voice. She called. I had to come. She's shown up for me, more than once, when I needed help. Especially when my kids were in real danger. Kez's quiet support means the world to me, and if I can repay that, even in a small way . . . I will.

I park and get out. The early-morning chill gnaws at me, and I zip up the fleece jacket I put on and raise the hood. I don't normally mind the cold so much, but now? It just adds to the surreal feeling of dread. There's something very, very wrong here. Maybe it's the darkness, the mist, the pervasive smell of mildew and rotten, stagnant water. This isn't close to Stillhouse Lake, but it isn't far away, either; it occurs to me, as I try to fit the geography together, that I couldn't be more than five miles from the compound that the Belldene family calls home. And I have to suppress a real shiver. The Belldenes and I have a truce, but that truce is very contingent on me *not* being up in their business, or bringing more attention to the area where they make their home and run their illegal drug trade.

I'd rather not open that hopefully closed chapter of my life again. But I can't shake the feeling of being watched from those dark trees, and it's deeply disturbing.

Kezia meets me before the lone county officer—lounging in his cruiser—even spots me. We hug briefly, and that's a rare concession from her in a professional setting. It's over so fast I don't think anyone else sees. I spot the strain in her too-composed face when she draws back. The coroner is setting up some portable work lights, and we both flinch a little as they blaze on, casting a milk-white clarity over what this place is.

Just a pond, I think. But I know it isn't.

"What happened?" I ask her.

She gives me a sharply professional timeline. "County got a call from someone who said they thought they saw something suspicious happening out here. Didn't leave a name. Deputy Dawg over there didn't see anything special, but then he happened to park here to take a leak. That's when he saw the car."

I look around. "What car?"

She points to the pond, the one with mist twisting on the surface. I send her a questioning glance, then step up on the rise just enough to see what the work lights are illuminating. The water is dirty green, verdigris with a ground of rust, but it can't conceal the car under the water. It smells of mold and algae and a reek of dead fish.

I hear a sneeze from the cruiser and see the deputy wrapping a blanket around his shoulders. It clicks with me that the man looks wet, miserable, and stained from the water. He went in. Looking for survivors. But there's no ambulance here, just the coroner's van driven by a young African American man who's suiting up in crime scene coveralls. Nobody's in a hurry.

"So there is a body inside?" I guess.

"Two," Kezia says. She casts a look at the deputy. "He went in on the chance someone was alive. They weren't."

"Two." Well, that's bad but she's seen worse; it's rural out here, and prime meth territory. Mostly, I've been thinking on this long, dark drive about why she's called *me*. "Kez . . . does this have something to do with . . . with me, somehow? Or Melvin?" It's my worst nightmare, being dragged kicking and screaming back into the spotlight, along with my family. She knows that.

"No," she says. "Nothing like that. Sorry, I should've said on the phone. I just . . . there are some aspects to this that I think you might be able to help me with. Unofficially."

That seems wrong to me. Kez is many things, but when it comes to investigations, she is generally pretty by-the-book. "Okay. So . . . why do you think you need unofficial help?"

"Because it's bad. Bad as it gets." She takes a deep breath. "Two little girls still strapped in their car seats in the back. Maybe a year old, I don't know. Twins, probably."

She says it calmly enough, but I know she isn't calm at all. I feel it like a visceral spike that goes right into my lower abdomen, and I look wordlessly at the car again. I can't see the bodies. Thank God. Finally, I say, "But no sign of the driver?"

"No sign of anybody. They were just *babies*." Her voice shudders on that last word, but doesn't break. If anything, it hardens. Her eyes take on a shine like metal, and she doesn't blink. "I want this asshole. Bad."

It's hard to think past the coldness of the moment, the oppressive atmosphere of this place. When I blink, I imagine I see drowned babies in that car, and I feel sick. The cold, wet stench of the pond makes me dizzy. "You think one of the parents . . . ?"

"That's the thing. I just don't know. Could be the driver had car trouble and got abducted, then the kidnapper pushed the car into the pond to conceal it. Might not have ever seen the kids." She sighs, and I hear the frustration. The anger. "I'm just guessing. We have to evaluate all the evidence up here. It's pretty clear where the car went in; forensics will tell us whether it was pushed in or driven."

I clear my throat of the taste of this place. "It could be that the driver—mom, maybe—made it out but couldn't get to her kids. She could be injured, wandering around in these woods."

"Could be, but it's not likely. Deputy Dawg left one hell of a mess coming up out of that water; he swears that bank was undisturbed when he went in. Nobody crawled up out of there without leaving a trail."

I hate having that possibility closed off, and I can see she does too. If the mother were wounded and wandering, it would have been an accident. A tragedy, yes. But this makes it so much worse. Sinister and terrifying.

"You calling in state?" I ask.

"Have to. But I'm going to try to make it my case. This pond is just inside Stillhouse Lake boundaries."

"Half the pond," the sheriff's deputy says from where he's shivering in his car. I wouldn't like to get the look she gives him. "Other half is county."

"Car's in my half," she says. "I'll work with county and state. But I *want* this."

I nod. I still don't know why I'm here, not really. I'm a private investigator, not a cop. I'm a friend, yeah, but the Tennessee Bureau of Investigation won't take that for much. So I say, very gently, "Kez? Did you know them?" It's the only thing I can think of that would make her this . . . invested. But she shakes her head. "Then why . . ."

She doesn't want to tell me, and it takes her a long moment to find the words. "Javier and I have been talking about having kids for a few months now," she says. "Just took the test yesterday, and . . ." She lifts one hand, palm up, and her smile has an edge of sadness. "Turns out I'm pregnant. When I got this call, I was happier than I've ever been, and now, seeing this . . . I don't know, Gwen. I just know I can't let this go. I can't."

I take her hand, though I don't think that was what she was offering, and her fingers lock around mine.

She takes in a sudden breath. "I haven't even been able to tell Javi yet. I didn't want to just send an email. Our scheduled call's coming up in a little while. God. I'll probably still be here. With this."

I can't imagine the chaos of emotion she's feeling right now. I try to put all the compassion I feel into my voice. "Is there something you need me to do? Off the books."

"We're going to be chasing up the owner of this car," she says. "But I need a name and address for the 911 caller who called in the tip. Our system's so old it's practically antique. I know you've got much better tech to put on it." She takes out her phone and types, and in a few seconds I feel my own phone vibrate. "I just sent you the full recording and data we got. The caller ID didn't register a name, just a number and general location. I'm guessing it was a pay-as-you-go."

"I can check," I tell her. "You're thinking if the person who called was out here, they saw more than they said?"

"Or it was the killer himself. Sometimes they do that. Play games."

I shudder, a fine little contraction of my insides, because she's right. Melvin Royal was a game player; it amused him to no end to taunt the police with clues that led nowhere. But mostly what makes me uneasy is the mental image of someone—someone who is just a shadow right now—making that call, enjoying his moment, while the mother of two murdered children struggles in the back of his car, or his trunk. It's horrible, but I'd rather think of her as abducted and endangered than complicit.

The coroner comes over, and Kez straightens up. Visibly putting on her professional demeanor. I don't know if he notices. "We're ready to drag the car out, Detective. I've got all the pictures, including the bank on all sides," he says. "And we need room on the road to preserve and sort evidence, whatever the water's left us. Going to have to move all these cars."

Kezia nods. "Tow truck's on the way. How long do you think the car's been down there?"

"I'll tell you once we get the bodies out, but not long. Couple of hours, maybe. Cold night. That's good, but the faster we can get the victims out of the water, the better."

I realize that my vehicle is the last-in-first-out piece of the traffic puzzle; they'll need me gone to squeeze the tow truck into position. "Kez, I'll do whatever I can," I promise her. I'm still a step removed from this horror; I haven't seen the bodies. I desperately don't want to get closer, because dead children hold a special kind of trauma, of heartbreak. A heavy weight of responsibility for those who bear witness. "Call me later?"

She just nods. Her attention is back on the pond. The car. The babies hidden from view.

I imagine myself in her shoes: newly pregnant, with a boyfriend deployed on reserve duty. Facing this horror. I would have done anything for Kez before coming here, but now . . . now I'll do anything and *everything*.

Because I know she will give this her whole heart and soul.

I back out carefully; it's nerve-racking on the narrow gravel road, and I find myself holding my breath and praying I don't put a tire in a ditch. It feels like relief when I spot a dirt side road, and I quickly three-point a turn so I have headlights to illuminate the way out.

Behind me, the pulsing red-blue glow of the flashers looks like the start of a forest fire, something that will consume everything near it.

Who could do this?

Why?

Like Kez, I want to know.

Whether the mother of those children is abducted or a killer, she still needs to be found.

3

KEZIA

The tow truck takes its sweet time getting here, but it finally arrives. I hate the sound of it, the shrill beep as the muddy old wrecker backs up. I know it doesn't make any damn sense, but I wish it were a clean truck. This one is caked in weeks of filth. The driver of the truck is a tired-looking, big white man with a greasy trucker hat on, and he gives Deputy Dawg a hearty hey, but completely ignores me and Winston, the coroner. "What you want me to do?" he asks the deputy, who looks over at me. I step up.

"We need to get that car out of the pond," I tell him, as if that isn't completely obvious. "Carefully as possible. It's evidence in a crime."

He doesn't like getting orders from me. Too bad. I hold his stare until he nods and looks away. "Gonna take a while," he says. "Hope you like the cold. I damn sure don't." He pulls out a pair of hip waders from an equipment box on his rig and jams them on. "Could've waited for goddamn morning. Gonna need that car moved off down the road, far as possible." He points to my unmarked sedan. I've already moved it to what I thought was a safe distance.

"It's mine," I say. "I'll get it out of the way."

"Well *thank you*, Officer," he says. There's a lot of sass in that, and I'm tempted to respond. I don't. The South has never been friendly to my particular shade of folks, and bad things happen out here in the dark. I'm wearing a badge and a gun and I still feel it, like an ache in your bones when the weather shifts.

Last thing I need to do is start something. I need to focus on what's important: those two little babies, and getting them justice. Ignoring another Klan-adjacent asshole is just part of the rural landscape.

I realize that I'm not being completely rational about this. That I'm prickly in all the wrong ways, noticing things too much and giving the normal way too much power over me. I don't know if that's hormones, or just awareness of the world I'm bringing a little miracle of a child into. Our child will be loved, at least. But safety is a long way off.

I move my car and drive it to the side road I spotted on the way in; I park it and leave the portable red strobe light on top, in case someone comes barreling down from up-mountain. I walk back. The tow truck operator, cursing under his breath, has already waded into the pond. "Gonna get that brain-eating amoeba shit being in here," he says. I don't tell him that he wouldn't notice much of a change. Even if I don't care for the man, he does seem to know his business; he attaches the chains, grimacing when he has to crouch down and immerse himself in the pond. He curses as devoutly as most people pray. He scrambles up the bank, and the deputy offers him a hand when he slips. We'll have to document that shit, too, but there's no help for it. The driver gets a dirty towel from his truck and dries himself off, not that it helps the green gunk clinging to him. He gets to the controls and starts the work.

He's good at this. He balances the slow, careful drag against the weight of both car and water. Gears grind. I grit my teeth and have to bite the urge to tell him, *Treat that car like your own babies are in there.* I don't even know what that would mean to him. I want some damn reverence in this nasty process.

My cell phone buzzes. I grab for it and check; it's Javier. I let out a little sigh of relief as I accept the call, and then feel the weight of this place crush that relief flat. "Hey, Javi. I love you."

Javier Esparza's warm baritone voice glides through me like waves of summer heat, so welcome right now in this cold place. He sounds husky. "I love you too. You okay?"

It's in my voice, the creeping dread. Must have been for him to ask. I make an effort to shove it away. "Yes," I say. It sounds convincing. "Is it late for you right now, or early?" I don't know where he's deployed for his weeks of Marine Corps reserve training; I often don't. Safer for him that way. He's in the hands of the marines right now. They could have taken him anywhere.

"Querida, where I am, it's late morning already. I forgot it would be so early, but this is my slot. We don't get a lot of choices." He's been gone only a few days, and I already miss him so bad I feel he's been gone a year. "Everything okay there? You sound like you're outside."

"I'm on a case," I say. "I—" *Tell him.* But I'm weirdly reluctant now that he's on the phone. I feel fragile and out of control and he feels so very far away. I glance at the deputy, who's taken shelter again in his cruiser with the heater running. The coroner, standing by. I take a couple of steps away as the tow truck cranks gears again, metal on metal. My gaze fixes on the slow emergence of the car from the pond. The back bumper breaks the surface, and the roof of the car. Ripples flow sluggishly. "I need to tell you something," I say. I walk off a little bit, farther from the noise, farther from the ears. "I'm not sure it's the right time, but . . . I don't want to wait. Javier . . . we're pregnant."

The time lag feels like it has extra weight this time. Like he's speechless, not just far away. "Wait, what? We're—Kez! Oh my God!" The delight in his voice fills me up, drives away the cold and the desolation. I feel it like I'm standing in sudden sunlight. "Kez, baby. We're going to have a baby." His voice goes shaky on that last bit. Big strong marine, reduced nearly to tears. "You okay? Really? Damn, I wish I was there. I wish I could just *be there*."

"You will be," I tell him. "I'm okay. So's the baby. I'm setting up a doctor's appointment in the next couple of days. I'll send the sonogram to your phone so you can see it when you get to turn it on again." For now, his phone is off. Safety reasons, again.

"Kez." He sounds more somber now. "You don't sound that happy. Are you? Happy?"

"Very," I say, and I hear the emotion in the single word. "I want this so much. It's just . . . it's a bad one, this case. It's hard to be completely happy right now like I should."

"Sweetheart. I'm sorry. You do what you gotta do, Kez. I love you. Always."

"I love you too." I let the silence run a bit, warm and sweet, then see the tow truck's finally got the right tension, and the back wheels of the car are starting to come up the slippery side of the pond. "Be safe, Javi. For me and the baby."

"*You* be safe too. Get some rest if you can—" The connection drops in the middle of the last word. I'm used to that; communications from some of the places he goes are difficult. I'm just lucky he was able to connect at all.

The predawn morning is colder with him gone. I exhale slowly, trying to avoid that ghostly puff of mist, and watch the tires as they roll up the bank. The sedan is finally out of the water. The tow truck driver is better than we probably deserve to have, out here at this hour. He manages to get it completely out, on the road, and then unhooks and backs his rig away. "You want me to wait?" he asks. Not me, of course. The deputy.

"Please," I say. "If you don't mind."

He shrugs. "They pay me by the hour."

Water cascades from open windows and runs in streams from the door seals. All four doors are shut. I force myself not to look in the back

24

as Winston adjusts the lights around the new site, and I focus on the exterior. It's not a new car, but it looks well kept. No damage. It's a pale beige, a color most people avoid these days, but maybe I'm unkind—maybe it's more of a light gold. Hard to tell in the work lights, which are harsh for a reason.

The deputy and coroner both look at me. I step up and help Winston unroll a clean blue tarp that we position on the driver's side so it'll catch anything that comes out; he gives me paper foot covers I snap on over my shoes. I glove up and approach the leaking bucket that was once a vehicle.

I lean in the open window to take a look at the seats. There's still at least a couple of feet of murky water trapped inside.

"Help me with the mesh trap," the coroner says, and I hold my end of the fine net; he rolls it under the car, holds his side, and uses a gloved hand to carefully pop the passenger side door open as I open the driver's side. Swamp comes out in a firehose gush, but is quickly down to a muttering trickle. He pulls the net to his side carefully to preserve any potential evidence that will have been trapped in it, and takes it off to the side to go pick out anything that might decompose if left damp: paper, particularly. I move the work lights so they shine on the interior of the car. I still don't look in the back, though it pulls at me like a magnet; I can see the unfocused pallid forms out of the corner of my eye, but I know that once I look at them directly, I won't be able to look anywhere else.

I focus on the front.

The seat's pulled up, which means a shorter person was driving. On the passenger-side floorboard, drowning in muck, is a woman's brown purse. It's a hobo-style, shapeless thing that seems stuffed. I mark and photograph the bag in situ and put it up on the seat. This doesn't look good at all. No driver, no mom, purse left behind. My instincts immediately bend toward abduction.

I carefully open the bag, and though the contents are wet they're not completely saturated, which gives me a good guess how long it's been in the water. I tease out a wallet and flip it open. "Sheryl Lansdowne," I say out loud, though why it would matter to anyone else in earshot I don't know. I lay the wallet out and take a photo of the driver's license. Sheryl's twenty-seven years old, slender and delicate and mildly pretty. Blondish hair worn in shoulder-length, soft curls. Skin tone's pale but burnished by a tan. Not the worst DMV picture I've ever seen. I open my notebook and write down the name and address. That needs to be my next stop. I'm already bracing myself for the relatives.

There's nothing else in the front seat of any relevance. The upholstery looks clean, and if there was any blood, it's been soaked away by the pond. Forensics will go over it for trace evidence. I pop the glove box, then take out the wet documents inside and give them to Winston to lay out for preservation. Looks like standard stuff: insurance paperwork, registration, car manual.

I've run out of distractions, and I feel a knot of tension wrapping up in my chest, tighter and tighter.

I take a deep breath and turn my head to focus on what's in the rear seat.

My first thought is, *They're so pale*. White babies, yes, but they're an unnaturally luminous color now. One has her pale-blue eyes open like a little doll, but she's not a toy, and the wrongness of it moves deep in me like an invisible snake. The other, eerily similar girl next to her has her eyes closed, thin lashes beaded with water. Their identical little pink outfits are stained from the green water.

They're so still.

Even seasoned cops lose their stomach over something like this. But I can't. One wrong step, and the deputy won't shut up about the black woman who couldn't hold her nerve. It's not just me I'm holding together. It's a line of women coming up behind me.

"No sign of obvious injuries," I say. I can't look away, now that I'm staring. Limp hair plastered against their soft little heads, probably blonde when it dries. One has a little yellow ribbon tied in her hair, but the other doesn't. Maybe that's how the mother tells them apart; I can't really spot any other differences. I swallow hard. "Winston?"

The coroner steps closer. "Foam at the mouth and lips," he says, "but don't put money on it yet."

He's telling me he thinks they drowned, and that's . . . worse. These babies strapped in, helpless and crying while the car rolls and splashes into this pond. While cold water spills in through the windows and around the door seals. While the compartment fills up.

Someone wanted these children to suffer. Or, at the very least, didn't give a shit if they did.

There's nothing else to see here, but I can't stop staring. The one with closed eyes looks like she's just fallen asleep, except for the water dripping from her hair, from the feet of the pajamas she's in. I was shopping for baby clothes earlier. I saw some just like these.

My mouth feels sour when I step away, and the air smells filthy and close. For a second I feel perilously dizzy, and I find my hand pressed to my stomach. I don't know if I'm trying to soothe myself, or the child still hidden deep in there.

"You okay?" Winston asks.

"Sure," I lie. "Call me when you get ready to proceed."

"Gonna be a while," he warns me. "I got two suspicious deaths came in earlier this afternoon."

I meet his gaze and hold it. "Those cases can wait."

He pauses for a second before he says, without a flicker, "Okay. You sure you want to observe the autopsies? Pretty tough. I could just get you the report."

Somebody needs to be a witness, I think. These two girls died alone, not even their momma by their side. Alone, cold, terrified. The least I can do is stand that lonely watch. "I'll be there," I say. "Call me when you're ready to start."

Winston nods. The deputy climbs out of his car and says, "I'll secure the scene. Y'all want the pond searched?"

"If there's so much as a tadpole in there, I want it," I tell him. "You're here until relief comes. Don't leave for *nothing*."

He nods, miserable, cold, and unhappy as hell, but he knows better than to cross me on this. Or should.

I head down the road while Winston loads the two limp bodies, still in car seats, into the coroner's van. Once I'm in my car with the door safely shut, I just sit and shake and breathe for a while. It feels like I'm decompressing after walking on the bottom of a very deep sea. I find myself sucking in short, shallow gasps, and force them slower. My hands are too tight on the wheel.

I need to go to Sheryl Lansdowne's address in Valerie. Someone will be waiting there, I hope—a husband, a father, a mother. Not that I'm looking forward to breaking the worst news of their lives. Fact is, every day in this job I see people at their lowest points, but nothing's as difficult as delivering news of a death.

Like attending the autopsy, it isn't something I can turn away from. Not and stay the person I want to be.

I put the car in gear and go.

4

GWEN

I get home again before dawn, but not before Sam's up; I hear him in the shower as I enter. I dump my purse and coat and move off down the hall; I check the kids and find them still sleeping soundly before I get to my office. Kez's unease haunts me, and however tired I am, I can't lay myself down and catch an extra half hour. I can't keep Lanny from taking stupid risks, but maybe if I can help ease Kezia's burden, even a little, that will make me feel less helpless.

I open my laptop and log in to the office's mainframe. One of the less-than-comfortable perks of my job is the ability to trace cell tower pings on a number, and sometimes, *sometimes*, trace the movements. It's only quasi-legal, one of those services that's a loophole if you know which buttons to push. It's an open back door for people like me if they know how to navigate it.

Kezia's sent me a written transcript and an audio file. I transfer both to my laptop and pull them up. I read as I listen.

"911, what is your emergency?" It's a marvel to me how most emergency operators sound bored and impatient. Male or female—and this one is a deeper male voice—they share a detachment I sometimes envy. "Hello?"

The second voice is fainter, but I think that it, too, has a deeper timbre. Male? I think. "Y'all need to send somebody out to Crease Road and Fire Road Twelve," he says. "Something's goin' on up there." The most important impression I have is that the accent is fake. Very fake. Definitely a bad actor's version of the rural South. Not even Vee Crockett—with the most backwoods accent I know—would sound like that.

"What's going on, sir?" The operator sounds like he couldn't possibly care less. But at least he's asking.

"There's a car up in there stopped. I heard a scream. Woman driving out here alone, bad things can happen. You'd best send someone." I tense up. The caller hasn't said anything about a woman until now. A scream, yes. But still, it seems off the way he phrases it. So does the tone . . . almost flat, which seems odd.

"Sir, can you describe the car, or the driver—" Maybe the operator's picked up on it, too, because suddenly he sounds engaged and interested.

But the caller hangs up. I listen to the operator try a callback. No one answers. But the operator did manage to snag a number, and I look at the entry on the transcript. *Bingo.* Kez was almost certainly right, it's likely a burner phone, but at the very least I can trace other towers where the cell pinged, if the caller keeps it on.

I log in to the J. B. Hall system and access the proprietary program; it's plugged into all carriers in the area, and it works like a charm. Like I said: Not exactly legal, but not illegal either. It's a dark shade of gray that sooner or later will be completely erased by new legislation, but the government moves too slowly to keep up with a lot of innovation in the tech industry. Private investigators don't need warrants, just access agreements since we're paying for the data use.

I put the phone number into our reverse database on another screen, but as expected, it comes back without a registered name and address. I switch back to the tracking and try that.

I watch the program as it highlights the path of the call. Not surprisingly, it's hitting towers close to Stillhouse Lake, but the interesting thing is, when the call comes in, it's already moving *away* from the spot where the car was discovered in the pond—and along a different road than the one where the pond is located. Logically, it's already made at least one turn away from the crime scene . . . if it was ever on that road to begin with. It keeps moving, but not toward the lake, and not toward Norton. It navigates narrow back roads, then turns east.

I get a sinking feeling as I watch it steadily move forward. I know where it's heading, and sure enough, the signal pings near a major freeway.

Then I lose the track completely. He's almost certainly switched it off and removed the battery; he would have pulled off to do that before entering the freeway. Heading north or south? I have no way to know unless he activates the phone again.

Unless he's already ditched it, I think. I imagine him rolling down the window and tossing the phone off on the side of the road. I mark the coordinates of the last signal. It might be worth a look. If Kez can retrieve the cell itself, it could reveal call logs, photos, texts, DNA, all manner of interesting information. Not to mention old-fashioned fingerprints.

He was enjoying himself. That impression makes shivers move over my skin. He said just enough to tease, not enough to give anything away. I'm honestly a little amazed the 911 operator sent a patrol at all, or that the county cop was lucky enough to spot the drowned car. God wanted those girls found. But what about the driver of the car? I imagine a mother bound and gagged in the back of that second car, screaming for her children. Not knowing, hopefully, what's happened to them . . . though I don't know which would be more torturous, knowing the fate of her babies, or not knowing at all. I can't imagine. I don't want to. I identify way too closely with it. I'd honestly thought that as my kids grew up and became more independent, I'd be less anxious. Instead, I find myself endlessly cycling through a horrific *what-if* catalog of disasters now more than ever, because I can't protect them like I once could.

Maybe I'm wrong about the abduction. The other, colder possibility is that the woman was the one who rolled her own car into that murky water and watched her children struggle and die. That she had a ride waiting to take her away.

I don't want to place bets on which scenario is worse.

But in that case, why make the 911 call?

I put everything I've got into an email and send it to Kezia, along with a note that I'm available if she needs anything, anytime. No immediate answer, but I don't expect one. I'm hoping she's finished up at the crime scene, and heading to rest a little . . . but I know it's unlikely. A homicide is a ticking clock.

I shake it off with a sigh and prepare to shut down the laptop, but a message alert catches my attention. It's not from an email I recognize, but I do get things in from other investigators, even client referrals; there have been more of those recently. I look at the message without any particular worry about it; the trolls who tend to come after me and the kids seem to have mostly moved on, though there are always a few showing up.

The message, I realize a tick too late, is not a client referral. Not from a colleague or a fellow investigator.

Too late to stop reading it now, so I dive in.

You've always been on my mind. But never really at the top of my list either. What a strange coincidence that our paths are crossing now. That does make everything so much more difficult, and so much more interesting.

The only thing that's held me back has been doubt—doubt about whether or not you truly were guilty of helping Melvin Royal commit his awful crimes. But there's enough reason to think you did. I know you walked away once. Let's see if you really are innocent, Gina Royal. Once and for all.

He's eloquent, I have to give him that. Proper spelling and grammar, which isn't usual for this kind of thing. It doesn't have the fetishization that most of the other trolls display; he doesn't tell me how he plans to hurt me, kill me, kill my kids. There's a certain measured rationality to it that alarms me more than if he'd indulged in the standard-issue lurid death fantasy.

I look at his handle, but it's just a string of anonymous letters and numbers. Most trolls are fairly careless in their internet habits. They use all or part of their not-very-clever false identities in other, mundane places. I caught one who changed only two numbers on the end of his screen name and posted with his regular handle on hockey forums; from there I was able to track him back to his real name, address, workplace. I didn't do anything with that information. I just make it a point to have it . . . in case things get worse.

So far, I've tracked down about 60 percent of my stalkers. The other 40 percent are smarter, cleaner, and better at their trollcraft. But they'll screw up or get bored and move on. Eventually. I'm playing a long game.

But I'm not sure this one is anything like the rest. He unsettles me in ways that are entirely new.

He's an original. And he's smart. I need to take him seriously. And I need to tell Sam, and loop in the Knoxville police.

I print out the email and close the laptop. Still thirty minutes before I need to start breakfast and wake the kids for the day, which is always something of a battle, especially when neither of them is really a morning person. They're great kids, and they love each other deeply, but they're also at that age where every little slight feels like a mortal wound, and the last few weeks they've been more reluctant about school than ever. I'd thought they'd adjusted well to the move, the new classes, the new friends . . . but I constantly worry I'm missing something.

I take a minute to think about it, then reach for the phone and dial.

"Office of Dr. Katherine Marks, how may I help you? You've reached her answering service."

Of course it's too early for Dr. Marks to be in. I feel momentarily stupid, and realize I'm just dull with weariness. Not enough sleep, and I need more coffee. "Hi," I say. "I just need to make an appointment with Dr. Marks for family counseling for later this week. Gwen Proctor, I'm already a client."

"Okay, I can help you with that. Would you consider this urgent, ma'am?"

"No." Hopefully.

"How about Wednesday at four? It'll be for you and which of your family members?"

"Me, Sam Cade, and our children, Lanny and Connor Proctor." *Better if we do it together this time,* I think. It feels like cracks are forming—small, subtle things. I want to keep them from growing any worse. The kids already have their own counselors, but Sam and I see Katherine Marks on a fairly regular basis to deal with our own deep-seated traumas.

None of us are in denial about our damage.

By the time I've confirmed the appointment, Sam comes out of the bath dressed in a towel, hair damp and gleaming tiny jewels of moisture. He looks, frankly, fantastic, and I sit on the bed and unashamedly watch as he drops the towel and reaches for his clothes. He notices. "Really?" he asks, with just a hint of encouragement. "You know I can't be late. Private client? Money in the bank?"

"I know," I say. "Just enjoying the view." We understand each other perfectly, at least the vast majority of the time. When we don't, it's trouble, but little things? We've grown well past all that. It's good. It's even fun.

"How's Kez?" he asks as he skims his soft blue T-shirt over his head. "Not like her to call you out at that hour."

"She's got a tough case," I tell him. "You'll probably hear about it on the news. Two little girls drowned in the back of a car, no sign of the driver at the scene."

He hesitates as he puts on the flannel shirt to go on top. "Was the driver abducted, or do you think it was an accident, or what?"

"God knows," I say. "The 911 call is suspicious, for sure. It's creepy to listen to."

"So Kez is asking for your help?"

I shrug and don't answer, because right now I don't know how much more involvement I'll have. He sits down to tie his boots. "What's your day like?" I ask him.

"Eight thirty private lesson. The guy's pretty steady, shouldn't be eventful. This afternoon, sessions in the simulator for the A-320." The simulators, I know, are stressful, but he enjoys them most of the time. The stress comes from the fact that every single sim he does is going in his record, and affects his ability to make the leap to where he wants to be. But I know how steady he is, and how good. He'll be okay.

I think about telling him about the new and dangerous troll, but to be honest, I don't want that to poison his whole day; better to talk tonight, once we're home and relaxed and everything is quiet.

I head for the kitchen. It's my day for breakfast, and I make eggs and bacon and toast; Sam eats fast and heads out. The kids are a shambles, as usual, but I get them up and dressed, and make sure they have enough food and juice in front of them to give them strength to face their school day. They keep the sniping to a minimum, thankfully.

They haven't managed to finish before the doorbell rings, and I have to take the alarm off to admit Vera Crockett. She's wearing pajamas and ridiculously oversize house shoes and God only knows how she got here, because our house is five blocks from her small, cheap apartment. Walked, probably. Vee doesn't give a crap what people think. She's always had that dark, defiant streak since I first met her in Wolfhunter as a girl wrongly accused of her own mother's murder, and it's only grown wider as she has matured. She's *almost* an adult now.

One who wears battered, enormous yeti house shoes out in public.

"Breakfast?" I ask her, and she yawns and nods. She's still wearing the ghost of last night's party glitter. Lanny, at least, has washed hers fully off. "You're lucky there's any left."

"I ain't picky," she says, and winks at Lanny. "Anything's good."

"Tell me you didn't walk all that way dressed like that," Lanny says as Vee pulls up Sam's empty chair and I get her a fresh plate. Lanny looks genuinely worried, but Vee doesn't answer, just digs into her eggs and bacon like a starving wolf. The girl's got manners, somewhere, but she doesn't usually bother with them. And in truth there's something satisfying about seeing someone so completely in the moment, every moment. Doesn't mean I don't worry about her, and her influence on my daughter.

"Hey, Ms. P," Vee says. "You got any ketchup for these eggs?"

I provide it and try not to shudder. "Vee, what are you doing today?"

"Nothin'." She pops ketchup-soaked eggs into her mouth. "Killin' the patriarchy."

"Killing it by not having a job," Connor says. "Good one."

"I got a job," she says, not quite defensively. "Part time, anyway."

If she does, it's news to me. Vee's record of jobs since being ruled independent is . . . spotty. We gave her the deposit on the apartment, and she's on her own for rent, which luckily isn't much; she seems to do okay. I'm not her mom, and I know her well enough to know she won't welcome me pushing in and interrogating her. Instead, I observe. She doesn't seem wired or high, which is good. I can't stop her from doing what she's going to do, but I have let her know how much I worry about it. And she's actually listened. Changed from that wild, angry, occasionally chilling child I met in Wolfhunter, at least a little.

I accept progress, even when it's in small steps.

"I got a letter," she announces suddenly, and pulls it out of the pocket of her pajamas and slides it over to me. "Thought you ought to see it."

"Actual paper letter," I say. "Wow. Old school."

"I guess." There's something solemn in Vee's expression. I look at the envelope; Vee's name and address are carefully written on the outside, no return address. I slip the thin copy paper out and unfold it.

> *Dear Vera Crockett,*
> *Don't be fooled. They aren't who you think they are.*

That's it. Not surprisingly, it's unsigned. And there's no stamp on it. "This came to your apartment?"

"Yep. Bastard knows where I live, put it on that rusty clip thing at the door where they hang late-rent notices and stuff like that."

"Who do you think he's talking about?"

She rolls her eyes. "Do I got to spell it out for you? I ain't got too many friends around here. Seems pretty plain to me."

"You think it's about us. Me and the kids."

"'Course I do."

I put the letter and envelope aside. They're going in my files. I know this is a problem; how large a problem, I don't yet know. "Vee, you knew this could happen; you come over here all the time, you hang out with Lanny. You've been in the news. Sooner or later, you were going to get a troll interested in you. The good news is, ninety-five percent of the time these people are cowards who'd never dare try anything. They feel big and brave threatening from a distance." That's all true. But this, I'm all too aware, wasn't delivered from a distance. It was at her front door. "If you want me to take it to the police—" Though I know full well the Knoxville police will just dismiss it. There's no threat even implied here, much less openly stated. Free speech applies.

"No!" She snaps it instantly, just as I thought she would. "I can handle it." Vee has had far too much contact with the police in her life, and in Wolfhunter, the cops were as bad as the criminals, if not worse. She doesn't trust a badge unless she absolutely has no choice. And truthfully, this time it wouldn't help anyway.

Lanny takes Vee's hand and squeezes it, which is more comfort than I'm offering. Vee gives her a ketchup-smeared smile and makes a kissy face, and Lanny flinches away. *"Ewww,"* my daughter says. "Gross. No."

"Definitely no," I say. "Wipe your mouth, Vee."

"You ain't my momma."

"You parked your ass at my table like I was. Wipe your mouth."

She does, grudgingly. Vee doesn't like doing anything that isn't her own idea, which is something I hope she'll grow out of. It may take another eighteen years of growing before she achieves anything like balance. I like and admire the girl—love her, in some ways—but I'm wary too. Vee's all edges, and no comfortable place to hold on to. I don't want my kids—especially Lanny—getting hurt.

Then you shouldn't have quasi-adopted her, I tell myself. Fair enough. But I couldn't just abandon her to the spiral of destruction she was headed down either. At least this way she has a chance. And someone watching her back.

"I'm gonna get a gun," Vee announces. "For protection."

Oh shit. "No, you're not," I tell her. "If you want one, you follow the same rules as anyone in this house. You train, and I don't mean the bullshit online checkbox courses. You go to a gun range and you get *good* with it, and then you keep training to stay good at it. Understand?" I have zero authority to say this; Vee can sneer at me and do exactly as she wants. But she's got her feet under my table, and I use my severest tone.

To my surprise, it works. Vee chews thoughtfully on her eggs a second before she says, "Well, I don't know much about guns. Might be a good thing to have somebody like you tell me what I ought to be doing."

"Guns are for offense. They can't shield you. They're not for show. The only thing they do—and they do it very well—is to kill somebody first who you believe is trying to kill you. But that's the problem right there: judgment. Because you have to be prepared to make that decision in a split second, without real information, in a situation where your adrenaline is screaming through your veins and you're scared to death."

"*You've* got guns," she says, and it's surprisingly not confrontational.

"I do. Because I have kids to protect, and because I don't romanticize firearms. They aren't ego props, Vee. They're tools to kill, and the damage they leave behind is real and brutal. Often final."

"I know that," she says. And she does—she's seen far too much of it already. "But I think I need one, Ms. Proctor. And I'd like it if you'd help me get one."

She's thrown it right back, and I feel Lanny's gaze heavy on me. Lanny doesn't own a gun, but she's been taking classes once a week; she and I practice together. She's getting to be a decent shot too.

"Here's the deal," I tell Vee. "You do classes with us at the range, starting tonight. You only get to buy a gun when I say you're ready to have one, and that means when you're officially eighteen. And when you do get one, you keep the practice up. I'll check. Understand?"

She nods and doesn't answer, too busy chewing. I'm not sure I've made a good decision. Vee Crockett isn't a stable personality; she's got volatile peaks and spikes, and she's been prone to self-harm before, through pills and booze and just plain recklessness. But she's also vulnerable, and that letter is proof that something's up. The fact that he knows where she lives . . . it's worrying.

Best call I can make, for now.

Vee finishes her breakfast, and I offer to drive her to her apartment so she doesn't have to walk back in those ridiculous house shoes. She accepts.

Once the kids are headed into their classes, it's just her and me alone in the car. I say, "You already have a gun, don't you?"

She flinches and turns her head too fast. "Why'd you say that?"

"Because I know you, Vee. You don't ask permission. You *might* ask forgiveness, sometimes."

She shrugs and turns away, but I see the color's warmed in her cheeks. "My business," she says. "Ain't it?"

It is. Vee Crockett is an emancipated adult, and though she can't legally own a gun yet, I'm not inclined to turn her in for it either. There's no time in a woman's life that isn't dangerous, and that's just a fact of life. "You made it my business this morning. I'm going to the range tonight here in town. I'll pick you up and we'll look over your gun and see what you can do with it. All right?"

She hesitates, then nods once. Her jaw is stiff. She doesn't like this; I'm coming close to her limits of obedience. She'll like it even less once we're at the range, but I intend to train her properly.

When I pull to a stop at her apartment complex—a cheap place, but clean—she gets out and marches away in her ridiculous floppy slippers without another word. A man outside smoking on the walkway gives her a long, appraising stare. She flips him off, unlocks her door, and slams the door after.

I don't like the look on the man's face, and I sit idling in the parking lot until he discards his butt and heads into one of the apartments. I make a note of his room number.

I'm a suspicious bitch, but I've found it works for me.

5

KEZIA

Dawn's just breaking when I make it to Sheryl Lansdowne's hometown. Valerie's not much, just bumpy streets and clapboard houses; whatever overflow Norton and Stillhouse Lake have from the K-ville commuters, they don't make it this far out. The place has a depressed look, but that could be just the gloom. The few streetlights struggle against it and lose.

I know, because I know these towns, that everybody awake is rubbernecking at my car cruising down the street. They'd know everybody in town, and every set of wheels on the road. I see a few lights coming on in houses as I glide past, and then I take two more turns and pull to a stop in front of the address for Sheryl Lansdowne. I don't see another vehicle in the driveway. Lights are on inside, though, frosting the white curtains. It's a nicer house than I expected. Bigger than the others.

I park and take a second to get ready. This is the unknown, whatever happens: either I find a person waiting who's about to get a horrible shock, or I find something else that makes this whole puzzle clearer, or I find nothing at all. I'm tired, but I get my head clear. I have to.

The air outside is chilly but doesn't have that oppressive stench the pond did, and I'm grateful. I take it down in gulps as I head up the path. The lawn's a little overgrown, needs a good shape-up, but that's not significant. I go to the front door and look for a bell. There isn't one, so I knock—forceful, unhesitating knocks. No point being indecisive.

I hear a dog race toward the front, barking. Sounds like a small one, at least. I make a note in my book and put on evidence gloves before I even consider touching the doorknob. Evidentiary value of the outside doorknob isn't much, though, so I go ahead and turn it.

Locked.

No other lights come on inside the house.

Just to be on the safe side, I knock again, louder and longer. There's no response, though I can see lights flashing on in neighboring houses. I'm waking up the whole damn town. Great.

I head around the side, making my way carefully with the help of my flashlight, and sure enough, there's a back door. It's locked too. I see what I can through the curtains; nothing out of place except the clearly unhappy dog, who charges into the kitchen area and sends dry food flying when he kicks the bowl. He's a little terrier of some kind, I think. Loyal, at least.

Whatever's happened to her, Sheryl Lansdowne didn't leave herself vulnerable here; plenty of rural folks leave windows open, doors unlocked, but she has this place secured. So why did she take her kids out there on the roads so late at night? I don't know. I didn't see suitcases, or even so much as a diaper bag, in that car. She couldn't have been on the way somewhere, or she wouldn't have left all these lights burning and the dog alone. It's a fair-size house, and I doubt she had money to waste on an unnecessary electric bill. Nobody out here does.

I retreat from the back door and take another look around. All the windows are locked down. Nothing to do here. I don't see anything suspicious at all.

I go back to my car and I'm starting it up when I see the next-door neighbor's front door open, and a big, older man in a checked robe steps out to stare at me. I roll down the window and gesture, and he comes over with a deliberate, heavy gait. He stops a couple of feet away, still staring. He's white, with a well-worn face and a red drinker's nose, though that could charitably be because of a cold or the chill. "What you want 'round here?" he asks me bluntly. I pull out my shield and show it to him. It saves time. His mood alters a little from *suspicious black woman* to *suspicious black woman with a badge*. I know he's got a handgun in the pocket of that robe; it's pretty damn obvious.

He grunts and cinches the frayed belt a little tighter. "Well, you ain't local," he observes. No, I'm not. Few black people in this little town; it's the legacy of the sundown laws officially in place until the sixties, where people like me had a curfew to be out of town every night. Still unofficially enforced.

"I'm Detective Kezia Claremont from Norton PD," I tell him. "You know your neighbor there?"

"Sheryl? Sure. She's got two little girls. Cutest you ever saw." His body language alters again. Worried. "She all right?"

"She isn't home," I tell him. "Does she live alone?"

"Since that no-good bastard of hers left she does. Been more than a year since he took off."

"Name?" I ask, and write down *Tommy Jarrett* when he gives it up. "You know where Mr. Jarrett moved off to?"

"Somewhere up around Norton, I expect. He's got family up in there."

Interesting. I don't know of any Jarretts. "And you are, sir?" I've let him get comfortable with it. I keep my tone polite.

He relaxes. "Hiram Trask. Me and my wife, Evie, live right there." He points to the house he exited—smaller than the Lansdowne house, and in poorer condition. "Last I saw Sheryl, she was off driving the girls. She does that, time to time, when they get cranky. Says the car noise puts them to sleep. She get into an accident or something?"

"I'll check into it," I tell him, and dutifully take down the make and model of Sheryl's car when he tells me, though I already know. I don't want to give him any reason to complain. "Thank you for your help, Mr. Trask. Y'all have a good day, now."

He nods and steps back, and I back out and head for Norton. He watches me all the way to the turn, to make sure I'm gone. I expect nothing else.

It's a short drive back to Norton, but one thing I'm already certain of: I have a lead. Tommy Jarrett, if he was the babies' daddy, might well want Sheryl dead, and the children, too, especially if child support was involved. Worth looking into, at least. Always start with the closest person to the victim and spiral out.

Before I can make it to the station to start running checks on Sheryl Lansdowne and Tommy Jarrett, I get another call. This one from the morgue.

"Hey, it's Winston," the coroner says. "I got your girls ready. You comin' in?"

"Yes," I say, before I can convince myself otherwise. "I'll be there in a few."

◆　◆　◆

The county coroner's office doubles as the Norton Funeral Home; I ring the old bell and wait until I hear the grate of the lock. Winston stiff-arms the door open for me and I duck in before it slams.

The place stinks of cleaning products, with a low undertone of something else. Old meat, like a butcher shop. Same as always. I take a deep breath, then another, trying to flood myself with the stench so it just becomes background. Normal.

It never really works.

Winston is not a big talker. He just heads down the wood-paneled hall and off to the left, where the county coroner's small work area is located. It's not terrible, and he keeps it well up to anyone's standards. Gleaming metal, shining porcelain. Perfect, neat lines of blades and saws and needles, everything just so. Winston's conscientious, even though they pay him shit—two-thirds what the county coroner over in Everman makes, though he's got the same training and experience. We don't talk about it.

He nods over to the right, where a small set of paper bags is already filled and sealed. "Clothes over there," he says. "I left the car seats as they were. Cut the straps close as I could to the sides, in case there was any foreign DNA left on the catches." The two seats are still wet, but he's set them out on sterile towels to catch anything that might drip off. I leave it for now, and turn toward the single autopsy table.

It's still empty.

"I thought you said you were ready. Where are they?" I feel an oily sickness bubble up in my stomach. I can handle shit, but I hate anticipating it.

"Ran into a problem after I called. I need to find a different scale," he says quietly. "I've got to weigh the bodies before I get started. The built-in scale on the table won't register them. I was going to call the hospital and get a baby scale, but who knows how long that'll take. They're giving me the runaround, saying it's not protocol—"

I can't. I can't let those babies get colder; I know Winston's kept them in the bags, in the dark, and everything in me rebels against the inhumanity of that. Not one more hour. Not one more *minute*.

I tell him, quietly, "There's a way to do it. I'll help."

He gets what I'm saying immediately, and turns to stare at me with wide eyes. Says, "You sure?"

I just nod because I don't know if I can say it again. I feel cold and heavy with dread, but there's a terrible, warm tenderness boiling up in me too. These lost babies need to be held. To know, even this late, that someone cares for them.

Winston helps me up on the autopsy table. The surface is cold and smells of bleach, strong enough to make my eyes water. I let him record my weight, and then I hear him unzip the first body bag. I take a deep breath and close my eyes and hold out my arms.

The cold, limp weight settles in against my chest, and I instinctively hold her close. I don't care about the fact that she's dead and gone. I just care about *her*. My mouth goes dry, my throat tight, and I feel tears clumping thick at the edges of my lids. "It's okay," I whisper to her. "You're not alone. It's okay." But I'm talking to both this lost child and the barely begun one hidden deep inside me. A promise I'm going to try to keep forever.

I hear Winston quietly recording the combined weight, subtracting mine, and then he takes her away. For a split second I want to fight to hang on to that poor baby, to hold her until she's warm again, but then I let go.

The second body lies heavy and cool against me, and this time I can't stop the tears. I brush my now-numb fingers across the little girl's drying hair.

God help the one who did this. God help him because I'm going to find him.

6

SAM

My eight-thirty client is a rich older man who doesn't mind paying my rates and—luckily—takes his responsibility as an aspiring pilot seriously. He comes early, and he comes prepared, and the hour and a half I've allotted for him goes by fast. Ten in the morning, a beautiful, clear day. When I taxi the Cessna back to the hangar, we finish up and shake hands, and he's on his way with a spring in his step.

My mood has improved too. Flying is an irresistible joy for me, a kind of therapy that brings me real peace. Doesn't last once I'm on the ground, but it does help.

I'm doing a check on paperwork before quitting—I don't have any more clients scheduled—and it catches me by surprise when someone says from behind me, "Hi. Are you Sam Cade? The flight instructor?"

I turn. "Yeah," I say. "What's this about?" I'm a little sharp because I don't like strangers walking up on me. Then I revise it a little—he doesn't exactly look shifty. He's casually but expensively dressed in khaki pants and a polo shirt, a bomber jacket he probably thinks makes him look aeronautical, along with the *Top Gun*–style Ray-Ban Aviators. White, young, maybe thirty. Short-cropped dark hair that barely shows under a Florida Gators ball cap.

"I was wondering if you had any openings for me," he says. "To learn how to fly, I mean. I'm Tyler Pharos."

"Sorry, but this isn't a good time," I tell him. "But we can set an appointment to go up and do a discovery flight with me as pilot, and I can explain the process. We'd also need to get you enrolled in ground training. It isn't particularly cheap, and it takes about six weeks to complete it for most people, in addition to the flight instruction." I reel it off fast because I know it by heart; I do get a lot of callers who think learning to fly is easy and fast. Walk-ins are kind of rare at this airport, but I'm not really surprised by it either.

"Oh," he says. "Sorry. I guess I should have called before I came." He's got a medium kind of voice, with a regional American accent I can't immediately identify. He offers his hand, and we shake. We're just about of a height, but I can't read his eyes behind the sunglasses.

"Interesting name, Pharos," I say. "Where's it from? Greece?"

He doesn't seem bothered by the guess. "Huh. Most people don't know that it comes from there."

I shrug. "I've done a lot of traveling." That's one way to talk about being in the military, anyway. See the world, kill people. "I can give you the paperwork to fill out for ground school, if you're interested—how's that?"

"Would you be the one to teach it, too?"

"I can, sure. Usually best if the same instructor does the ground school and flight training, because then we can be sure it's all consistent."

"I think that would be okay," he says. We walk over to the small office I share with a few other people, and I get out the paperwork and price sheets. He goes through them slowly and intently. I'm feeling less bothered, but not a whole *lot* less, which is odd. I'm usually better with people, but I can't seem to get a feel for this guy. He's a blank slate, emotionally. Neutral.

I'm not disposed to doubting him, but one thing about teaching lessons: you have to evaluate people from the jump. I don't care whether he's rich or poor, as long as he can pay for the lesson, but it goes beyond that . . . I need to see his temperament, his level of tension or relaxation. In the back of my mind, too, is the ever-present urgency of finding out *why* they want to fly. I don't want to train a suicidal person or, worse still, a terrorist.

He doesn't hit either of those alerts yet, but I'm picking up *something*.

"Sorry, Mr. Pharos, but that's all the time I have right now," I finally tell him. "I have another place to be. You can fill out the paperwork and send it back to me, if you decide to proceed."

"Okay," he says. "I understand." We shake hands again, but he doesn't go. He just stands there, looking at me. I can't read his expression.

Then he says, "I know who you are."

Oh man. I brace myself and try to keep my voice light when I say, "A licensed pilot? You'd better hope so if you want me to teach you to fly."

"You live with the serial killer's wife."

I was going to blow it off, minimize where he was going, but suddenly I feel my hackles go up, sharp as nails. "Gwen Proctor is my partner, yes. Not *his wife*."

"Ex-wife, I meant," he says. "Sorry." I want to snap off something else, but I don't. I just wait. I still don't get any particular emotion from him, even now, when most people would show *something* . . . discomfort, at least. "I didn't mean to offend you."

"I can see that," I say, and miracle of miracles, my voice sounds pretty even. "So yeah. That's me. And I'd rather leave my personal life out of this, if you don't mind."

"Of course," he says. "I'm sorry. I shouldn't have asked."

"It's okay," I say. I've not had anyone recognize me before out of the immediate context of being with Gwen or the kids, and it stings unpleasantly; I'm starting to understand, in a very minor way, how Gwen feels all the time. "Sorry. I really do need to go. And I think you should find another flight instructor. Nothing personal, I just . . . like to keep it separate."

For the first time, I see a little flicker of something like feeling in him. "I understand. It's just . . ." He shakes his head and turns away. "Never mind. I'm sorry I bothered you. I just thought you might be able to help."

I know I shouldn't do it, but there's something about the subdued tone that gets to me. I say, "Help with what?"

"I—" He takes in a breath and lets it trickle out slowly before he manages the rest. "My sister was murdered too."

I feel that go through me like a bullet, and for a second I can't breathe. A jumble of things floods through my head—crime scene photos, my sister's horrifically mutilated body, Gwen's face, Melvin Royal's mug shot—and I realize I've let the silence go on too long. "By Melvin Royal?" I thought I knew all the victim family members, and he doesn't seem familiar.

"No," he says. "Just—by someone. They never caught him."

That's a nightmare that I've never lived . . . not knowing who killed my sister. Not seeing him brought to justice. For a second or two I can't even attempt a reply, but then I say, "I'm sorry. That must be really hard." It hits me, then. "You . . . didn't come here for the flying lessons, did you?"

"No," he says. It's almost a whisper. "I . . . somebody told me about you, and I thought you might understand. Might be somebody to talk to about it. Because I can't talk to anybody else about her."

I've been reading him wrong, I think. He isn't emotionless. He's locked up, wearing an emotional straitjacket. Afraid to express *any* emotion because once he cracks that door, he might not control what comes out.

And I feel that because I know that place. It's where I lived for a while, before I moved on to darker places that I don't like to remember.

"Have you tried seeing a professional? Doing therapy?" I ask. I know a lot of men are resistant to it. Particularly if they blame themselves. It took a lot to get me moving in the right direction. "Because if you need somebody, I have some good contacts—"

Tyler's already shaking his head. "No, no, it's okay. I just—I thought maybe you'd understand. That we could talk a little bit. But I understand if you're busy."

I am busy. But not that busy. I could spare him a few minutes, at least. Grief twisted me into something bitterly wrong, and I've taken years to come back from that. A long, tough climb to get to a relatively stable place. The instructions from flight attendants keep running through my head: *put your mask on first before you help others.* I'm not sure my mask is completely on yet. Or that oxygen is flowing.

But at the same time, I can see this kid's damage, even if I can't feel his pain. Maybe because he doesn't dare feel it himself.

So I say, "Let's go get a coffee and talk about it. Okay?"

Tyler lets out a low, shaking breath and nods. "Thank you, Mr. Cade."

"Sam," I tell him. "Call me Sam. What was your sister's name?"

"Clara," he says. "I don't—I really don't want to talk about her so much. Just . . . just about how you handle it. Especially when you can't get it out of your head. You can't, can you?"

"Sometimes," I say. "Sometimes for hours. A couple of times for a whole day. But you're right. It doesn't go away."

We walk to the small coffee area set aside for the hangar, get cups, sit. Tyler seems uncomfortable still. He finally takes his sunglasses off, and behind them he looks very young. Vulnerable. His eyes look tired, and like they've seen far too much. "I get angry," he says. "About what happened to her. Is that normal?"

God, it's so normal.

And I take a deep breath and start explaining to him why that's bad.

I'm not sure how well I do. He's listening. His reactions are small, but I see the significance of the slight flinch, the way he looks at his hands. He doesn't break down, though I can almost feel how much he'd like to do that. The mask stays in place.

When he gets too close to my own wounds, I turn the conversation another direction. And when my watch buzzes a reminder, I'm surprised to find that a whole hour has gone by. The coffee in front of me is still full, and cold; Tyler's consumed all of his. I dump mine and tell him that I really do have to go.

Tyler thanks me for my time, and doesn't offer to shake hands this time. But just like before, he hesitates, and has one last question.

"Do you think your sister would be upset?" he asks me. "If she knew about . . ." He doesn't finish the question; maybe he realizes it's crossing a line. Because it is, and I know I ought to be angry about it. But somehow I'm not.

"If my sister knew I was happy with Gwen?" I guess. He nods. "Honestly? I don't know. I'd like to think she'd want me to be happy, because I wish she was. But I don't know."

He nods. "Thank you, Sam. I—I've never talked about it before. Not like this, with someone who understands." He rocks back and forth on his heels, and for a second I see the real suffering he's been concealing. Then he takes his sunglasses from his pocket and puts them on, and just like that, he's armored again. "I know that wasn't easy. Thanks for talking to me."

He doesn't wait for me to reply. He just turns and goes.

It feels strange, having let that conversation happen. And oddly good too. Maybe . . . maybe I'm actually starting to heal that part of myself. It's been long enough.

But I find myself wondering if I really just helped someone, or hurt him. Because I don't know.

I just don't know.

◆ ◆ ◆

It's just about quitting time and I'm headed back home, having passed my simulations and breathing easier and feeling almost, *almost* back to normal. I'm halfway there when my cell rings. I don't recognize the number and nearly let it go, but I finally hit the hands-free and answer. "Hello?"

"Hi, I'm looking for Sam Cade."

"You're talking to him."

"Oh, thank you. I'm Emory Osgood from the *Tennessean*." The woman on the other end sounds young and almost artificially subdued. I'm instantly on guard, but it doesn't sound like one of those damn robocall spammers. "I'm calling to double-check the spelling of a name, if you don't mind. Gwen Proctor. I normally wouldn't call, but it's spelled two different ways in the text I have." *Why the hell is she calling me?* I consider asking, but I spell it out for her. Before I can ask what the story is that she's writing, she hurries on. "Oh, thank you so much. It's really important we get the announcement right, of course. And could you confirm the name of the funeral home?"

My mouth goes dry. I don't think; I just pull my truck off the road and into a grocery store parking lot and the first empty spot I see. My hand is shaking as I put the engine in park. "What are you talking about?"

"I'm calling about the death notice," she says. "For Ms. Proctor?" She sounds taken aback now. Uncertain. My heart's pounding and I feel clammy. Sick.

"What happened to her?" I ask. I can't even recognize my voice—it sounds like a stranger's. "When?"

"Oh, sir, I am *so* sorry, I thought—wait, didn't you submit the notice yourself? This isn't supposed to happen, I just—I don't know what to say. I apologize for doing this to you, are you okay?" She sounds utterly horrified.

"Am I—" I bite back the sudden fury I feel. My eyes are burning. Whole body shaking. "What the *fuck happened*?"

"I—" I hear her take a deep breath. "Sir, I really don't have all that information. I have a computer submission via email that has the death notice request and lists you as the party to contact. That's why I called. I don't understand what's going on—"

I hang up on her. It takes me three tries to stab the number in to dial Gwen's cell. I struggle for breath while I listen to the distant, empty rings. It feels like the whole world is falling away from me down a dark well.

And then she answers. "Sam? Hey, how was your day?"

Like nothing's wrong. Like nothing's happened.

Because nothing *has* happened.

Thank God.

I can't even speak for the relief filling my throat until I clear it and say, "Fine, honey. Everything's fine. I'm—I'm on my way home. You there?"

"Yes," she says. "About to start dinner. What do you think about—"

"Whatever you want," I say, and I mean it. I can't tell her what just happened. I don't want to ruin her mood. "Got to go, I'll be home soon, okay?"

"Okay," she says, and I can hear the slight shift in her tone. She can tell something's off. I hang up before she asks anything else.

Then I redial the number for Ms. Emory Osgood, and get transferred to her from the main number of the *Tennessean*, our local newspaper. "Emory, this is Sam Cade," I say. She starts another flood of apologies, and I cut her off without listening. "Somebody sent in the death notice. How?"

"Well . . . it's a form online. You fill it in, and then we double-check it—that's what I was doing when I called you because her name wasn't spelled the same way in one place as it was in the other, and the funeral home number isn't working. The order's got your name and phone number attached to it. Sir, what exactly happened—"

"Gwen Proctor isn't dead," I tell her. "And I didn't send that in."

"Oh my God, Mr. Cade, I am so sorry—I—why would anyone *do* something like that?"

"Cruelty," I tell her. "Just delete it. And don't accept any other death notices for me, Ms. Proctor, or her children, Lanny and Connor, unless you verify it with me or the police first. Treat everything like it's a vicious prank, because it probably is. Okay?"

"O . . . okay. Wow. I've just never heard of such a thing happening. Again, I'm so sorry . . ."

"It's okay." It isn't, but I don't want her to agonize about it. She didn't do anything wrong. I rub the back of my stiff, aching neck. "Somebody's learned a neat new trick, I guess. Something to think about for the future. For both of us."

"Yes sir," she says. "I'm glad everybody's okay."

"Me too, Emory. Me too."

Now that the shock has passed, reality sets in, and it's grim as hell. I'd been hoping nobody was going to start up shit against Gwen again, but I was wrong.

Dead wrong.

7

GWEN

When my phone rings at around eleven a.m., I'm half-asleep in my office chair, and the buzz jerks me wide awake. I'd nearly dozed off going over a background check, but then again, it's been a long damn night. I scramble for the phone and see Kezia's name.

"Kez?" I answer instantly. "Everything okay?"

The silence that follows is far too long, and feels heavy. "Not really," she says. "Autopsy on the two little girls just finished. I got their names from the birth records. Mira and Beth." There's more to it, but I don't push. Kez will tell me if she wants me to know.

"How are you?" I ask her. "Really?"

I catch the shake in the breath she takes in, and it hurts me. "Okay," she says, and I hear the lie loud and clear. "The TBI is taking the case, I just got word."

"And you're just going to step off?" I ask. I know better. Her silence confirms it. "Kez—"

"Can't just walk away from this, Gwen. Those little girls . . ."

It *is* about the little girls . . . but it's more than that, and we both know it. The child she's now carrying was a joy, and it's become a reminder that life is so terribly fragile, and tragedy so unspeakably final.

I understand why she's obsessing; I'd probably do the same. But it's risky. Kez has done plenty of things on her personal time that a larger police force than Norton's might find questionable; pursuing her own investigation will be something massive enough to put her job in danger if she doesn't get buy-in from her chief, and we both know that. The Tennessee Bureau of Investigation won't welcome her poking around, either . . . any more than it will welcome Gwen Proctor, the ex-wife of a serial killer, PI license or not. But I wasn't planning to ask their permission, and I'm guessing Kez isn't going to either.

"So what's your plan?" I ask.

"Thought I'd head up that road in both directions," she says. "There have got to be a few places out there. Maybe somebody saw something."

"And maybe you should let the TBI do that?"

"They're doing a grid search of the woods around that pond today," Kez says. "Just talked to Prester, and he's going on out there. I tried to talk him out of it. Best I could get him to agree to was to split the hours, so I'll take over as soon as I finish doing this check."

"You want company?" I ask her. "Kez. You need it. Especially if you're knocking on doors out there all by yourself."

"I'd love some. But you have to hang back. House rules."

"I'll meet you at your office," I tell her. "Give me forty-five minutes."

"Okay," she says. "Drive safe and text me from the parking lot because you *know* the looks I'd get if you came inside."

"Oh, I know. I'll be careful. Mind if I give you some unasked-for advice?" I say.

"Go ahead."

"Take some deep breaths. Clear your head. Then get your boss on board. I know you want to dive right into this thing, but fact is, it looks to me like it'll be a long, tough haul. Conserve your passion. You're going to need it."

"Oh," she says, "I got enough passion. Believe that."

I do. There's a hardness in her voice I've never heard before. This has got its claws deep.

She hangs up with a quick goodbye, and I give up on the sleep-inducing background check and get my things together for the drive. I'm actually grabbing a bottle of water out of the fridge to take on the road when the doorbell rings. I go to the security camera feed to see who it is.

The feed shows a delivery driver holding a handheld device, looking impatient. Behind him on the street looms a dark-colored van, no logo. I stare at him for a moment. No emblem on his shirt, but he's got some kind of ID badge clipped on. I liked the old days, when the only delivery people came in clearly marked vans, with recognizable uniforms. It's too easy for someone to gain access these days; all they need is a clipboard and a box.

I ask the delivery person, through the doorbell microphone, to hold up the ID to the camera. It does look legit. So I go to the front, turn off the alarm, and open the door. Situational awareness, as always; I've automatically identified how far it is to the nearest weapon, and I brace myself in case of attack. That's what PTSD does to you; it makes you constantly evaluate your chances of survival against the normal as well as the unexpected. It's exhausting. In my case, it's also been pretty necessary.

The driver just shoves the device to me and says, "Sign here, please." I take it and scrawl something with my finger that doesn't remotely resemble a signature, but he doesn't even glance at it, just hits a button and hands me a slender, folder-size cardboard envelope. He's halfway back to the van before I can turn it over and see that it's not addressed to me . . . or, not to Gwen Proctor.

It's addressed to Gina Royal, my old name. No return address visible.

I feel a hot and cold wave splash through me. It leaves me furious. My first impulse is to yell at him to come back and refuse delivery, but then I get control of that instinctive flinch. *Better to know than not,* I tell myself, and grab a picture of his license plate before I shut the door. I engage the alarm and settle on the couch. I turn the envelope over and rip the easy-open tab straight across, then carefully, with the envelope facing away from me, open it wide and shake out the contents.

What falls out is a smaller white paper envelope. It lands facedown. I check the package, and there's nothing else in it. I set it aside, take a breath, and flip the envelope over.

I know this handwriting. It makes me go feral inside, rolls in my stomach like a ball of razor wire. *He's dead. Melvin Royal is dead.* I tell myself that, but it's like a whisper into utter darkness. Swallowed up and gone.

I keep staring at the envelope as if that will make it go away, make it not happen, but here it is and here it will remain. *I should burn it,* I think. *Or shred it unopened.* It's thin enough I could do that in the office without trouble. And there's a certain freedom in the idea that's seductive.

Melvin has nothing to say that's meaningful to my life now.

And yet, my hands reach for it. I'm almost observing it, not directing, as I rip open the top and slide out the letter. Unfold it.

The cramped, precise writing that stains the page makes me flinch so badly that the paper makes a faint, protesting flutter. Without willing it, without wanting it, my eyes focus on the first line.

Dear Gina,

It's always Gina.

I know this will come as a shock to you, but I'm not angry anymore.

That's a lie; he was always angry, a beast waiting to pounce, even when he hid it behind smiles and calm words and charm. He was angry the night I killed him.

I forgive you for all the harm you did me.

I make a sound in the back of my throat, half a laugh and half a gag. Harm I did *him*, a monster who claimed an appalling number of lives. Manipulation and control, gaslighting, Melvin's stock in trade. I can feel him on the other end of this letter, calculating effect.

If you're reading this, I've died. Maybe that was just karmic justice; maybe it was something else. I've always thought that if I die it'll be because of you. Was it?

Yes, you asshole. Yes, it was. I shot you in the face.

Doesn't matter, dead is dead. But you know I can't let go that easily, don't you? I loved you once, Gina. Not that you were ever worthy of that love. But I can't help it. We were meant for each other. Made for each other.

The poisoned honey in those words. I'd wanted to believe in him for the longest time, craved the affection he showed me, and I'd swallowed the bait every time. I'd believed I wasn't worth much, that no one could ever love me but Melvin, that my only happiness lay with him. And here it is again: control.

He's dead, and he's still trying. You can't say he isn't dedicated.

I made arrangements in case this happened, obviously. Letters, so you don't forget me and what we were together. Enjoy what you think is freedom, because it's just a long leash I've let you run on. Soon you'll get to the end and that will be a short, hard stop. And in that moment, you'll know that I've never really let you go. Never.

I'm breathing faster now. My fingers are crushing the paper, nearly tearing it. But I keep reading.

Till death do us part, that's what we said in our vows. I'm going to hold you to it.

Bye for now, my beloved wife. Kiss our children for me.

His signature sprawls at the bottom, taking up space with spiked arrogance. I stare at it for a moment, then ball up the letter and drop it to the table, where it sits like a paper grenade.

I have a choice. I can give this more time, or I can think about it later. Kez is waiting.

And Melvin's still going to be dead.

I take the letter to my office and put it in my desk drawer, and I feel a half a ton lighter when I leave Melvin's shadow behind, locked in the dark.

◆ ◆ ◆

I text Kez from the NPD parking lot, as promised, and I keep a low profile to avoid being spotted by any of the uniformed cops. I have something of a local reputation in Norton. It's not exactly favorable.

Kez walks confidently across to me and slips into the passenger seat. "Best be on our way," she says. "Shift change is about to start."

I drive us out onto the Norton main drag, which is just a two-lane state road; being back in town makes me feel unsettled, a little strange. Although maybe that really has more to do with Melvin Royal's ghost darkening my door again. It isn't unusual; he's got acolytes all over the country who got packages full of letters he prewrote to me before his prison break, and they all enjoy sending me his twisted form of love.

Kez is giving me a cool, assessing look. "What?" I ask.

"You don't seem like yourself."

"Really. How does myself usually seem?"

She lifts one shoulder in half a shrug. "Calmer," she says. "Something happen?"

I don't want to lie to her, but I also don't want her to know Melvin Royal still haunts me. I don't want anyone to know that. "No. Not really."

She probably doesn't believe that, but she lets it go. "Thanks for making the trip. I know this is twice in just a few hours. And I ruined a good night's sleep."

"Oh, my daughter ruined it before you did." I explain about Lanny's late-night club date. She just smiles.

"That sounds like her," she says. "Hope you're not going to be too tough on her. She's growing up fast."

"Too fast," I sigh. "Anyway. Did you talk to your chief? Let him know you were going to keep working the case?"

"He's fine with me working it until the TBI says we can't. Then I may have to have another conversation."

"Maybe the TBI will want to work with you on it."

"I get the feeling they think us rural folk don't have the skills."

"Well, that's a dumb mistake."

She quirks a smile, barely. "Not necessarily. You met Deputy Dawg this morning; beyond pissing in the accidentally right place, there's not much he actually did right. Maybe they'll see past that and look into my record. I don't think they'll bother."

Or they'll look into her record and worry she might turn out to be all too effective. She might take the shine right off them if she solves it. The TBI is a bureaucracy, like anything bigger than three or four people; there's a chain of command, there are clearly defined roles, and there are always politics in play. In her present frame of mind, my friend doesn't care about any of that, and while I'm with her, I wonder if she's thought through the consequences.

I open my mouth to ask, then shut it without uttering a word. She has. And she's made her decision regardless.

"What were the autopsy results?" I finally ask her. Her eyes lose focus, and there's a significant chill that settles through me even before she answers.

"What we expected," she says. "Death by drowning. Marks on both bodies show they struggled."

It conjures up a nightmare, which I imagine she's seeing in terrible detail. I can feel the cool breath of it on the back of my neck, but she's faced these ghosts directly. I don't reply. I can't think of anything comforting to say.

"I went to her house," she continues after a moment. "Sheryl Lansdowne's house. It doesn't look to me like she was planning a trip, and there weren't any suitcases in the car, just her purse. You ever drive your kids around in the middle of the night?"

"Sure, when they were little," I say. My mouth has gone dry, and I take a restoring sip of water. "Mostly Connor. There were more than a few nights I couldn't get him settled, and I didn't want to wake up . . ." My voice fades out to a thin thread that breaks on the last word. I'm Gina again, frustrated and exhausted, afraid the baby will wake Melvin. I leave my daughter asleep in her bed and I put my son in the baby seat in the back. I drive him around the dark neighborhood, singing nonsense songs, until he finally is limp and peacefully dreaming.

I left my daughter *with Melvin.*

I haven't thought of that horribly vulnerable moment until now, and it chills me deep. She was just a little thing, and I'd checked on her when I put my son back in his crib. She'd seemed peaceful and undisturbed, but I hadn't thought *once* about the risk to her. I'd had no reason to then. But I hadn't even thought of it later, when I found out what Melvin was, what he did.

Oh, I'd had generic, unfocused terror over what he *could* have done, but for some reason this one memory of her lying so defenseless in her bed, face round and innocent, little hands clutching the Care Bears blanket she loved so much . . . it breaks something in me with an audible, ringing snap.

I didn't protect her then. And in a very real sense, I'm horribly aware that I can't protect her now. Not from this carnivorous world.

Kez has seen it.

"You're thinking about being with Melvin, aren't you?" She's too perceptive. I swallow and nod. "Sorry. I didn't mean to dredge all that up again."

"He's like a zombie," I tell her. "Keeps coming back no matter how many times I put him down. It's okay." I don't think the smile I deploy is especially convincing. "Anyway, the answer is yes. I did drive my baby around in the middle of the night sometimes. And I remember how exhausted I was, and how surreal everything seemed. When you're a new mother, you're just in a fog of hormones and exhaustion most of the time."

"Yeah, already feeling some of that," she sighs. "So that's likely what she was doing out there in the middle of nowhere. Getting the kids to sleep?"

"Or she was meeting somebody."

"I thought about a drug deal, but honestly, nothing about that car or her house screams junkie to me. House needed some outside work but seemed pretty orderly inside."

"We both know of high-functioning addicts, especially opioid addicts," I say, and she nods. "But you're right—that seems an especially lonely place to go for a drug exchange. Pretty strange when truck stops and convenience stores exist."

"Could have been some kind of romantic rendezvous," Kezia adds. "Though I can't imagine that as a make-out spot even on a damn sunny day."

I have to agree with her. If ever a place had a bad spirit, it's that one. And now it has claimed two lives . . . or two more. You'd have to be exceptionally high or drunk to have some kind of consensual encounter out there. "So, if not a drug deal gone bad, we're looking at a straight-up abduction of the mother that he covered up by pushing her car into the pond?"

"That would have to be random, wouldn't it?" she says. "What are the odds of some predator trolling those back roads and scoring at that hour?"

"Depends on how often she drove those babies around," I say. "If she had a routine, a route . . ."

"Then it wouldn't be random at all," she finishes. "He'd know her habits. Damn." She sighs. "But we haven't got shit as far as evidence of any of this. We're just guessing."

"Is this the turnoff up ahead?" We've already passed the exit to Stillhouse Lake, and I'm weirdly relieved not to be headed that direction . . . and at the same time, a little sorry too. It's such a strange, mixed feeling for me. Longing and loathing in equal measure.

"Yep, that's it. Take a right. We've got about twenty minutes before we get to the crime scene."

We arrive there exactly on time and pass the flapping crime scene tape; the TBI's attention must be elsewhere, because there's a minimal presence. We drive past without pausing, and Kez says, "Okay, should be about five possibilities. I'm not sure any of them will check out, but it's worth looking into."

"How many of them have a view of the pond?"

"None. But they *may* have a view of the road. Best we can do."

Driving on this road takes concentration; the flicker of light and shadow seems more disorienting than usual, and the road curves and loops and wanders, with steep drop-offs on either side. Barely big enough for two cars to pass, if they do it carefully. My SUV seems monstrously large in the space, and I don't know where I'd pull over if someone came from the opposite direction.

It takes the better part of an hour to strike the first two off our list. The third time seems to be the charm. It's new construction set far back from the road, almost embarrassingly large, with double-paned windows and solar panels on the roof and a tidy garden on one side. A suburban McMansion dropped into the hills, immaculate and deeply out of place. Even though it's overdone, I still feel a guilty twinge of house envy as we pull to a stop on the evenly paved driveway. "Jesus. They know where they live, right? A double-wide trailer is luxury around here."

"Feels like a middle finger of a house," Kez says. "So I'm guessing they do know. And don't care what folks think about it. But we're in luck. Cameras."

She nods toward the eaves. She's right—there are two aimed at the driveway and, hence, the road.

"Doorbell cam, too," I note before we get out. "Let's hope they don't greet us with guns."

"Out here, that's a solid bet. You go first," she says, and shoots me a wicked grin.

I do.

The doorbell rings inside with a soft chime, and a woman's tentative voice through the speaker says, "Yes?" Even the one word sounds guarded. I make sure she can see me clearly on the camera.

"Hi, my name is Gwen Proctor. I'm investigating a crime that happened down the road," I tell her, which is technically both true and a lie. "I just need to ask you a couple of questions and, if at all possible, look at the camera footage from your security cameras. Would that be possible, ma'am?"

There's a long silence, and then she says, "Go on. Ask your questions." She's not going to come out. Fair enough.

"Did you see any cars pass early this morning? Maybe after midnight, but before dawn?"

"No." She's lying. I can feel it.

I try a different tack. "You didn't hear anything either?"

"No. What kind of crime are we talking about?"

"We may have a missing woman," I say. "She's a mom, two baby girls. We're just looking for any description of vehicles that passed on the road. That's all." I play a hunch. Something in the way she asked *what kind of crime* makes me think she's worried that we're here about . . . something else. Something she definitely knows about. "This isn't about Belldene business, nothing like that." She knows the Belldenes. She'd have to, living up here. And having this much cash? She probably knows them real well, either on the business or buyer end of things.

"I—" She hesitates, then says, "There were two cars out last night. One was a regular sedan, kind of old. The other one was a dark SUV. A nice one." She says it like she knows she shouldn't be talking. It comes in a rush, and then she takes a deep breath. "That's all I know."

"Thank you. That's very helpful. Would you mind emailing me that footage, then? Just in case we can spot something on it, like a license plate?"

She doesn't sound happy about it. "Give me your email. Just . . . don't tell my husband. Okay?"

"We'll keep it confidential."

Kez glances my way, and I gather she doesn't want to give her official contact account, and I know she never gives her personal one. I spell my PI company email out, and make sure the woman repeats it back to me. I thank her again, and there's nothing left to do but go. As we're strapping ourselves into our seats, Kez says, "She's not going to send anything."

"You're sure?"

"Ten bucks sure. She'll be afraid of having her name in the records, testifying, something like that. I've never been up here myself, but this address comes back to more than one domestic complaint, and looks like her husband's deep into the pill business. Bad combination. I'm surprised she said anything at all. Fear runs deep when you're alone out here."

She's right. Women who live this remotely are either under the oppressive control of a partner, or independent as hell. Not a lot of middle ground. And getting out of a bad relationship is tough at the best of times. Out here, in the sticks, with a husband with criminal ties . . . that would be infinitely harder.

"Maybe she'll call," I say. "I'm an optimist."

Kez shakes her head. She knows me better than that.

The last two houses are a bust; one's a hunting cabin, locked up tight and no sign of inhabitants. The other is a broken-down trailer rusted on the sides, and we raise no response when we knock. Kez sticks her business card in the door, and we head back down the mountain. I have to admit, it feels like relief. I don't like being up here in Belldene territory. They've told me, in no uncertain terms, how unwelcome I am.

"So what did we get out of that?" I ask.

"We got confirmation that there was a second car," Kez says. "So either our missing woman set it up as her ride away from the crime scene or we have an abductor who might or might not have been stalking her. God, I hope he was. Her little town is just full up on busybodies. Somebody will have seen him. Probably got his damn license number too."

"So . . . where to now?"

"I should probably join the grid search. Prester's not up to it right now, tramping around through the woods. I'm taking over from him."

"You want me to go to her hometown, then? Talk to her neighbors?"

Kez cracks a quick, grim smile. "Better you than me. Doubt I'd get a whole lot of cooperation." There's a thread underneath that, one of resentment and resignation. I understand it, at least to a very small extent.

I just say, "Of course, I'm happy to help. Is that going to screw you up with the state boys?"

She shrugs as her whole answer, and I can see she means it. She doesn't care about the consequences. There's a sharpness to her expression, the set of her jaw, that makes me think this is one of those cases that will haunt her for the rest of her days. She wants to solve it any way she can. Maybe she wants to do it for the child she's bearing, the one who will change her life so completely. Maybe she needs to prove something to herself.

I hope that doesn't put us both in real danger.

8

KEZIA

I have a secret I never tell anybody: I appreciate nature, but I hate the goddamn woods. I like the city, I like the brick and steel and sweat of it, and being out here in the wildest part of the green to me always feels like I've been scooped up by aliens and dropped in the middle of a *Predator* movie. God help me, I spend a damn lot of my time out here too. I pretend I don't care.

I do. Violently.

Gwen drops me off to get my car, and I hook up with the TBI again, who offer to let me tramp the hills with their grunts; I take the opportunity mainly because I know Detective Prester is already up there, trying to hold up our end. Sure enough, when I pull up, I see Prester coming out of the woods. He's moving slow. His color—never real good—has an ashy undertone I don't like. God help me, I love the crusty old bastard; he's a smart, capable detective, and more than that, he cares about victims, and he's made me care about them too.

He doesn't want my worry, but he gets it anyway.

I walk up to him, and he—of course—waves me back like I'm a fly bothering him. "I'm okay," he says, which he isn't. "It's the heat is all." It isn't that hot, and we both know it, but I let it go. I've been nagging him to see his doctor, but he's having none of it. He'll just snap at me if I push, and I can't really say I'd blame him. If I make it to his age, I'd like to be that independent, not have my bossy young partner ordering me around.

"I'll finish up for you," I tell him. "Not a problem."

"You hate the trees," he says, which is accurate, and I've never told him that, but somehow I'm hardly surprised he knows. "Too much imagination, Claremont. You think bears lurk every-damn-where."

"What, you mean they don't?" I flash him a grin, and a corner—just a corner—of his mouth quirks in response. "How long you been out there?"

"Few hours," he says. Which is bad, given how he looks right now. I try not to tell him that. "You been out with Gwen?"

"I've been following up leads," I say, which isn't an answer, and he doesn't take it for one either. "Any luck out there yet? Found anything?"

"Oh, found plenty, all of it junk. Old condoms, rusty cans, beer bottles. Nothing about our missing lady. Not a trace."

"They'll keep going until it's dark," I say. "Go on home. Please?"

He doesn't like it, but he nods. I stand up and walk away without another word. I can feel him watching me, but I don't turn around. I hear his engine start with a loud, rattling roar, and he backs that boat-size sedan out with the ease of a lifetime of driving these narrow roads.

I'm double-checking the laces on my boots when a young woman in the outfit of the sheriff's office comes over. I silently produce my badge and ID, and she makes a note in her logbook. "Detective." She nods. "Uh, the boys are all up in the hills right now. You want to wait at base or—"

I want to wait at base, damn right I do, but I put on a heavier jacket, then add a fluorescent vest. Don't want to get mistaken for a damn bear. Or a black woman. "I'll take the grid Detective Prester was walking," I say. I strap on a flashlight; it gets dark under the trees even in full sun, and clues can be easy to miss. And I keep my sidearm handy, because there are indeed damn bears. And predators on two feet, too, who might enjoy a potshot at a cop. Bears don't shoot back. I will.

I follow the accommodating deputy uphill to her small folding table. She's got a map spread out that's weighted down at the corners with rocks, and still rippling a little in the strong, chilly breeze. "Okay," she says, and points to a spot on the paper. "This is your section. Grid search, north to south, then east to west, no more than three feet apart on each pass—"

"Thank you, Deputy; I know how a grid search works," I say. "Channel?"

"We're on seven," she says, and hands me a walkie-talkie. It's a brick of a thing, heavy enough to use as a baton in an emergency, and built so sturdy it would probably work if you ran over it with a truck. I turn the dial to the right channel and do a radio check. At her nod, I head uphill into the tree line.

Darkness drops a cloak on my head, and I pause to let my eyes adjust. It's oddly warmer here, mainly because the breeze isn't as strong and direct; I take a few breaths and flip on the flashlight to look for the marker Prester would have put in to show where he stopped his search. The fluorescent hit of the neon yellow flag jumps out at me. He didn't get too far.

I walk to it, alert to the whisper of the woods. There are other cops out here doing their own grids, but I can't see or hear them; I might as well be alone, as far as it feels. I love Javier, but if he laughs at me *one more time* about feeling vulnerable out in the wild . . . I shake that off and pull up the marker flag. The deputy's given me neon orange flags to use if I find any potential evidence; the number of them in the bag is damn optimistic, seems to me. But I've noted which way Prester had his flag pointed, and I start slowly walking that grid. I frequently refer to my compass to be sure I'm straight on the path; too easy to get turned around out here.

I pause when I spot a glint in the light and crouch to examine it. A broken beer bottle, label long tattered from being out here for years. I mark it anyway and move on.

Prester's grid is not rich in clues. I finish north to south, start east to west, and I'm halfway through (and an hour in) before I spot something odd. I examine it, trying to figure out what it is; it's just a shape half-hidden by a scramble of ferns, but it looks wrong. I carefully move the plants and take a closer look.

Smooth. Pale. Curved. Organic.

This has nothing to do with our missing woman, but this is bone. My heart starts beating faster, but I talk it down. *Probably just an animal,* I tell myself. That would make sense; it *is* the middle of the damn woods. I know it's risky, and the TBI boys will probably, righteously, scream about me tampering with evidence, but I don't want to be that stupid local who fussed over a deer skull either. So I crouch down and start carefully working the dirt away from the sides.

It's a human skull, buried in the ground chin down. Whether it was fully covered before and rain washed it visible, I can't tell, but when I get to the brow ridge and orbital sockets, I know for a fact it's human, and probably male, since the brow ridge is large. I stop, back off, plant an orange flag, and key my radio.

"Got something," I report to the deputy manning the table back down the hill. "I'm going to need the scene commander up here, now."

"Yes, Detective," she replies crisply. "I'm sending him now. Y'all need forensics up there, too?"

"Absolutely," I say. I think that's the end of the conversation, but after a short pause she comes back.

"Did you find her?" She asks it tentatively, almost reverently.

"No," I said. "Something else. No sign of our missing woman."

She doesn't respond this time. I wait, staring at that half-buried skull.

Who are you? I wonder who put him out here in the dirt too. And why the hell he's so close to the drowned car in the pond. Because something—nothing logical, something deep at the base of my brain—is whispering that it can't be a coincidence. We like things to make sense and be logical, we cops. I know this probably won't mean a damn thing except some drunk hunter broke his leg and got eaten by the proverbial bear, but . . . still.

It's connected. I know that, even if I can't prove it yet.

◆ ◆ ◆

My grid quickly turns into a crime scene, and after initial questioning by the scene commander—a TBI lieutenant, white and brusque, who demands to know why I partially uncovered the skull and doesn't much listen to the answer because asking is enough to fill in the box on his mental form—I drop back to lean against a tree and watch from a distance. Their approach is pretty clean, all things considered, and it being an old crime, not a fresh scene, they don't have to worry about footprints. Hairs and fibers, though, they do worry about, and everybody hovering over the skull ends up with forensic paper coveralls, or they don't make an approach at all. A tech approaches me to gather hair and fiber samples in case I've shed on the dirt or skull, and I'm fine with that. It's just protocol.

What isn't protocol is the way the scene commander throws out opinions like he's shaking off water. *Probably a drifter.* Out in these woods? Unlikely. Homeless folks don't hang around in the woods by preference, and if he were homeless, he'd have had a pack, some kind of tent, something. There's nothing I can see anywhere nearby. *Some drunk who decided to sleep it off in the wrong place. Or a suicide.*

Accidentally dead people and suicides don't generally bury their own skulls. I know the skull could have gotten separated from the body by scavengers; could have rolled here from uphill, come to that, and gotten buried in mud naturally. I wonder if I should mention it, because not one of the people on scene is looking that direction yet.

I don't. Instead, I head up the hill.

It's a tough climb, friable rock shattering into gravel under my feet, slick vegetation nearly sending me down again, but I manage. I arrive at the top breathing hard, sweating under my jacket, and put my hands on my hips as I slowly turn a circle. Here at the top it's still shady but not the same nightfall it was down below, and I don't need the flashlight to identify the grave. It's old, but not more than a couple of years, I'd judge. Shallow, and disturbed plenty by scavengers, which explains the skull tumbling down the hill. I don't dig into the dirt this time, just observe; I don't have to touch a thing to see three rib bones sticking out. Tattered fabric flutters in the wind.

I solemnly plant one of my neon flags, stand up, and key the radio. "Got something up the hill," I say. "Looks like the rest of the body."

From where I'm standing, I can see everyone stop, turn, and look up at me.

I don't say anything else.

◆ ◆ ◆

The TBI agent is on a slow boil now, not because I've found the body but because I've disproven his popped-off theories. I'm told to fall back and keep going with my grid search . . . although the bootheels of all those officers have left me with a mess that will make it ten times harder. I don't argue. I slip and slide back down the hill, flick on the flashlight, and start where I stopped. There's a lone deputy standing guard down there, roping off the area around the skull; we nod, and I keep moving. It's another hour before I'm to the end of the pattern, and I report in what little I've come up with—couple more glass bottles, a plastic water bottle, and a shotgun shell casing that looks too weathered to be of much use. I head back through the trees to the table, and I'm surprised to see the sun's already sliding toward evening. Didn't feel that long, but when I check my watch, a wave of exhaustion hits me. I haven't slept much in the past forty-eight, and while I *can* keep going, it's not real smart. I'll start to miss things. My reaction time will turn to shit, which when you carry a sidearm is a real problem.

I phone myself off duty with the station and head to Pop's warm, cozy cabin up the hill from Stillhouse Lake. I bounce my car up the steep gravel road to the flat parking area—just big enough for my dad's truck and my car—and when I step out into the chilly evening air, I catch the smell of the place. I breathe it deep, closing my eyes. Fresh, clean trees, and no lake scent this far up. Dad's cooking up fish, and I have to swallow a sudden burst of saliva as I realize how damn hungry I am. When did I eat? I can't remember anymore.

I knock, wait for his yell, and enter the side door. Javier's dog, Boot, bounds to his feet, panting, and comes to me for his welcome petting. He's well behaved, even in the face of the smell of food. I hug his big, muscular neck, and he gives me fond licks. "Lock your damn doors," I tell my dad as I stand up again. He doesn't turn around from the stove, just waves a big iron fork over his head.

"Anybody comes for me in here, I'll stick 'em on the grill," he says. "Filleted."

"Catfish?" I guess, and come to look over his shoulder. My father used to be taller, broader, before age shrank him down; it's always a little disorienting, and a little sad, to reconcile this wiry man with the big, booming one who used to pick me up in one arm. Ezekiel "Easy" Claremont. One hell of a father, even in the worst days. And we had some bad ones after Momma died: not enough money, way too much grief. My pop gave up a lot to take care of me. Time for me to do the same for him, as much as he'll allow.

"You back off now, I only made enough for me." He shoots me a sharp look, though. "You skip lunch, girl?" I just shrug, which I know he'll take for *yes*. He shakes his head and reaches for a big metal spatula that he uses to cut that generously sized sizzling fish portion in half. He turns both pieces in the pan.

I wash my hands and get down plates and set the table, an old ritual that still conjures up the ghost of my mother, long gone, though the memory of her smile still lingers. These were her plates—worn, chipped in some spots, but precious to her. I get him a tall glass of water and set out his pills, and grab myself a Coke.

"Least you can do is get me one of those beers, since I'm cooking for you," he says.

"You know those meds say you can't drink alcohol with them."

"I know that beer ain't got much alcohol in it anyway."

It's a familiar grumble, and I let it go. I know—and his doctor knows—that he sneaks beers time to time. Hasn't hurt him much, though I worry. I find the potatoes and spinach he's already made warming in the oven and put them on the table, and by that time, the fish is done. Pop carries over the heavy skillet and slides the portions out; I stop myself from taking over when I see his arm shaking. He doesn't need that out of me, not right now.

"Your leg's a little better," I tell him. It's true. His limp's not as bad as it was a week back.

"Be better still once it warms up and stays warm," he says. "That cold's a bastard. Sit yourself down, get some food in you. You need it."

Pop is right, of course. I'm ravenous at the smell of the fish—blackened Cajun-style—and I barely wait for the prayer before I dig in. Home spice melts on my tongue, and for the first time all day I feel right. Safe. We eat without talking much, and every bite of it feels like love from him to me.

I'm torn about telling him about the baby. On the one hand, I know he'll be so happy about it he could bust . . . and yet, I want to tell him when Javier's here with me. I want to share this with Javi, the joy my father's going to feel. It's just another week. It's all I can do not to blurt it out, but I hold back. Somehow. And I know part of the reason is that I don't want Pop to fuss over me and nag me about dropping out of this case.

"Anybody stop in?" I ask him. Our friends often do, just to make sure my father's okay all alone up here, though since Sam and Gwen moved off to the big city, they don't come as often as they did. A couple of other neighbors make a point of it, though; one especially nice older lady from Norton drives all the way out once a week to have coffee and pick up his grocery list and make sure he's set up. I feel guilty about that, but I think she's sweet on him and I don't want to step in the middle of whatever *that* is.

"Sam just checked in," Pop says. "He's been off flying today. Guess it makes him happy." Pop's voice sounds grim, and I remember how much he hates to fly. Always has, as long as I can remember. He'd rather spend days on a bus going to visit relatives than take an hour on a plane. "And you can stop telling people to call me all day. I've got my damn cell phone, and I know who to call if I fall and can't get up."

"You call 911," I tell him briskly. "Not friends."

He sends me a look that tells me I'd best step back. "I know that."

"Fish is tasty, Pop," I say, and that mollifies him a little. "What'd you put in the spinach?"

"Garlic and lemon. Fresh lemon, not that stuff in the bottle." He lets a little space go by before he says, "You're into a bad one, aren't you?"

"Pretty bad," I tell him, and eat the spinach. It's lost its taste now. I'd forgotten about the little girls for the span of a whole few minutes, and it hurts like a betrayal. I know the little baby inside me right now is too small to feel, but I still *think* I feel the flutter of its tiny forming heart. I should tell him, but at the same time, I don't want to tell him. Not until this thing is over, and Javier is here. "You don't want to know."

"I know you don't want to tell me."

"Pop."

"Can't bottle that up inside, you know that. Javier's gone off to the Marine Corps, ain't he? Who you talking to about the case, then?"

"Gwen," I say. "I talked to Gwen. She's helping me out on this." He grunts, which is his way of saying he both approves and still wishes I'd put it on him. But I can't, not this. I just don't feel right about that. "I'm probably going to be doing some long hours on this. I'll make sure people come by and help you out if you need it."

"I'm not a damn shut-in, and I don't need folks coming up here all hours knocking on my door. They can call if they got something to say." Once my father's feathers get ruffled, his spurs come out, too, and I hold up a placating hand.

"Okay," I say. "We got any dessert in here?" Dessert always diverts my dad. He's got a bit of a sweet tooth.

"Chocolate cake," he says. "Myra brought it by last week." Myra is the Norton woman, and maybe my father's side piece, but I don't want to think about that. I just get up and get us slices of the cake, which is homemade and rich as hell. Myra's a good cook. We eat it up and forget our rough edges, and the rest of the half hour I spend there is easy and calm. I wash up and put things away and leave him tuning in to a boxing match. Night's fallen dark and heavy around the lake, but the stars are out, stark and beautiful. I lean against the car and finish up the last of my Coke before I three-point it into the recycling bin. I whistle for Boot, and he comes bounding down the stairs and into the back of the car.

Cruising around the lake road is a strange experience now; I always look over at the house where I first met Gwen Proctor. It looks the same. Odd I won't find her there now.

I check my phone in the car. No calls, but Gwen's emailed that she's heading out to Valerie tomorrow to interview neighbors and see if there's any sign of a stalker in Sheryl's life. It's late, but I need to run down Sheryl's ex, Tommy Jarrett. The old detective theory of "it's always the husband" is cliché because it's mostly true. If not the husband, it's almost always someone close—family, friends, ex-partners, neighbors. I'd have to eliminate Tommy anyway to go anywhere else. An investigation is a spiral, moving out. And when you miss something, you have to go back to the beginning.

I prefer going at odd hours if I plan to doorstep somebody, but it's closing in on ten at night, and that's pretty late in these parts. Still . . . I have the nagging feeling I'd best push on. I don't locate an address for Tommy, but there's an Abraham Jarrett living out in the sticks beyond Norton. Good bet. I head there and text Prester once I roll to a stop at the destination. I give him the address and what I'm there to do. He sends back BC30 . . . which, in Prester-speak, means *be careful*, and that he expects a check-in thirty minutes from now. Good enough. If I don't have backup, at least I'll have someone alert for trouble and getting help rolling fast.

The Jarrett place is . . . pretty typical. Half-farm, half-junkyard. The small farmhouse on the property hasn't got a roof, and I don't think anybody's lived in it in decades, but there's a seminew single-wide trailer sinking into the dirt not far away. It's maybe half a mile out of Norton proper, but it might as well be in the heart of the wilderness, it's so dark and quiet around here. Lights are on in the trailer, though, and that gives me a little confidence.

I walk up the steps and knock briskly on the flimsy door. I hear heavy thuds, footsteps moving toward the front of the home, and then the door flies open with such force I'm glad I moved a few treads down, out of respect. An old, grizzled white man glares down at me. "What you want at this hour? Jesus wept, it's late." But then he blinks, and sees the badge I'm holding out, and his body language shifts. "You here to tell me you found him? My boy?"

"You're talking about Tommy?" I ask, and he nods and comes out on the steps. He's wearing a checked bathrobe that's too thin for the cold, but he doesn't seem to care. Weathered old house shoes on his feet. I glance behind him inside the house—habit—and see that it's fairly neat. That's unexpected. "I'm here about him, yes. You're saying he's missing?"

"I'm saying he left a long while back, and nobody believes me when I say he wouldn't have done that," Abraham says. He squints at me. "You must be new. Never dealt with you before."

"I'm Detective Claremont," I tell him. "Can I ask you a few questions? I know it's late, but it may be important."

He rocks back and forth in his slippers for a minute, then nods. "You want to come on in? Have some coffee?"

"I'd be much obliged." I'm guardedly pleased to be welcomed. At least he's talking. That's a good start.

Inside, the trailer is just as neat as the glimpse implied. The carpet's old, but there's very little clutter. Photos on the walls, and some generic dollar-store art. Nothing in the place makes me think there's been a woman living here for years, if ever; the small touches all seem masculine. My gaze catches on a framed Confederate flag as I turn, and I take a beat, then move on. Not exactly unusual in this part of the world, but indicative of several things.

He's getting out a couple of mismatched mugs, and there's a half-full pot of coffee in the machine. He pours and, without looking at me, says, "Cream or sugar?"

"Black is fine," I say. He sends me a look, as if to figure out what I mean by that, then nods and carries the coffee over to the small two-person table. We sit. "Late to be making these kinds of calls, ain't it? You're lucky you didn't get shot."

"I know it's late," I say. I let the implied threat slide. "Sorry about that, sir. I know you were probably just settling down for the night." I put some warmth in my voice, and it helps; his shoulders come down a touch. Anything I can do to disarm him right now is useful. "I didn't know about your son's case. Can I ask—"

"He's been gone over a year now," he says. "And I'll tell you what, I think that woman of his killed him. I said as much to the other detective, but I don't think he even listened." I hear the anger, and see the muscle harden in the line of his flabby jaw. "Damn shoddy job he did. Said my son just ran off and left his pregnant wife. If that's true, why'd he sign over his damn car *and* house to her first? And his whole bank account too? Man's going to run out on his responsibilities, he takes what he owns."

"You're right, that sounds strange." I say it, but I don't mean it; lots of men dodge their duties as parents but try to make up for it by leaving shit behind they don't want or need. I can see Tommy Jarrett thinking that would absolve him, and I imagine the bank account could have had some withdrawals prior to his disappearance. Maybe Tommy had saved up for his dash for freedom.

I'll pull the file. Odds are good that Prester was the detective, unless it was the last days of the other white detective I barely knew, the third one in rotation who barely came to work at all. He's now retired and off to Florida, and he never gave me the time of day. Not looking much forward to questioning his judgment if that's the case.

"When's the last time you saw Tommy, sir?" I ask, and take out my notebook. He takes a gulp of his coffee and gets out his cell phone.

"About fourteen months ago. Here," he says, and puts the phone down and slides it across to me. There's a photo on the screen: Abraham in a plaid work shirt and jeans with his arm around his son, both grinning at the selfie camera. Sweet. I look hard at Tommy, trying to see past the easy grin, the shape of his face. Does he look like a man who would abandon his pregnant wife? I have no idea. One thing being a cop will teach you: nobody looks like it, and everybody looks like it. We contain multitudes, and at least half of that multitude is made up of assholes.

"Nice-looking young man," I say, which is true. "Mind if I get a copy of this picture? I can send it to my phone." That'll give me the date and time it was taken, as well as the location.

"Please yourself," he says, and I see a little flash of unease in his face. I make sure he sees I'm not snooping as I forward the picture, and I hand his device back. He immediately pockets it. I doubt it has anything to do with his son; everybody's got something to hide, and I'm not interested in his secrets. "So, you actually intend to look for him this time? Not just file some piece of paper about how my son's a cowardly piece of dog shit?"

He sounds aggressive, but I see the glint of tears in his eyes. Hope's a hard thing in cases like this. He's fronting to try to hold in that fear, that desperation, and I get it. I'm very respectful when I say, "Mr. Jarrett, I'd be very glad to look into it. It'd speed matters along if you'd give me permission to take a look around where he was living, give me permission to access his phone and bank records as his next of kin—"

"I will," he says before I'm even finished. "Whatever it takes. Tommy lived in the house he bought with his own money with that woman—I ain't even calling her his wife. When he disappeared, he was still living right there. He never moved."

"You know that for a fact?" I ask him, and I'm gentle about it. "That he didn't throw some stuff in a bag and get a friend to pick him up?"

He doesn't answer that, and I didn't really expect him to. He doesn't want to believe it, but men can do strange things when their women get pregnant. Some bolt for the hills. Some get mean. Some get possessive and strange.

Some kill their kids.

It hits me with a small, significant chill that one person Sheryl Lansdowne would have stopped her car for out there in the dark was her missing husband.

I keep a bland expression, but now I'm alert for any signs that Abraham is trying to cover up for Tommy. A prickle on the nape of my neck says I should check the house for any sign he's been here, but I need to be careful; if he is here, I could be in a fatal situation, fast. Best I come back prepared, with backup.

But even as I decide that, Abraham gets up and says, "Come on with me. I'll show you his room. Nothing in there but what he left when he got married, but maybe it'll help y'all."

There's no clue in his body language that things could pop off, but I follow at a distance, hand close to the gun I've got concealed beneath my jacket. I'm fast and accurate, which is never a guarantee of surviving a gunfight, but it helps. My heart ticks up to a faster rhythm, and I breathe deep to slow it down. I'm hyperaware as we move through the small kitchen, down a dark, narrow hall, past a bathroom. There's a single closed door at the end. Abraham swings it open and goes inside.

In or out, girl—decide.

I go in.

There's no ambush. And no Tommy Jarrett waiting with a child-killing grin to finish me off. Abraham jams his hands in the pockets of his bathrobe and stands back after turning on the overhead light, and I'm looking at a teenage boy's room. It even smells like one—that lingering scent of old socks, testosterone sweat, dirty sheets. The bed's made, with a cheap Wal-Mart comforter over the sagging mattress. Posters of white country artists I barely recognize, and muscle cars. A miniature basketball hoop in the corner that's probably seen a lot of use; the net looks ragged. I make a slow circuit of the room, then glance at his father. "Mind if I open the drawers?"

"Do as you please," he says. "Ain't got nothing to hide."

He's right. There's not much in the small dresser except some extra sheets, a pair of old running shoes that stink of years of service, a pile of papers that, when I look through them, mostly seem like schoolwork. Tommy was a solid B student. Not exceptional, but he paid attention. "Your son do anything in school special? Like football, or—"

"Basketball," he says, which I could have guessed. "Real good too. Could have gone off to university, he had some offers."

He had indeed; I've already found the letters. But none of them offered a full ride, and I knew Tommy would have had to give up on that dream. No way Abraham could afford college for his son without a scholarship. Tommy, I guessed, was a solid player but not a star. Same as his schoolwork.

I check the closet. I half expect to find Tommy hidden in there like some nightmare, but it's empty except for old wire hangers swinging gently on the rod, and a collection of abandoned high school tees. A letter jacket with his name on it. I understand the message of this room: when Tommy left, he put childhood things away. He left fully intending to become a man on his own terms.

And then he ran away when it got too real? Maybe. But instinct is starting to pull me in a different direction.

Abraham suddenly says, "You didn't come about Tommy, you said. What brought you out here?"

He's going to find out anyway; it'll be all over the news soon, if it isn't cooking already. So I say, "His wife, Sheryl, has gone missing."

"Oh lord," he says, and looks briefly taken aback. Then worried. "Did she leave them girls? Who's got them?"

I break it to him very, very carefully, and there's something especially grim and sad about seeing an old, proud man like this break down. He sinks down on his son's bed and puts his head in his hands and cries—huge, heaving sobs. I sit next to him. Don't touch him, but I wait for the storm to pass. He's lost everything now . . . his son gone, and now his two grandchildren.

He finally whispers, "She never let me see them girls. Not even once."

I swallow a painful lump in my throat and say, "They didn't suffer, sir." That's a lie, but I can't tell the man the truth. Not now. "I'm looking into what happened to them, and to Sheryl."

He nods. His whole body is shaking with the force of his grief. I stand up, finally, and put a hand lightly on his shoulder. I take my business card out and place it next to him on the bed.

Then I leave, shutting the door behind me on the hell that I've brought. Once I'm back in the car, I take a deep breath and reach for my phone. I text ACOM, which Prester will read as *all clear old man*. Prester's recently discovered emojis, a fact that amuses me to no end, and I smile when he sends me back the cussing smiley face. It's not much of a smile, but it's something.

The smile fades fast, and the small comfort along with it. I'm almost sure that Tommy Jarrett is dead.

Which means in the morning, I need to get into Sheryl Lansdowne. Hard.

9

GWEN

By the time I'm home, it's pretty late in the afternoon, so I dive right into Sheryl Lansdowne research. Kez is going to be tied up on that grid search outside Norton until dark, so best I make some headway for her with basic stuff.

It doesn't turn out to be basic at all, because it quickly becomes evident that Sheryl isn't who she seems to be. In fact, records for Sheryl Lansdowne begin just three years back.

It's a false identity, and not a very good one at that. Good enough to get her a real driver's license, but the social security number she's using is false. She'd be kicked out fast if she had a job, claimed benefits, or had an employer who'd ever paid in for her, but it doesn't look like Sheryl worked in any official capacity at all. Didn't even apply for assistance, as far as I can tell, which is rare around these parts. Maybe she had some kind of gig that paid her cash? It's not really possible to tell yet.

I use our firm's proprietary facial recognition software to try matching Sheryl to the driver's license databases.

My first hit comes from Iowa.

Sheryl Lansdowne's original name is Penny Carlson.

Penny is a missing person. Last seen driving off, but she never arrived at the university she was scheduled to attend. Extensive searches were conducted for her car, and she was considered endangered missing, but since she wasn't a child—she was eighteen at the time—there wasn't much more to be done. As a legal adult, she had the right to disappear if she wanted. She packed up her life, got in her car, and vanished like a bad memory. I find a website dedicated to finding her, probably put up by family or friends, but it doesn't look like it's been updated for a long time. Several years, at least. They've given up.

Maybe Penny had decided that college wasn't for her, that she wanted to start over entirely differently. But my instincts catch fire when I realize the time gap between Penny Carlson and Sheryl.

Ten years from Penny's disappearance to Sheryl's arrival in Valerie. So where was she during that time? What had she been doing? My brain keeps trying to connect random dots, but I don't have enough to go on, just a deep sense of unease. None of this makes sense.

Sometimes it just doesn't, part of my brain says calmly. And while it's right, I'm not about to admit defeat. Not yet.

I widen the search to more states. Results slow down, and I get too many false positives. I've lost track of time when I finally hear the kids come home. Lanny appears in the doorway to say, "School's boring, Connor aced a test, nobody's bleeding, in case you're interested. Did you eat?"

I hold up the empty plate that once held pie, gaze still fixed on the computer screen. I see her shrug in soft peripheral focus, and then she turns to go.

I wrench myself away from the screen and say, "Honey? Thank you for asking." It disconcerts me to realize that she's trying to take care of *me.* "Is it your night to cook?"

"Yeah, and it'll be pizza because I'm a basic bitch," she says. "Calm down, with salad, so it's healthy. I just have to watch out for Connor trying to sneak his habanero hot sauce all over it. What are you working on?"

"Stuff," I say, and realize how dismissive it sounds. "Sorry. It's for a case that Kezia's working, actually. It's a little urgent."

"Can I help?"

I instantly reject that idea. I don't want her anywhere close to this. "Thanks, but I'm almost done with what I have to get together. Last of it right now, then I'm all yours. We can protect the pizza together."

"Then the range with Vee, right?"

"Right." In all honesty, I'd nearly forgotten about it. I want to ask her more about her day. I want to have her sit down beside me and give me a hug. But I'm derailed in the next second by the notice of facial recognition matches out of Kentucky.

Ten possibles come up, but I spot her immediately, right in the middle of the pack of similar features. Penny Carlson took an improbably good driver's license photo as a blonde. She'd also changed her makeup style, going for something dramatic and glam, and she looks older and much more sophisticated, though according to the new driver's license in the name of Tammy Maguire, she was just twenty years old at the time of the picture.

I realize that we don't know Sheryl Lansdowne at all. Not her name, not her age, not anything except her face . . . and plastic surgery could put an end to that tracking, if she had enough cash.

I don't know if she's running from something, but if she was . . . it's caught up with her this time. And that's a sickening, horrifying prospect that makes me sweaty with memory: A decaying Louisiana manor. A camera watching me. My demented ex-husband's face.

I know what it's like to be the prey. And the hunter.

But I still don't know which of those identifies Sheryl.

The search doesn't turn up any more results before I have to leave it and help Lanny with dinner; Sam comes home in the middle of that process and pitches in, though I can see he's tired. He tells me about his day, the training session in the late afternoon; I get the sense that he's leaving something out, but I don't press him on it at the dinner table. He's aced the simulations, as usual. Sam doesn't fail much, though he's the first to say crashing in sim is the best teacher. I know he's concerned about reactions slowing as he gets older, but so far, his twitch-times are damn good. Better than mine, I think.

There's something on his mind. Something on mine too. We're both holding something back for a quiet conversation later.

We eat, we talk. Lanny's bright one moment, down the next. Connor's quiet and a little sullen. Teens. I remember feeling those storms of emotion, and I know there isn't much I can do to help him through it other than be understanding. It stings, though, and I miss the days when Lanny and Connor couldn't stop excitedly talking except to shovel in food. The later teen years are different, and now I have two to deal with, and God, I don't know how it should work.

But at least they seem relatively normal these days. Therapy has worked magic on Connor; he seems much less anxious, more relaxed. Lanny's still a firecracker ready to pop at the first perceived slight, but she laughs more often, and I think she's going to find her balance. But it frightens me how little time I have left to make sure she's safe and well and protected, prepared to survive alone in this world. Her and Connor both.

Lanny eats a small bite of the pizza and says, "Mom and I are going to the gun range with Vee."

"We," Connor says. "I'm going too."

"Excuse me, when did you suddenly like guns again?" Lanny frowns at him. "Don't they still freak you out?"

It's an attack, but not a mean one, and he doesn't take it too badly. "That's why I want to go, *sis*. Because they still freak me out. Mrs. Terrell thinks if I get familiar with them, it'll help."

Mrs. Terrell, his therapist, has talked to me about that. I'm a little worried about the effectiveness of that treatment. Connor's problem

isn't rooted in an unfounded fear so much as it is trauma; he had a seriously violent reaction to a school-shooting drill, and that was *before* he
was abducted and caught in the middle of an actual gunfight. Aversion
therapy seems like the wrong move to me.

But taking control back after trauma sometimes works. It did for
me. Connor wanted his own therapist, not to share mine; I'm not sure
I altogether approve of Mrs. Terrell, possibly because she's a part of
my son's life I don't control, and I don't understand why she's advising
some of the things she does. But the feral-animal part of me, the part
that never quite goes away . . . that part wants Connor to learn to shoot
properly. Because my son will always be at risk, given who I am. Who
his father was. Who *he* is. The future's coming at us fast. I just want to
reset the clock. Slow it all down.

I hate it when I feel this tug-of-war inside me. I like clarity.
Certainty. And I know I will almost never have it when it comes to the
best thing to do for my kids.

Lanny and Connor are both looking at me. So's Sam. His is the
hardest expression to read; he's going to let me make this call without
weighing in. Lanny's wanting me to tell Connor no, of course; she's only
recently won the right to learn to shoot, and the last thing she wants
is to lose that special status. But Lanny hasn't been through the same
things Connor has, especially back in that grim compound at Bitter
Falls. I lock gazes with my son and say, "Fine. We'll all go to the gun
range. But you need to understand: if you start to feel uncomfortable,
even a little, you tell me or Sam, and we will get you out of there. All
right?"

He nods, and I see tension ease out of him. Sam's still watching
me, and when I transfer my attention back to him, he nods once and
digs into his salad.

Lanny drops her fork. Loudly. She sits back in her chair with her
arms folded. "Wow. Really. Not even a discussion?"

"Not even," Connor says. He's way too smug about it. "What? You don't think I can handle it?"

"Like I worry about you at all." Lanny shoves her chair back from the table and leaves. I hear her door slam.

"That was mature," Connor says. When I start to slide my chair away from the table, he rolls his eyes. "No, Mom, don't go talk to her. She'll be okay. Trust me. She's just pissed off at me."

"Just because of the gun range? Or something else?"

He shrugs, gaze on his food, and I know there's more to it, but sometimes the kids need to work it out without me in the middle. I just shake my head and finish my pizza. We wrap up Lanny's last slice and put it in the fridge.

Sure enough, she shows up when we're loading the car for the trip to the range. I say hello, she silently takes the back seat, arms folded, face a stone mask. It's unsettling, because I can see the shadow of the adult she's becoming. There's nothing dramatic about her just now. She's centered, even in her disapproval.

Please stay my baby. Just a little while longer. Please.

Connor, oblivious, calls shotgun, which leaves Sam to slide into the back next to Lanny. When Connor and I get in the front, I check my daughter in the rearview mirror. Sam's leaning over and asking her something in a calm, quiet voice; I see her lose a little of her stiffness as she answers. He puts his arm around her in a half hug.

And just like that, she's okay. It breaks my heart that I don't know how to do that anymore with her, make it all . . . fine. We sometimes clash like mismatched gears, my daughter and me. I know that's normal, but it feels like failure, and it makes me want desperately to make it right.

Vee's waiting at the curb when I pull the SUV in, and Sam gets out to let her in to sit between him and Lanny. She climbs in encumbered with a battered old black satchel, and she seems wired, as usual. "Cool,

cool, cool," she says, and wiggles in the seat as she gets comfortable. "This is going to be fun! Hey, Lantagirl."

"Hey," Lanny says. She's relaxed a little in Vee's presence, at least. "What's in the bag?"

Vee reaches in and pulls out a far-too-large-for-her semiautomatic. I feel a kick start of urgent, wild adrenaline. A nightmare lurches into motion in my brain. I imagine Vee's finger tightening on that trigger, a bullet firing through the seat, my son bleeding.

"Drop it!" Sam's shout is sudden and shocking in the confines of the SUV, and she puts the gun down on top of the satchel and raises her hands high. "Jesus, Vee. *Never do that.*" He takes the gun, carefully pointing it toward the SUV's floor, and checks it over. "Loaded," he says. "One in the chamber. Vera—" His tone is grim and angry. He methodically ejects the cartridge that's under the hammer, then takes out the magazine.

"What? It's in case that asshole letter guy comes creepin' up!" We're all staring at her, even Lanny. Vee hunches in on herself, and grabs the made-safe gun back from Sam when he offers it. She shoves it into the satchel along with the magazine and loose bullet. "I'm just tryin' to protect myself is all." Her rural Tennessee accent has come back thick. "Wouldn'ta shot y'all or nothin'."

"Accidents happen," I say. "And you need trigger discipline. We'll go over all that once we get to the range." My heart's still hammering, my hands unsteady, but I take a couple of deep breaths and glance over at Connor before I put the vehicle in gear. "We're going to get you a gun case."

She mutters something under her breath, and I doubt it's complimentary, but I'm focused on my son. He's staring straight ahead, and I see the hard shine of his eyes. "Connor," I say gently. "You all right?"

"Sure," he says, in a voice utterly devoid of emotion. "Fine, Mom." He isn't, but I see him taking slow, regular breaths, and he blinks and smiles. It isn't totally convincing, but it's better. "I'll be fine."

It hurts. I want to wrap him in cotton and tuck him in bed and never, never let anything hurt him again. But that's my screaming instincts, not my rational brain. My son has overcome a lot in his young life; he copes with what he can't control far better than I have. I have to trust him, and trust his therapy process. He chose it. I have to respect that, even if it makes me weep inside.

So we go to the gun range.

It isn't the comfortable, familiar place Javier operates back at Stillhouse Lake; that one is small and extremely well run, even though it's a backwoods haven. Former military like Javi don't tolerate sloppiness.

I don't love this one nearly as much. It's large, it's loud, and in my opinion it's slipshod on safety processes. But it's close to us, and if the instructors aren't the best, Sam and I can teach the kids properly ourselves. After we kit Vee out with the right things to have—a transport case, a small quick-access safe for home, a holster—we go back to the car and get all the weapons we're going to use: my Sig 9mm, Vee's gun, Sam's revolver. All packed into cases the way they should be.

We're just locking the car when Vee says, "Do you know that guy?" There's something odd about the way she says it, and I turn to glance over my shoulder at her. She's staring off to the right, and I follow her gaze.

There's a man in a car parked across the street, but even as I see him, he puts the car in gear and drives away. I don't get more than a glance at him, but I can see he's white and is wearing a dark-colored ball cap. That's the extent of my impression. The car's a completely anonymous dark-blue sedan, a Toyota, and I see the rental car sticker in the window. It's too late, and the angle's too bad, to get a license plate. He turns the corner and is gone.

"Why?" I ask Vee. She's still staring after the car, but she shifts her attention back to me. I see something odd in her gaze, something I've rarely seen in her. Vee's all steel and smoked-glass strong until she breaks. She rarely shows weakness.

Right now, she looks afraid. And that wakes something deeply primal in me. We're exposed out here. Far, far too exposed. My mouth goes dry. My pulse speeds up. And I find myself watching the street, waiting for something to happen.

Hypervigilance. It's dangerous. I back it down, breathe deep. Panic is contagious.

"It's okay, Vee," I tell her. "We're fine. Right?"

"If you say so," she mutters, and grabs the case that holds her gun from me. "This one's mine, right?" There's no mistaking it. She chose a shiny paisley-patterned case in neon colors. Before I can ask her anything else, she's moving for the gun range door, as if she doesn't want to spend another moment out in the open.

I desperately, desperately want to be inside, in a windowless concrete room. Safe.

But I stay. I feel the cool wind on my face. I watch the traffic on the street, a river of metal and lights. I'm facing it down, the beast that comes for me out of the back of my mind. And it always, always has Melvin's face.

Behind me, Sam says, "Gwen? You coming?" He says it gently, as if he understands, though I don't know how he could.

"Yes," I say, and I turn my back on my instincts and go to teach my kids—even Vee—how to properly handle a weapon that I pray they never need.

◆ ◆ ◆

Connor does better than I could have imagined. He barely flinches at the sound of the shots. He's steady and deliberate when I teach him proper arm position and stance. When he finally fires his first shot, he hits the target. Not dead center, of course, but in the ballpark. Most kids would celebrate that, but not my son. He looks at the target critically, makes the gun safe, and puts it down as if he's been doing this his whole life. "I missed," he says.

"You didn't. It's on the outline."

"It wouldn't stop him," Connor says. Just that, and it tells me everything about my son and what his attitude will be toward guns. He's not in this for sport, or fun, or excitement like the teens who are squealing and clapping in other lanes as they even come close to a good shot. Like it is for me, this is survival for him. Pure, simple survival.

I hate it. I mourn for what it says about how bleak his world seems to him. How inevitable it is that he's going to need this skill, a thing he doesn't want but will not flinch at learning.

My son is so brave it steals my breath.

I put my hand on his shoulder, and while he doesn't pull away, I still feel the muscles tighten. Guarding. That's another heartbreak for me as his mom, the knowledge that my touch can't soothe away the pain anymore. That it might, in fact, add to it. I have to let that strike me and fade before I can master my voice to something like normal. "You'll get better," I tell him. "But let's stop there for tonight, okay?" I check my watch; it's been an hour and a half. Lanny looks incandescent with victory over her accuracy, and she and Vee share a high five while Sam looks on, shaking his head. I show Connor how to stow the gun properly in the case, then have him sit with the girls on a bench in the back as Sam and I take a quick turn in adjoining lanes.

Shooting feels like freedom to me. The world goes quiet inside my head—even the constant racket that soundproofing ear protection can't quell. Everything narrows to me, the target, the weight of the gun in my hand. There's a certainty to it that I don't find anywhere else.

I brace, aim, and quick-fire, alternating shots between head and heart. Next to me, Sam does the same. We put our guns down and glide the targets. I step back with him to compare.

Evenly matched. His is just a hair closer on one of the head shots. Damn. I need to get in here more often.

I don't realize that the kids have joined us until Lanny, at my elbow, says, "Jesus, Mom." She sounds shaken and impressed. I put my arm around her, and all the arguments are washed away.

"Don't fuck with the fam," Vee says.

"Vee!" I chide.

"What?"

I just shake my head. After all . . . she's not wrong.

As we're packing up, the alarm sounds, and everyone steps back from their lanes, guns down and made safe—or, at least, most people obey the protocol. I see the range master coming down the row, making note of those who were sloppy about it, but he's heading straight for us.

I feel my shoulders brace as he comes to a halt facing us, and I see Sam look up as well. Neither of us is aggressive, but both of us are on guard. The kids don't seem to get it, but I see it in the man's light-blue eyes before he says, "Look, I'm sorry to do this, but I've had a complaint."

"About us," Sam says.

"No. About her." His gaze is squarely on me. "I'm going to have to ask you to come up front. I'll refund your membership fee."

"You're kicking my mom out? What for? She obeys all the rules!" Lanny gets it fast, and as I might have predicted, she isn't about to stand for it. She thrusts herself forward, chin out. Her cheeks are flushed, her eyes flashing, and I'm glad Connor puts a hand on her shoulder to hold her back. I'm too wrong-footed to intervene, too taken by surprise. And yes, too exposed, too humiliated; I hate the people watching me, whispering. One or two have taken out their phones to film it. I know this all too well. Just another recurring nightmare. I feel a sick, weightless darkness forming in the pit of my stomach.

"Simmer down, kid," the range master tells Lanny, and of all the things he could have picked to say, that's the worst. I see Lanny's volcano building up to blow. Connor's hand tightens on her shoulder, but she shrugs him off. "Okay, all of y'all, follow me." He doesn't want a scene any more than I do.

My daughter opens her mouth to say something none of us can take back, and I quickly say, in as even a tone as I can, "Of course. I'm happy to comply. But just me, please. Sam will stay with the kids." I'm not calm. I feel like everything's turned to quicksand under my feet, but getting out of here, away from the watchers . . . that's the only thing I can control about this moment. More than that, I need Lanny to cool down. She needs to learn control if she wants to survive long-term in a world that will happily push her right over the edge. If nothing else, I have to show her that.

But I see the disappointment and disbelief in my daughter's expression before I turn away, and it hurts like a slap. Sam moves to stand close to her. Good. I need him to be a calming influence right now. I'm trying, but I can feel the jitter under my skin, the churn in my guts. I know what's coming; I've faced it often enough. I'd just hoped that in a town as large and diverse as this one, it would take longer to manifest.

Once we're in his office, the range master doesn't look comfortable having this conversation. So I save him the trouble. "Let me guess. Someone—you don't need to tell me who, it doesn't matter—identified me as Gina Royal, ex-wife of a serial killer. And they don't like having me around. Bad press."

"Ma'am, you've been arrested in connection with not just one major case, but *three*."

"Never convicted," I say. It sounds flippant, but he has to know I have no actual criminal convictions. I was arrested originally and put on trial as Melvin's accomplice; the fact that I was judged not guilty will never be proof of innocence. "Look. I have a dark past. Lots of folks do. But I need a place to practice."

"That place can't be here, ma'am," he says. "I got investors who don't like bad press." He hesitates a second, then reaches down to open a drawer in the plain military-surplus desk that sits in the center of the office. He takes out a piece of paper and slides it across to me.

I know what it is before I touch it. I recognize the style, the layout, everything. It's a wanted poster, and it's got my picture on it. In smaller pictures, my two kids. I don't bother to read it; it'll spread the lies about how I helped Melvin Royal get away with murders, and how my kids are just as sick. I not only know what it says; I know who designed it.

Sam made it, originally, years ago. Part of a long harassment campaign by the Lost Angels online group he was part of, and helped found, for the families of Melvin Royal's victims. It's our shared horrible past, yes, and we've put that behind us . . . but this still hurts. I feel wounds coming open and dripping fresh pain.

The flyer used my mug shot from my arrest on the day Melvin's crimes were discovered. I look like that woman, still, though I barely recognize her at the same time. The flat look in her eyes that I recall as shock . . . it comes across as hard and emotionless. Gina Royal was a different person, and I never want to be her again. And I hate the echoes this wakes in me, the earthquake it unleashes.

I realize I haven't said anything. I look up at the man and say, "Where did you get it?"

"They went up today on telephone poles in the neighborhood. Word's getting out, Ms. Proctor. Ain't no escaping it."

"You've got surveillance in the parking lot. You could tell me who put them up."

"I can't do that, ma'am."

Won't, more like. I don't push him. There's no point. I pick up the flyer and ask if I can keep it; when he nods, I fold it and put it in my pocket. Then I let him write me out a refund check for the whole family's fees, and I put it in my pocket too. I don't say anything else, not even when he apologizes and offers to shake my hand. He's trying to ease his own feeling of injustice, and I don't want any part of that. I just nod and leave.

I can't speak because if I do, I'll scream.

Leaving the office, I walk right past Sam and the kids. I ignore his questioning look. I finally swallow and manage to say, "Let's go," and head toward the building's exit.

Outside, the monster attacks. Not the physical kind of assault; this is far worse. I feel the panic of being outside, vulnerable, *watched*, hunted. My brain is reacting to a threat by dumping survival adrenaline into my blood at near-toxic levels, and there's nothing for me to fight. Nothing but myself.

I can't breathe. I try, but it feels like my diaphragm has frozen solid, like my lungs have filled with heavy ice. My pulse is pounding so hard I can't hear anything else. I know I should control it, *can* control it, but nothing works. Nausea slides over me like grease, but I don't even have the ability to vomit it out.

I collapse against the wall, gasping for air, and see Sam rushing to me. I read his lips as he crouches beside me. *Breathe. Try to breathe.* He turns his head, and I think he's shouting at Lanny, who's hovering a step behind, hands clenched into fists. She takes her phone out of her pocket and drops it, picks it up, finally makes the call. I want to say *I'm okay*, I need to, because I know I'm not having a heart attack, even though that's how it feels.

I'm having a full-on panic attack. Haven't had one in years.

I hear Melvin's cold voice, clear as hail on the roof: *I always knew you were weak. Look at you, you sniveling little wreck. You can't protect our kids. You can't even stand up.*

I shut my eyes and search for peace in the storm. And this time, I hear different voices.

My daughter saying, "Mom? Mom, it's okay, the ambulance is coming. Mom? It's going to be okay."

And my son's unsteady, soft voice near my ear saying, "It's okay, Mom. I understand."

I know that he does most of all of us.

Feeling comes next. Sam's arms around me. Lanny's hand fever-warm against my face. Connor holding my hand.

The storm fades. Silence sets in.

I gasp in a sudden, convulsive breath. My head is spinning and aching, but *I'm here*. I'm with the people who love me. My circle of protection. It blindsides me that I've been so busy trying to protect all of them that I've utterly failed to protect myself.

I burst into tears and hug them close, all three of them. Vee's hovering on the edges of this, part of it but separate, and I wish she'd come in, I wish I could be better, I wish this sudden, melting peace could last.

But I hear the siren of the ambulance coming, and I know it's already starting to disappear.

The paramedics don't find anything wrong with me, other than elevated blood pressure and low oxygen saturation, but they advise me to see my doctor about it. I thank them and wince at what this will cost us, but at the same time, Lanny did exactly the right thing. Better a bill than a funeral.

Sam's standing with me as the ambulance pulls away. People in the parking lot and across the street are watching us, and I feel their eyes on me like groping hands. I suddenly, desperately want to be out of here. "We should go," I say. "You drive." I hand him the keys. He kisses me gently on the forehead, pulls back, and gives me a long and searching look. "What?"

"You're all right," he says, and I feel the quirk of his smile tug at something deep inside me. "And you'll be all right."

Lanny and Vee are standing near the SUV, shoulder to shoulder, and they turn as one as we walk toward them. "You scared the *shit* out of me," Vee says. Her surveying look is not kind. "What the hell was that?"

"Panic attack," I tell her crisply, as if I'm not ashamed of it. I shouldn't be, but it's hard, hard for me to admit weakness, especially to her. Vee's got a predator's unerring instincts, and though she's not cruel, when she goes in for an emotional kill, she's efficient about it. "Come on, let's get you home."

"Guess I won't get more lessons," she observes. "Seeing as you're famous again." She reaches in her pocket and pulls out a folded piece of paper. "I took it off one of them other cars."

I know what it is before I unfold it. The flyer. The same one that I got from the range master.

When I look up, I see pieces of paper fluttering under windshield wipers all around the lot.

I want to howl. I don't. I just say, "Let's put it on hold until I find another shooting range. It's Knoxville. There are plenty." About a dozen, in fact. But I know that if my stalker continues to come after me, it'll be easy to find me no matter where I go. He could cover a dozen places in a couple of days. I need to stop him. Now.

Sam glances over and sees the flyer that Vee's handed me. I hear his intake of breath, but he doesn't say anything. I see the blood draining from his face. This hurts him, too, in ways that I can't truly appreciate.

"You want to talk about that?" he asks. I shake my head. I don't want to talk to *him*, and I know that's irrational and cruel; it isn't his fault someone resurrected his favorite form of punishment and used it against me. It isn't his fault, but it feels like it is. And I need to settle that in my head.

But I don't get that chance because from the back seat, Lanny leans forward and grabs the paper. "Oh my God."

"Give it back," I tell her, and my voice is too loud, too tight.

She doesn't surrender it. She knows what she's looking at—she remembers it very well. She says, "They're doing it again." Her voice sounds like a little girl's again, shocked and traumatized. I feel my breath catch hard in my throat, and my eyes burn with tears. I see Connor take the flyer and examine it, then carefully fold it up and give it back to Vee. For once, Vee sensibly keeps her mouth shut.

There's not a sound in the car but road noise. If I can't help blaming Sam, he also can't help blaming himself. And this time, he's going to see the toll this takes directly on my—*our*—children. I have to suppress the vile impulse to think he deserves that for his past actions.

"Wait, y'all have seen these before?" Vee finally asks.

"People put them up other places we lived," Connor says, and his tone is calm and uninflected. "They wanted us to leave, and we did."

It's the calmness, and the inevitability behind it, that makes my heart ache. I did let the Lost Angels . . . *Sam* . . . hound us from place to place, for years. I did that for my kids. But I also did it *to* my kids.

"We're not leaving," I tell Connor, and hold his stare in the rearview mirror for a second.

"We just started getting *normal*," Lanny says. "I just found *friends*." She sounds too shattered to be angry. The rage that sweeps over me is breathtaking and weirdly freeing. It steals my breath and clenches my hands, and I think, *Fine. Come at us, you assholes.*

Even Vee is quiet now, realizing this is way deeper than she can swim, with currents fast enough to drown the unwary.

That river of silence, fraught with rage and pain and fear, flows continuously, unbroken, until we arrive at Vee's apartment and let her out. I watch her walk to her door with her absurdly bright gun case and safe and let herself in before Sam puts the SUV back into gear and heads us home. *Home.* It feels less like that now, more like a fortress bracing for an attack.

I never should have let my guard down.

Sam pulls the SUV into the garage, and we all stay in the vehicle until the door rolls closed. Usually Lanny or Connor is the first to bail, but my kids are quiet and still.

Finally Connor says, "Are we going to talk about it? You knew about the flyers, didn't you? That's why you had the panic attack."

"Not here," I say. "Inside."

Sam nods and gets out first. The rest of us follow him, and I see the too-rigid set of his spine, the linebacker angle of his shoulders. Sam's got a great poker face, but his body language gives him away if you know how to look. I've retrieved our guns, and I carry them into the bedroom with the main gun safe to store them away. I put his favorite sidearm in the fingerprint-locked safe on his side, and then mine in its mate on the other. The larger gun safe holds other things as well: a hunting rifle, a shotgun, and two more smaller pistols. Ammunition and cleaning equipment. I seal everything up and go into the kitchen, where Sam is pouring two generously sized glasses of red wine. He slides one over to me, but doesn't meet my eyes.

"We're not okay, are we?" He asks it quietly, but I hear the heartbreak in his voice.

I take the glass and turn toward him. The kids are in their rooms, and I keep my volume low as well. "Sam, did you know the Lost Angels were ramping this up again?"

"No." He says it definitively, and I believe him. "I thought they were letting it go. Last time I checked, we weren't high on their list of monsters anymore."

"But not off it."

"I don't think we'll ever be off it."

"Sam," I say gently, but with purpose. "It isn't *we*. Me and the kids are the ones on the posters."

That silences him. He squeezes his eyes closed, then says, "I know. I'm sorry." I hear the guilt. He started this. He knows how much damage it's already done, and will continue to wreak. But there's also little he can do about that, and I take a breath to acknowledge it.

He opens his eyes, and we hold that gaze for a long moment before he says, "Gwen, what are you going to do?" I can feel the solid ground between us trembling and eroding, and I hate it with every muscle fiber.

Someone did this to us. But not Sam. I know that. I wish I could *feel* that, but I know it takes time.

So for now, I reach across that uncertain ground and take his hand, step close, whisper, "Stay." It's a promise from me, and a question for him.

I feel the relief that floods his body as he hugs me, a long and warm embrace that soothes the screaming parts of me. I hope it does the same for him, but that's the hell of being human: you never really know. Never.

You never know what the person you love might do. Or could be capable of doing.

Sometimes you don't even know that about yourself.

We seem better as we get the kids settled for the night; we take our wineglasses out to the porch. It's not the same as it was back on Stillhouse Lake; the view's of a cul-de-sac and a neighbor's front window, not the soothing, cool ripple of the water. But we still have a covered porch, and our two rocking chairs, and we sit together and sip in silence.

I ruin the mood by telling him about my new, worrying stalker. After a fairly significant pause, he tells me about the call from the newspaper.

I nearly spill my wine. "Someone called in *my obituary*?"

"Probably the same guy, don't you think? Hell, he might have gotten busy with the flyers too."

I take in a deep breath. "You took care of that obituary, though. It won't—"

"Show up online, or in the papers? No. But we should be aware that's a tactic that's out there. Stay alert."

I feel sick at the thought. There's so much *viciousness* to all this. And I understand the impulses behind it. It's so easy at a distance to pass judgment, to feel satisfaction when someone else receives pain you think they deserve.

What this man—if it is just the one man—is doing is the bigger, more toxic version of that common, petty feeling.

"Anything else?" I ask him with a sigh. It's been a hell of a day. I take a big gulp of wine.

"Thank God, no. That's all I've got. We're going to get through this, you know." He takes my hand, and we sit quietly, connected. "You trust me, right?"

"I love you, Sam."

"But do you *trust* me?"

I turn to look at him, and find him staring straight at me. I feel the impulse to lie to him. To protect myself. And I fight that with all my heart. "Honestly? I'm trying as hard as I know how. Sam . . . *I hate this.* I hate that all my instincts tell me to grab my kids and protect them from everything, everyone, even *you.* I know it isn't right. I know that you're the love of my life, the man I ought to trust above anyone else. But I have to *learn* that. It doesn't come naturally."

I'm afraid, when I say it, that he's going to take offense . . . and I realize that fear, too, is part of what I have to unlearn. Melvin got in me as deep as cancer, but if I have to claw him out by the bloody hand-fuls, I will.

It feels like a piece of that rot falls away when Sam says, steady as always, "It didn't come naturally for me either. You'll get there, Gwen. I trust you to find the way. And I'm not going anywhere."

The gift of that makes tears burn in my eyes. I lift his hand and press my lips to it in silent gratitude.

"Now," Sam says. "Somebody's fucking with our lives. What are we going to do about that?"

I take a deep breath. "Go get him," I say.

"Damn right."

We clink glasses and drain the last of our wine.

10

KEZIA

I'm so damn tired that night when I get home, I fall asleep on the couch without doing any of the normal things I'd take care of before bed.

Like putting my phone on the charger.

I wake up at 5:00 a.m. and instinctively reach to check messages only to find the damn thing's dead. *Shit*. I plug it in and go off to shower and make coffee; when I come back it's got enough power for me to see that I had just one missed call.

Gwen. I call back while I take my first, life-saving sip of coffee, and I forget about the cup altogether as she tells me about her night. About the damn wanted posters, the gun range expulsion. That has to hurt, and it's worrying. My coffee gets significantly cooler while she tells me about the new internet stalker she's acquired, but I take a big gulp anyway before I say, "You think it's the same guy?"

"Seems pretty likely," she says. "Sam's going to check on the Lost Angels site and find out who's agitating against us right now. This guy . . . seems pretty devoted, and pretty capable. I'm worried, to be honest."

"About how the kids will handle it? Or about how you will?"

"Shit, Kez. You get right to the heart of things, don't you?" She lets out a breath. "Both, I guess. You know what my impulse is, don't you?"

"Grab what you love and run?"

"I can't do that anymore. I can't do it to *them* anymore."

"'Stand your ground' didn't work so well out at Stillhouse Lake."

"That was special circumstances," she counters. "Unless the NPD finally decided to get serious about the Belldenes, it was the right decision to go."

"We haven't, and we probably won't unless they do something real stupid," I say. "So you're likely right. You think the kids can handle that pressure?"

"I think we all have to learn to live with it. Somehow. Sorry to add to your burdens, Kez, I didn't mean to do that."

"Look, I called you out to a crime scene at God Knows O'clock, so you get to drop whatever you need on me. I'm so sorry. You don't need this shit."

"I really don't," she says. "But I'm shoveling. Listen . . . I should have said before, but I turned up something you need to know about Sheryl Lansdowne." Then she launches into the story, and I grab pen and notebook and find myself taking quick, furious notes, writing down names in sharply slanted handwriting that tells me my hunter's blood is up. I'm completely focused on what she's saying, and deep down I'm not even that surprised. I believed Tommy's father last night when he told me his son didn't just run for the hills. There's something here. Something dark and twisted and very, very dangerous.

"Thanks, Gwen," I tell her at the end. "Take time, okay? Take care of your fam. I got this."

"I'll keep digging when I can." She seems calm and practical. I don't know if I would be. "It's good to have something else to think about."

"Gwen. You got through it before. Stay strong."

"Just once, I'd like to not have to," she says, and I'm a little surprised at how vulnerable she sounds. "I still plan to head to Valerie once the kids are in school today and find out more about Sheryl Lansdowne. I'll get back to you tonight, most likely."

"You just watch your back." I mean that on every level, from the regular worries about poking around in things that aren't her business to the threats hanging over her.

When we end the call, I stand there staring at the coffeepot for a long few minutes before I dump what I've made in a travel cup.

I need to get to work.

◆　◆　◆

Detective Prester is there ahead of me. He looks tired, and he looks worse than yesterday. I worry for him. "Hey," I say, and put my bag and travel mug down on my desk. "Coffee?"

He nods without speaking, and I go fetch it. I know how he takes his; I made it a point to find out the first day on the job. He sips and turns another page. Still doesn't speak until he finishes reading, and then looks over at me. "Sorry I dumped this on you," he says. His voice sounds rougher than usual. "Getting old is no picnic."

"You been to the doctor like I asked you?"

"No, and I'm not going, so you can just drop that right now. I just got tired. I need some damn vacation. I heard you found another body to add to the tally. Anything come back on that yet?"

"Nothing from TBI. They took the skeleton in for dental forensics and such. DNA if they can get it. My guess is it'll turn out to be Sheryl Lansdowne's ex, Tommy. His disappearance sure doesn't smell right."

"Neither does hers." He shakes his head. "Those two little girls. My God. So what you thinking?"

"You saw the file."

"You don't put it in the file. I know you, Kezia."

We spend half an hour talking through it—nothing either one of us wants to put on paper. Gwen's call this morning has definitely put Sheryl in a new light, and not a good one; Prester had already been leaning toward Sheryl as a perpetrator, not a victim, and now—though

I hate it with a real viciousness—I think he's probably right. But we have no actual facts just yet.

He finally sighs and closes his eyes for a few seconds. "So what do you make of the dead husband, if those bones turn out to be his?"

"If Sheryl's a killer, maybe she did for him, too; she did end up with a house, bank account, and car free and clear."

"Next steps?"

"I'm going to follow up on Gwen's leads, see what I can turn up. If the TBI comes back with a positive on Tommy Jarrett, we may have something to really sink our teeth into on this."

He nods in agreement. "I'll finish up reports on that domestic abuse case and the car theft at the bakery, then I'm going to take your advice and go home to rest. Kezia. You watch your ass on this one. Like you always say, there are bears in these woods."

What he means is that there's no clear direction, and when that happens, attacks can come from anywhere. Killers want to stay hidden. Dragging them into the light is a dangerous business sometimes.

"Bears better watch their furry behinds," I tell him, and he laughs. "I got this."

"I know you do." Prester hands the file back and says, "Send me a copy?"

"I'll put it in email."

I get to work as Prester does his two-finger typing on his reports. I consider going back to the morgue, but I know I shouldn't do that. It's agonizing, and it won't be productive in any way. But the thought of those two little girls all alone in the dark . . . it still haunts me. I feel chilled to the bone from it. Maybe I'm still coming to terms with having a small, fragile, helpless life depending completely on me, but I want those girls to know somebody loved them. Cared about them.

I guess right now it will fall to Abraham Jarrett to see to their burial when they're released, if their mother's still gone—or worse, if she's the one who caused their deaths.

The second I focus back on the piece of paper where I've taken down the notes from Gwen's info, I feel everything else fade away. The chase pulls me in like nothing else ever has done; it's a little unsettling how right this feels to me. *You're not a damn superhero,* I tell myself. *You're just a cop doing a job.* Which is true, but not completely. Something happened to me back at that lonely, misty pond. Something important. It put motherhood—something that until that moment had been distant, misty, and unformed—into a very real, very emotional shape.

It's not just a job. Not this time.

I start diving in, tracking down the information that Gwen's found about Penny Carlson. Her work's solid, but it's still a clue, not a conclusion. I've got access she doesn't, and I find two more aliases besides her Maguire discovery that match Sheryl's general profile. It fills in some of the time gaps. If all this holds up, our girl's been busy. She's got only two arrests in the past ten years, each under a different name and in a different state. Both were for small offenses, and in both cases, she paid the fines and left town not long after.

The record looks minor, but it's wrong. My instincts tell me that Penny Carlson's been on the wrong track for a long, long time. Her juvenile records are sealed; it'll take a court order for me to gain access, and I doubt I'll get anybody to sign off on that yet. I've got plenty of other things to run down in the meantime. Gwen's set one hell of a table, and I'm about to eat some lunch.

◆ ◆ ◆

I start from the beginning. With Penny Carlson of Rockwell City, Iowa. It's a dot of a town, isolated by lush fields of corn and soybeans. The kind of place where everybody knows everything, but as a stranger I'm not set to learn much. Still, I give it a try with a call to the local police department.

The chief of police answers after just a short delay, which tells me how busy a town it is; he's pretty cordial when I explain things, but when I mention Penny Carlson, there's a long, fraught silence. Then he says, "Ma'am, do you think you know where Penny is? Is that what you're telling me?"

"No sir, I don't know where she is right now. I think I know where she *was*," I say. "Might be able to confirm her identity if you send me her prints and file. We'll be processing a car shortly, and if the prints match up, then this could help close your case."

That makes me his new best friend, and I hear his tone warm way up when he says, "Well, Detective, I sure would like to be of help to you. Happy to send the file along. Email okay?"

"Yes sir, that would be just fine." I give him my contact info, and we shoot the shit a little, meaningless pleasantries that small towns still value, and then I tell him I have to get going. I can read this man even over the long expanse of telephone wires; he's not telling me everything he knows, and it may not be in that file either. It could take some honey and a crowbar to get the rest of it out of him, and I'll need to be careful about when I apply either of those. Small-town chiefs like to keep a town's secrets, in my experience. And Penny may have had good reason to be shut of the place.

I'm going to need to play this game with more than one police department. I tap my pen against the pad in front of me as I consider strategies, but really, I don't know enough yet to get fancy with it. I don't know how long it'll be before the Iowa chief sends me his file—*if* he sends it; cordiality is no guarantee—and I feel time burning away with every second.

I pick up the phone and call the police department associated with the second name Gwen provided . . . in Kentucky. I feel a little knot of tension ease when I hear the familiar notes of a black man's voice on the other end of the line. "Detective Harrison," he says. A nice voice, deep.

"Hello, Detective, I'm Detective Kezia Claremont, Norton Police Department out in Norton, Tennessee. How y'all doing today?"

He makes a sound that isn't quite a laugh, isn't quite a sigh. "Same as usual, ma'am. What's up?"

"I need to see if you've got an open file on . . ." I check the name again, just to be sure. "Tammy Maguire." I spell it out for him, and hear keys clicking. "This would have been about seven years ago, maybe eight."

"You ought to work for a mining company," he tells me after a moment. "'Cause you just struck gold. Tammy Maguire's wanted here for felony theft. You got her in Tennessee?"

"Not quite," I say. "She's a missing person."

"Here too. Skipped out before we could make the arrest, no sign of her since."

"Out of curiosity, what kind of theft?"

"She cleaned out her boyfriend's bank account—wasn't that much, a few thousand—and stole his car on top of it. Plus, she swiped checkbooks from a couple of old ladies she was cleaning houses for, pretty much drained their accounts as well. Real piece of work, this one."

I think about her husband, Tommy. Bank accounts, car, house, all transferred to her just before his disappearance. Maybe Sheryl had stepped up from stealing and ghosting to something more brazen. "You think you could send me that file? I'd like to compare the prints you have on file."

"You're welcome to it," he says. "I'd love to see this one taken down. Stealing from your boyfriend . . . well, okay, fair enough, we all get burned time to time with bad choices. But she had no call to ruin those old ladies who trusted her in their houses. Cold."

"Very," I agree. I'm starting to think I understand how Sheryl sees people: obstacles and opportunities.

But if that's so, why have the babies? She must have known they'd tie her down, commit her to a life that was infinitely riskier than the one she'd been living even if she hadn't killed Tommy for his cash and belongings. Staying put means a chance arrest, getting fingerprinted, maybe even for something as simple as speeding. And that leaves her wide open to being discovered, especially since she's got a felony on her record.

I provide my email to this detective, just like before, and check my in-box ten minutes later. Detective Harrison from Kentucky is fast on the draw; I have the file on Tammy Maguire, and it's fairly thick. I print it out and start reading the particulars, including complainant statements. It's fairly pathetic stuff, even through the dry language of a police report. *Mrs. Rhodes states that she did not realize her checkbook was missing until she went to the bank to withdraw money for shopping and was told her account was overdrawn. This caused Mrs. Rhodes to miss payments to her electric and water bills, and these were only paid due to the charity of her fellow church members.* In other words, Tammy had left an eighty-year-old woman dead broke in the wintertime in Kentucky, without giving a single shit if she froze to death.

Like Harrison had noted: cold.

I'm mostly done reviewing that file when the Penny Carlson file comes through, and unlike Harrison's thorough and concise documentation, this one . . . isn't that. The statement is written longhand, and whatever patrol officer wrote it down wasn't exactly a calligrapher by nature; I have to puzzle over scribbles until my head hurts to figure all of it out, especially since he was no wordsmith. I finally start transcribing it into a document for clarity, making my best guesses at some of the words.

It's verbose, with lots of digressions about Penny's family members, her grades, friends, and general state of mind. The Rockwell City police are used to dealing with other kinds of crime . . . probably the same we have here in Norton: petty thefts, domestic violence, drugs. Missing persons investigations are not their specialty, and I could drive a truck through the holes I spot in the questions they asked.

But it boils down to a simple set of facts, in the end: Penny Carlson didn't much like her life. For all that her friends and family claimed to think the best of her, nobody had seemed overly upset—or surprised—when she'd suddenly pulled up stakes and vanished. I wondered if that had ever changed with the years she'd been gone. The word *cold* resonates with me again, because Penny clearly hadn't cared anything about the worry she'd cause the people she left behind. Maybe because she knew that while people professed to love her and like her, they'd move on pretty quickly.

I find myself doodling a note to myself. *Some people are hard to love.*

Interesting. Not that I'd put it in the file, but I wonder if her folks sensed something about Penny/Tammy/Sheryl that wasn't that obvious to most. I'm on the fence about calling the family to find out; on the one hand, if they *have* moved on—and the file kind of indicates they have, since they stopped pestering the police after just a few months—then I don't want to open up healed wounds. But if they haven't, if they're existing in a hell of not knowing, maybe I can help them grab a breath of free air.

And what if Sheryl's really dead this time? Or a child murderer?

That's what stops me. Until I know more, I can't pull that string. I don't know what it would unravel, and I don't want to be responsible.

Prester would tell me that I'm being stupid, that maybe the reason her family stopped asking about Penny was that she got in touch. Maybe so. But I have other things to do before I have to take that road.

Gwen still hasn't gotten anything in the way of video yet from the woman we talked to out in the sticks, and though I know it might not be smart, I'm too restless to stay still. I tell the sergeant where I'm going and head out.

It's a long, cool drive out into the budding green hills, and I have to stop and check my directions twice along the way. It's easy to get turned around out here. I don't pass many cars on that tight little back road, just one rusted pickup that looks like it's mostly held together with Bondo, and a shiny SUV that makes me briefly curious before I recognize the tags. It takes up most of the road, and I have to drive right on the precarious edge to avoid getting my mirror taken off as it whizzes past.

The SUV belongs to the Belldenes, our local Dixie Mafia hill folk with a compound not too far from here . . . and a pretty substantial drug business. We play tag with them pretty often, but I don't bother to pull them over today. One thing about the Belldenes: they aren't going anywhere. They succeeded in driving Gwen Proctor out of Stillhouse Lake through threats and leverage, and I'm not giving up that grudge anytime soon, but I got other fish on the line right now.

To the Belldenes, drugs are just business, and business is good. I can't imagine them drowning two little girls in a car, no matter what other crimes they'd condone. Deep down, they've got some kind of morality, and this is so far over that line you can't spot it from space.

Which, it occurs to me, is why it's possible that they *did* see something; they'd be out all hours in rural areas. Maybe *they* made that 911 call. But chasing down that lead will be dangerous, and I'll need a hell of a lot more than just a hunch.

I pull into the driveway that Gwen and I visited. The McMansion looks quiet, no cars visible. I step out and walk up to the door, careful to stay in range of the cameras. I ring the bell and step way back, holding my badge.

Apart from the chirps and songs of birds in the trees, I don't hear anything from inside the house. I wait for a solid two minutes, then step back up and knock. Forcefully. "Norton Police Department," I say, and I know it carries. "Hello?"

Not a damn thing. I feel a cool breath move across my neck, and hair stiffens. I listen to my instincts and tuck my badge onto my belt, draw my sidearm, and try the front door. Locked, which I expected. I go to the big picture window in front, but the blinds are shut.

It's a risk heading around the side, but I do it, driven by something I can't really define. That's where I see the curtain blowing in the breeze behind an open window. The mesh screen is five feet away, discarded on the grass.

Shit.

I don't touch the window, just lean in to look. I don't see anything in the room, which seems like a spare, crowded with boxes and filing cabinets. "Hello! Norton police, call out!"

Still nothing.

I debate going through the window—it's plenty big enough—but I could destroy valuable evidence doing that, if there is something amiss inside this house. I pause and call the station, and tell Sergeant Porter that I may have a situation. He snaps from laconic to professional in an instant, and dispatches a patrol car toward me.

It'll take a while, so I continue around the side and to the back of the property.

The blood shows up thick and dark red in the sunlight. It's smeared over the grass of the backyard in a long streak. Been there long enough to turn dark and clotted, and the cloud of insects buzzing over it is delighted with the bounty. I hold my breath for a second, then deliberately let it out in a slow hiss.

There's no body visible, but that's clearly either a drag mark, or someone crawling. It heads into the trees. I follow it in parallel. It goes from a thick trail to a thin one, then to drops and smears here and there.

I see the soles of her feet first, shimmering in the gloom under the trees. Ghostly white, those bare feet. Her body's an eerie, cold shade, and I know before I put my fingers to her pulse that she's long bled dry. There are ants on her, and some trundling beetles. Flies swarming. I swallow hard and move back, careful of my steps, and call it in.

I don't touch her again. And I don't leave.

"I'm sorry," I say. My voice sounds tight and resigned.

Because I think, deep down, that the visit Gwen and I paid got her killed. Whether it was done by the husband, or by someone else, I don't know and can't dare guess.

But she was alive, and now she's lying here naked and dead, and I crouch down, breathing hard, and try not to feel the guilt that pounds at the door in my head.

◆ ◆ ◆

It takes another ten minutes for the cruiser to arrive, sirens wailing. I walk back around to the front to meet them, and ask the two patrolmen to help me clear the house. The back door's hanging open; stepping inside, the first thing we see is the kitchen.

It's neat and organized . . . and covered in blood. Blood splattered on the walls, streaked in frantic marks on the floor. Some on the ceiling. Directional spatter on the clean, white refrigerator and blue countertop and shelves. "Shit," I whisper softly. "Heads on a swivel. Let's clear this place, and watch your feet." I have to say that; these local boys probably haven't seen too many bloody crime scenes like this one. Can't say I've seen all *that* many myself, and I take deep breaths to manage my racing heartbeat. Adrenaline is making me jumpy, and I have to consciously work against it. Last thing I want to do is shoot some innocent person hiding in a closet.

I wave the two men one way while I take the other. My way leads me down a dim, narrow hall lined with pictures. I don't look at them. I can't spare the attention. There are drag marks clearly visible on the carpet, with blood thickly beaded and dried crusty on top. I hug the wall until I get to the first doorway, take a quick second, and then ease in with my gun ready, finger close to but not on the trigger.

It's a bedroom—probably, from the look of it, an extra one. It's set up with a full-size bed topped with a beige duvet and fluffed pillows. A dresser against one wall. No evidence of blood in here, but I check the closet anyway. Empty except for some coats and shoeboxes.

I check under the bed and clear the room. Back to the hallway. There are no other doors my way except a bathroom, and it, too, is sparkly clean and orderly.

The blood rounds the corner. I follow it, and at the end of the hall is another body.

Male, fully clothed, lying facedown, arms outstretched like he's about to swim. I wince when my brain reconstructs that blood trail; somebody pulled him facedown by his feet all this way. I can see a small gunshot wound in the back of his head. I imagine the exit wound in his forehead will be a hell of a mess.

I check his pulse. Cold as stone. I clear the bedroom—the master, just as clean and neat as the other one—and the closets and the attached bath.

Killer's long gone.

We have two people dead, and when the other two officers join me, I read from their faces that they didn't find anybody else. I shake my head and stare at the body.

"Hell of a lot of killing going on right now," one of the patrol officers says. It's not helpful, but I let it go because he's right. Norton's murder rate for the year just doubled. "Sweet Jesus, there's a lot of blood." He's the younger of the pair, and he looks pallid and sweaty.

"Go on outside," I tell him. "Radio for the coroner's office and get forensics moving. Better advise the sheriff's office and TBI, too—we don't need some jurisdiction bullshit right now."

He nods and walks out. Grateful for the chance to be out of here. I don't blame him; the rank smell of old blood hangs heavy.

"Stay here," I tell the other officer. I go to the other end of the house—the side the officers checked—and find a home office with a cheap desk loaded with computer equipment. There's a separate monitor for the surveillance system. I'll need a warrant to seize the stuff, but if they have a hard drive saving the recording, then we're in business.

But I look down and realize that though the display is still showing a live feed, there are dangling wires beneath it.

The killer took the evidence.

I'm on the phone to Sergeant Porter as I walk back out to stand guard over the dead woman to tell him I'm going to need a warrant that covers cloud storage of data, too, just in case.

But our killer would have thought of that too. Maybe he forced one of those two dead people to give him access so he could scrub his dirty fingerprints, just like he probably has in this house.

I can't help but feel a little tingle of unease. Nobody was following me and Gwen out here, I'd stake my life on that. We'd have noticed a car tracing us. So how the hell did anyone know we'd been here at all?

I can feel invisible eyes on me, though. Watching.

And I shiver.

11

GWEN

The morning starts early. I don't know what wakes me, just that it brings me instantly awake; I listen, and I hear nothing. It's still dark and, as far as I can tell, peaceful.

I get up anyway to wander the house like a ghost for the next two hours—putting dishes quietly away, cleaning counters, sweeping floors. Busywork, meant to keep my mind off those damn flyers and the consequences that are most certainly coming for us. When I run out of household tasks, I head to the office, shut the door, and tap into the rushing river of hate that's always running our direction.

Our new stalker's been busy. I see him popping up in various troll-friendly hotbeds to leave messages, and when I check, he's done the expected: he's posted the wanted poster, complete with our new address. In short order, of course, someone got hold of our home phone number. I'm not terribly concerned; I have a device attached to block unknown numbers, and a one-button block for harassers. So far, no sign of our cell phones being compromised, which is my biggest worry. I do *not* want these assholes getting to my kids.

He hadn't signed his earlier work, the initial email, but now he has a handle he's using. MalusNavis. I make a note of it. That's striking enough that I'm confident I can track it down.

I take a little while to decompress, and go back to Kez's case. Sheryl Lansdowne and her shadow identities. Kez doesn't answer her phone, so I start putting it all into an orderly email document.

Kez calls me back before I finish. It's a short conversation, but I can hear the stress in her voice. She's relieved about the new leads I provide, but at the same time, she can't fail to understand how much this complicates her investigation.

I'll need to help her however I can. It isn't like Kez has unlimited resources in Norton, and I'm well aware of the TBI's jurisdictional supremacy. They won't want her in their business, and she isn't going to give it up . . . so I'm in it too.

It occurs to me that I've done nobody any favors opening this up as a multistate investigation; the FBI will have their hands on it soon, and that sidelines Kezia even more.

I'm making tea when I hear a door open quietly, and the pad of footsteps coming down the hall. I look up to see Lanny standing there. She's got on a black Henley tee, Halloween bat-themed pajama pants, and a pair of battered bear-feet slippers that Vee bought for her about the same time Vee's white yeti slippers made their first proud appearance.

I make her a mug of hot tea, too, and add honey just the way she likes it. We sit down in the living room—the farthest point from the other bedrooms—together on the couch.

"Couldn't sleep?" I smooth her hair back from her face. Instead of the rainbow colors she's been dyeing in, she's redone it to a softer hot-pink shimmer in the front, darkening to purple at the edges; it looks cool, I have to admit.

"Not really," she says. "You know what the flyers mean, don't you? When we go to school today, somebody's going to have it. And it'll blow up all over the place. Next thing you know, people will be sending me clips from true crime shows. Like I haven't seen them."

"You watch—"

"No shit, Mom. I mean, we're mentioned in at least four of them. You know that, right?"

It's more than four, and I don't tell her. "Language, Atlanta." My heart's not in it.

"The actress playing you was crappy in the one I watched. They played her like she was probably guilty. And they had that prosecutor on, you know the one. He thinks you got away with murder."

I've seen every one of the documentaries, listened to at least half of the podcasts. Most of them think I got away with it, or at least that I was aware of what Melvin was doing. I wasn't, and the injustice of it still burns, but I've grown a lot of fireproof skin for that kind of stuff. It hurts that my kids have to walk the same inferno. But I know I can't keep them out of it either.

I put my arm around her and hug her close. She doesn't pull away. We lean against each other, sipping tea, and it feels good and peaceful and right until Lanny says, "School's going to be awful today."

"It'll be awful for a while," I agree. "And yet you're going to go. Right? Head up, shoulders back, face the world. You know how we do it."

She gulps the last of her tea. I do mine as well. "How come we always have to be the brave ones? How is that fair?"

"Because we can," I tell her. "Because we have to. And no. It isn't fair, not even remotely." I relent a little bit, because I can feel the tension in her. "Let's make a deal: half a day at school. Then we do something fun."

"You'll be here?" She glances over at me, then quickly away.

"In the afternoon I will," I tell her. "I have to do some work this morning, sweetie. But this is Sam's day off, so he'll be here until I get back. Okay?"

She nods and takes our cups into the kitchen. I check my watch—it's nearly 6:00 a.m. now—and as I do, she yawns and pauses in the doorway. "I think I'll go back to bed for a little bit," she says. "Thanks for the tea, Mom. Next time, just come talk to me, okay? I'm not a kid. I can help with stuff."

I've known that for a while, but I've been looking at it completely wrong. I've seen it as conflict, as pulling away. But people change. God knows *I've* changed from the naive child I was when I married Melvin Royal to the terrified, paranoid person I was when I arrived at Stillhouse Lake to the woman I am now—who's maybe got a handle on the fear, if not the paranoia.

Lanny has filled in the spaces of her own life. And she *has* helped. She can be my ally, and so can Connor. I only need to let go of the fear that keeps me from seeing that clearly.

At least I know what's holding me back, even if I can't get there instantly.

So I hug my daughter and tell her I love her, and I put her in charge of getting her brother up, ready, and to school. I've never done it before, but I give her the keys to my SUV. She looks at them, shocked, then at me. "I—I can take them?"

"Yes," I tell her. "I'll borrow Sam's truck. He won't mind. I know you'll be careful." The urge to tell her *how* to be careful is strong. I manage to resist.

She clenches those keys so hard I think she'll hurt herself, and her smile is a golden reward. "Thanks, Mom. I promise, no cruising, no giving rides to friends, no bullshit. Straight to school and back. And I'll look after Connor."

I just nod, like it's an everyday thing that I let my seventeen-year-old drive my car. It isn't. I know a lot of kids drive by themselves far earlier, but I've always been so . . . in their lives. It's tough.

But this is the clearest sign I can give that I trust her, and right now, she needs that.

When that's settled, I talk to Sam about borrowing his truck for the day; as I thought, he's just fine with it, barely even pausing before he agrees. He adds, carefully, "Do you need me with you?" And I realize that he's trying not to express an actual concern, trying to give me the space I need. I put my arms around his neck and savor the gentle kiss we exchange.

"I always need you," I tell him. "But *with* me might not be helpful this time. Two people looks more threatening than just little old me, and I'm doing some door-knocking in a small town."

"And having a strange guy with you may tip the scales the wrong way," he says, and nods. "I get that. But you know I worry, right?"

"I know." I trace the line of his chin with my finger, relishing the feel of his morning stubble. "I'll be careful. And Kez will know where I am too. I'll call in after each stop and tell you where I go next. Deal?"

"Deal. You can bring me back breakfast. What's good in Valerie? Doughnuts, maybe?"

"Doubtful," I tell him. "But I can stop for them once I'm back to civilization. Might be two or so, by the time I make the drive to and from. Then maybe we can take the kids to a movie."

"Got to be some kind of normal life out there waiting," he says. "I mean it. Be careful."

"I will."

◆　◆　◆

Coming back into the area around Stillhouse Lake feels like both a homecoming and a trauma. I can't really separate those two, not anymore, but I still love the scenery even if I know I'm not welcome in it. I pass the turnoff to the lake, and our old house, and have to resist the impulse to see what the new residents are doing with my old place. I don't need to stir up old memories and ghosts. There are too many to count.

Besides, the truce might not hold if the Belldenes spot me out here. I don't need that trouble.

I take the tiny road that leads to Valerie.

As with most rural towns around here, it's seen better days. Most of the small downtown is shuttered; the rest is filled with junk stores and nostalgia for a past that was never as good as it seems in the rearview. Kez has sent me the address, and I find it easily enough, though GPS is predictably unreliable around here, and Valerie doesn't much believe in investing in street signs. Why should they, when everybody who lives there knows where everything is?

I slow in front of Sheryl Lansdowne's address. There's a TBI van parked on the curb, so they're likely inside processing the place. I leave that alone and head down the street. Kez has updated me on her conversation with the immediate next-door neighbor, so I skip him for now and text Kez and Sam to let them know that I'm starting at the house one down.

I get a timid little old woman with a mild, seamed face and frizzy gray hair who seems to live in her housecoat. She invites me in for iced tea, that grand southern tradition, and I accept. It's a good decision. The tea's just standard Luzianne, but she's an avid gossip, and she has homemade cookies. Perfect.

I tell her who I am, of course; I show her my private investigator's license, which she thinks is fascinating, and after we get the usual questions about what I do out of the way, she's quick to tell me about the flaws of people living on the block.

But not, I notice, Sheryl. When she finally pauses for breath and a sip of her iced tea, I ask about that. She gives me a sharp look. "I don't speak ill of those who are gone to rest, and Lord knows, she may be. Missing, ain't she? And those two darling girls of hers gone?" She shudders and shakes her head. "Don't know what this world is coming to—these things just never happened when I was younger and people feared God and believed in America."

She's wrong, of course; I could reel off a solid dozen hideous crimes from the 1950s onward that happened just in this county, but I'm not going to change her mind, and I'm not interested in wasting my time.

"Well, Mrs. Gregg, it sure would help if you'd tell me something that could help me find Sheryl," I say. "And anything might do that. Anything at all."

"Would it? Really?" Her pale-brown eyes go wide behind her old-fashioned glasses. "I don't know anything much except that her husband lit out on her some time ago. Damn shame when a man does that to an expectant mother, don't you think? Abandoning her and the children?"

I can tell she's poised for another *back in my day* lecture, so I head her off. "Absolutely," I say firmly. "Damn shame. Did you see him go?"

"*See* him go? Well, I really don't know, now, do I? I didn't see no suitcases, but I did see him get in his truck and leave, and I don't recall him ever coming back."

"And Sheryl was home then?"

"Lordy, how would I remember a thing like that?" But she puts a finger to her lips and taps it thoughtfully. "Well, maybe that was the day she went for her doctor visit. I just don't know. I don't write it down, you know. And I'm not a snoop."

"Of course not," I lie smoothly. "You're just interested in your neighbors. That's normal."

"It's just being friendly," she says. "Unlike these young folk. All they do is stare at the TV and their damn phones and such. Don't even go out on the porch in the evenings like normal people. I just don't know—"

What the world is coming to, I finish mentally, and jump in. "Do you know who Sheryl's obstetrician would have been?"

"Only one around here," she says. "Dr. Fowler, and he's even older than I am, probably still pushing cod liver oil on those poor babies." She makes a face. "Your mother ever make you take that stuff?"

"Past my time," I tell her, and she pats my hand.

"Well, good for you, dear, good for you. Anyway, Dr. Fowler would be the only place she'd go if you're asking about that." She gives me a too-sharp look. "You know some folks 'round here think her husband didn't just leave, don't you? That it was something else?"

"Like what?"

She leans over the table, and her eyes are bright with interest. "Some say he was *murdered.*"

"No!"

"Well, that's what I heard. Not that I'd know for sure, of course. But some folks say it sure was convenient how she got his money and house and car easy as pie. He weren't wealthy or nothing, but she came here poor as country dirt, and now she's got a roof over her head and a car to drive and money to spend."

"You knew her when she first came?"

"Before she got married? She came in on the bus, just some rough little baggage. Got herself a job at that Sonic near the edge of town. That's where she met Tommy Jarrett, and I guess that was all it took. Don't know anything about her other than that, though. Maybe she was just down on her luck. I was born just before the Depression, did you know?"

"I didn't," I say, and I listen politely to her tales of growing up amid poverty even more desperate than it is today. I don't know how much of it is true, but it doesn't matter, and it makes her happy. I leave her my card, in case she thinks of anything else. Mrs. Gregg is nice enough, and a busybody is always useful.

I'm on my way out the door when, out of the blue, she says, "And you know about that man, don't you?"

I turn to face her. "What man?" I feel my heartbeat kick up to a higher gear.

"The one in the white van, of course. Used to drive by her house quite regular. Always at night."

"And did he stop at her house?"

"Never. But he always slowed down." Mrs. Gregg looks very pleased with herself. I want to kiss her.

"Think hard. Did he stop at anyone else's house that you know of?"

"Not on this block, no."

"And you didn't recognize him?"

She snorts. "Well, of course I did! You didn't ask *that*."

Jesus take the wheel. I force myself to be calm. "Okay, now I'm asking: Who was in the van?"

"Douglas Adam Prinker. Lives over on Adams, out near the old Dairy Queen, the one they closed down about ten years back."

I take out my notebook and write all that down, along with *white van* and several exclamation points. "Thank you, Mrs. Gregg. That's helpful. Anything else?"

"No, I don't think so," she says. "Y'all be safe out there. Those poor, poor little children." She clucks her tongue and closes the door.

I start for my borrowed truck, but I spot a man loitering near it. He looks like a cop, and I don't want to get into that. Not until I make a bit more progress. So I hit a few more houses, taking precautions every time as promised. Two want nothing to do with me and close the door in my face. One asks if there's a reward. I tell him there's not, and he immediately loses interest. Sheryl's next-door neighbor is surly and makes me damn glad I've texted my whereabouts, but he does support what Mrs. Gregg's told me about the day Tommy left; nobody saw any sign he was packing, and the neighbor describes Tommy as an outdoorsman, often gone fishing or hunting. Not unusual around here at all.

He doesn't seem to have any suspicions about Sheryl. In fact, he's adamant that she's a good woman and a good mother, and seems very certain of it.

I wonder how he'd feel if he knew about her past.

Nobody else seems to have noticed Douglas Adam Prinker or his white van, and I sure hope it's not made up out of whole cloth. That's the drawback of busybody neighbors; I was the victim of one when the news about Melvin first broke. She swore up and down that she saw me helping him carry a woman into the house. It was a lie, told for attention and because she was certain I deserved the punishment anyway.

I don't *think* Mrs. Gregg is lying. I just have built-in wariness that's hard to shake.

I get met at the last door I knock on with a shotgun, which persuades me it's past time to be going. The phone lines, I'm certain, have been burning up, and Mrs. Gregg will have spread news of my interest far and wide. That *might* be useful. But for now, it renders me persona non grata.

Unfortunately, the cop I spotted earlier is still waiting by Sam's truck when I approach, and I slow down to figure him out. He's a youngish man, tall, paler skin than most, and developing what looks like an uncomfortable sunburn. Blond hair and very blue eyes. He's wearing khaki slacks and a button-down, and he straightens up when I come closer and offers me a handshake. I don't accept. "That's my truck," I say.

"Technically, it's not. I checked," he replies, and takes a card from his pocket. "Randall Heidt, Tennessee Bureau of Investigation. I'm one of the investigators. And I don't much appreciate you interfering in what we're doing, Mrs. Proctor." But I notice he didn't stop me from doing it either. Interesting.

"Ms.," I say, and I'm thankful he hasn't deployed *Mrs. Royal*, because he clearly knows who I am, and a quick Google search would show him who I've been. "I'm not interfering."

"You're interviewing potential witnesses."

"Sheryl Lansdowne wasn't abducted from here."

"She might have been stalked here," he says. "I'm advising you to back off. Look, I don't want to be on your bad side, but you really can't be doing this. Understand?"

"Am I doing anything illegal?"

"Potentially obstructing an investigation."

"Good luck proving that in front of a judge. Having iced tea with an old lady and knocking on some doors isn't a crime."

"I'd like you to share your notes with me, please."

"What notes?" I say. "I didn't take any. And I'm under no obligation to tell you about my conversations unless you want to arrest me and take me in for questioning." The notebook's burning a hole in my pocket, but I try to keep from giving that away.

I must be successful, because he sighs and says, "Just give me something. Come on."

So I give him the information I've gathered from Mrs. Gregg . . . except for the bit about Douglas Adam Prinker. I hold that back only because I want Kez to have it, and the second this man gets his fist on it, he'll clench it tight. I tell myself I'm doing the right thing, but truth is, I'm not really sure I am. *Well, shit, they weren't even canvassing properly yet. If they talk to Mrs. Gregg, they'll get it themselves.* That's not really an excuse. And I feel a little ill when I don't disclose.

It's also Heidt's fault that he doesn't push me at that point, but mostly it's mine.

I call Kez immediately and tell her where to meet me. I drive the short distance to Norton's pretty decent bakery and order some cake; I'm carrying it to the table when Kez enters the door, spots me, and heads over. She seems tired, but energized. She slips into the chair opposite me. "This lunch for you? Because there are still vegetables in the world."

I pass her a fork. "It's carrot cake."

"I'll allow it." She takes a bite, heavy on the cream cheese frosting. "What'd you find out?"

"Ever heard the name Douglas Adam Prinker?"

"Should I have?"

I tell her Mrs. Gregg's story, and she pauses eating to take out her notebook and write it down in swift, flowing lines. Kez has better handwriting than I do. "One thing," I say. "I couldn't get anyone else to verify that story about the van. Maybe she just said what I wanted to hear. She did love to talk."

"Uh-huh, I'll check it out. If it seems viable, I'll get the TBI on it." Kez sounds low-key excited, though. It's a real possibility. "You didn't prompt her about the van?"

"She brought it up all on her own."

"Anything else?"

I tell her the rest of Mrs. Gregg's saga, though I'm not sure how probative it is. She makes a note of Dr. Fowler's name, which might be useful in giving Sheryl an alibi—or disproving one—on the day her husband went missing. I tell her about Heidt too. "Watch out for that one," I say. "Seems territorial, but that could just be because I'm me. Maybe he'd be more welcoming to you."

"Yeah, I doubt that," Kez says. "Penny Carlson's prints came in, by the way. They're a match to Sheryl, and two more aliases. Starting to look like Penny was some kind of rolling-stone grifter."

"But a murderer?"

"Don't know." She eats some more of the cake, for which I'm grateful; the slab is the size of Rhode Island. "The woman we talked to out in the sticks? At the big house?"

"You got the video?"

"I got a double murder," she says grimly. "And the camera hard drive's gone."

"Killed how?" I ask.

"Shot," she says. "Up close and damn personal. Autopsies are pending, but that's how I read it, anyway. If I had to guess from the scene, she was surprised in the shower, killed in the kitchen, and dragged out into the trees. Husband was either home or got home, and he was shot in the back of the head. Totally surprised, looks like."

"Jesus." She just nods. "Kez—that's four dead, one missing."

"Five dead," she says. "If you count Tommy Jarrett, which is starting to look more likely all the time. That's a whole lot of bodies dropping way too fast." She sighs. "Maybe the TBI's the right agency for this one. I don't have the resources, and Prester's not well and isn't about to admit it."

"But he's okay?"

Kez licks some frosting off her fork while she thinks. "At his age, I'm not so sure. I wish he'd get himself checked out, honestly. If something happens because he's being a stupid, stubborn man, I'll kick his ass."

"More likely bring him soup," I tell her, and she shrugs. "I don't have much on my plate at the moment—"

"Aside from your stalker problems?" Kez has a point. I was thinking caseload.

"Well, I was trying to avoid that for a little while longer," I say, and sit back. We've demolished the cake by this point; like all diners sharing a dish, we've left a little strip in the middle of the plate. No-man's-land. "You're right, though. I should be focusing at home." And on getting back there. It's time for me to start the drive.

"Anything you can do from there, I'll gladly accept," Kez says. "But I don't want to put you or the kids in more danger either."

"What about you?" I ask her. "With Javier off to training, Prester not his best, you don't have any backup. I'm worried about that, Kez. Whatever's going on—"

"It's not clear yet that the murders at the house had anything to do with the car in the lake. Easy to suppose that, but we don't know what these folks were into, or who they were into it with. I saw a Belldene car up on that road."

That stops me. I'd considered that the woman who'd promised us video might have been in the drug business. It could make a lot of sense, and it might explain why they turned up dead, nothing to do with Sheryl's case. "Even worse," I say. "You think the Belldenes won't pull the trigger on you if it means protecting themselves? They would. They might even get away with it."

"Not if Prester has anything to do with it. And that's my problem, Gwen. Not yours." Kez goes for the last bite. She's going to need the energy. "Got to bounce. You go home and take care of the ones you love, okay?"

"Kez?" I draw her direct gaze with the seriousness of my tone. "I love you too. And I don't want you left vulnerable out there."

"Damn, girl, I've got the whole Thin Blue Line on my side," she says, and acknowledges the irony of that with a quirk of her lips. "Well. It is pretty thin. But they'd put on the black armbands and give me a nice send-off. That's some comfort."

It's no comfort at all to me, but I keep that to myself.

◆ ◆ ◆

I head home, and arrive to relative calm . . . or so I think. Lanny and Connor are playing a video game and body-slamming each other to try to throw each other off; I settle them down and go look for Sam.

I find him in the office. He's just . . . sitting. When he looks at me, I feel my steps slow in response. It isn't that I know that look, but I don't like it. At all. "Sam? What is it?"

For answer, he holds up an envelope. One glance at it, and I know what it is. My heart drops.

It's the letter I received. The one written by Melvin, delivered post-humously. The sight of it makes my mouth go dry, my knees weak. I don't like that Melvin still sparks this physical revulsion in me, but it's also more than that. It's fear. Not of Melvin, not anymore . . . Fear that he's still got the power to destroy something I love even if he's six feet underground.

Sam says, "Why didn't you tell me?" His tone is as hollow as a struck bell. "I saw it in the drawer."

"I was going to, and then this thing with the flyers—"

"Gwen. You had plenty of time to tell me."

He's right. I did. I kept it from him because . . . I don't know why I did, really. It felt private. Horribly personal. *I didn't want to worry you* is the first thing that I think of saying, but I don't, because it's disingenuous. There's something about receiving letters from my dead ex-husband that makes me want to keep them to myself, and I know that isn't right, or fair.

And I know it's wrong when I jump to the attack, but I still do it. "You went through my drawer?" My words are sharply pointed, and they draw blood. Sam sits back in his chair, staring.

"I needed staples, and that isn't the point. Gwen."

I'm instantly sorry, and I know I'm wrong. Damn, I wish I could flip a switch and turn off this darkly aggressive streak I have, just be *different*, but I have to work at it. Hard.

But after counting to five, I finally try. "Sorry. I—you caught me by surprise with it, and when it comes to Melvin, I still have places that aren't really healed. You know that, right?"

He nods. "I've still got some sore spots there too. Maybe more than sore."

"He's not your rival, Sam. In any way."

I know, as soon as I say it, that I'm wrong, and I see it flash in his eyes. He leans forward and looks at me intently. "I wish that were true, but Melvin's still here. He's standing here right between us. Can't forget him if he won't go away. You have to let him go, Gwen."

He's absolutely right. And it's the scariest thing I've done so far, it feels like jumping off a cliff into the dark, but I take the envelope and letter out of his hand. Then I walk over to the crosscut shredder and feed it in. Watch it chewed to random bits. Utterly gone.

Turns out that wasn't a cliff. It wasn't even a fall. It was *easy*. I feel a strange surge of release and wonder, like stepping out into the sun after a long, long darkness.

I feel Sam's hands on my shoulders, Sam's warmth at my back. He kisses me gently on the side of the neck. "Thank you," he says. "I know that was hard."

"It wasn't." I thought it would be. I thought it would hurt, or be terrifying, that there would be some kind of consequences for the action. I've been bracing myself for a long, long time. Treating Melvin Royal like a threat even when he's gone.

Treating him like junk mail feels astonishingly like freedom.

"You've still got the address it came from?" Sam asks.

"I have the mail center envelope. That gives me a place to start looking for the sender. If we can find the source of those letters . . . we can put a stop to it. Maybe, finally, forever. We could shred every single thing that's left of Melvin Royal." I swallow. "I'd like that. That would be *great*."

"It would," he says. "We start tomorrow. We owe the kids a movie today. I don't want to let them down."

Neither do I. So we wait until they are ready to pause the game, and we load up the SUV, and we spend a glorious couple of hours not home, out of our too-full heads, transported to another world.

It's a temporary escape. But God, it matters. Happiness, however brief, always matters.

Even if it makes things that much more jolting when we get home.

The night's chilly; people are still burning fireplaces, and I smell the pleasantly pervasive scent even through the closed windows as we turn off into our neighborhood. It's calm, well lit, quiet, totally normal. Our house sits at the far end of the block, and we glide past glowing houses and neatly kept yards, and I make the turn into the driveway.

There's something taped to our door. I focus on that sheet of paper and feel the hair raise on my arms, pull tight at the back of my neck. *No. Oh God.* Then I get hold of my anxiety and push it down, hard. *Maybe it's a pizza delivery ad. Or a note from a neighbor. Or . . .*

It isn't. I know it isn't.

I pull the SUV into the garage and take the alarm off as everybody crowds into the house after me. Relocking the garage door is second nature, and so is scanning the place to be sure everything's just as we left it.

Nobody mentions the note on the front door, but when I look around, they're all staring that direction. Connor says, "Should I get it?" His tone is so calm and adult that it almost scares me. He is facing things head-on.

Lanny doesn't wait for anyone to give permission; she just stalks straight ahead, unlocks the door, opens it, and grabs the flyer as she kicks the door shut again. Even as she's studying it, she's turning deadbolts and setting the alarm. My girl.

"Anybody want to guess?" she asks. "Because this is a super easy one."

"Wanted poster," Connor and I say at the same time. Sam doesn't speak.

"You win the awesome prize of *even more harassment!*" She brings the flyer over and puts it into my hand. "So. What do we do?"

"We check the video and see who thought they were being clever," Sam says. "Doorbell camera." He's already walking down the hall, and the rest of us follow.

Sam pulls up the feed and scrolls back. It happened about an hour ago, just after dark; the front door camera shows two people in black hoodies with bandannas over their faces. From their build, I'd say teens, maybe a little older. One has the piece of paper, tape already applied. They're both wearing gloves. Once the paper's on the door, they both back up and flip off the camera.

"And another country asshole heard from," Lanny says. I don't try to police her language, not now. Maybe not ever again. I like the dismissive, pissed-off way she says it. "Where are they going now?"

They run to the right, toward the garage. Sam switches cameras to follow the progress. They bypass the garage and go around to the side of the house. The fence meets the house halfway down the length, and I keep the gate padlocked from the inside.

They don't get that far. They take out cans of spray paint. From the camera's angle, I can't see what they're doing, but it's pretty obvious it's not Banksy creating a masterpiece on our south wall.

"Great. So original," Connor says. "They must be freshmen at Troll School." He doesn't sound shaken either. Or scared. He just sounds . . . normal. I spare a second to mourn for the fact that this *is* normal for them, that they have a connoisseur's appreciation for the finer points of vandalism, but honestly, in the next second I'm completely okay with that. They're steady. They're ready.

All of us are. I wait for the panic to grow inside me, but this time, I'm actually okay. Angry, but—like my kids—grounded.

"Any guesses about their identities?" I ask, and freeze the picture at the best moment to get a view of their clothes, the bandannas they're wearing.

"Well, for a start, they're from our high school," Lanny says, and points to the taller one on the right. "See his sweatpants?"

I'd missed it. Her eyes are better, but when I grab my glasses, I make out a logo—black on dark gray—of a small stylized Viking's head. Her school's mascot.

"That could be a brand mark," I say, but she shakes her head, grabs my laptop, and quickly navigates to the school's website. She finds a shot of the boys' track team.

Same logo. Same sweatpants. She's absolutely right.

On-screen, the vandals finish up and run off into the dark, fleeing through a neighbor's yard, and then out of sight.

"Well," Connor says, "we know for sure they're not on the track team." We all look at him. He raises his eyebrows. "Come on. You saw them run. *I* could beat that time, and I'm kind of a nerd. But anyway, all the athletic teams get the same basic workout gear. We can find them, though. These idiots will be sharing this like crazy."

"Go find them," I tell him. "Just get their names. Let Sam and I take care of the rest. Clear?"

He and Lanny both nod, and they head off together. Little soldiers on a shared mission.

"They're so strong," I whisper. "Aren't they?"

"Yeah," Sam says, and gets up to put his arm around me. "I was hoping you'd start to recognize that. Come on. We've got work to do too."

We go outside, around to the side of the house, and Sam turns on the flashlight.

Bloodred paint in wobbly letters. From the difference in sizes and slants, one teen did the first word, the other did the last two.

PSYCHO'S LIVES HERD. I can only assume the writer meant *here*, but his graffiti penmanship is as bad as his grammar.

"Well," I say, "we know they're not on the honor roll."

Before we start, I take photos, and a sample of the red spray paint—which, thankfully, has already dried. Then we silently, methodically, paint out the evidence. It takes four coats of thick masking paint and then two more topcoats. When we're done, it's a decent job. A little trim work, and we'll be back to normal. It takes most of the evening, and by the time we're done, I'm feeling every inch of the day that's rolled over me hard.

We finish, put the paint and rollers away, and head to the bedroom to dump our sweaty, paint-stained clothes. Without discussion, we both get into the shower, and I lean back against Sam's chest with his arms around me and let the hot water beat some of the aches out of my body. Sometimes—many times—this shower is our personal fun zone, but not tonight. Tonight it feels like shelter from the storm.

When the water's running lukewarm, we finally shut it down, dry off, get dressed, and find the kids. They're both in Connor's room, cross-legged on his bed, both with laptops. Neither looks up at us as we enter, though Connor says, "I was right." He keeps typing one-handed, and holds up his left; Lanny meets it for a high five with her right. A well-oiled machine. "I've got their names."

"And *I've* got their address and all their social media accounts," Lanny says. "They're brothers, and they live two blocks over. Couple of total vacuum brains, by the way. I mean, they're both on the baseball team and got a C in Prevention of Athletic Injuries. Who does that?"

"And how do you know their grades?" I ask her.

"Mom. How do you think? They posted about it. They were pissed that not showing up for class earned them a C. Should have failed their stupid asses, but a C is as close as it gets for jocks, I guess."

I sit down on the edge of the bed. "And you know that this means—"

"Means we'll be targets of all the *best* bullies now that the popular kids are on it? Oh yeah. We know," my son says. "The flyers are all over the place. People are taking pictures with them and posting them on Instagram. We're the hot meme. Want to see a photo of somebody taking a dump on one?"

"No," Sam says. "We really don't. And you need to stop looking at it too. It's not good for you."

Connor looks like he wants to argue, but Lanny reaches over and shuts his laptop, then her own. "What did they tag on our wall?" I show her the photo I took. "Wow. Three words, three words wrong. That's a new record in the *Guinness Book of Fail*." She busts out laughing. Then Connor gets a look, and *he* laughs, and it's ridiculous and we're all laughing somehow. Angry, cleansing laughter that leaves us gasping for breath and clinging to each other.

We're almost done when Sam, out of nowhere, says, "That's it. I'm putting my foot down. Homeschooling."

And we cling to each other and feel, in this strange and ridiculous moment, like the trolls are *nothing* to our power when we're together. Sobriety finally hits when Connor says, "I don't want to be the baby here, but—"

"But you are, baby bro," Lanny says, and ruffles his hair. He smacks her hand away.

"But were you serious? About homeschooling?"

"Was I?" Sam looks at me, eyebrows raised. "That depends on how the two of you feel."

"Homeschooling sucks," Lanny replies, and sinks back, boneless as a relaxed cat, against the headboard of the bed. "Well, RIP my social life again, not that I actually have one. But . . . we can't go back tomorrow. It's going to be a horror show until they get bored and move on to somebody else. And I'd rather not beat some cheerleader's popular ass for getting in my face."

Lanny, in fact, has rarely lost a fight. She's rarely started one lately either. They're strong, but I don't think either of my kids has a bullying instinct. They don't stand still for it either. Connor's strategy used to be *run*. Lanny's was always *fight*. But neither of them is a passive victim.

It's a recipe for disaster, sending them back to that school in the morning.

RIP my social life, too, I think. But it's the right thing to do for my kids, until this whole thing passes over like a spring tornado. Lock us away in the storm cellar and hope for the best.

"You're staying home," I say. "That doesn't mean no schoolwork. I'll talk to the principal in the morning and get your studies from your teachers. Call it an extended vacation."

"Bored already," Connor says. "Can't we help *you* do something? We're good at looking things up. Obviously. And we know how to find weird stuff."

I don't ask how weird, because I don't want to know. I shudder to think of them getting involved with Kez's case, even in the slightest; there's a darkness there too deep for kids their age, whatever their personal history. "It's late, and you must be tired. So let's settle down and get some sleep tonight, and tomorrow we'll find you something useful to do. *Plus* schoolwork."

"Not tired," Lanny says. I check my watch. It's only ten. It feels later, but that's because I've been sleeping badly. "C'mon, let us do something? It's that or I kick his ass in *Fortnite* again."

"Like you can," Connor says. "Ever."

I make the decision without thinking hard enough about it, because I'm tired, and because the interest in their faces is so sincere. I go and get a notebook and write down a name. *Douglas Adam Prinker.* I bring it back and hand it to them. They both lean over to read it together.

"So who's this guy?" Connor asks.

"That's what I want to know. He lives in Valerie. He drives a white van. That's all I have right now. I *do not* want you to message him, engage with him, or in any way interact, not even if you think you're anonymous. *And* I want you to use the anonymizer protocols when you do it. Understand? Information. Not interaction."

"Got it!" Lanny chirps. She looks far too thrilled. Connor, at least, looks like he's evaluating the risks appropriately.

"Keep your eyes open," I tell them. "And *be careful.* Screencaps only. Okay?"

"Got it," my son says. "Lanny, calm down. We're not solving crime. We're just doing background."

"Still cool," she says. "Isn't it?"

"Kinda."

Sam and I leave the room, and I heave a sigh. "Did I just make a mistake?"

"Trusting them? No. I don't think so. Having something to do never hurts. So . . . who's Douglas Adam Prinker? Really?"

"I really don't know. One of the witnesses in Valerie mentioned him. I'm just covering some bases for Kez."

He looks at me carefully, searchingly. I see the real concern in his eyes. "But *you're* being careful. Right? This isn't a good time to be risky."

"I know. This is the last of it, and then we can focus on our own problems tomorrow." I feel a grin emerge. It feels sharp. "And boy, our mystery mailer is going to be sorry he ever took us on."

"Amen," he says, and kisses my forehead. "Come on. I need to show you something."

For a hot half second, I think he means that playfully, but that isn't the case. He closes the office door and goes to his laptop, boots it up, and navigates. I lean over his shoulder, and then I find myself drawing back when I see where he's going as the banner flares on the screen.

The Lost Angels website.

"Sam . . ." I say it as a caution, but he shakes his head. I feel my stomach muscles tighten, like I'm bracing for a punch. I *hate* this website, partly because I know how much damage it generates, but also because I know it represents a part of his past that's so complicated and difficult for him. He helped form the Lost Angels—the core of it being the families and friends of Melvin's victims. He and the mother of one of those victims fueled and refined a lot of the rage those poor people felt . . . and aimed it straight at me and the kids.

But Sam walked away from them. To me. And he's told me his credentials for the site were canceled . . . but now he's logging in, and the private message boards are opening, and I don't know what to think.

"I was going to tell you," he says, and I hear the regret in his voice. "Should have. I wanted to dig around and see what crawled out of the woodwork."

"You *went back?*"

"Not as myself. It's a new account. Anonymous. I took precautions." He pauses for a significant second. "I did it a while ago. I just wanted to . . . keep tabs. Try to spot trouble before it exploded, maybe defuse it a little."

That's not how we agreed it was going to be, but it's not the time to fight about it either. "Sam, did you know about the flyers?" I sound sharp. I feel sharp, like I'm shaped into a knife and ready to cut. "Somebody must have updated them."

"Somebody did," he says. "And I missed it. He wasn't on the usual threads. He was over in a general forum, and he was pretty clever about it. I found him while you were out today. He posts under the name MalusNavis." Same handle as the posts I found on other sites. Sam pulls up the message board in question and does a name search. "I didn't find it because he never explicitly mentions your name. Just asks about wanted-poster templates. Someone gladly provided him with a copy of the original." The one that Sam designed. "Everything else he did before yesterday was about other cases. Nothing to do with you."

"Wait, he was on the LA board before yesterday? What other cases?" He shows me the full list of MalusNavis posts. It's pretty sizable. There's nothing overtly violent about any of them; they're all more clinical, more investigative, like he's an armchair detective, not a troll. He's asking about odd cases . . . unsolved murders, mostly. Disappearances. As Sam's scrolling down, my eyes fix on a name, and I instantly put a hand on his shoulder. "Hold on. Open that one." I point.

"Okay." He does.

It's a discussion about Tammy Maguire, one of the aliases for Penny Carlson / Sheryl Lansdowne that I turned up for Kez. That cannot be a coincidence. I feel my focus sharpen as I read what MalusNavis has posted. He was inquiring whether there had been any forward motion on the case. Someone broke it down and copied in the link to the felony warrant for her arrest. He didn't comment after that. Not directly, not about Tammy Maguire.

But he did post a general question, never answered, about someone else: Hannah Wheeler. I grab a pencil and write it down. I open my own laptop, log in to the office's mainframe, and do a name search. Lots of Hannah Wheelers, but one's listed as a missing person suspected in defrauding the elderly. I get a link to a story from a regional newspaper out of Georgia. It's a few years old, but there's a photo attached, a smiling candid picture of a young woman. She's got short brown hair in this picture, carefully shaped eyebrows, dramatic makeup, but I recognize her anyway. "Sheryl Lansdowne," I say. "AKA Penny Carlson. AKA Tammy Maguire. He was looking into her."

"You think he found her?"

"I think he did more than that," I say, and push back from my desk to face him. "Sam. Why would he switch from tracking her to focusing on *us?*"

He's silent for a few seconds, thinking, and then he shakes his head. He doesn't know. Neither do I.

And then I do, with breathtaking clarity. *He saw me at the pond.* He knows I'm looking into the case.

This? This is all my fault.

I can't say that out loud, but down in my bones I feel that it's true. Irrational, maybe. Paranoid, certainly. But *true.*

Sam says, "I might know a guy who can shed some light. He's . . . I can't even call him problematic because that's an understatement. But if anybody knows this MalusNavis guy, I'll bet he does. But I need to talk to him face-to-face. He won't do it on the phone, or any electronic device. And I can't do it here, for obvious reasons."

"He's from the Lost Angels boards?"

He clearly doesn't like telling me. "He's a serious troll. I—let's just say we had a business relationship a few years ago." Meaning, Sam used him to get to me, in some way. He doesn't want to say how. I don't want to make him either. "Let me make a call."

"We should do this tomorrow."

"If you're right, if this guy started attacking you and the kids because you got involved in Kez's case . . . we can't wait. We need to push hard. Now. Before things get any worse."

He's right. I'm so tired I could cry, but he's right. "Okay," I say. "Sam? Is it safe to do this? I mean, safe for you?"

He doesn't hesitate this time. "I've met him a few times. Never had any trouble." That doesn't answer my question, and we both know it.

But this is a test too. A test of my ability to trust. And I have to say, "Okay," and let him go. Because it's his risk to take, not mine to prevent.

He steps away for a couple of minutes, and comes back putting his phone in his pocket. "He's willing to meet," he says, "but not tomorrow. Has to be tonight. I need to go now. He's not the kind of guy who waits."

"Sam—" I bite my lip to keep the rest of it in, and finally say, "Just be careful, okay? Write down where you're going?"

"I'll text you when I get there," he says. "But *don't* follow me. And *don't* do anything for at least an hour if I don't answer a call or text. Okay? He likes to talk. And he likes phones to be silent while he does."

I just nod. It sounds to me like Sam is allowing this man to set all the terms, and I don't like that at all.

Trust me, his expression says.

I hope mine says, *I do.*

He kisses me, whispers that he loves me, and then he's gone.

12

SAM

I don't want to do this, not on any level. Everything, *everything*, is shouting at me to turn the truck around as I drive away. I know I'm going to regret it—that's not even a question.

But sometimes you have to do the tough thing knowing it's going to leave a scar.

The instructions I've been given lead me to a barely operational motel on the outskirts of a rough part of K-ville; it's one step away from rent-by-hour, and nothing's ever looked more like a trap to me. This isn't Dr. Dave's normal routine. We've always met in public before . . . but then again, I haven't met Dr. Dave in years, and that last time was only because it was necessary; I was already pulling away from the anti-Gwen crusade. Still a deeply unpleasant, disturbing memory.

I know this will be worse.

I sit for a minute, wondering whether I should do this at all, and then I text the motel address to Gwen. She texts back ILU.

It means a lot in this moment that she does love me. It means even more that she trusts me to get this done for us. Letting go, stepping back . . . that's something that takes one hell of a lot of courage for Gwen. And I can't let her down.

I text the burner number that Dr. Dave gave me: Here.

I get a response that says, 4.

I make sure my handgun is in place on my belt. I don't want to need it, but I'd be an idiot not to come armed to this, and besides, he'll know that I will. Dr. Dave is many things. He's not stupid.

Room 4 is at the far end of the first level, isolated. As I stand ready to knock, for a disorienting second I have a sense-memory of another motel like this. Gwen and I stayed in several while we searched for Melvin Royal. I blink and see Gwen coming out of the bathroom, fresh from a shower. That was the first time I knew, *really* knew, that I was completely in love with her. That moment is fixed in my mind, eternal and bright. We weren't lovers then.

But it was the start.

I knock on the door, and the memory breaks apart under the hollow sound. I don't hear footsteps, but the door swings open.

Dr. David Merit smiles at me. Good-looking white guy, strong face, great teeth. He looks normal, and that's the terrible thing about Dr. Dave. He's a fairly prominent local dentist. His patients have absolutely no idea that the man they're letting put his fingers in their mouths is a vicious, amoral, sociopathic troll. He likes to cloak himself as a "victim defender," but—like many of the Lost Angels hangers-on—he really just likes any excuse to cause harm, and directing it at those the site identifies as abusers and predators and killers is perfect cover for a sadist.

It is *never* a good idea to put yourself at Dr. Dave's mercy. And I don't. I stare him down, as emotionless against his false warmth as I can be, and I move my jacket so he sees the gun. "Just so we're clear," I say, "I don't like this."

"Nice to see you, too, Sam." He steps back to allow me in. The gun, as I expected, bothers him not one bit. I keep my gaze fixed on him, alert for anything that might tell me he's about to shift his affable mask, but he just calmly closes the door and turns with his arms folded. Still smiling. "Been a while, buddy. But I understand why. Fucking the woman who fucked your sister's killer must be one hell of a drug." His opening shot, looking for a weak spot. It's accurate, but I'm ready. He gets nothing but silence. After a long moment, he rolls his eyes. "Fine. Down to business. What do you want?"

"Let's talk terms first," I say. "Because I've still got the recordings from three years ago. Before you try it, Tennessee is still a one-party consent state. You admitted to things that you really don't want the public to hear. Or the cops."

"That again." Dr. Dave waves it away like a bothersome black fly. "Lots of people say things. It's another thing to prove I did any of it. You know that."

"I know your business depends on your reputation. And I've got your reputation by the balls." I hate doing this so much. But dealing with Dr. Dave means staying in control, staying ahead, because he's a hyena who'll crush your bones and laugh while he's doing it.

"Okay," he says. He's still smiling. "What brings you here, this time of night? Because I'm guessing it has something to do with Gina Royal. It always does these days."

It's so strange talking to him; my skin crawls every time I do it, *because he sounds so normal.* His patients love him. He's got high marks on all the ratings sites. And he wouldn't blink as he killed you, if it came to that. I don't *think* Dave's ever killed anyone, though he's hurt plenty of people. He's a controlled kind of sociopath, one who understands how to work within the rules, even if he can't really, emotionally, comprehend why the rules are there.

But I wouldn't want to meet him in a dark alley either. Bad enough meeting him in this isolated motel room.

"MalusNavis," I say. "He's on the LA boards. You know him. You replied to him and gave him the wanted-poster template."

Dr. Dave's smile gets wider. It makes him look a lot less normal. "And? It was a public service. That bitch has been left alone for a while. Time to heat things up, don't you think?"

"What do you know about MalusNavis?"

"Not a lot, if you're asking for personal details. But he's . . . let's say, exceptional. I've had some interesting private chats with him. His ideas are extraordinary."

I feel the hair raise on the back of my neck. I've seen what Dr. Dave posts in public. What he says in private chat must be unimaginably worse. "He give you any contact info? Any hint where he's from? Anything?"

"Not really. If I had to guess from his grammar and syntax, I'd say he's college educated or very well read. He's got money, that's obvious from some of the discussion points; cost doesn't seem to be an issue for him. And I think he's from a coastal area."

"Why do you think so?" I ask.

He sounds smug when he answers. "Why, Sam, I'm sure you'll work that one out if you try hard enough. And you're right not to sleep on this one. I'd place a nice-size bet that he'd very much like to do something nasty to your girl. Not *see* it done. Actually do it."

I flinch at the pleasure in that last part. "Anything else you know? Don't hold out on me. You know there will be consequences if you do." There have been. I've hurt him before. He needs to believe I'll keep on doing it, or I'll move from the predator to prey column.

His smile disappears like it's been wiped off a whiteboard. What's left is only really human in its basic form and function. Dr. Dave doesn't possess empathy, or if he does, it's so stunted and malformed that it serves no real function beyond making him cautious. "He's bad news," he says. Quite a statement, given who I'm talking with. "Don't take him lightly. He's . . . dedicated. And she's hardly his first project."

"Who else?"

"Work that part out. You have the pieces. I put it together; so can you if she hasn't fucked your brains out." The scorn he puts on *she* is obvious. Gwen is, to him, a thing. An object he would very much like to see hurt, just for the simple entertainment of it. I'm not sure he thinks of the kids as even that. They barely exist to him, except as tools to hit Gwen with.

This bastard's got children of his own. Three of them, according to his website. His wife is pretty, glossy, and I'm sure she's absolutely terrified of him. But leaving him would probably be even worse for her. He doesn't like losing to me, but he *really* doesn't like women.

"Spell it out for me," I say. "Why did he look into Tammy Maguire?"

"Because she's easy pickings," he says. "Why do you think?" He says it like it's blindingly obvious; it isn't to anyone but a true sociopath. From what Gwen's told me, the woman she first knew of as Sheryl Lansdowne seems like a predator herself.

A house cat is a predator, I realize. But it's also prey to a pit bull.

He seems impatient now. "It's late. Are we square, Sam?"

"No," I say. "But I won't be looking to hurt you unless you step out of line. Not just with me. With *anyone*. I mean it, Dave. Play nice."

"Of course," he says, and there's that smile again. "And you should also try being nicer. It'll get you a lot further than your threats."

No, it won't. Not with him. And we both know that.

He opens the door and leaves. Before he closes it, he says, "I hacked your credit card, by the way. The room's on you."

I don't know if he actually did. His lies read as true, every time. I'll just ask at the office on the way out.

I need a long, hot, disinfecting shower. Instead, I check the room for any nasty surprises, and he doesn't disappoint me. Tucked under the bed is a thick stack of horrific child pornography—movies, crudely printed magazines, photos. It's deeply disturbing stuff. *Christ.* Even in this place, they'd call the cops on that. And of course he'd put the room in my name.

I grab a plastic trash bag from the bathroom and shove it all in, then check the rest of the room. He hasn't bothered with anything else that I can tell.

I head straight for my truck, toss the bag in the bed, and call the office. Dave, thankfully, was lying; he'd paid cash for the room. Just another of his little mind games. I'm much more worried about the shit he's left me with; I can't just dump it. So I drive outside K-ville to a lonely road, build a small fire, and start tossing the filth on top of it once it's burning briskly. I break the DVDs. I rip apart the videotapes. I tear the magazines. Destroying it feels better.

As it all burns, I take out my phone to do a quick search. Dave taunted me about having plenty of clues to put together. So I start doing that. *Malus Navis* refers to a navigational beacon. So that's why he said our stalker probably lives on the coast. Though which coast, and in which state . . . who knows. But Dave's suggestion is sound: I need to look closely at MalusNavis's public posts and see what they can tell me. Maybe they can give me some directional hints, after all.

I take a deep breath and slip back into the emotional torture that is the Lost Angels site.

It doesn't take me long to see it. MalusNavis's language is spare, measured, but in a way it's as inexorable as an avalanche. He never seems to have much emotion about what he's doing, but he does have an enormous interest in the concept of an eye for an eye. I find him posting on several different boards—Tammy Maguire is one, but he's also interested in other names. I write them down. Not all the people he's been interested in are female; most are names I don't recognize. Some barely rate a mention, even on a board obsessed with crime.

But he's there, gliding from board to board. Hunting.

I write down *avenging angel* and stare at that for a few seconds. It makes me go quiet inside, because if this person *is* that, I've been him. I know him. I know how it feels to have an inner truth that takes over your whole world . . . even when that all-consuming conviction isn't true. You'll compromise your ethics and your morals, cheat, lie, steal, hurt, kill . . . all in the name of justice.

It took coming face-to-face with Gwen Proctor and her kids to break that iron illusion for me, to see that what I was doing was harming me as much as I meant to harm her.

MalusNavis sounds like a man on a mission. I just don't know what *kind* of mission. Maybe he, like Dr. Dave, knows where the line is, and stops at harassment. I remember the drenching horror of that phone call asking me about Gwen's death notice: that could have been our guy. It's cruel, not illegal, just amoral. Like many of the things that come streaming through the internet aimed at Gwen and the kids. Like the flyers I created.

But it makes me wonder, because Dr. Dave, a sociopath, seemed to think MalusNavis is *worse* than him. And here in the dark, burning up the horrifying stash of incriminating evidence he meant me to be caught with . . . that's really something.

I make sure it's all burned, twisted, distorted, unrecognizable for the filth it was, and douse the fire with dirt. I bury the ashes, and feel horribly like I'm a criminal burying a body.

I text Gwen while I wait for the smoke to clear. **All okay. Coming home.**

The call comes almost immediately after that. I expect it to be Gwen, but it isn't. I don't recognize the number, and I nearly let it go, but then some instinct tells me I'd better not. Not this late.

"Hello?" I make it a one-word challenge. Subtext: *this had better be urgent.*

"Sam? Mr. Cade? It's Tyler. From the airfield." He's agitated. I can hear his breathing rattling the speaker.

"Not the time, Tyler."

"Okay," he says. He sounds subdued, within the limited inflections he seems to possess. "I just wanted you to know it isn't your fault."

I pause in the act of opening my truck door. "Excuse me?" A million things race through my head, and all of them are bad. Most of them infuriate me.

"You're the only person who really tried," Tyler says. "To understand what was happening to me. And I appreciate that. I just don't want you to think this is because of you."

"What are you talking about, Tyler?"

"I'm on the Gay Street Bridge," he says, as if it explains everything. And after a second, it does. I feel my heartbeat speed up, my mouth go dry.

"Tyler, what are you going to do?" The Gay Street Bridge is just outside downtown, over the Tennessee River. A low, green-painted steel railing. A long drop down to the river.

"I can't do it anymore," he says. "I really can't. It will be better for everybody."

I yank my truck door open and climb in. Start the engine. I put the phone on speaker and drop it on the seat. "Tyler, I'm coming to you, okay? Let's sit and talk awhile. Can we do that?" I know that thin edge he's on. I stood there many times in the past few years, before Gwen stretched out a hand to me and pulled me back to the world. Lots of times nothing seemed worth it, nothing seemed *real* enough. It's a very bad place, when you hear the dead whispering to you that things will be easier if you join them.

A fall off that bridge might not kill him, but he'd drown. This time of night, traffic on the bridge is low, and it would be the work of a few seconds to step over the rail and into the dark.

Tyler isn't answering me. I speed up. "Tyler? Still there, man?"

"I'm here," he says. "I'm just tired, Sam. I'm just real tired."

"I know you are. I know how it feels. But I'm coming, and you won't be alone. Okay? Promise me you'll wait for me. Please. You don't know me real well, but you know I've been where you are right now. I can show you a way back. Okay?"

He thinks about it for an agonizing, silent few seconds. I glance at my speed. Well over the legal limit.

Then he says, "I'll wait."

"It's going to take me about ten minutes. Stay on the phone with me. Tell me what's on your mind."

He starts talking. I'm listening, but mostly I just want him to stay engaged. He talks about finding a photo online of his family, about how it took him back to one particular Christmas just before his sister was taken away. I understand that. Memories are a drug, and sometimes they have a rush to them that brings a horrible, hollow emptiness after. I still remember the last video call with my sister while I was deployed. I'd had to cut it short. I still replay it in my mind and think about what else she might have said, what else I could have done to keep her in my world just a little bit longer.

Tyler is doing the same thing, but he's got nothing to hold on to. His sister's killer was never caught, and that never-ending suspense and despair makes people lose faith, lose love, lose hope. My mystery was solved.

His may never be.

Five minutes away. I keep an eye out for patrol cars. If I dared, I'd try to make a call to the cops and send them to the bridge, but the trust I've established with Tyler is as fragile as a smoke ring; if he thinks I'm going to betray it, he'll be gone before they can stop him.

And what if this is something else? A little voice in the back of my head, a cold one, has doubts. *You don't know this kid. What if he's luring you?*

If he is, I'm armed, and I'm not going down easy. Tyler doesn't strike me as someone who'd be physically aggressive, but if he is, I'm ready for that.

"Sam?" His voice is faint now. Tired. "I just want to go now. Thank you for trying."

"No, Tyler, don't do that. Come on, man, stay with me. I'm three minutes away. You can wait three minutes, right?" I'm hurtling there like a comet. I can see the lights of downtown. The bridge isn't far. I blow through a deserted red light and keep moving.

"I don't want to wait."

"But you called me for a reason," I say. "You wanted me to know. And I do want to know. You've got more to tell me. I know that."

I keep talking, not even sure what I'm saying anymore; I see the green superstructure of the bridge up ahead; it's built under the bridge, not over. The lights illuminate the roadway, and I can't see any cars stopped in the narrow breakdown lane on either side. It's only a two-lane bridge, and no traffic at all.

I slow down, afraid I'll miss him; even so, I spot him at the last second. He's wearing dark pants, a dark hoodie, and he nearly blends into the night.

He's standing on the concrete ledge, legs pressed against the green steel. It's an easy, effortless step over.

I hit the brakes and fight the wheel to steer the truck into the narrow space of the breakdown lane, and I bail out fast, phone clutched in my hand. My instinct is to run at him, but my next impulse is to stop, slow down, approach carefully. So I walk, though it seems to take forever.

Tyler is staring out at the river, not at the lights of downtown. And as Nietzsche said, the abyss is looking into him. He knows I'm here, but he doesn't break that stare.

"Tyler?" I see the phone is in his hand, still active. I shut off the call and hold up both hands. "I'm going to put my phone in my pocket, okay?"

"Okay." He sounds fine. That's the worst part. "You didn't need to come."

"I know." I lean against the railing. I'm ten feet away, trying to figure out how to get closer without triggering a deadly reaction. I put my phone in my jacket pocket, and as I do, I hit the emergency dial function for 911. I wait for a few seconds, and hope that it's connected before I say, "Why did you pick the Gay Street Bridge to jump from?" God, please let the operator pick that up.

"It's quiet," he says. "I like this bridge. And it's high."

It is. There's a strong, cool wind blowing. The stars are out, the moon behind a rising cloud bank. It'd be beautiful if I were standing here with Gwen. It's ominous now.

"You want to explain to me why you decided to do this now? Tonight?"

"I told you. The pictures."

"But there had to be something else. You've seen those pictures before."

He turns his head toward me. He's wearing his Florida Gators baseball cap, still, with the hoodie drawn over it. He puts his hands in his pockets. The blank expression is no different than it was at the airfield, and that chills me deep. "It's her birthday," he says. "My sister's, I mean. She'd be twenty-one today. I would have bought her a drink. Made sure she got home safe after."

That guts me. I can feel the crumbling edge of that emotional cliff. Tyler looks back at the river.

"Tell me about her," I say. "Did you two get along?"

"Not always. She was kind of a bitch the day—the day it happened." I see his Adam's apple bob as he swallows. I see him waver forward a little, and I tense up. I can be fast if I need to; I *might* be able to get to him and grab his hoodie before he's out of reach. But stopping a falling body his size is tough, and I'll probably rip a ligament, maybe dislocate my arm.

That isn't a deterrent. Just a factor. I carefully, hopefully unnoticeably, edge closer. "Did she know you loved her?"

"What?"

"Did she know you loved her, Tyler?"

I get his stare back again. "Why?"

"Because it matters. It mattered to me. The last thing I told my sister was that I loved her, and that helped. But she would have known it anyway, I hope."

"I don't know," he says. "I don't know if she thought that. I bought her a Christmas present, a nice one. She never got to open it."

I can hear a siren in the distance. *No no no . . .* if they run lights and sirens, they could send him off the edge fast. I move forward a little more. He doesn't react. "I'd really like to talk to you about my sister. I could use that help, too, talking to somebody who understands. Do you want to get down and go grab a coffee, maybe? Come on, Tyler. Let's talk it out. You can do this anytime. But I'm here, right now. And I care."

He seems to sigh, and for a terrible red second I think I've lost him. Then he says, "Yeah. Okay."

And he jumps down off the ledge.

I'm not really prepared for that, and the relief that fills me makes my voice a little unsteady. "Thank you, Tyler," I say. "Come on with me. Let's go find someplace quiet, okay?"

He says, "Did you call the cops?"

I don't blink. "No. Maybe someone else did, though. Someone could have seen you up here."

He nods and walks over to my truck. While his back is turned, I hang up the call. I open the door for him and get him inside just as the Knoxville patrol car glides to a stop nose-in toward us. The strobes stay on, but the siren stops. Two officers get out. I hold up my hands and walk toward them. "Sam Cade," I tell them. "I'm the one who called. He's down, and I'm going to take him for coffee and then try to get him some help. We're okay. Thanks for coming."

One of the officers breaks off to talk to Tyler. The other moves me up against the railing a little farther off. It doesn't take long. They're just relieved not to have to be talking someone out of an irrevocable decision.

When I get back in the truck, Tyler seems okay. Quiet. He's staring down at his hands. "Thanks for coming, Sam," he says. "You didn't have to. That means a lot."

I don't know how to answer that, so I just nod and start the engine. There's a twenty-four-hour diner not far away; I've hit it several times, and it's usually quiet. He doesn't talk on the drive there. We pull up and walk in, take a seat in a yellow leatherette booth, and get coffee pours. Tyler orders a waffle, which surprises me a little.

Now that my heartbeat's slowing down, I realize that I'm already late coming home. I text Gwen stopping on the way, home soon, will call. I put it on silent, not even vibrate. The responsibility of Tyler is pretty big in my mind right now. I don't want him to think I'm not completely invested in this conversation.

"I've been thinking about whether or not she knew I loved her," Tyler says. "That's a good question. I guess she didn't, Sam. I never was good at showing things like that, even before—" He points toward his head. "Big brother, little sister, I got annoyed at her a lot. I wish that wasn't true, but it is. Did your sister—"

"We didn't grow up together," I tell him. "We were separated in foster care when we were both really young. We reconnected while I was overseas. Mostly, we just talked on video calls and the phone. She probably annoyed me before we lost our folks, but I don't really remember that part so well."

That gets his attention. He pauses with his coffee cup halfway to his mouth. "Your parents died?"

"How about yours? Are they still—"

"No. They're both gone too."

We sit there, two orphans, both hurt in different ways. I don't know that I like the mirror that I'm looking into. But I understand the black, wounded desperation he feels, and that's enough to make a bond.

I tell him about my sister. I do it slowly, a little haltingly, because I'm afraid it's going to unleash all the nastiness I've buried so deep. But it doesn't, beyond a couple of uncomfortable twinges. That's a wonder. I talk about how it felt to come back, to deal with the loss, to fall in with

Miranda Tidewell—the mother of another of Melvin's victims—and go down that unhealthy, entirely destructive spiral.

I talk about Gwen, and how she's pulled me back out of it, or at least been a signpost on the way. He takes it in silently, eating his waffle with mechanical efficiency and no real sign of pleasure. My coffee sits untouched even after his is empty.

When I finally stop talking, he meets and holds my gaze for long enough it feels uncomfortable. "Thank you," he says. "I needed to know that."

I lean forward and rest my elbows on the table. "Point is, Tyler, there is going to be a way up and through this. I found one, and believe me, I was in a very, very dark place. I believe you want to find a way out too. So if you want to keep meeting and talking about it—"

"I don't think that'll be necessary," he says, which sets me back a little. "I mean . . . you're right, Sam. I should get help. Real help. Like you have."

"I'd like to help you do that," I tell him. "How about I call a counseling crisis center and you talk to them? They're going to have better advice than I do."

He shakes his head. "I already know where to go," he says. "There's a doctor I know who can help me. I just . . . didn't want to go there, that's all. But I guess I have to, really."

"Can I drive you there?"

He blinks, like he didn't think I'd offer. "That would be nice."

I pay the check, since he's done. I walk him out to the truck, and he gives me quiet directions. We pull up in the parking lot of a small hospital; the sign says it serves behavioral health urgent care. That's exactly what he needs.

"Sam?" He unlocks his seatbelt and turns toward me. "You've been real kind to me. Thank you. Can I ask you a question?"

"Sure."

"Do you trust Gina? I mean, Gwen?"

I don't know why he's asking, and it makes me wary again. "Yes."

"All the time?"

I want to lie, but I know this is some kind of a test for him. "I didn't always, but now? Yes. I trust her."

"Do you think she really is innocent?"

"Tyler, I don't want to talk about Gwen, she really isn't what we're about here. This is about you, me, the people we've lost. Okay?"

"I know. But . . . I need to understand. Why do you believe her? When other people don't?"

"I choose to. I think she's a good person."

He nods, as if that settles something, and he opens the truck door. Before he closes it, he says, "I wish I could believe that too. About myself, I mean. Maybe someday."

Then he slams the door, and I watch him walk inside. I wait a little bit, but he doesn't come back, and I finally put my truck in gear.

I pull my cell from my pocket and realize that in my focus on Tyler, I've missed text messages and alerts.

An alert from our security system.

Our home alarm's been triggered.

"Shit," I whisper.

I put the truck in gear and leave rubber as I head home, fast as an arrow from a bow.

13

Gwen

I'm sitting tense, watching my phone and waiting for Sam to get home.
Long minutes tick by. Half an hour. I tell myself to be patient; he was
pretty far out when he texted me from the diner, and maybe he's hit
traffic, a road closure, something like that.

But I'm really starting to worry when it closes in on an hour, and
there's no word. I text him, but I don't get a response.

It's well after midnight when the home alarm goes off.

The siren is so loud it's almost like being punched in the head
with sound waves, shocking and nauseating in its intensity. I roll off
the couch, fall on my knees, and press my thumb to the sensor on the
lockbox. My gun's in my hand in less than five seconds, and I'm on my
feet and heading down the hall, no thought left but for my children. I
glance at the alarm panel as I move past it.

The alarm was triggered in Lanny's bedroom. My whole body is
shaking, but I know how to control it, how to *use* it. Fear is a sharp,
metallic taste in my suddenly dry mouth.

I open the door to Connor's room, and Connor's right there, bracing himself with the baseball bat in his hand. He's put himself between
danger and his sister, who he's shoved into the corner, I realize, but she's

backing him right up, and holding her laptop like she intends to smash it into the first skull she sees. Recognition makes them both relax. I mouth, *Lock the door*, and Connor nods. I shut it, and go across the hall.

I take a breath, a second to get my gun in position, brace, and I ease Lanny's door open.

Moonlight catches on curtains blowing in the breeze. Her window is up. I see a shadow moving, and for a hot chemical second I feel the twitch go through me, and I almost, *almost* pull the trigger. But something stops me for just long enough that the lamp next to Lanny's bed switches on, and spills its light over Vera Crockett, who sees me with the gun and staggers back, holding up both hands. Her face has gone milky pale, a few freckles standing in stark relief. Her eyes are wide and scared, and I quickly lower the gun. I stalk past her, slam the window, and give her a glare that would probably melt steel; she looks appropriately chastened.

Then I go the nearest alarm panel and turn the siren off.

The silence flows over me like cool water, but my ears are still ringing, my nerves still burning from the stress. And I turn that right on Vee as she comes out of Lanny's room. "Jesus *Christ*, Vee, what the hell did you think you were doing? I nearly shot you! I could have killed you!"

Before she can answer, I hear the home phone ringing. It's the alarm company. I get to it and tell them, in clipped tones, that there's not an emergency, and to call off the police response. They're likely halfway here already. I don't like showing up as a false report, especially now.

As I hang up, Vee says, "Ms. P, I am *so sorry*, I thought—I texted Lanta to ask her to turn off the alarm, I thought for sure she'd do it . . ." She trails off because now my attention is on her again, and it's not kind. She swallows hard.

"Tell me she didn't leave her window unlocked."

"Uh . . . she didn't? I kind of know how to slide those locks?" She looks ashamed to say it, but I'm actually relieved a little bit; at least this time it isn't my daughter's doing. Not completely, anyway. Though

Lanny should have warned me that Vee was planning this. "It really wasn't Lanta's fault. It was all mine."

"You're damn right it was. Vee, why didn't you just come to the front door like a normal person?" But I think I know, from the way her cheeks turn a bit pink. *She was hoping for a little make-out session with my daughter,* I think. I have no idea if Lanny's agreed to it or not, but either way, it's just throwing fuel on the fire. Both of them should know better. "Sit. Down. I need to tell my kids they're not about to be murdered, thanks to you."

"Sorry," she mutters. "Bright side is, you didn't even shoot anybody."

She's getting her equilibrium back. Far too quickly for my taste.

I knock on Connor's door, the usual signal pattern to let him know it's me and I'm not under duress; he unlocks it and peers out, still wary, until he sees me. Then the door flings wide. "What was that?"

I look past him at my daughter. She seems completely clueless. "What? What did I do?"

I sigh. "Check your phone."

She does, whipping it out of her pocket, and I see her expression go from guarded to shocked to utterly horrified. "Oh no."

"Oh yes."

"*Vee?* She broke my window?"

"Not broke," Vee says quietly from behind me. "Kinda jimmied. Didn't know you'd ignored my message."

"Dumbass, I didn't even know about it! You can't just . . ." She's actually angry. Lanny, for the first time I can remember, is holding her friend—maybe even her crush—to account. "Do you know what kind of trouble you could have caused? Oh my God, you're lucky Mom didn't shoot you!"

Mom almost did, a fact that makes me shiver. The gun feels heavy in my hand, and very, very lethal. "Go lock your window," I tell my daughter. "Vee. Couch. Now."

I trail her on the way back, and stoop to put my gun away. When I straighten up, she's trying so hard to look inoffensive that it's nearly comic. "I just wanted to make sure she was okay," Vee tells me. "She texted me about the boys who put up that flyer on your door. There's one over 'round my place on the telephone pole too."

"Did you take it down?"

"'Course I did, what do you think I am?" She seems offended I'd even ask, but with Vee, honestly, I kind of had to. "I expect that guy who sent me the letter put it up. Right?"

Her instincts are good, but I just say, "I don't know for certain. I guess since you're here, you might as well stay the night. I don't want you walking around in the dark." The fact she was foolish enough to do that makes me itch, but that's Vee: smart and stupid at the same time. That's also being a teenager. Lanny's growing out of it. I hope that Vee will too.

"Where's Sam?" she asks. I notice that Vee's usually *Ms. P* when it comes to me, but she treats Sam differently. Not sure what I make of it, or if I should make anything of it at all . . . and then it hits me, and I suck in a startled breath.

Sam.

I grab for my phone. There's a notification from the alarm company on the screen; I swipe past it and see a missed call from Sam. He must have seen that the alarm triggered.

He's okay.

I shut my eyes for a second in real relief, and then hit dial. He picks up on the first ring, and I hear the roar of road noise immediately. "Gwen?"

"Slow down," I tell him. "We're okay. It's okay. Vee set off the alarm. Everything's fine. Are you all right?"

"Oh, thank God. Yeah. I'm fine. I'll be there in five minutes."

"Take your time. The crisis is canceled."

"In our house, it's always just postponed," he says, but he sounds better. More relaxed. And I can tell he's slowing his speed to something reasonable. "I love you, Gwen."

"I love you too. Please get home safe."

"Oh," Vee says as I hang up the call. "He ain't here? Wow. Guess I really did put my foot in it. Y'all didn't have a fight, did you?"

"No, Vee, we didn't have a fight." In her world, violent breakups seem far more likely than happy relationships. "You didn't just come here to make out with my daughter, did you?"

"What? That's ridiculous." She lies pretty well, now that she's settled. "I wanted to tell you about the flyer in my neighborhood. And make sure everything was okay here."

"And you wanted to tell me something you found out," Lanny says from the hallway. How long she's been there, I don't know. She's looking at Vee with very adult eyes right now. "That was really, really dumb, Vee."

"I know. Sorry." Lanny sinks down on the couch near Vee, but not next to her. I notice the space. So does Vee. "You're mad."

"Disappointed. What did you find out?"

I shift my weight as the meaning of that hits me. "Wait, what? What is Vee doing looking into anything?"

"Vee," Vee says primly, "is *helping*. I told you I had a part-time job, didn't I? Well. I work for Mailboxes For You, the one with all the storefronts all over town, which Lanta says is where you got mailed something you wanted to trace—"

"Wait, *what*? How do you know about that, Lanny?"

"I'm not blind," she says. Cool as spring water. "I know the look you get when something to do with Melvin shows up. So I looked at the footage on the security system. You got a package. I saw the mailing envelope on your desk. Mailboxes For You, return address in Knoxville. It isn't the place that Vee's working. I just asked if she could find out who paid to send it. Just looking up a receipt, Mom. Nothing dangerous."

She doesn't know that. *I* don't know that. But we're well past that now. I look at Vee. "And?"

She pulls a piece of paper out of the pocket of her tight-fitting skinny jeans and hands it to me. It's folded small, and clammy with sweat. I open it carefully. It's a printout of a receipt, a courier package addressed to me here on Monday.

The return address is the Mailboxes For You on the other side of the city. But the credit card charge has a name on it.

The name is *Penny Maguire*.

It takes me a second to link the last name back to Sheryl Lansdowne, but once I do, I stare at that name hard until my eyes burn. Then I fold the paper up and put it on the coffee table. "Thank you," I say. "And if I could ground you, you'd be grounded for a month, Vee. Best I can do is tell you that you do nothing else. No poking around. No asking questions. *Nothing*. Is that clear?" I don't even wait for her answer. I turn to my daughter. "And you're damn lucky that I don't have time to ground you, either, because that was *not* a safe thing to do, Lanny. Not for Vee, not for you, not for this family. Do you understand me? *No going off on your own*. We communicate, and we stay together."

I see a muscle tense in her jaw, but she nods. "Sorry," she says. I'm not sure she's sorry enough, but there's nothing I can do to make her understand how much of a risk both of them took.

Lanny, after a beat, says, "Was I right? Was it from him?" She knows I've gotten other letters. I've tried to be open about it, to the extent I thought was wise.

"It's the last one," I say. And that's not a lie. I'm going to make damn sure it is.

"Can I read it?"

"No, honey." I hear my voice soften, because I understand this impulse. All too well. My feelings about Melvin Royal are both clear and complicated; my kids are struggling with reconciling a dad they still feel they should love and a monster who doesn't deserve it. Reading his letters is like touching a hot stove for them. Sometimes they feel they have to hurt themselves to prove they can take it. "I shredded it. It was meant for me. It wasn't about you or Connor."

"You *shredded* it?" She seems surprised. I guess she ought to be. "I thought you . . . kept them."

"Not anymore," I tell her, and put my arm around her. "I don't need them. And neither do you."

Connor, I realize, is in the kitchen pouring himself a glass of water. When I look over at him, he just nods. "I'm okay with that," he says. "I said goodbye to Dad already. I try not to think about him at all."

That hurts and soothes at the same time. We sit quietly for a few seconds, and I hear the purr of the truck's engine as it comes closer. Garage door opening. The second Sam's inside, I reset the alarm, and I'm in his arms two moments later. He holds me tight.

"I was so worried about you," I whisper right in his ear, so close my lips brush skin.

He hugs me tight and doesn't say anything. I don't need him to. He moves on to embrace the kids. "Did the alarm scare you?" he asks them.

Lanny snorts. "I'm Supergirl. I don't get scared."

"More like Squirrel Girl," Connor says.

"Who's even *more* awesome, so thanks." She shoots that back without hesitation, and that's when I know they're okay. Finally. Sam lets them go and turns to Vee, who's on her feet, hands on her hips.

"What?" she demands. Cocky as ever.

Sam shakes his head. "You're staying, I assume? You know where everything is. Don't throw wet towels on the floor this time. And no hair dye in the shower."

She gives him a mock salute and goes right to the hall closet, where she takes out a pillow and blanket that she throws in the general direction of the couch.

Everything seems normal, but I can see from the look Sam gives me that it's anything but. We head back to the office, and he closes the door.

"I need to tell you about a guy named Dr. Dave, and a guy named Tyler," he says. "And you're not going to like any of it."

◆ ◆ ◆

He's absolutely right. I hate it. I hate that he knows someone as slimy as Dr. David Merit, Dentist Troll. I really hate that he met him alone, in such a terribly vulnerable place, and narrowly avoided worse things happening.

And having to talk a young man down from suicide . . . that is a hell of a night. I can tell that Sam feels an affinity for the kid, a bond that I can't really understand. And though he doesn't say it, I can tell he's uneasy about that too. Anything that touches on that pain, that loss . . . it's deeply uncomfortable for him.

But Sam's okay, and at least the evil dentist has given us something to work with. Sam tells me his theories about MalusNavis, and they make a dreadful kind of sense. Even to the avenging-angel part . . . especially alarming if this person now has his sights fixed on me. On us.

Why does he have a credit card that sounds like it probably belongs to Sheryl Lansdowne / Penny Carlson / Tammy Maguire? Is she *with* *him*? Does he have her prisoner? What the hell is happening here?

It's too late—or, by this time, far too early—to solve any of those questions. I carry them with me to bed, into an exhausted sleep that seems to drag me down like a weighted net.

I wake up later than I intended—almost seven, sunlight streaming in through the blinds. Wednesday morning, and I try to think through the day for a second. Nothing urgent comes to mind. That leaves me a window to do something about Melvin's letter.

Sam's side of the bed is empty; I usually wake when he moves, but not today. I put my hand in the hollow of his pillow. Cool. He's been up for a while.

I find there's a pot of coffee already made, so I pour and head for the office, still in my sleep-time T-shirt and flannel pants. Vee's sound asleep on the couch, curled like a fall leaf under a snowy white blanket. She looks relaxed and very young, and I'm careful not to wake her.

Sam's in the office. Fully dressed. I shut the door behind me as I enter. "Well, I feel like a slacker."

"The kids sent you an email," he says. "Copied to me. Isn't Douglas Adam Prinker the guy in Valerie?"

"It's for Kez's case."

"Are you still sure that's . . ." He searches for the right words for a second. "Good for them?"

There's no good way to answer it except to say, "They can handle a little more responsibility. Besides, you saw what happened when I *didn't* give permission. All of a sudden Lanny's asking Vee to go look up records from a place where she's already well known. Vee cannot keep a low profile. And it's about *Melvin*. I need to keep them out of that. Completely."

"I'm thinking it's not separate, though. Aren't you?"

I hate that I am, actually. Kez's case started early Monday morning. I was at the pond before dawn. And just a few hours later, I have Melvin's letter served on me like a subpoena. That doesn't feel random. And now Vee's provided a link—at least a strange and tenuous one—with a credit card that looks like something Sheryl Lansdowne might have had as a new identity. How would MalusNavis—if it's him—get his hands on Melvin's letter? From what Sam's uncovered, he's hardly likely to be someone Melvin would have attracted as a fan.

Between that, the word from the loathsome Dr. Dave that Monday was when MalusNavis asked for the template, the fake obituary, the letter Vee received on her door, and the posting of flyers at the gun range . . . it all looks very, very bad. Like I'm now in the crosshairs of someone who's very serious.

But it *also* looks like a patchwork of coincidence that could fall apart like mist under the spotlight of a real investigation. So I can't tell. I have a confirmation bias, a thumb on the scale.

We need some real proof, like getting a picture of the person who sent that package. If it's Sheryl Lansdowne, then there's something real to chase. If it's someone else, there's still a lead to follow, a face, *something*. But as I well know, Knoxville PD is not going to be helpful. They tolerate me just fine, but they're certainly not bending any rules on my behalf. Posting Melvin's letters isn't a crime. And if the credit card is valid, using it might not have been a crime either. And they'll just shake their heads at the Lansdowne connection until I have real proof.

No way to get a warrant, or official action. And I can't put Kez into that position either. *No help for it,* I think. *I'm going to have to be creative.*

"Hey, Sam?" I say, and he looks up. "How do you feel about staying here with the kids for a while?"

"Fine, they're sleeping until noon anyway, at this rate. I'll take care of whatever needs doing. Why? You going to see Kez?"

"I . . . don't think I should tell you. That way, if you're asked, you can truthfully say you have no idea." I hit print on the document I've pulled up. It looks official, but it isn't. Good fake, though. I don't intend to leave it behind, just flash it and a fake badge I keep for real emergencies and hope the store clerk isn't very savvy. I pause in the act of folding it up and look at Sam. "Shit. What's today?"

"Wednesday," he says.

"I made an appointment for us with Dr. Marks for this afternoon," I remind him. "All of us. I can change it if—"

He's already shaking his head. "No," he says. "I think we need it. We might need it a *lot.* And Gwen? I would really rather that neither of us goes to jail right now. Understand?"

"Yes," I say. "Don't worry. I'll be fine."

I sound far more confident than I feel, but Sam gives me the incredible gift of letting me get away with it.

I kiss him, finish my coffee, and head off to shower.

I dress in a black knit pantsuit with a plain white button-down shirt and my nicest pair of flat shoes. My hair's grown out to shoulder length; I tie it back in a plain, no-nonsense ponytail. No makeup. My shoulder holster goes on under the jacket, and while the tailoring isn't perfect, it's pretty decent. I look professional. And a wee bit intimidating.

I don't dare take either of our cars, so I catch a ride-share to a random location; it drops me about six blocks away from the place where the package originated. In a hidden inner pocket of my pants are my necessary ID cards. I have cash. I have a disposable phone with emergency numbers preprogrammed in my left jacket pocket. I'm as unidentifiable as possible.

In the right pocket, I have the document I printed out, and that costume badge. Neither is perfect, but they look and feel solid. I put on my sunglasses and a black cap as I leave the ride-share and walk for a while, staring in store windows and just generally looking casual.

I make my way to the right block, and stay on the opposite side of the street. I'm watching the door of the mail establishment, counting the number of people entering and leaving. It doesn't look busy. I see only two people in thirty minutes, and both are in and out in under five minutes each. It's ten in the morning . . . after the theoretical morning rush, before the lunch hour crowd runs errands. Best guess, the place is empty.

I walk confidently to the door.

My eyes, hidden behind sunglasses, have to adjust to the dimmer light inside. It feels warm, and the smell of old cardboard makes me wrinkle my nose. There's a long counter on one side, and some smaller standing tables for people to prepare packages.

I was right. Nobody home but the man behind the counter. He's in his early twenties, tall and thin and gawky. He's busy sorting out some packages, and says without looking up, "Hi, can I help you?"

I take the paper out and unfold it on the counter, and set the gold badge on top of it. "Detective Karen Fields," I tell him. "That's a warrant to view your video."

That gets his attention. He looks up at me, and I smile. He won't remember me, more than likely; he'll remember the template. Black suit, white shirt, businesslike, professional ponytail. Gun visible under the jacket. Badge. But mostly the gun.

"Uh . . ." He stares at the fake warrant. "I should call my manager."

"Okay," I say. "But he'll tell you that you have no choice but to cooperate. Look, I'm not here to ruin your day. I just need to access your video. I can do it from the cloud if you don't want to give me computer access, but that means a bigger hassle. We'll probably have to seize your computers and probably close you down for a while. What's your name, by the way?"

"Dale."

"Okay, Dale, call your boss. I don't want you to get into any trouble."

He has no idea what to do, but he picks up the phone and dials. There's a hurried conversation. I'm *so* lucky the manager is out. He hangs up and says, "Okay, he says I can let you look. Uh, I need to keep a copy of that thing. The warrant."

"Sure." I take the entirely fraudulent warrant and go to the copier. I turn the paper to the blank side and make a copy. I wipe the panel with my sleeve, covering that with my body, and then fold up the blank paper that comes out, making sure to slide my fingers so that the prints won't be clear on the surface. If they go to the extent of DNA, I'm screwed, but that's not likely unless this goes completely, horribly sideways.

I staple it shut, and write *Detective Karen Fields* on the outside, with a phone number I make up on the spot. I slide my palm down the pen as I put it back in the holder to smear any prints I've just left.

Dale seems entirely satisfied. I put the original fake warrant and the badge I got at a costume shop in my pocket. "After you?"

He leads me down a short hallway to a claustrophobically small closet with a folding table, a folding chair, and a computer. He logs me in, and I'm looking at just one feed from the store that covers the door and the counter. "There you go," he says. "What day?" I tell him, and he scrolls back to it.

"The guy I'm looking for came in early on Monday. Probably right when you opened up. He'd have paid for a courier service. You do that, right?"

"Yeah, not real common," he says. "But we guarantee two-hour service in the metro area. Definitely narrows it down." He scrolls to the opening time. While he's still cooperative, I ask him to write down the cloud storage information so I can easily access it. He does.

I scroll as fast as I dare as he dithers behind me; he hears something in the other room and leaves, and I realize I've probably gone too far forward into the morning. I need to back up again and scrutinize every single person. There are a surprising number, but I didn't recognize Sheryl Lansdowne in any of the faces. So I try again, focusing hard.

I nearly miss him anyway, because he's just so . . . bland. A man with a manila envelope walks in. I can tell he's white, medium build, nothing special about him in particular; he's wearing blue jeans and a checked shirt and a ball cap. I'd pass him on the street and never even notice.

Like Melvin, I think, and shiver.

He talks to the guy behind the counter, gets a courier envelope, and opens it up. I freeze it, and the image isn't fantastic, but I see a white blur. He's dropping a letter into the package.

Melvin's letter.

I take the thumb drive out of my pocket and copy the digital footage from the moment he comes into the shop to when he leaves. He hands over the credit card, and the clerk on duty doesn't seem to even hesitate, or look at the name, before running it.

Why do that? Why not just pay cash? He's exposing himself. He's not that stupid.

Unless he wanted me to find this. Wanted me to be here.

I felt clever until now. And suddenly I feel exposed, and manipulated, and very worried.

While my unwitting coconspirator is gone, I flip back to today's recording and make sure I erase my presence on entry, and at the counter. I'll be sure to keep my face turned away now that I know where the camera is. I wipe the keyboard and mouse clean of fingerprints.

I've just finished when Dale comes back. "All done," I say. "Thanks so much for your help." I feel a little bad for him, but his boss can't hold him accountable, not when Dale did his due diligence and called. Not his fault I'm leaving him holding a blank piece of paper and a fake phone number.

"Is he some kind of killer or something?" Dale asks. "If you can tell me, I mean."

"I can't, sorry," I say. We come out of the hallway, and just as we do, my luck runs out. The bell dings as someone opens the door and walks inside.

I only get a glimpse of him, but my gut kicks hard, and I know it's him. *It's him.*

I've just locked eyes with the man who sent Melvin's letter.

"Hey!" I shout.

He looks around, as if he's not sure if I'm talking to him. I launch myself at him, and he backpedals, shocked, and then quickly turns and runs.

I hit the door hard with my shoulder and stumble outside, off balance. He went to the left. I see him twenty paces ahead of me already, but I start closing the distance fast. My vision narrows, red at the edges. He speeds up after glancing back, but I'm still gaining on him.

I reach out to grab his shirt, and I'm close enough my fingers brush fabric, but I can't get a grip. He twists and pulls free, and momentum sends me stumbling desperately for balance. By the time I get myself right again, he's around the corner. But I'm not about to give up. No way in hell. I put my whole self into it, tap into every reserve, and I gain on him again. Fast.

I catch up to him halfway down the side street. It's not busy here, and I don't hesitate. I grab him and drag him into the closest shadowed alleyway, out of sight of anyone who was watching us.

Then I slam him to the ground so hard his ball cap flies off and rolls unsteadily away. He lets out a breathless, injured "Hey!" but stops talking as I twist his arm up behind his back with my knee pinning his opposite side. He's not going anywhere. "Ow!"

"You sent me a package on Monday," I say. "Remember?"

"I *what?*" He turns his head, and I realize there's something . . . wrong with it. For a second I think, *Oh my God, I've crushed his skull,* because it's oddly flat under the blur of close-cut dark hair. But the scar that twists through the skin is old. Several years old. "Please, lady! Please don't! Please don't hurt me!"

He sounds panicked. And a little odd, a little off, his tone strangely flat. I start rethinking what I'm doing. *Oh God. What if I've just made an awful mistake?* I ease up a little, but I keep holding him down.

"My name is Gina Royal," I say. "Did you send me a package on Monday? Yes or no."

"Uh—yes?"

"You're sure?"

"I guess so."

"Why?"

"Because—because a guy paid me," he says. "Cash, two hundred bucks, just to pick up an envelope and take it in and mail it. He even gave me a credit card to use. You want it? You can have it! Take my whole wallet!" He sounds scared. "I didn't—I didn't do anything wrong, did I? I didn't mean to! I was just doing what he said! It was a job, just a job! I don't work steady!"

Oh Jesus. What have I done? I'm still cynical enough to tug the wallet out of his back pocket and flip it open. His driver's license says his name is Leonard Bay, and he lives here in Knoxville: 250 Beacon Street. I take a photo with my phone, then check the credit cards. He has only two. One's a pay-as-you-go debit card, and the other is a credit card in the name of Penny Maguire. I slide it out, careful to hold just the sides, and slip that into my pocket. "Okay," I tell him. "Relax. Relax. I'm sorry. Are you hurt? Do you need an ambulance?" I wince at the thought, because what I've done is most certainly assault, and even if I dump the fake warrant and badge, the damage is done because the clerk will be able to identify me and swear he saw me chase this poor man out of the store.

"I think I'm okay," he says. He still sounds shaky. He's not fighting me at all. "Are you going to take my money?"

"No," I tell him, and put it back in his pocket. "I didn't take anything but that credit card, and only because it isn't yours. Okay?"

"Okay."

"What can you tell me about the man who paid you?"

"I met him on the street," he said. "I was—I'm going to be honest with you, ma'am, I was panhandling. I was low on my rent money. He said he'd pay me, and he did. I was worried about that credit card. I wasn't going to use it for fun."

I don't think that last part is true, but I let it go. And after another hesitation, I let *him* go. I loosen my grip on his arm and lever my weight off him. He doesn't move for a second or two, as if he's afraid something worse is coming, and then he turns on his side to look at me. There's a fresh scrape on his cheek, but other than that, he doesn't seem hurt. Not much emotion in his face. Maybe, with that kind of frightful head injury, he's lost a lot of ability to communicate expressions, even fear. I try to remember whether he looked scared before he started running. I don't know.

"Okay, Leonard."

"Len," he says. "I like Len better."

"Len," I say, and nod. "Do you remember anything about that man? How tall he was, maybe? You can sit up if you want to. Do you need help?"

I offer a hand, and after a wary hesitation, he takes it. He sits up and scoots back until he's sitting against the brick wall. It's cool in these shadows, but I can see him clearly. We're now blocked from street view by the dumpster, which eases my nerves. I crouch down to put us on a level. "What do you think?" I ask. "Was he tall or short?"

"On the tall side, I guess."

"How about his skin color?"

"White," he says immediately. "Kinda tanned, though."

We go through the rest of the questions, and Len seems utterly calm by the end of it. His answers come slowly sometimes, but I never get the sense he's lying. I'm sweating, aware that people could have called in the foot chase to the police, and I'm on the alert for any sound of sirens. So far, nothing. But I'm well aware of time pressure.

Unfortunately, for all my coaching, what I end up with is a completely unremarkable profile of a ghost. There's nothing I learn from Len except for the credit card I've confiscated. And for the risk I just took, I'm not sure that was at all smart of me.

I help Len up, dust him off, and impulsively dig cash out of my pocket. "Here," I tell him, and hand him two twenties. "If I hurt you at all, I'm very sorry; I never meant to do that. Are you sure you don't need a doctor? I'm happy to take you to an ER, or a clinic, and pay . . ."

"No ma'am, I'm all right. I get knocked down by people a lot," he says. The matter-of-fact tone makes me feel even sorrier for him. I pick up his ball cap, and he puts it on; it disguises the odd shape of his skull, the damage of his terrible injury. I do think about the man in the rented car, the white man in the ball cap . . . but this cap was battered and old even before our tussle. Well worn and dirty. I didn't get the same impression from the man in the car.

It strikes me that the man in the car is MalusNavis, and Len . . . Len is his bait. Chosen for the likeness, especially the ball cap I'm sure he always wears.

Len holds out his hand. "Thank you for helping me. That was real nice of you."

I didn't help him. I chased him and knocked him down, and *he's* thanking *me* for paying him guilt money. I'm honestly taken aback, and worried about his ability to cope in the world, especially with what must be a significant cognitive impairment. "Len, do you have a real place to stay? Like, a home?"

"I do," he says. "When I want. I like to be out, though. It's better. Most of the time it's nice." There's a certain flatness to his affect and, at the same time, a kind of weird innocence. I think he means it. And that's even more worrying.

"Please be careful. Len? If you see the man again, would you give me a call?" I hand him my card. It goes to a J. B. Hall number that forwards to my regular cell, anonymously.

"I will," he says, and puts the card in his pocket. "You take care, ma'am."

I can't believe that the man I chased down on foot is somehow wishing *me* well. Or that he's walking away with my cash in his pocket. This has all taken a very odd direction.

"Hey," I call after Len. He stops at the end of the alley and turns toward me. "Why were you going back into the mail shop today?"

"I had another thing to mail for that man," he says. "You want it? I should have said, I guess."

I come forward as he holds out a thin white envelope. It has my old name and address on it. But it isn't Melvin's handwriting this time. I don't recognize it at all.

"When did he give you this?" My tone's sharp now. And Len shuffles back a step, sensing trouble. I try to moderate my tone. "I need to know this, Len. Please."

"I saw him this morning," he says. "Real early. Like, before dawn. I was staying the night at that mission over there. I was too tired to walk home." He points vaguely off to the right, but I don't know this part of town. "I saw him outside. Like he was waiting for me. He gave me more money for doing it, do you want that?" He starts fumbling in his pocket. I hold up a hand to stop him.

"Keep it," I tell him. "Thank you."

He nods and moves off, shuffling at first, listing a little, then moving more smoothly. A glitchy machine remembering how to walk.

MalusNavis picked him because of the general resemblance. Because that would bring me here, eventually. He wanted to see if I was clever enough to find the card. And his damaged, innocent bait.

I open the envelope and pull out a letter. I instantly recognize the computer-printed prose.

> *I know you're hunting me. Good. You and I were always meant to meet.*
>
> *Everything that follows will be because of you. You have a chance to save the lives of the people you love, but that's going to be your choice, not mine.*
>
> *I'm your destiny, Gina Royal. I'm what you've earned.*

I swallow hard. This feels . . . different. Cold, methodical, *driven*. His earlier email felt more like casual cruelty, but this is a change. A direct challenge. I can feel it all around me, like a fog.

I look the direction that Len has gone, but he's out of sight. I don't think there's much else he can offer up, but I'm hopeful that he'll call me if he's approached again. I hope he stays safe; I have the ominous feeling that MalusNavis is very good at covering his tracks.

I head the direction of the shelter he indicated he stayed in last night. It's four blocks down, in one of the very worst areas of Knoxville, and I stand out in my unofficial cop clothes like a neon sign. The area's full of homeless people, grubby tents crowded together in clusters under bridges and in alleys. People give me a wide berth, avoiding looking at me at all. I look like the law to them. It's more protection than I'd have if I'd come here just in my regular jeans-and-work-shirt look, but it doesn't guarantee that someone won't get aggressive. A significant portion of people out here are high, looking to get high, desperate to get high, or mentally ill. And cop or not, I look like I might have something better than what they have.

I'm glad it's daylight. But I'm also aware that the storefronts around here are mostly empty except for the convenience store on the corner. And one look at their antiquated camera system tells me it's not worth the try. I doubt it even works.

I check at the shelter and ask about Leonard Bay. The tired young woman on duty checks the register and shakes her head. "Not on here," she says. "But they don't usually put their real names, either, and we don't ask for ID; most of them don't have any, or if they do, it isn't their own. Can you describe him?"

I do, including the damage to his head. That's memorable.

She blinks and says, "Oh, *him*. He did come here last night. Stayed the night. Left early."

"What did he say his name was?"

She looks at the register, then turns it toward me and points. "That's him."

It's an illegible mess. I can't make out a thing. He's far from the only messy writer on the page, but this seems worse than normal, more . . . chaotic.

"He has some kind of brain damage, he took his hat off and showed me," she says. "Real sad. I don't think he's regularly homeless, though. He dresses too neat, and he's too clean."

I ask for surveillance, but she wasn't born yesterday; she wants a warrant. The fake one's in my pocket, but I know better than to serve it on her, or show her the badge. She's seen far too much of the world.

"Thank you," I tell her. I don't really need anything else. I have Len's home address.

I need to get back to Sam and the kids, because I feel it in the air: this is going to get bad.

14

KEZIA

Wednesday starts with problems. Car problems, which are no damn joke out here in Norton; our cabin is a long way from town, and getting a tow truck out could take hours. No Uber or Lyft out here either.

Luckily, I grew up poor with a dad who knew how to fix things. I find a loose wire and fix it with electrical tape and a prayer. Seems to work.

I'm half an hour late to the station, and I find Prester there looking considerably better. We nod to each other, and I get coffee, and when I come back Prester says, "You might want to check your messages. Phone's been ringing off the hook for you."

I meet his gaze for a second, then nod. I have a wild impulse to tell him about the baby, but I control that fast. Like telling my father, I want to wait. There's some strange dread in the back of my mind; I want Javier with me to make this real. Until that happens, I want it to be my secret. Well, mine and Gwen's. It just feels . . . right.

I hit the voice mails on the office phone. I have six messages. One's from a TBI detective complaining to me that one of my friends (that would be Gwen) has been up in Valerie interfering. I ignore it. The next is from his commander. I pay slightly more attention, and make myself a note to kiss and make up. Don't need that TBI commander crawling up the chain of command. I'm doing a good job, but success is a fragile thing.

The other four are from different cities I called yesterday about potential matches to Sheryl Lansdowne's identity. The fact that all four gave me a call back is shocking, but what's even more concerning is that every one of them leaves me a name and direct number and says they want to talk. Not just "send info," but *talk*. Three out of four of these are small towns, granted, but still . . . that's one hell of a batting average for cases that should have been long gathering dust.

I start from the top: with the detective from Wichita. She tells me that their missing person fits Sheryl's description, and I confirm it from prints they've sent in. Then the detective starts telling me what isn't in the missing person's notice. "Took about two weeks for us to locate a relative of the old lady who passed on," she says. "He came into town about a week after that to settle her affairs, and found out that she'd been writing a hell of a lot of checks out of her savings account—about ten thousand dollars' worth—to our gal Mary Hogue here. Who by that time had been reported as missing by a friend from down the block. The old lady kept a good supply of cash at home, and all that was gone, as well as a few pieces of nice jewelry."

"And Mary?"

"Gone like a summer breeze. She left all her stuff behind, but it wasn't much at all . . . a bank account with just enough to keep it going for another month, rental furniture, an old car that turned out to not be worth what it cost to tow it off. First glance, she *looked* normal as anything. But when you dig into it, she really had no roots."

"Just had to look presentable long enough to find somebody to con," I say. "Jesus. So, the old lady—"

"Yeah, getting to that. The son demanded an autopsy and got one. The old lady was poisoned. Antifreeze. A real bad way to go too."

I've never worked such a case, but I've heard how painful that is, and how deadly. It can take days, weeks, months. Poisoners are some of the coldest murderers there are. "Any idea how she ingested it?"

"Drinks are the easiest method. Iced tea. Pop. Anything like that. It tastes sweet."

"Let me guess, Mary was a real good neighbor who had that nice old lady over for a glass of iced tea before she turned up sick?"

"We think so."

"But you didn't charge her with murder?"

"Couldn't," the detective says briskly. "There was never solid evidence Mary Hogue poisoned the old lady, only that the old lady was poisoned; hell, the coroner wasn't even sure it wasn't accidental or suicide. If we'd been able to get Mary in and really press her, we might've been able to build a case. But we had nothing—no evidence, no leads on where she'd gone off to. Everything went cold. But trust me, we remember."

The Wichita call is a template, as it turns out. Sheryl's name changes, but the circumstances are always similar. She moves to town, builds up a good reputation, lives a normal but poverty-level life . . . and finds some kind soul to pull her out of her desperate circumstances. Who's left dead broke, or dies of apparently natural or accidental causes, or just plain vanishes. But there's never enough to put out a murder warrant on her. Never.

In every case, the prints match to Penny Carlson / Sheryl Lansdowne.

I put the phone down, finally, and turn to Prester. He's waiting expectantly, fingers poised over his keyboard. "Sheryl Lansdowne might be one of the coldest damn serial killers nobody's ever heard of," I say. "I figure we can pin at least six prior victims to her easily, and there are likely more. That's not even counting the number of people she's stolen from and conned but didn't kill. She always uses hands-off methods, seems like: poisons, falls down stairs, drownings."

We both think about that for a while. What it takes to embark on a career of ice-hearted murder like that and slip away without a trace every single time. She's never been arrested for anything serious enough to get her into a national database, and by moving state to state, she's been keeping herself off the radar.

We may never know exactly how many people she's killed. Only that it's probably more than we have found.

"Best write it all up and send it to TBI," he says. "They're going to want to take it federal, most likely, since it's a multistate investigation now. This goes far beyond our little town, Kez. Let it go. If she's out there somewhere, she's going to be found."

While I'm finishing the write-up, an email comes in from the TBI. The bones we found on the grid search belong to Tommy Jarrett. He's been lying up there in those hills since the day he disappeared. He didn't leave Sheryl and those soon-to-be-born kids. And I sincerely doubt it was any kind of an accident.

Sheryl. It keeps coming back to Sheryl.

I don't want to just trust someone else to do these dead children justice, but Prester's right: I don't really have any choice.

It's over.

It doesn't feel over.

Gwen calls just as noon approaches, and she's got a lot to give me, because she's got the 411 on Douglas Adam Prinker. I'd honestly just about forgotten about him in the rush of revelations about Sheryl, though she'd mentioned the name and I'd intended to get into it. But Gwen's beaten me to it.

Turns out Mr. Prinker—who's alleged to have been doing slow rolls past Sheryl's house, according to the neighbor Gwen interviewed—has a shady record, including multiple domestic violence complaints.

Currently newly married with one child, and I feel for that woman; Douglas isn't likely to change his ways.

There's a white van registered in his name, but it's so old it's got to be on its last thousand miles. His credit report is littered with unpaid bills, and his trailer is threatened with foreclosure. Breaking four hundred on a credit score would be a really good day for him. To him, Sheryl must have seemed like she had it all.

Could be it's just that simple. Maybe Prinker saw an opportunity to grab a woman with money, meant it for a robbery, and something went hard sideways. Given Sheryl's history, that would be ironic. But if so, why take her? No action on her bank account, nothing on the two credit cards active under Sheryl's name.

Gwen's included Prinker's employment history. He's working part time at the Norton landfill, and when I call, he's at work.

"Landfill?" Prester leans back in his chair. "I assume you got this."

I'm putting on my jacket and wishing I'd worn older clothes. "Yeah, I got this," I say. "Unless you're so bored you can't miss this chance to smell the sights."

"Kezia Claremont, I searched that damn landfill *twice* looking for two different murder weapons in my career, and I have done my stinky-garbage time. You enjoy yourself." He goes back to typing, but then glances up as I pass. "And watch your back."

That's our version of a warm hug.

I turn back when I hear him make a sound. It's an odd one, a groan, and when I walk back, I see that he's sitting hunched over. His face looks ashy, and he's pressing a hand to his stomach. He grimaces when he sees me back. "I'm all right," he says. "Ulcer's acting up, that's all. I'll be fine. I made an appointment with the damn doctor, I see him next Monday. Stop hovering."

He means it. I don't like it, but at least he's actually sensible enough to seek some medical care, thank God.

I look around, and see Sergeant Porter watching us both. I point to Prester, then to my eyes, and he nods.

Porter will watch over him while I'm gone.

◆ ◆ ◆

I head for the landfill, which is situated far enough out of town that the smell hardly ever drifts to downtown. But it's easy to know you're getting there. Between that and the sewage plant situated close by, it's a full, stinky experience.

Seagulls circle the dump like vultures, swept-back wings riding the currents. I don't like the damn things, and I just know I'm going to get crapped on out there by one of them. But as Prester said: you got to put in your garbage time, and this is part of mine.

The stench is like to knock me over when I get out of the car, but I power through the invisible fog over to the small, yellow-painted office. Incredibly, they keep the windows open. Maybe it's to keep their tolerance level up.

I lean in the window to the big man crowded at the desk and show my badge. "Hey," I say. "Afternoon. Kezia Claremont, NPD. Here to talk to Douglas Prinker."

"You mean Junior? He's up on the ridge driving the compactor. Big thing with the roller. Can't miss it. Just finished lunch, so he should be back up there by now."

"Can I drive up there?"

"Only if you got a tractor. No cars allowed."

He points out on the map where I'll find Junior, and I go outside. There's a wide path winding up the hill, pale dirt that's kept hard-packed by tractors running daily. Not a hard climb, except for the stench. Seagulls shriek and dive into the jumble of white, blue, green, and red bags that litter the slope, ready to be pushed down flat. One man's trash is a flying rat's treasure.

Douglas Prinker is dwarfed by the giant machine he's driving. I watch him a minute, then get close enough that he can hear my shouts. The roaring engine dies with a rattle, and the cries of birds take over the empty space. He climbs down onto the step of the compactor . . . but not all the way down. I hold out my badge and point at the ground. He jumps and lands two feet away from me.

He's bigger than he looked up on that machine. Broader. Wiry strong. He's sweating, and he takes off his battered, dirty helmet and tucks it under his arm. Beneath it, his blond hair is dark and matted. "What you want?" he asks. "Ma'am."

"Detective Claremont," I say. "Y'all know me, Douglas. Don't you?" Most folks who live and work around Norton do. And he nods. From the wary look in his eyes, he thinks he's about to be collared. "I need to ask you some questions. You want to do it here, or come down to the station with me? Either is fine with me."

Nobody chooses the station.

He says, "Go on then. I'm on the clock. They're gonna dock my time."

I think about clever approaches, but doesn't seem like it'd be worth it. "You acquainted with Sheryl Lansdowne at all?"

"Sheryl who?" I see a vein start to throb in his temple. I wish there were about two more feet between us, but I'm not about to step back either.

"Lansdowne. Married Tommy Jarrett a while back?"

"Don't know her."

"Then why do we have video of your van cruising by her house on several occasions at night, Douglas?" We don't, of course. But he doesn't know that. I see him shift uncomfortably. "You sweet on her, maybe?"

"She was pretty, that's all," he says. "I didn't do nothin' to her. You can look at that video. I never even stopped at her house for long. And I damn sure never went inside."

Just sat outside in his van long enough to get off, I suspect. That doesn't surprise me. It does disgust me a little. "You happen to be there on Sunday night, early Monday morning?"

He puts some thought into it, then shakes his head. "I was at the Low Dog until about closin' time. Then I got myself pulled over on the way home and was in the Valerie jail until mornin'. You can check that."

"I will," I say. It sounds depressingly likely and true. And he wouldn't give an arrest as an alibi unless he was confident it would hold up.

"I heard what happened to her girls . . . ," Prinker says. I look up. "I got a little girl. That's just plain evil. I'd never do a thing like that. Never."

He's got a record of battering one ex-wife and one ex-girlfriend, but somehow, I believe him on that one. Even bad men have limits, and that's his.

He puts his hat on. "Hope you find Sheryl," he says. "And I sure hope you catch that asshole what did this."

I nod and thank him, and he climbs back up in his machine and fires it up. The rumble shakes the ground I'm standing on, and I back away and head down the hill.

I'm convinced already that Douglas Adam Prinker is a waste of time, but I'll close the loop and check the box. And that doesn't leave a whole lot of room to keep moving forward. Maybe Prester's right. Maybe I should let the TBI take this one.

But maybe there's one more distant possibility to run down.

Instead of heading back to the office, I stop off at home and shower to get the reek of the dump off me; I can't stand it, and can't imagine anyone else could either. I find there's a big fat seagull dropping on my jacket, and scrub it off and curse the damn sky rats. Fresh jeans, shirt, suit coat, shoes. I feel much, much better.

I turn to Boot, who's been watching me run around with great interest and a good deal of satisfaction at having me home. I rub his head, and he looks up at me with big, brown eyes and pants softly. He can smell something coming. He gets to his feet and trots to the door, looking at me expectantly.

"Absolutely right. Road trip, boy," I tell him. I get the leash but don't put it on him; he doesn't need it on the property. I open the door and say, "Car."

He bounds out and straight for it, and pauses by the back door of my plain black sedan like the good boy he is. One foot in the air, polite as you please. "Go pee," I tell him, and point at his favorite tree. He looks at me, then the tree, and then his ears go down and he snuffles his way there, circles it three times, and does his business. By that time I've got the back door open, and he launches himself into the car at a dead run. The car bounces on its springs as he lands.

Boot is about seventy pounds of solid muscle, and as far as backup goes, he's better than most of the local officers I know around here. Listens better too. I have a twinge of worry as I start up the car, and I pay attention to that. I call my pop. He's gruff and fine. Talking to him, even in a mood, makes me feel better.

Boot puts his head through the gap between the headrests and rests his chin there.

"Such a good boy," I tell him, and he grunts deep in his throat. I laugh. "Should have named you Prester, you sound like him."

Another doggie grunt, and I hear the slap of his tail against the upholstery.

"Okay, partner. Let's do this."

I put the car in drive.

My plan is pretty simple: follow the track laid down by the 911 caller's burner phone as traced out by Gwen. I know this is probably a huge waste of time, but since Sheryl Lansdowne's case is being tossed up the food chain well above my reach, this is the last lead I can follow. I call Prester to let him know where I'm going; he tells me it's probably a boondoggle. I don't care. I keep driving, since there's nothing more urgent demanding attention from me.

I hit the spot of the hidden pond. Yellow crime scene tape flutters and flaps in the wind, but the place is deserted now. TBI's long gone, and FBI hasn't yet arrived. I expect I'll be requested to face-to-face once the feds hit town, so I figure I should make use of what time I've got. I check the map Gwen emailed and start driving the route.

Boot changes to staring out the window; I roll it down so he can stick his head out, but not enough that he can jump if he gets excited. He seems content. We pass the broken-down wreck of the two abandoned houses. Then the crime scene of the McMansion; this one's still active. I don't stop. A couple of deputies eyeball me as I drive past, and I don't acknowledge them. They don't know me, and the closed expressions tell me they're not giving me any benefit of the doubt.

The hill slopes down. The road curls through dark trees and not a lot else, and then we emerge into full spring sun. The meandering rough track meets a positively spacious blacktop farm-to-market road. I turn south. It leads me past fields and distant farmhouses, and then a couple of businesses. I slow down and check the map, and yep, I'm nearly to the end of Gwen's track. Right on target.

I stop at the first business—a gas station—and buy a soda. Once the elderly black proprietor makes it to the register, we do some friendly chatting about nothing in particular. When I show him my badge and ask kindly to take a look at his camera recordings, he looks crestfallen. "Ma'am, I'd be glad to help you out if those cameras were real. They ain't. Just there for show. I can't afford the real stuff."

"What if you get robbed?"

He shrugs. "Get kids in here all the damn time," he says. "Mostly polite since I know all their mommas. No black boys robbing me out here. Only white tweakers, time to time."

"Okay. Here's my card, you call me if you get in trouble," I tell him, and slide it over. He nods and pockets it. "You recall anybody coming by here early morning on Monday, maybe? What time you open up?"

"Five," he says. "But Mondays I stock shelves 'round three thirty or four. And I live right upstairs." I'd suspected that, since it was a two-story building. "Cars don't usually come by here that early, but I saw one that day."

"What kind?"

"Some kind of big black SUV. Sorry, I don't know nothing else. Didn't see the driver, and it didn't stop in, since I didn't have the lights on. Just kept on going."

"Heading where?"

He points wordlessly in the same direction as the rest of the map track. I nod and thank him and add a couple of bottles of water, snacks, dog treats, and a shallow plastic bowl from the shelves. I don't intend to be gone so long, but this place looks like it could use the money. I pay and go, putting all that in the trunk except the soda for me, water for Boot, and the doggie bowl. I fill it halfway with water for him on the ground and let him out; he makes straight for it and sloppily drinks, then noses around excitedly and leaves a few territorial squirts. When I whistle him back, he comes at a run. I toss the rest of the water, and we're back on the road.

Two miles down I approach the distant, sedate traffic of the freeway. There's nothing between the small convenience store and here except a broken-down old car repair shop that's been boarded up for a while, and a shiny new truck stop right close to the intersection. When I check the map, the truck stop is where the GPS track ends.

This is where my man stopped and got rid of his phone, or at least took out the SIM card. I feel my pulse quicken. If he stopped, could be that he needed gas; no reason he would have chosen a busy location like this otherwise if he was up to no good. And I know from experience that this is a gas desert for about a hundred miles in either direction, so he'd have to get it here.

I fill up myself and head inside. The place is in a lull just now, but there are probably half a dozen truckers and a few civilians shopping the snacks and drinks. More lined up at the Arby's counter in the back. I go straight to the register, pay for the gas, and ask for the manager.

He's a slender Asian man in his midthirties, and he seems pretty cooperative when I show him my badge and tell him I'm just looking for a quick peek at his surveillance. He clearly knows the value of keeping in the good books. So he leads me to the back.

They have a pretty elaborate setup—no fewer than seven cameras outside covering the pumps and the building's exterior, plus more for the inside of the shop. I doubt my guy would have come inside. Not worth the risk. So I focus on the gas pumps around the time the phone signal was lost.

And I get him. *I get him.* I feel my heartbeat jump into a race, and I lean forward, intent on the black SUV that's gliding into a spot on the very far pump at the end of the lot. He stayed as distant as possible from the cameras. I'm not sure if the resolution is good enough to get us a plate; it looks to me like he's deliberately dirtied up the front and, likely, the rear to obscure details like that. But there he is: your average white male, features not distinct, wearing a baseball cap with no logo I can see, jeans, a checked shirt.

Then I lean forward, because a movement in the vehicle has caught my eye.

There's someone in the passenger seat. I can't see clearly . . . and then the passenger door opens, and someone gets out.

Goddamn. It's Sheryl Lansdowne. And she's not in distress. She's not tied up in the back of that SUV—she's on her own two feet, calm as you please. I see her toss something in the garbage can that sits on the island beside the gas pump, and I hit pause. I don't know if the FBI can work with this, but it's possible. Very possible.

I turn to the manager and say, "How often do you empty those garbage cans out on the pumps?"

"Every couple of days."

"Any chance you haven't gotten to that one yet?" I point.

He leans over to look and shrugs. "Maybe? Depends how full it is."

"Then go pull that bag right now, tie it up, and set it aside. Do not let *anyone* touch it. I'll have someone from either the TBI or FBI come get it. They'll want to go through everything. Keep this footage. Mark it and show it to whoever comes." I turn back to the screen and scrub through. Sheryl finishes her little walk-around and gets back in the car. The man uses a credit card at the pump, so I tell the manager to pull those records and get them ready as well.

I watch the screen. The SUV pulls away, makes a broad circle, and exits the lot. It's a stretch, but I think I can see it turn the corner on the farm-to-market road and head toward the freeway.

I roll it back to when the SUV comes into view. "Tell them to watch from there," I say. "Thank you. You're doing a real good thing, sir. Guard this with your life. It's important."

He nods. He seems unsure and pale, but steady enough.

I call the TBI on my way out of the truck stop and tell them what I've found. The agent who takes my call sounds impatient at first, then intrigued, then downright eager.

I make sure the manager collects the trash, and then I head over to the car. Boot's fallen asleep in the back, but he wakes as soon as I open the door. "Hey, boy," I tell him, and he licks my face. "Stop that. We're fine. It's fine."

I'm putting the car in drive when I see it.

A pristine black SUV. Dirty plates. It's idling at the edge of the parking lot.

"That's impossible," I say. "Can't be." I seriously have to think about my sanity for a second, because I have to be seeing things. Or it has to be a completely different vehicle. SUVs out here are a dime a hundred, never mind a dozen. Odds ninety to one that it's some suburban family headed out on vacation, and not . . . not what I think.

I roll the sedan slowly toward the SUV.

It backs up and speeds away.

"God*damn.*"

I hit the gas, fumbling for my phone as I take the curve and accelerate. He's already hitting the on-ramp to the freeway. Hell of an engine in that thing, and my detective's sedan isn't built for high-speed pursuit. I voice-dial TBI again. I tell the agent I'm in pursuit of a black SUV suspected in the Lansdowne case. I try to catch up to get part of the plate, but he slips away before I can make it out; he's put some kind of blurring filter over it. Illegal, but few probably even notice under the mud.

There's enough traffic on the road that I have to concentrate hard on the driving; I flip on the bumper flashers and hit the siren for good measure, and most people give way. A semitruck blocks my view of the SUV for a few critical seconds, and when I blast past it, I see the vehicle just ahead, already on an off-ramp. No way I can slow and make that turn. I yell the exit number into the phone and put my foot to the floor, heading for the next exit a mile away. I make a U-turn, and head back as fast as my car will go.

He's picked the wrong damn off-ramp, I think. A fierce hunter's instinct hammers my heart faster. I know this area; nothing out here but roads and fields and trees, and no real turnoffs to speak of for miles. The road goes two ways from the freeway—north and south. I turn north because I see fresh black tire marks that direction; he left rubber. The road takes me into trees fast, and I tell the TBI agent what road I'm on when the sign flashes past, a barely readable blur. I can't see the SUV. The road's empty, but it turns sharply just up ahead. I can't let him slip me.

I'm in the middle of the sharp curve when shit goes wrong. I don't see the spike strip, but I feel it when I hit it, when the car lurches and the wheel whips hard in my hands, hard enough to burn, and the world spins, glass cracking, metal crunching. Boot yelping.

I manage to keep us from turning over, but the sedan spins off the road and hits a tree in the left quarter panel with the force of a pile driver. Airbags flash, and I snort blood and taste acrid powder.

I'm trying to blink back stars and get it together. Boot is barking, a raw and constant sound of alarm, and I hear his claws tearing at upholstery as he tries to reach me. I drag in a shockingly painful breath—something stabbing deep, probably a rib—and I manage to say, "Hey, boy, hey, it's okay, I'm okay." In the next second, I panic. *My baby.* No no no, not like this, no . . . I'm shaking. Gasping. Horrified and scared to death, not for me but for the child I've barely begun to meet. Oh God, God no.

Boot tries to stick his head between the seats—the gap is narrow, the frame's bent—and frantically licks the only part of me he can reach. My hand. I look down and see the blood drops on it shimmering like rubies. Can feel the bloody nose now, aching like a day-long sunburn. I caught a good one from the airbags, but they kept me—*us*—from getting slammed around too badly. Maybe I'm okay. Maybe the baby's fine.

I don't think I'm okay. I need help.

The windshield is an opaque mess of cracks. Can't see a thing. Somehow, the car landed on its tires, but it's tilting badly to the right.

I fumble around for my phone, then remember I slotted it into the cradle on the dash. The whole cradle's gone. I try to bend across to grab it when I spot it wedged half-under the passenger seat, and have to pause and gasp against the pain, and once again, terror jolts through me. *Stay with me, baby. Stay with me.* My fingers graze plastic, and I manage to hook the cradle and get it onto the seat. My phone's screen is cracked, but it lights up when I tap it. *Thank you, Lord.* I dial 911.

My head is hurting, and when I reach up to touch the left side, I find blood. That explains some of the mist that keeps fogging up my brain. I grab the phone and push my door open—it's cranky, but not jammed—and fresh, cool air floods over me and helps me focus. I experiment with standing up, one hand gripping the frame of the door. It hurts, but I manage. I look through the back window. Boot seems all right—he's barking and whining and scratching at the door. "Just a minute," I whisper to him. "Hang on." I don't know if I'm really talking to him, or myself, or the baby. Maybe all of us.

That's when I see the black SUV.

It's idling near the next curve, maybe a quarter mile out. Just sitting there. I try to get a picture of it, but it's already in motion when I snap the shutter; I don't know if I got anything useful. *Dammit.* I'm suddenly shaking with fury, and for a half a second I even think about chasing it down on goddamn foot, but then sense comes back. Fear. The baby, helpless and dependent on me not being stupid. I just cling to the door and try to stay upright. I'm tired. So tired.

I've forgotten that I dialed the phone, so it's a little surprise to hear a scratchy voice coming from somewhere near my right hand. I lift it, stare at the active call in confusion, then lift the phone to my ear. "Hello?"

"This is the 911 operator. What is your emergency?" She sounds cool and calm as the fresh air. I scramble to get my thoughts together.

"This is Detective Kezia Claremont," I say. At least I remember my damn name. "I've been in a serious accident." I sound pretty good, I think. Until suddenly my knees give way without any warning, and thank God I have hold of that door, because it slows my fall into more of a kneel. It hurts. Everything hurts. "I need help. I'm pregnant. Please send somebody. Leaving phone on." That's all I can manage to say. I put my arms on the driver's seat, rest my head on them, and slide away into the dark with only Boot's frantic whines for company, and the voice of the 911 operator as distant as the stars as they whirl me away.

15

GWEN

I'm boiling with frustration on the ride home, and the letter from MalusNavis burns in my pocket like an ember. I call Kez but get her voice mail, and I leave her a message to call me. I find myself reading the letter again. *You have a chance to save the lives of the people you love, but that's going to be your choice, not mine.*

I don't know what he means, but I know he's talking about Sam. Lanny. Connor. Even Vee. I call home. I can't do anything else. And I'm relieved when the phone is answered on the first ring.

"Hey, Ms. P.," Vee says. "Good news. Ain't had to shoot nobody yet." She sounds ghoulishly cheerful.

"This isn't a game, Vee," I snap. "You understand?"

"Yes ma'am." Her tone goes instantly cooler. "Ain't like I'm stupid. I get it. I just thought you'd like to know everything was all right. We just ate some lunch. Sam sure does make a mean chili. Saved some for you, I think."

I let out a slow breath and try again. "I didn't think you'd stick around, Vee."

"It's my day off. I get to do what I want."

"Can I please talk to Sam?"

She yells his name so loud that I have to pull the phone away. I'm sure the ride-share driver can hear it, but luckily, he's not the chatty type. While I'm waiting for Sam to get to the phone, I run down the mistakes I've made. I'll be on the exit video for the store, but I was moving fast, and I wasn't facing the camera; if I'm lucky, I can get to the cloud data storage for the mail center and delete that footage. Can't do anything at all about other surveillance cameras on the street, though, and I surely attracted notice chasing after Len. I walked a long way before I called a ride-share, so hopefully that puts me well out of any search circle . . . but all in all, I know I got lucky. Len doesn't seem like he's going to call in a complaint, and the mail clerk will want to keep things low key. The manager might kick up a fuss, once he realizes he's got a blank piece of paper and a fake phone number. Hard to know.

Right now, my best defense, if the police come asking questions, is to just face it down and lie. They won't like it, but with the fake badge gone, and the warrant deleted from my computer and search history, they won't waste their time trying to prove it.

Unless something else comes up that's a bigger problem. Like Len turning up dead.

"Hey," Sam says, and I relax a little. Didn't even realize I was tense. "Are you okay?"

"Fine," I say. I don't want to tell him about the risks I took. "I have some video of the guy who mailed the package, but . . . turns out he was paid to do it, and I don't really have much of a lead on the one who hired him. Got a credit card that Kez may be interested in, though."

"As long as you're all right. We're fine here. Lanny's agitating to get out of the house, but I'm making her finish her English class reading first."

"English isn't the problem. Make sure she's done the math. She always leaves it for last."

"Yeah, I've got my hands full making sure that she and Vee don't decide to sneak off somewhere, but thanks for the advice." He sounds mostly amused, thankfully. "Connor's fine. He's already finished with classwork, so he's taking a nap."

It all sounds so lovely and normal, and I hate to break that illusion, but I need him on guard. "Sam? The guy I talked to had another letter to deliver. I have it."

His tone shifts, goes lower and darker. "And it's not good. Right?"

"It's not. We need to find this troll. I don't know how he got his hands on Melvin's letter, but . . . maybe that's a way to track him, somehow. Melvin didn't give it to him. He took it from someone."

"How can you be sure he wasn't one of Melvin's little helpers?" Melvin had assembled a sickening little cadre of fans, no doubt. Some of them had been willing to smuggle out letters for him, aimed like poisoned arrows at me.

"I just know," I tell him. "Everything he says points to seeing himself as some sort of . . . white knight. He may be on the dark side, but he sure thinks he's the hero. Hey. He talked to a fair number of people on the Lost Angels forums. Any chance he might have also been talking to people on the boards where Melvin's fans like to lurk?"

"Maybe. Want me to check?"

"No," I tell him. "I will." I don't want Sam to have to dig through that filth. People who worship Melvin Royal are in many ways worse than the ones who hate him. The things they say about the victims . . . no, I don't want him to have to experience that. If our troll—MalusNavis, whatever he's calling himself—is there, I'll spot him even under another name. The one thing he can't seem to change is how he writes.

Or maybe that's another puzzle designed for me to put together. He seems to *like* to have me following his clues. I wish I could see another way past this, but . . . I can't.

I sit tense and silent the rest of the ride until I'm dropped at my house.

Sam's putting his keys in the tray on the table, and I can't help but notice that he's wearing his gun on his belt. He looks down at it, noticing my glance, and unclips it. "Yeah," he says. "I guess I'm a little jumpy. I'll put it away."

"Where did you go?"

"I took Vee home. She said she wanted to change clothes. I'll pick her up later."

"She get inside okay?"

"Yes. And her new alarm system was installed yesterday; I made sure she set it after she went in. But it's anybody's guess how diligent she's going to be with it. You know Vee."

"You see anything odd?" I'm transferring the contents of my pockets to the table, and taking off my shoulder holster to put that away too. "Anyone watching her?"

"Nothing," he says. "But God knows it's easy enough to set up a surveillance camera these days. Our guy doesn't even need to be close to be watching her. Or us, for that matter."

That is a particularly specific paranoia that I hadn't tripped over until now, and I have to resist the urge to storm out the front door and check the trees for cameras. And our neighbor's trees and eaves too. Which will just make me look strange, so I rein myself in. If he's watching, there's not much I can do about that.

I wasn't going to tell Sam everything, but now I realize that I need to. He needs to understand where things stand and what might happen, and so I tell him about chasing down Len at the mailing store, about tackling him, about being seen and noticed coming and going. And he takes it about as well as I could have expected.

"Gwen, dammit—" He stops, takes a breath, and shakes his head. "I know you didn't deliberately put yourself in danger, but *damn*. If he'd had a gun—"

"I had a gun," I point out. "And he didn't draw one. Which is good, because I don't know how I'd have played off a broad-daylight gunfight." I sound confident, but I'm not. "Sam. I'm okay. Really. But we do need to be aware that this could trace back to me, if the KPD really, really wants to take an interest. And then it could get rough."

He nods, but his eyes stay dark. "Okay. Would you consider handing all this over to J. B., or Kezia, or, well, anyone? Just get out of the middle of it, please. I don't like where this is going." He doesn't ask me for things like that often; he knows me all too well. But he's right. This isn't just a simple harassment campaign.

"I'll give everything I have to J. B. as soon as I look into the Melvin message boards and groupies," I tell him. My boss is damn good at what she does, and she hires people who are even better at specific things. One of them will be able to make this work where I might not.

He doesn't really believe me—as well he shouldn't, as obsessive as I usually am when it comes to anything Melvin Royal–related—but he lets it go. I take a few seconds to use the login info I swiped from the mailing store and find the footage of myself; I wince when I realize it probably would be a pretty clear tipoff that something was up, and erase it. I put the thumb drive containing the probably useless surveillance footage on my desk, kiss him, and go and hug my kids. They're fine, of course. Connor, ever observant, says, "You've got dirt on your pants. What happened?"

"Nothing," I tell him. "I brushed up against a dirty bumper." I don't like lying to him, but I don't want to spark any worry either. Bad enough for me and Sam to be on edge. I don't need the kids to be there with us. "Hey. So. Counseling. You ready?"

He nods and closes his laptop. I give him a pat on the knee and get up to get Lanny in motion, but she's already putting on her shoes. I don't know where my daughter gets her excellent taste in footwear, because I'm very utilitarian, and I'm always startled how well she coordinates. "Half an hour until our appointment," she says. "We should probably get going, right?"

"Five more minutes." I want to chase down the lead to Melvin's groupie hangouts, but I'm well aware that might take a while. I can't slack on talk therapy right now, in the midst of what's going on. We need it. So I just go change to a more comfortable outfit, brush my hair after releasing it from the ponytail, and we're on the road headed to Dr. Marks's office right on time. I feel a little better, having all of us together and apparently harmonious. We need this pressure release today, and then we can see where to go from there.

My cell phone rings when we're two miles from our destination; I ignore it and let it go to voice mail.

Then Sam's phone rings just half a minute later. I look over at him, and he looks at me, and we both know that's not a good sign. He looks at the number and says, "Norton Police Department," before he slides to answer the call and put it on speaker. "Hey, Kez," he says. "Is everything . . ."

"This isn't Kez," Prester's rough voice says. It sounds emotional. Prester is rarely emotional, and I feel a cold void form in my stomach. "It's about her."

"What's happened?" I blurt it out before Sam does. Dread bolts through me, and I taste blood and ashes. Feel every muscle in my body brace for impact.

"She's been in an accident," Prester says. "Some asshole set a trap for her on the road when she was in pursuit. She's alive. Got herself a head injury, maybe a broken rib. Lucky it wasn't one hell of a lot worse."

Oh God. I let out a shaky breath and focus on the good part. *She was lucky.* Head injuries are tricky and worrying, but I have to hope that she's going to be okay. But then I remember her new pregnancy. I nearly ask if the baby's okay, but I can't; I don't know if she's told Prester, and I don't want to violate that confidence. "Where is she?" Sam asks when I don't speak. "Norton General?"

"She was closer to y'all when it happened," he says. "They flew her to UT Medical Center. Javier's taking leave from his reserve unit to get here, but I don't know how long he'll be making it back."

"Did anybody tell her dad?"

"I'm stopping by there right now to give him a ride up to the hospital." Prester clears his throat. "I think this is my fault. And yours."

"Mine? Why?" I sound sharp and defensive, and I wish I could take it back. I admit it: I'm afraid of the answer.

"Both you and I let her push to keep after this damn case," he says. "The little girls in the water. Sheryl Lansdowne. She should have stepped back and let TBI take it. We all should have."

My heart pounds so hard it hurts. "She found something?"

"Guess she did," he says. "And whatever it is, it's going to TBI and we are *ending this*. Now. You keep poking around in this swamp, your ass is going to get gatored. Understand me?"

He sounds tired. Old. Worried. And I feel the same, suddenly. Overwhelmed by it all. I just want to turn the car around, take my children home, and never set foot outside again.

But I say, "We'll go to the hospital right now. And we'll stay until you and her dad can arrive, at least."

The University of Tennessee Medical Center has a fine trauma center, and I'm afraid as we arrive, breathless, to ask after Kezia's location that she'll be in the ICU . . . but she isn't. The elderly lady on duty at the front desk checks her computer and says, "Your friend's already out of the ER; they've got her up for tests right now, but she's listed as stable. If you want to have a seat, I'll let you know when they get her into a room."

Stable. That is a huge relief. Then, with a jolt, I remember. "She's pregnant," I say. I keep my voice low. "Do they know that?"

"I really don't know, ma'am, but I'll make sure to tell the nurse right now."

I was already scared for Kez, but now I'm sick as well. If she's lost the baby because of this . . . I don't know how she'll come to terms with that. What it will do to her. *Please,* I think, and send it up as a silent prayer. *Please keep them safe. Both of them.*

We start to walk to the chairs, and she calls me back. "Oh, I see there's a note in the file . . . apparently, the county sheriff says there was a dog in the car, and they need to find out who can take him. A big dog, apparently."

"Boot," I say. "His name is Boot. Was he hurt?"

"They took him to a vet, but he seemed to check out okay, according to the note. Just shaken up. They need somebody to pick him up from the vet's office." She gives me the address, and I text it to Prester's cell phone. It'll be on the way for him, and if I know Kezia's dad, he'll want that dog close to him anyway. A small comfort in what has to be a very difficult time for him. He doesn't often show it, but Kezia is his whole world. I've feared for my children before. I understand how agonizing it is, and how desperately, claustrophobically lonely.

Then we wait. Sam and I hold hands; the kids quietly whisper to each other and check their phones like their lives depend on it. I keep thinking, *what if,* but I don't let it get any further than that. I can't. It's hard for me to trust, to love. I can't afford to lose a friend like Kez.

"Ma'am?" My head jerks up as the lady at the counter motions to me. "She's been moved to a room. Here you go." She slides me a piece of paper with the number on it. "Elevator to the left."

They're taking this seriously. A uniformed Knoxville police officer is standing guard by her room, and he checks our IDs before he allows us in. "Don't get her riled up," he tells us, and I nod. "She's supposed to rest."

Kezia is, predictably, not resting. Oh, she's in bed, and she has a bandage around her head, and scratches and bruises visible on exposed skin. But she's got a tablet device and is blinking to focus as she types.

"Hey, friends," she says, and puts it aside with a warm smile. But it's fragile, I can see that. She's not herself. Seeing someone like her—someone so young—hooked up to an IV and monitors makes my heart race with anxiety. "First thing is, I'm okay. Just got a good knock on the head and some cuts and bruises."

"And a broken rib," I say. "That's what they told us."

"Only hurts when I laugh. Or cough. They've strapped it up."

There's absolutely no sign of giving up in this woman. She's still got her teeth sunk deep into this. I don't want to ask, but I have to. "Kez . . . the baby . . ."

"Baby's fine," she says, and blinks. Her eyes clear a little. Her left hand, the one not tethered to the IV, moves to cover her stomach. "Tough little thing, thank God. We're okay."

For now, I think. I am deeply worried.

A little sharpness comes back into her gaze as she reads my expression. "I was following him, Gwen. I nearly had him. Swear to God I did. Close enough to smell that bastard."

"Too close," I say, and take her hand. She feels warm—not feverish, thank God. Her fingers squeeze mine. She's broken off a couple of nails, and I wince when I see the ragged edges. "How?"

"I hunted down video along the way. I expect he was hoping to get it himself first, and when he realized what I was doing, he wanted to stop me." She pulls in a sudden breath, and winces. "Boot's okay, right? They told me he was, but—"

"Boot's fine," I say. "Don't worry."

She nods, but she's still frowning. Her gaze is distant, blurred by the medication she's on. "Gwen, he had me. I was down. He could have killed me *but he didn't.* Why?"

"I don't know. I'm just glad you're okay. Kez, no more, okay? No more chasing. No more poking around. It's enough now. Let the FBI and TBI take care of this. He's on the run, and he's not going to get away."

"He hasn't gone anywhere, and he could have. He *should* have."

"You need to promise me that you're giving this up. For real."

"Why?" She studies me for a second or two. "Will you?"

"I've got my own problems," I tell her. "I'm going to step back. And I'm asking you to do that too. Please."

"I'll be fine. This is my job, Gwen."

"No. Your job ended when this got kicked upstairs, you know that. And you need to stay safe. Hell, even the Knoxville police are taking this seriously. That's why there's a guard at the door."

"Is there?" She looks startled. "I didn't ask for one."

Prester must have called somebody and demanded protection. I know that, and she must realize it, too, from the way her expression changes. It's more of a cop mask now, trying to keep her feelings to herself. Pain medication renders it a little less effective.

"My cop daddy thinks I'm a target," she says. "I don't think so. I think he just wanted to warn me off. He could've taken me out if he'd wanted to."

"Maybe," Sam says, and steps up next to me. "But are you willing to risk your baby's life on that?" I didn't tell him—it was Kez's secret, not mine—but he couldn't have missed the discussion just now. I'm not sure she intended him to hear, but he has. I'm glad he knows.

Kez blinks slowly, and I see her realize that Sam's right. And I'm very glad Kez has protection stationed right outside. "Okay," she says. "Maybe you're both right. Maybe I've been going at it too hard." I see tears form in her eyes and spill over to form glistening tracks down her cheeks. She quickly wipes them away. "Damn. That's the drugs."

Drugs and stress. I squeeze her hand. We move back and let the kids talk to Kez a little while Sam and I linger near the door. I don't like how any of this is unraveling . . . Kez, hurt and sidelined, at least for a while. Me, frustrated and unable to see where my own enemies are hiding in the trees while they take potshots at all of us.

We stay an hour, and Kezia's already asleep before Prester and her father arrive; I warn them with a finger to my lips, and the tears in Easy's eyes make me swallow hard. "She's okay," I whisper to him. "Just resting right now." I hug him, and feel him shaking. Sam pushes a chair over so Easy can sit down, which he does, wincing as he favors his bad leg. He looks years older than he did when we last visited him just a few weeks ago.

Prester doesn't look much better, if I'm honest about it . . . his usually healthy dark color has taken on a silvery undertone, and he seems thinner. Slower, somehow. He gestures me to the other side of the room, and I head there with him. "She tell you anything about what happened?"

I give him as much as I can remember, and he nods and notes it down. When that's done, he pockets the notebook and gives me a bleak look. "She thinks Sheryl Lansdowne's actually a killer," he says. "Probably killed her own girls too. But I don't know why. Based on what the TBI's told me just now, Sheryl got in that SUV of her own accord early Monday morning; they've got video of her at a truck stop. Kez found it before she took off in hot, stupid pursuit."

"Was he *waiting* for her to find it?" I say. "Jesus."

"Don't know if it was that, or he was working out a way to wipe that footage somehow and they just crossed paths. If so, that was bad luck. Either way, Kez took the bait, and he reeled her right in. She's out of this. No more, Gwen. And you get out of it too."

"We're out," I tell him. What I can't tell him is that I don't think that means anything at this point. I think the man in the black SUV, the ghost Kez chased, is the same man who paid Len to send me those letters. He's been awfully busy, but I suspect Len's not the only help he's hired. Flyers could be posted by anyone; once he got them going viral, he didn't need to do more.

I have no proof that MalusNavis is the driver of that black SUV . . . except one thing.

I take the credit card that Len gave me out of my pocket, sealed in a plastic bag. "I ran across this today," I tell him. "Someone who was hired to harass me had it." That's close enough to the truth, without leading him into dangerous territory. "Look at the last name."

"Maguire. Jesus." He turns his sharp eyes to me, and as always, I'm sure he sees more than I intend. "Why's he harassing *you*?"

"Because I was helping Kez." Also true. Just not completely accurate.

"Well, like I said, you get the hell out. Now."

I just nod. I don't want to promise him anything, because I know that we've gone way past that particular exit. Maybe there never was an exit at all; maybe the second I went to that pond, the second he saw me there, he intended to come for me. I don't know.

But I do know he's coming. I just don't know how he'll do it, or how bad it will be. He promised I'd have a choice.

All I have to do is choose not to engage. I hope.

16

KEZIA

I hate hospitals worse than the woods. I hate being hooked up to tubes, and it's strange but I'm scared to bend my arm in case something tears loose. I have nightmares, bad ones, but I can't seem to wake up.

When I finally open my eyes again, Pop's there, with Prester looming in the background. If we talk, it disappears into vague smears when I start to drop off again. He holds my hand; I feel the warmth of it like a promise. I have a blurry, unformed impulse to tell him about the baby, tell him the baby's okay, but I don't act on it before I slip away into dreamless rest.

When I wake up again, they're gone. Instead there's someone in the room placing a gigantic bouquet of flowers on the ledge across from my bed. It's a vague shape in the dim light, and I blink to try to bring him—I'm pretty sure it's a him—into more focus. He's white, with close-cropped hair, wearing some kind of uniform jumpsuit and a baseball cap. I say, "Who sent those?"

"Don't know, ma'am," he says. "I just deliver them. There's a card if that helps."

I look over at the door, and the Knoxville police officer is there holding it open. He seems tired and impatient. "Okay, let's go, buddy, let her get some rest. On your way."

The deliveryman nods and half turns toward me. Says, "I hope you get well soon."

When I blink again, he's gone, the door's closed, and I'm halfway convinced that I hallucinated the whole damn thing, except the flowers are still there. A riot of color in the otherwise bland room.

I sleep again, and it's deep dark outside the window when I wake up. A nurse comes in and changes IV bags, takes my vitals. I need to pee, and she helps me drag my IV stand into the bathroom, then gets me back safe in bed. I feel pretty good, considering. Better than I expected. I tell her so.

"You'll be sore by morning," she tells me. "They're taking you off most of the medications, but you tell me if you start feeling too bad, okay? Oh, and you have a visitor who arrived. It's really late, and we don't usually allow them, but he says he's your boyfriend?"

"Javier?" I struggle to sit up. "Can you let him in, please?"

It occurs to me too late as the door opens that it might not really *be* Javier, that the man who crashed my car might have come back to finish the job, and I start to call out to the cop stationed outside . . . but then I just gasp. I cry hot tears of relief at the sight of Javier, *really here*, rushing toward me. Then he's hugging me carefully, and I bury my nose in the crook of his neck and take in a deep breath. It carries the scent of him—mint soap, leather, sweat, a whiff of gunpowder. He's still in his reserve fatigues. The hug turns to a kiss, and it fills me with warmth and the most perfect kind of peace.

I sigh into his mouth, and I think he feels that peace too. We don't let go for a long moment, until the pain bites again and I wince. Then he eases me back to the pillow and drags a chair over to hold my hand. "I'm so glad you're okay," he says. "You are okay, right?"

"Yes. And the baby's fine too." I have a vague, watercolor impression of most of the day, including the visit from Gwen, Sam, and the kids. I barely remember Pop and Prester's presence, but I know they've been here. But the knowledge that my baby's okay is completely, wonderfully clear. As is the love in Javier's eyes. "They did tests. Everything's going to be all right." But even as I say it, I know it isn't. Not unless I *make* it right. Now that I'm steadier, I'm also angrier. That anonymous driver meant to hurt me, and he also risked my baby, and rage shakes me hard.

Javier's fighting back real tears. He kisses my hand, careful of the tubes. He's angry, too, but he's hiding it better. "Bet you hate this," he says. "Being laid up."

"No bet. It's all I can do not to rip this needle out and go out the window."

"You'd bleed like hell, and you're on the third floor, so those are not good options." He smiles, and it's so beautiful it makes me lose my breath again. "You stay with me. Right here. Okay?"

"Okay," I say, because I can't do anything else when he smiles like that. It's powerful stuff. "How was training? Where were you?" I never ask in advance, because he's not supposed to say. But he's back now.

"Deployed on a ship," he says. "I caught a bird coming home. They dropped me at NSA Mid-South. I rented a car from there. Sorry I'm so late getting in."

From a ship at sea to here? "You're not late, baby. You're just when I needed you." I put my hand on his cheek.

He kisses my palm. "You're on the good stuff, or you wouldn't say that. Especially calling me baby."

"Probably." I feel ironed out flat. Warm and wrinkle-free.

"So what's the damage?"

"Crack on the head in the crash, concussion, could have been way worse," I say. "Cuts and bruises. One broken rib, but they've got it strapped. Did I mention the baby's okay?"

"You did. So basically you need a dent popped out, some paint work, and you'll be good to go," Javi says. "Except I don't want you going anywhere except home, Kez. You know that, right?"

"I know."

"Who the hell were you chasing?"

"How do you know I was chasing anybody?" He just gives me a look, and I have to smile. "Bad guy. I think a real bad one. Hard to be sure right now. This case is like fighting fog."

"You don't fight fog. You stay the hell home until the fog goes away."

"You're cute when you're all protective."

"Kez."

"You staying the night with me, or are you too tired?"

"This chair folds out," he says. "I'm not going anywhere until you are, *Corazón*. Besides, you didn't eat your dinner. They told me to call when you got hungry. Are you?"

I have no idea, but I feel like I ought to be. "Pudding is mine. Fruit cup? All yours."

"Deal. I'll have them bring it."

I've drifted off again, and I wake to a tray being pushed in toward me. Javier uncovers dishes like a waiter looking for a 30 percent tip. "Madame, your very late dinner this evening includes Salisbury steak— allegedly—some random vegetables, iced tea, a fruit cup, *and* pudding. We both win. But you win less, because you got to eat the Salisbury whatever."

"I don't have to do anything, mister." I don't feel hungry, I realize. I just want to sleep. But he shakes his head and starts cutting up the meat and threatening to feed me like a child, so I take the fork and do it myself. It's a little cold. It's not good either. We both get to the dessert pretty quick, and take our time over that part.

"Congratulations," he says. "That is *way* worse than a marine mess, and that's saying something, because an army marches on its stomach but marines don't march, so we don't eat that good either."

He's lying, but that's okay too. We debate what to watch—I choose a *Project Runway* marathon, over his objections—and sit together in contented silence until I fall asleep. Again.

It's about two in the morning when I wake again, and I swim up out of the darkness only because I hear Javi talking. I know that tone.

He's not happy, and that brings me out of my cloudy haze fast. It's two people at the door of the room, and Javier confronting them and saying, "No, man, you have to come back, she needs her rest—"

"I'm awake," I tell him, and hit the control after a second of fumbling to raise up my backrest to a sitting position. I hit the room lights and blink as they blaze on. "Who is it?"

"Prester," Javi says, and steps back so the shadows in the hall can step inside the room. "And some guy I don't know."

The second man is white, with blond hair; I don't know him, but I know the bearing and the type. He's police, no doubt about it. He's wearing khaki slacks and a white shirt, like some kind of door-to-door missionary, with a plain dark-blue windbreaker unzipped over it. I can see the outline of his shoulder holster under it, and the gleam of a badge clipped to his belt.

"Ma'am," he says. "Randall Heidt, TBI." He skips the hand sanitizer and comes straight at me. I hold up a hand to keep him at a distance. I'm not sure if that works, or if it's the fact that Javier steps in his way, blocking his access.

"It's not ma'am," I tell him. "Detective Kezia Claremont, which I guess you already know, since you dragged Detective Prester out to come at me this late." I fix my partner with a look. "You ought to be home resting."

"Ought to be," he agrees. "I took your father home to get some sleep. Boot's with him. Don't worry."

It does help knowing Boot and Pop are together and, I hope, not stressing over me right now. I just wish Prester had stayed home too. I love the gesture, but he looks worse than I do.

Meanwhile, there's man-drama going on behind Prester, and that keeps me from asking him to go and get himself in bed.

"Back off," Javier says to Heidt, who's standing way too close to him. Heidt locks stares with him for a moment, and I take back my first impression of a missionary. Now he looks more like one of those white-bread paramilitary types.

But he steps away, after a long enough pause to make it clear it's his own idea. He looks past Javier at me.

"Detective," he says, "what the hell do you think you were doing out there, meddling in our investigation? Again?"

"What investigation?" I ask. "You've had plenty of time to follow up with that truck stop and get the video. You didn't. I was just cleaning up after you. Did you get the trash? The video?"

"We did," he says. "We found a disposable phone in there that traces back to that 911 call. But you shouldn't have gone out there. Not by yourself."

I see Prester take that personally. He's here, I realize, because he feels guilty about letting me waltz off into danger without him. And that makes me mad.

So I take it out on Heidt. "Just trying to move things along, since your team wasn't getting it done. We got a missing woman and two dead kids, and it's my case from the start. So don't tell me I was off base. If you got questions for me, ask them."

He takes out his notebook and starts firing them at me. I have to concentrate, but the questions are easy enough. He walks me through my actions leaving the truck stop, spotting the SUV, the chase, the crash. I give him as much as I can remember about the make and model, and the fact the license plate was obscured.

Heidt asks me if I saw anyone and whether I can give him a description. I concentrate, but that part is a frustrating blur. I *think* I did. Didn't I? But if it was ever there, that memory's gone now. I know that happens in head injuries. Maybe it'll come back. Maybe not.

I finally tell him no.

Heidt snaps his notebook shut and stuffs it in his pocket. He doesn't have much of a range of facial expressions, but he manages something that looks like a scowl. "Okay. That's all I need. Detective, I don't know how many ways to say *back off*, so I'll just put this out there straight: if you continue to interfere in this investigation in any way, I'll put the full weight of the TBI on you. You'll get busted back to uniform so fast you'll wish you'd stayed in that bed. Same goes for your little friend Gwen Proctor; if she wants to keep that PI license, she'd better stay out of our way. Understood?"

I was ready to let it go. I was. But this only makes me want to pick it up again, because I get the feeling that at the very least, he just wants full credit for solving it, and at most, he's covering something up. Or maybe it's just pure stubbornness on my part. I don't like his tone much, and neither does Javier from the way he shifts and centers his weight, like he's getting ready to throw hands. Last thing I want is a fight in my damn hospital room, so I say, "You do what you got to do, Detective. I expect we'll hash this out somewhere else."

"Oh, we will," Heidt says grimly. "Count on that."

He turns to leave and finds Prester standing in the doorway, blocking his exit. It looks accidental, but I know the old man well enough to know it isn't. Prester looks Heidt up and down and says, "Son, you don't know shit about who her boss is, because her boss is *me*, and you can complain all you want. Now, I already told her that we're going to step back, but your ability to threaten anybody in this room is full zero. Clear?"

It's really, really rare for Prester to be that blunt, and for a second I think it's going to backfire . . . but then Heidt turns and looks at me, shakes his head, and says, "Locals," like it's a plague on his house.

Prester moves into the room. Heidt leaves, and the door silently closes behind him. "Staties," my partner says sourly. "Can't work with 'em, can't kill 'em. Kez, he's right. We are done with this case. I'm going to take my tired self home and get some sleep. You rest. That *is* an order."

He leaves, too, and Javier takes my hand again. Squeezes. "You all right?"

"Sure," I say, and yawn. "I got all the good drugs. Hey, who sent the flowers? You?"

"I would have, but I didn't want to stop to do it," he says. "Now I feel shitty because you've got a better boyfriend."

"I'd rather have you here than flowers any day."

Javi goes over to retrieve the card from the bouquet and hands it to me unopened. My name is label-printed on it: Det. Kezia Claremont. I flip open the envelope and pull out the small, flat card inside.

It's a graphic of a sad teddy bear, and the printed message says, *Choose to let this go.*

It takes a few seconds—I blame the drugs—before what I'm holding comes into real focus, and then I feel a red streak of alarm sizzle through me, head to toe. I drop the card to the sheet and stare it like I expect it to grow fangs.

"What?" Javi asks. "Who's it from?"

I look up at him without saying anything. He reaches over to pick up the card, and then I find words. "No, don't touch it," I say. "See if you can catch Prester before he leaves. Use my phone." I point. My finger's shaking a little from the rush of adrenaline.

Javier grabs my phone and calls Prester. He doesn't take his eyes off me while he tells Prester to get back up here, *now*. Once the call's done, he puts the phone down and says, "Are you going to tell me?"

I shake my head. "When Prester gets here."

It takes about three long minutes before my partner slams open the door. He sweeps the whole room with a look, and I see the officer who's been stationed outside the room has his gun drawn, ready to back Prester up. "It's okay," I say. "The flowers are evidence." I point to the card and envelope, both lying on my lap. "I didn't want to touch it more than I had to."

Prester takes his hand off the butt of his gun and turns to nod to the KPD officer, who looks sweaty and relieved. Prester lets the door shut and comes in, putting on blue gloves while he's walking with the unconscious precision of somebody who's done it too much. He picks up the envelope first, examines it, then turns his attention to the card. Without a word, he opens up a small paper bag produced from his coat pocket and slides both pieces into it, and fills in the evidence tag already attached to the bag with quick pen strokes. "If you needed another reason to step back, here it is," he says. "Getting flowers from somebody that ran you off the road is a pretty damn clear warning light."

"Wait," Javier says. "These flowers are from the guy who tried to kill you? Can't you trace him with that?"

"Good chance that they were internet-ordered, probably with a pay-as-you-go cash card; this guy isn't dumb enough to give his own name and address. But I'll run it down regardless."

My heartbeat picks up a painfully fast rhythm. "Prester, please be careful—"

"Kez. Don't teach your granddad how to fish. This son of a bitch came for you. I'll run it down, and I'll give it to Heidt after I do."

I don't like it, and not just because of the danger implied in that; Prester seemed okay when he was facing down Heidt, but now he seems . . . drawn. Tired. And I see a little flicker of pain contort his face. "What's wrong?" I ask.

Prester shakes his head. "Nothing. Tired. You rest." He leaves before I can push the issue. Javier stares at the shutting door, then at me. Then he takes the vase of flowers and carries it out of the room. I feel relieved. Strange how oppressive that gift felt when it was just colorful, lovely flowers. When he comes back, I ask him what he did with it.

"I put them in a hazmat bag in case the TBI wants it for some reason."

"*Hazmat* bag?"

"Not taking any chances, querida."

I realize that Javi is actually afraid for me. Really, really afraid.

And now I'm afraid for him too. And Prester.

All of us.

17

Gwen

Sam and I take the kids home. We're all tired and dispirited; seeing Kez laid up is hard on all of us, and I think it makes the kids feel especially vulnerable. I hug them both close before I get them off to bed. It's not even that late. But I'm flat-out exhausted, gray inside with the stress of the day.

But I can't sleep. I find myself lying awake, listening to Sam's even, slow breathing. I finally slip out of bed and wander like a ghost. This is happening too much. I don't want to develop insomnia, but I feel like that's a depressing possibility. There are medications, of course, but deep down, I fear being drugged, helpless, unable to meet a threat head-on.

That's why you're not sleeping. Because you can't relax for a second, Gina. You know I'm always going to be out there, maybe not physically, but I'm in the heads of people who can hurt you. Who want to hurt you.

I hate that I can still hear Melvin's whisper at low moments like this. I visualize shredding his letter, and I feel peace descend like a light, low, cool mist. I find myself yawning, and I keep visualizing the shredder chewing up paper, chewing up emails, and those damn wanted posters. I imagine putting in every picture ever taken of Melvin Royal, from baby pictures to the photo of him screaming at the jury, and watching them spin into fragments like grim confetti. Last, I imagine taking the photo of his grave off the wall. Watching it disappear too. Like he was never here at all.

When I close my eyes this time, I sleep soundly.

When I wake, it's because my daughter is shaking me. I blink at her tense face and sit up fast. Sam's doing the same. He finds his voice first, but keeps it low. "What is it, honey?"

"Cops," she whispers. "They're outside."

"What?" I launch myself out of bed and move to the window. I bend the blinds just enough to get a look outside at the street, and she's right: there are two police cruisers parked in front of our house. Neither has its lights flashing. *Maybe it's a coincidence,* I think, but then I see movement. There's an officer moving around at the side of the house. Another near the front door. "Sam. Better get dressed. Lanny, get in your room, but *do not* lock the door, and don't resist if something happens, understand? Do everything they say, when they say it."

"What if they're not really cops?" she asks, and that pauses me in the act of dragging a shirt over my head. I tug it down and turn to look at her. "Like back at Stillhouse Lake? What if they're fakes?" She sounds really, really scared. And I have to admit she ought to be, because we've had that experience before. But this . . . this looks different.

"Honey. We're in the middle of a city suburb, in a neighborhood. The police will not be fake. We'll ask to see their badges. Okay?"

She grabs a breath and nods. "Okay. Are they here for you, or—"

"I don't know." It's a horribly likely possibility, since I was just impersonating a police officer. Maybe Len did go to the police and file an assault complaint. Maybe there was a 911 call, and they somehow, despite all my precautions, traced it back to me. I don't know. I just know that we have to handle this right, and carefully. "Go tell your brother to do the same thing I told you. Go. Now."

By this time, I have my jeans on. My shoes. And Sam's dressed too.

Lanny flies out of the room and heads for her brother. Sam and I exchange a look, and he says, "Stay calm. Let me take the lead, okay?"

That's a leap of trust, and I know he's right. If they're here for me, better he go first and find out. I resist the urge to unlock the gun safe, to have a weapon in my hand. This is not the time.

I follow him down the hall to the living room, just as the first volley of firm knocks hits the front door.

Sam looks back at me to be sure I'm calm and okay, and I just nod. He swiftly disarms the alarm and opens the door.

The officer standing there has his gun drawn and ready, and he sweeps Sam with a head-to-toe assessment before he says, "Knoxville Police Department, identify yourself, please."

"Sam Cade," he says. "I live here. Can you show me your badge?"

The cop holds out his identification and looks past him, to me. *Here it comes.* I brace myself for the inevitable. "Gwen Proctor," I say. "I live here too."

The officer says, "Who else is in the home?"

"Lanny and Connor, our kids," Sam says. "That's it."

"Okay, sir, please show me your ID." Sam reaches slowly for his back pocket, removes his wallet, and displays it. The officer nods. "I need you to step out, please. Sit down on the curb by the police vehicle, there's an officer there waiting." He keys his radio and reports something I don't catch, because my pulse is thudding hard in my ears. I know what's coming next. I'm ready. I put my hands up.

But he gives me an odd look and says, "Ma'am, put your hands down. I need to see some ID from you too."

"In my purse," I say. "Right there next to you. May I get it?"

"Slowly." I take the purse down from the shelf and open it. I tip out my wallet on the side table and pull out my ID. He inspects it. "Ma'am, please join the gentleman at the curb and have a seat. I'll get back to you."

"Wait, what?" I blink. "What—why are you here?" At least I have enough presence of mind not to blurt out, *Aren't you here to arrest me,* but it's a close race.

"We have a credible threat against members of your household," he says. "Before you exit the residence, please tell me if there are any firearms on the property."

"Yes. In gun safes."

"And who has access to those?"

"Just me and Sam."

"Okay. I'm going to need you to exit the residence now. I'll bring out the kids."

I swallow hard and press my luck. "Officer, it's better if I get them. May I do that, please?"

He hesitates for a long few seconds, then nods. "Go ahead. I'm right behind you."

I knock on Lanny's door first and say, "Honey? Come on out. It's okay." She does, breathing fast. She's gotten dressed too. "Go outside and sit next to Sam."

She looks at me, trying to gauge if it's really okay or if I'm just saying it is, but she goes.

I knock on Connor's door. I'm not surprised to see he's calm and collected and ready too. "I heard," he says. "It's okay, Mom."

But it isn't. The policeman says, "Connor Proctor?"

"Yes sir."

"Please turn around and put your hands on the wall. Spread your legs. I'm going to need to search you for weapons. Is there anything in your pockets that might cut or stick me?"

"N-no sir."

It hits me hard, and late, that the officer didn't search *me*. Or Sam. Or Lanny.

Only my son.

My voice is sharp when I say, "What the hell is going on?"

The officer ignores me. He searches Connor with calm efficiency, steps back, and keys his radio. "Bringing him out now." Then he finally turns his attention to me as he puts a hand on Connor's shoulder, holding him in place. "Ma'am, you can ask the detectives about the specifics, but someone posting as your son threatened to kill you, Mr. Cade, and your daughter. We're going to need to question all of you. I'd appreciate it if you'd cooperate fully."

I barely hear any of that after *Your son threatened to kill you.* I hear a high, thin buzzing in my ears, and I have to brace myself against the wall. A photo of the four of us rocks on its hook, and I grab it to steady it. My voice, when it comes, sounds oddly flat. "That's wrong. Connor didn't do that. Let him go." I don't look at my son. I don't dare, and I can't even think *why.* Maybe because I'm afraid he'll think I'm doubting him.

The officer, of course, doesn't let go. He fixes me with a cool, assessing look that tells me he's ready if I decide to flip out on him. I get myself under control, though my muscles are all tense and twitching, desperate to grab my son and wrap him protectively in my arms. The officer must see that, because he says, "Ma'am, please go outside to the police vehicle and take a seat on the curb. We'll sort all this out when the detective arrives." It's not warm, but at least it's a little less than aggressive, and I take a breath, then look at my son.

"It's going to be okay," I tell him. He's pale, tense, and I can't read the expression on his face at all. I've never seen him like this before. He's never *been* in this place before.

"Don't worry, Mom. I didn't—"

"I know," I tell him, and I believe it to my bones. "Honey, *I know.*"

"Let's save it for the detective," the officer says. "Ma'am. Please go ahead. We'll be right behind you."

It's very hard to turn my back on my son, even though I hear the footsteps following me. I want to look back, turn around, somehow reset the clock to half an hour ago, to peace and safety and love.

I want to protect him, and I can't. *I can't.* It feels like it's going to end me, this need, but somehow I keep walking through the living room, out the door, down the sidewalk.

Sam and Lanny are seated together on the curb beside the police car, and Sam's got his arm around Lanny's shoulders. They both stand up when they see me, and I see them look past me, to Connor.

"Oh *hell* no, you get your hands off my brother!" Lanny shouts, and lunges forward. Sam catches her from behind, and I step in her way. She rushes right into me, and I throw my arms around her as Sam does the same from the other direction. She struggles. Hard. "Let go! Let me go, you can't let them do this—"

"I'm not," I tell her. I sound icily calm. "Lanny. It won't do anybody any good if you pop off and get arrested. You know better. *Sit down. Now.*"

I've never used that tone with her before, and it gets through. She goes still. Sam doesn't let go, and I don't either, until I feel her muscles unclench. "You'd better fix this," she says. I hear the fury in it. The betrayal.

I let go. Sam takes our daughter back to where they were, but he's watching me closely as the cop leads Connor past us. I reach out and put my hand on my son's cheek, very briefly.

He says, "I'm okay, Mom. It's fine." Empty words, and I've never felt that more than I do right now. He's putting on a brave face, but he's scared and I know that. I'm terrified.

I watch my son put into the back seat of the police car, and I force myself to sit down next to Sam. I pull out my phone with trembling fingers and say, "Lanny. What message boards does Connor post on?"

"He—he doesn't—"

"Don't bullshit me. Not now."

She's quiet for a moment, and turns her head to face the police car. Connor. Then she says, "Some of the crime boards, but not under his own name. Sometimes he posts on a forum that a couple of guys from school set up. It's called Loserville."

I search for it, and find it fast. I take in the content quickly—mostly complaints about school, mockery of teachers, some truly horrible harassment—and my heart sinks. I don't know why my son would post here at all. It's a cesspool of the darkest impulses of young men. There's a whole thread on girls at school. I don't read it. I can't. I'm afraid what I'm going to find out about my own child.

I feel sick. Sweaty. I blink and focus on the search bar, and ask Lanny what he goes by on the board.

She doesn't want to say, that much is obvious.

She's crying. Silent tears running down her cheeks. Angry at herself, disappointed in him, I don't know. Then she says, "Ripperkid."

I can't move for a few seconds. My muscles simply won't respond. The name drops into me and just . . . sinks. I shut my eyes and let the awful, sickening ripples of it go through me, then take a breath and type it in. I want to ask her why he'd choose that hellish moniker. I don't. I think, like me, he's choosing to stand and fight, and this . . . this is part of that.

He hasn't posted that much. Most of it isn't noteworthy. He's mocked a few teachers, insulted a few people, but thank God, he's never joined the pack of hellhounds in outright harassment.

But he's been talking about his father. About Melvin Royal. He's answered questions. Detailed the crimes. He knows far, far more than I ever thought he did. *He's only fifteen. He shouldn't know these things.*

But it's the message from today that catches my full attention, finally. I take a screen capture of it, and only then focus on the words frozen on the screen. I'm so sick of my fucking so-called family. Liars and hypocrites, just like my dad. I'm going to make it happen. One, two, three bullets to the head. By tomorrow I'll be an orphan.

I freeze as my gaze skims over the IP address that posted the message.

Because it's ours.

The post came from our house. But it couldn't have. I know Connor didn't do it.

My phone buzzes in my numb hand. It's a blocked number. I swallow, taste ashes, and say, "I need to take this."

"Now?" Sam's annoyed. "Really?"

I don't answer. I just get up and walk away, over near the corner of the house. I can still smell the fresh paint where we blocked out the vandals. I slide to accept the call and put it to my ear.

"What did you do?" I ask it with real ferocity. If I could reach through this phone and grab something, I'd rip it off. "What did you do *to my son?*"

"I didn't do anything," the man says. Bland tones. Calm. I'm anything but. "I provided his login information to a friend I know. He's very, very good at faking originating IP data. Your son will be inconvenienced. He's not in any danger. Yet."

"*Not in any danger?* He's being arrested!"

"He's a juvenile. He'll get the benefit of the doubt, and they'll eventually work out he didn't post the message. But this isn't about him, Gina Royal. It's about you. And I'm sure by now you've figured that out."

"You son of a—"

"It's time to start making choices. Tomorrow morning at nine o'clock sharp, you will either walk out your door, get in your car, and drive . . . or you'll stay home, fight a losing battle to protect your family, and everything will be gone. Everyone that matters to you. Besides . . . I think you want to find me. Don't you?"

"Yes." I hiss it, and I can hear the venom in the sound. "You came after Kez."

"I didn't. She came after *me*. I only wanted to stop her. I did stop her."

If you think that, you don't know Kezia. I think it, but I don't say it. I want his attention firmly on me now. "What do you want from me?"

"The truth," he says. "The truth about who you really are, deep down. People always reveal themselves eventually. All their darkness and damage. And you will too."

There's something so horribly *serene* about him. He thinks he's right. He knows it. And I know none of what he just said is empty threat; he's shown me that he has the ability, and the will, to come after me, my family, my *son.*

"I just get in my car in the morning and drive. Just like that. And where am I supposed to go?"

"I'll tell you once I see you go. And if you value the lives of Sam and the kids, you won't tell them where you're heading once you know. You can bring your guns, it won't matter. This will be over on Friday, one way or another. I promise. Think of it as . . . a retrial."

He hangs up. I stand frozen, listening to the sudden silence after the disconnection, and then I slowly put the phone back in my pocket and turn to look. A detective's sedan is pulling into our street now, lights flashing. All our neighbors are awake. Watching on their porches, or through their windows.

This isn't a refuge anymore. Everything we've built has become a noose, and it's tightening slowly around our necks.

I go back to Sam and Lanny. My daughter glares at me, and I feel the force of it like hot irons. Sam's looking at me too. He's gone unreadable. "Everything okay?" he asks me.

"Yes," I lie. I sit down on the cold concrete curb next to him as the police detectives come toward us. "Sam? I need you to be there for Connor. *Really* be there. Will you do it?"

He gives me a strange look. "Of course I will. Why? Where are you going to be?"

I manage a smile. "Here, of course. With you. But . . . if anything goes wrong . . ."

He puts his arm around me. Not wary or annoyed any longer. I lean against him and stare at my son, who sits quietly in the police car, not looking at anything in particular. Connor's a strong kid, but my God. My God.

MalusNavis will destroy him to get to me. And Lanny too. He'll find her cracks and break her apart. Sam too. I can already see the reality of it stretching out before me, and it's devastating. Horrifying.

He wants to see who I am.

Then I will show him. And it'll be the last damn thing he ever sees.

18

SAM

I shouldn't be surprised when the detectives separate us, but it still stings; I don't know what's going on with Gwen, but I find myself watching her at a distance, trying to read her stiff body language, wishing I'd had time to get her to tell me *what the hell just happened*. I'm missing half the questions the detective talking to me is asking. I don't know him, he doesn't know me, and he's not patient with my distraction.

"Hey!" I blink and focus on his face instead of over his shoulder, because he's snapping his fingers in my face. "You with me, Mr. Cade? Because the faster we get through this, the better for both of us."

The last thing I want is an express train to Connor being arrested. But I focus. "Sorry, what did you say?"

"Does Connor have access to guns in the house?"

"No. We keep them locked and secure."

"In gun safes."

"Yes."

"And do these safes have codes?"

"Yes."

"Okay. Does Connor know any of those codes?"

"No." I say it firmly, and I don't expand on that; embroidering is where people get into trouble. Fact is, I don't know that for certain. Connor's a smart kid; I have every reason to think that if he wanted into the gun safe, he'd find a way. But this? This is bullshit. Connor is not out to kill us. I'm not about to entertain the idea that he is.

"How often do you change them?"

"Every couple of months."

He's frustrated, I can tell; he's not getting the long-winded responses he'd like, where he can drive a wedge into a crack. He changes tack. "So, Connor has a history of violent outbursts—"

"Connor had *one* post-traumatic stress incident that he's gotten counseling to deal with." I stop there. I badly want to shout, *Do you know what this kid has survived? Do you?* But it won't do any good. He doesn't want to know.

"He was also involved with a cult—"

"He wasn't *involved*. He was kidnapped. Along with me." That's it. I'm done being cooperative. "Look, I've answered your questions. That's enough. I will take you in, we'll open the gun safes, I'll inventory everything against our records, and *we are done*."

"Sir," the detective says. "We're done when I say we're done. And Connor needs to come to the station to answer some questions."

"Not without his parents he's not."

"You're welcome to attend the questioning." He says that like it's a favor. It's not. It's the law that he can't question the kid without us present. "You know, you're not doing the boy any favors being uncooperative."

"I've been nothing but cooperative. Now let's go look at the safes and move it along. It's been a long damn day."

Gwen casts me a look as we pass; I give her a nod and a smile, trying to let her know it's all okay. She doesn't look okay, though. She looks like she is one thin nerve away from hijacking that police cruiser and driving her son away. That's the thing Gwen fights every day: the urge to run, the urge to protect her kids even when doing it isn't productive or smart. She doesn't think I see it, but I do.

I mouth, *I love you*, and lead the cop inside.

We hit the safes, and I show him the paperwork that has all our registered firearms. He checks them off, one by one. While he's doing that as slowly as possible, he says, "So, does the kid know how to shoot?"

"I assume you already know the answer to that."

"We're aware of the flyers at the gun range. Your son was observed shooting there. We heard there were . . . complaints."

"Not about him. He's not a criminal," I say. "Connor's a good kid who's been dealt a bad hand."

"Hell of a bad hand, if your dad's a serial killer."

I straighten up after opening the last safe and meet his blank brown eyes. Hold the stare. Then I say, "I'm his dad."

"No offense." The man shrugs and checks the last gun off the list. "Okay. All accounted for, like you said. Do we have your permission to search Connor's room?"

"Get a warrant." The one thing that could save or damn him is the laptop that they're certainly going to need a warrant to grab anyway. I'm risking them taking all our electronics, just to be pissy about it, but I'm not about to let them poke around unsupervised in my son's room. "I'd like to go back to my wife now." I realize, with a weird jolt, that I just called her my wife. I haven't done that before; we're common-law married, but somehow I've just never defined it that way.

It feels good to say it. And strange. But good.

He just grunts and leads me back out of the house. I make straight for Gwen, and she looks visibly relieved to see me. The detective who's been quizzing her has finished, and mine joins him; they'll be sharing info, and I feel like we need to do that too. So I draw her away from Lanny, who's still talking to a uniformed officer, and say, "The guns are all accounted for. I don't say that to mean I think Connor was planning anything; it's just less proof they have."

She just nods. She seems so tense, so pale, and I want to make things better for her. But maybe there isn't any way to do that, not right now.

"Honey, it's going to be okay," I tell her. "Connor didn't do this. You know it."

"I know," she says, and meets my eyes for a second. "The problem is that someone else did. And they're not going to stop."

She says that like she's rock-solid certain of it, and I let a couple of seconds tick by before I say, "MalusNavis?"

"He's watching us," she says, and I see the jolt that goes through her. It's one of her worst fears, and who can blame her after all those years of being stalked by people *I* helped set on her trail? "He's watching *all* of us. Sam . . . I think I have to stop fighting it. I need to let him have me. I'm what he wants."

"No!" It comes out of my mouth before I've even formed the word in my head. "Gwen, no. Not an option. Ever."

"Am I supposed to give him Connor? Lanny? Vee? *You?*" She shakes her head, and then she's hugging me tight. I hug her back. "I don't see how to stop him any other way."

"There's got to be another way." I smooth her hair, hold her, and try to put every bit of confidence into what I'm saying. "We're going to find a way, honey. We will. But together."

I feel her nod, but I don't feel her relax. It worries me.

The two detectives come back toward us, and we break, but I keep hold of her hand. Her fingers feel cold, and I can feel her trembling.

"We're ready to talk to Connor at the station," the detective who questioned me says. "Which one of you wants to stay with your daughter?"

I'm about to volunteer that I will when Gwen catches me completely off guard and says, "I'll stay with Lanny." When I look at her, she says, "It's better if you go with Connor. I'm not—you're calmer right now. You'll be better at it."

"Okay," I say, and I'm gentle with it. This is . . . not what I expected. Gwen is usually so completely in this kind of fight, whether that's right or not, and to see her step back is surprising. Progress, I hope. "I'll take good care of him. I promise."

"I know you will." There are tears in her eyes, and I can see how this torments her. But she takes a deep breath and blinks them away and says, "Bring him home safe, Sam."

The detective stops at the police cruiser and has a word with the uniformed officer standing there; he opens the door and gestures Connor out. The handcuffs are removed. I put my arm around him, and we follow the detective to his cruiser, and when I turn around to see Gwen, she's standing with her arms around Lanny. It looks like they're holding each other back this time.

Maybe that's good for both of them. God, I hope we're not making a massive mistake here. She's put a staggering amount of trust in me.

Now I need to live up to that.

◆ ◆ ◆

"This is complete bullshit."

I say it bluntly to the detective who enters the room. We've been waiting only a few minutes, and I'm a little surprised; generally, the tactic is to keep people on edge, let the silence and time work on them. Not now. It makes me worry.

"Probably is," the detective agrees blandly, sliding into the chair on the other side of the table. Connor's no longer in handcuffs, and so far I've been able to keep myself from getting into some, so I suppose that's a win. "For the recording, this is Detective Aaron Holland, speaking with Connor Proctor and his legal guardian Sam Cade. Mr. Cade, Mr. Proctor, I know this ain't the best of times for you, and I apologize for that, and for keeping you waiting. Wanted to be absolutely sure I had all the facts before I came in here. Now, Mr. Cade . . . you're Connor's adoptive father, is that correct?"

"Yes."

"And his mom is Gwen Proctor."

"Yes. Where's the warrant?"

"What warrant, Mr. Cade?"

"The arrest warrant. Do you have one?"

"Mr. Cade—"

"Because if you don't, we're not saying one damn thing more."

"That's totally understandable," Holland agrees, with every sign of real sympathy. He fakes it well. "I can't even imagine the stress of comin' up like you did, Connor, with your family history. Plus moving, having people threatening your life all the time. And last year, getting abducted like that. Dealing with all that at such a tender age, that can't be easy at all."

Connor just shrugs slightly. He's not meeting the detective's steady gaze. He scratches a thumbnail on the smooth surface of the table like he's found a spot.

"You know why you're here?" Holland asks. His voice is profoundly gentle.

Connor says, "Because someone faked a message post."

"Connor, don't answer him."

Holland looks at me, then back to the boy. "So you're saying you didn't make that post, then?"

"I'm calling a lawyer," I say, and take out my phone. "I don't like any of this. He's not answering questions. Connor, be quiet—you don't need to say anything at all." I have a criminal lawyer in my contacts; we've needed her before, and I know she'll show up fast. I don't know what Gwen would do, but the last thing I want is for Connor to make a deadly mistake. "Connor, he's not on your side."

"But I didn't do it," Connor says.

"Then you've got no reason not to talk to me," Holland says.

"No." I say it flatly, and put a hand on Connor's shoulder when he tries to respond. "We're done. You want to prove that he did it, go ahead and try to do that without the help of a fifteen-year-old. That's your job."

Holland sits back in his chair and crosses his arms. "Let me just lay my cards on the table, all right? Then you can decide what you want to do."

"Pass. Because legally, you get to cheat at cards." I hit the contact number and get an answering service. "Yeah, I'm going to need Ms. Moore down here for Connor Proctor at KPD Central. He's not under arrest, but he's going to need representation." I give my callback number and hang up. Holland has a hangdog, disappointed look. I don't care. "Go ahead. Lay it out if you still want to."

He shakes his head, sighs, and gives Connor a look that clearly says he wishes I hadn't done that. I care even less. "Okay," Holland says. "Well, as you know, we have an internet post under Connor's name in which he threatens to go on a killing spree—"

"I didn't post that!" Connor says. I put a hand on his shoulder, and he subsides, but I can feel how tense he is.

"He knows you didn't," I say. "Don't you, Detective? And he also knows about the vandals at our house. And the flyers. Kind of wonder why he thinks *you* should be the one in handcuffs, considering all that."

"I didn't want to bring you in here," Holland says. He's still directing it toward Connor, not me. "Tried real hard to avoid it, in fact."

I snap my fingers and tap the table. "Hey. Talk to me. Not to him. He's done answering."

Holland does, finally. He meets my gaze squarely and holds it. He looks genuinely sorrowful. They've deployed their A game on this, I can feel it; he probably cracks a lot of suspects just through sheer empathy. It'd work with Connor, if I'd allow that.

I smile. "Go ahead and tell me what you think you have. Because I guarantee you, you have nothing worth pursuing."

"I have a witness who swears he saw Connor with a gun. Showing it off at school last week, in fact. He goes by Ripperkid on that message board, did you know that? And we've also got another witness who heard Connor publicly state on multiple occasions that he intends to kill a whole bunch of people. We take that seriously, Mr. Cade. I sure hope you do too."

"That's a lie!" Connor leans forward, his face flushed, fists clenched. I tighten my grip on his shoulder and get him to lean back. "Dad! I didn't!"

"Maybe it is, son," Holland says. He seems sorrowful about it. "But those two people called in complaints *yesterday*. Before this post was ever made."

"Convenient timing," I tell him. "You have any corroboration on that? Other kids who back it up?"

Holland doesn't say anything. He just sighs. "Mr. Cade, we both know that I can lie about that to you—tell you I've got twenty kids all on the record, tell you there's school video, tell you all manner of things. And even if I wasn't lying, you'd obviously believe I was. So I don't know how you want me to answer that question in a way that makes sense. But I'll tell you this, and I'm being as straight as I can: I have corroboration."

I open my mouth, then close it. I need to take my own advice. I don't look at Connor. I stare straight at the detective, and he stares back, and then finally he scoots his chair back. "I'll let you know when your lawyer gets here," he says.

The door shuts behind him, and I hear the lock click. We're not going anywhere.

Connor says, "Sam, I didn't—"

"Don't," I say. "They have cameras in the room, and they can hear anything we say. Tell me once your lawyer gets here because they'll have to turn them off, but not until then. Okay?"

He looks miserable, pale, absolutely wretched. But he nods. I put my arm around him, and we lean together in silence. I'm scared for him. It's hard to read Holland. He *might* be telling the truth about a witness, and about having more than one. I don't know. I still believe Connor, but . . . this isn't looking good.

It takes an eternity—well, two and a half hours—for our attorney to arrive and the police to decide they won't try to charge Connor. Which tells me that if they do have witnesses, they're not confident about them. Not yet.

We drive home. I'm so tired I feel lightheaded, and I have to focus hard on the road, but I say, "Ripperkid?"

Connor winces. "I know," he says. "That—doesn't look great."

"Want to tell me why you picked it?"

"It's what they call me at school," he says. "Once word got around. And word always gets around. I figured I probably should own it. I talked to Lanny about it. She thought it was cool."

Oh, Lanny. Of course she did. And the fact that neither of them told us . . . shouldn't surprise me, really. They're both at an age where what they tell their folks and what they actually do are two divergent courses. "That's why you answered questions about Melvin," I say. "To own it?"

"Yeah. I mean . . . better they think I'm kind of edgy than somebody they can kick around."

As coping strategies go, it actually isn't terrible. I know Gwen won't like it, but I see the point very clearly. "Hey, kid? I love you. You know that, don't you?"

"Thanks, Dad," he says. "I love you too." He doesn't often say it. I don't either. It's a guy thing. But it seemed right, in this quiet moment, and I feel better for it. I hope he does too. "Mom's going to kick my ass."

"I'll talk to her," I tell him. "She's just scared for you. Hell, I am too. So be a little patient, okay? We're trying to handle this the best way we can."

"I know," he says. "But I really didn't do anything. That makes me want to break something."

"I know the feeling. Hardly ever helps. You still feel pretty bad, and then you have to clean up the stuff you broke. Not great."

"I still want to try it."

"I'll hand you some ugly mugs we don't use anymore. But you'll be on broom duty."

He laughs, and it eases the knot in my stomach a little. I reach over and ruffle his hair. He squirms away.

When we pull into the garage, Gwen's already standing there, spotlighted by my headlights. I kill the engine and close the garage door. Her body language is stiff, but not angry. She's worried.

"Everything's okay," I tell her, which is not quite the truth, but close. "They let him go."

Gwen silently embraces our son, and looks at me over his shoulder. When did the kid get that tall? He's nearly her height now. I hadn't noticed, but in a few years, he'll make her look small. She says, "Thank you, Sam. God, thank you. I couldn't have done that." She lets out a shaky laugh. "I'd have launched myself like a rocket and ended up under arrest. One hundred percent chance." She pushes Connor back and studies him with that unmistakable tenderness mothers have. Puts her hand on his cheek. "Are you all right? Really?"

"I'm sorry, Mom," he says. His voice sounds choked and tight. "I—I know I shouldn't have gone on that board. I just wanted . . ."

"To belong," she finishes for him when he can't. "I know. I'm not angry. I'm just worried." She straightens up and looks at me, then back at Connor. "I called my boss. It took her crack IT guys ten minutes to locate the fake IP redirection and track it back. Guess where it ended up?"

I shake my head. So does Connor.

Gwen smiles slowly. It's a wicked kind of smile, with an edge that cuts, and I love it. "Remember our two brothers that you and your sister came up with on social media? The vandals?"

"*They* did it?" Connor sounds shocked, but I suspect he's just surprised that they were smart enough to pull it off.

"I'm not sure, but Lanny and I gave the cops their names as somebody to look into. Apparently they also called in tips that said you had a gun at school last week. Let's just say they're not having a very good night."

I know it wasn't them. I'm absolutely certain it wasn't; they aren't bright enough to pull this off, by all indications, or one of them wouldn't have worn school athletic gear to tag our house. What was it Lanny said? They got C grades in a class that should have been a walkthrough A. But I don't want to raise that right now, not when there's real relief on Gwen's and Connor's faces. Later.

I'm bone tired. But I feel like we're okay.

And I sleep the sleep of the dead.

19

KEZIA

The nurse was right; I feel horrible the next time I wake up on Thursday morning. Bruised, aching, cranky as hell. But finally my head is clear, and when I groan and squint against the morning light and hit the control to raise my bed back up to a sitting position, I see that Javier's getting my clothes out of the closet. They're nasty and bloody, but at least they're mine.

"I would've gotten you fresh stuff, but I didn't want to leave you," he says. "How you feeling?"

"Great," I say. "Better once I'm out of here."

"The doctor talked to me. They're pulling your IV, all your head CTs were good, so they're kicking you out. He says to avoid strenuous activity. I'm going to say that means no sex, no kettlebells, and no foot pursuits. Anything else ought to be okay, right?"

"It bugs me you put sex first in that list, Javi."

"Love, the way we do it, it *deserves* to be first." He grins and kisses me. Long, warm, sweet. A little bit hot, but he's trying to hold it down. "Good news, I don't have to go back to training. No sense burning more helicopter fuel getting me back again at this point." That's a relief. I like having him here always, but especially right now.

Getting dressed hurts, but it also feels like getting control of my life back. Gun, badge, purse. I top it with a jacket and pull on my low-heeled leather boots, and I feel like myself again. Moving around is helping with the aches and bruises.

The sunlight hurts my eyes. I slip on sunglasses and try to ignore the throbbing headache as I plug my phone into Javi's rental car charger. The battery flashes a red image as the phone starts powering; it'll take a few for it to restart.

"So catch me up," Javi says as he puts the car in gear. "What the hell is going on in this town? A lot, right?"

"Yeah, you leave, and look what happens."

"I'm serious. Two dead kids, three dead adults, you getting nearly killed, Gwen harassed again. Seems like a *lot*, right?"

"It is," I say, and then I repeat it, thinking hard. "It *is* a lot. Especially for a small town like Norton."

Any piece of this could stand on its own, but adding all of it together seems like . . . seems like a plan.

But I don't know what it means. Any of it.

I'm lost in my thoughts, and we're at the edge of Norton when I think to check my phone. I have missed calls and texts. No surprise there. I start looking through them.

Prester called me at three in the morning. *What the hell?*

I immediately dial the phone as we pass the city limits sign, and the town's in our rearview mirror. Two rings, and then a click as it picks up. I expect to hear Prester's deep, laconic voice.

Instead, I hear Sergeant Porter's. "Kezia?" He doesn't sound like himself. I hear a tremble in his voice that shouldn't be there.

I go cold and still. My voice, when I speak, sounds unnaturally cool and calm. "What's happened?"

"He's dead, Kez. Prester's dead." His breathing is ragged. I feel something crush inside me. *God. God, no.* "Been dead for hours, looks like. I shouldn't be answering this phone. Shit. Call me direct."

He hangs up. I just sit there, gripping the phone, staring at the trees whipping by. Javier's asking me what's going on. I can't answer. I can't.

I pull up Porter's number in my call list and dial. He answers on the first ring. I drag in a breath and let it out. "Where is he?"

"His car," he says. "He's in his car. They're processing it right now. Chief's on it. But you should be here."

"Where the fuck is *here?*"

"Sorry. His house. He never made it out of his car last night."

I don't reply. I hang up and turn to Javier, but I'm not really looking at him. Or anything. I'm seeing Prester's face the way it was last night. The way he looked last time I saw him. "Prester's house," I say. "Now. Go. *Go.*"

He drives like a madman, and it's still not fast enough for me.

◆ ◆ ◆

When I see the shadow of my partner's body still in the car, I feel my knees go weak. Javier catches my arm and steadies me, and I press against him for a few seconds until I can get myself right.

The chief is standing off to the side, talking to Sergeant Porter, but he breaks off when he sees me come up to the tape line separating crime scene from lookie-loos . . . only there aren't any, not yet. Prester's house is isolated, an old farmstead, plain and well kept. Been in his family a hundred years, give or take. I've eaten at his table. There's no one waiting inside, no grieving widow. His wife passed a few years back. He's been alone awhile. "Kez," he says. "You shouldn't be here. Go on home."

"What happened?" I ignore the rest of it. I let go of Javi and duck under the tape before anyone can stop me, and even though part of my brain is screaming at me to stop, I walk toward the car. They've already marked footprints in the dirt, and I'm careful to stop outside that perimeter. A forensic tech—Lewis, I think, can't really tell because I can't focus—murmurs at me to stay back.

I couldn't go closer if I tried. But I force myself to look at Prester.

The body is a mannequin made of flesh. The face is ashy and relaxed and calm. It's wearing Prester's suit, the same one he had on when he left my room. His second-best. I can see the small fray at the left-hand tip of his lapel.

"Somebody killed him," I say.

"No, Detective, we don't think so. There's no sign of violence on the body, no blood, no sign of strangulation, nothing like that. It looks like he drove in here and just . . . died," the chief says. He's very gentle about it. "We both know he hasn't been well, Kez. I'm sorry."

"Prester tried to call me at three this morning. What time did he die?"

The coroner—Winston, my God, again—says, "I can't tell you that exactly. Somewhere between two and five, that's my best guess right now. If you say he called at three, then from three to five. That helps narrow it down."

I remember the cases. Sheryl Lansdowne's go-to methods of murder. All indirect. Accidental. Natural causes. "Check him," I whisper. "This isn't right. It can't be right. He was going to look into who sent me flowers—"

"Kez, you're just out of a hospital bed," the chief says. "Please. Let us do what we've got to do for Prester. He wouldn't want you out here right now."

Prester would want me to find his killer. I'm the reason this happened. I have to be. It can't just *happen.*

Except it could. I know it could, I've been worrying about him, we've all seen how bad he's gotten these past few weeks . . .

I look down. There are footprints in the dirt here, but they're all large, old-fashioned men's dress shoes.

No. Not all of them. There are smaller prints. Some kind of sneaker. I wordlessly point to them, and the chief nods. "We marked them," he says. "But Kez—they're about your size. You come up here sometimes, don't you?"

I feel sick, hot, drifting. I force myself to *think*. "About three days ago. I brought him—" My voice fails. I try again. "I brought him out a case file."

"Were you wearing the same shoes you have on now?"

I just shake my head. I can't remember. I don't know. *I don't know.* What size are Sheryl Lansdowne's shoes? No sign of violence on him—they just said so. "Look for an injection mark, something like that," I say. "In case."

"In case what?"

They're all looking at me with concern. "In case *somebody killed him*, damn, what do you think?" I feel raw. I just want to sit down and cry right now. *Those aren't my footprints. Can't be.* I look again, and it hits me like a brick to the face that Prester has walked the last step in those stupid Florsheim dress shoes he must still have on. The ones I mocked him about just last week. *Come on, old man; treat yourself to something new.*

The chief pauses, face pale and older than it was the last I saw him, and then nods. "I'll get it done. Kezia—go home. Please." He's humoring me. He doesn't believe me. And there's no damn reason he should; even I know I'm not thinking straight right now.

I don't argue the point. There's nothing here for me. Nothing but what I've already noticed. I walk with Javier back to the rental car, and before I get in, I check my phone, which is halfway recharged now.

There's a voice mail from Prester. My heart lurches. I look wordlessly across at Javier, and he pauses in the act of opening his door. "What?"

I hold up a shaking finger to ask him to wait, and I hit the button to play the message.

Prester's voice takes my breath away. "Claremont, I finally got hold of some-damn-body at the flower shop that made the bouquet, but they don't have . . . it was an order off the . . . off the internet like I . . ." I gasp and put my hand over my mouth, because he's struggling. He's gasping. I have a recording of him dying. I can't listen to it, I *can't.*

Javier is by me in a second, taking the phone from me; I'm crying too hard to speak, and the weight of anguish inside me feels like it might take me to the ground. He listens to the recording, and I watch the grim shock settle on his face. He finally stops it and says, "Get in the car, Kez. Let me talk to the chief for you, okay?"

I can't do anything else. I collapse into the seat, and I feel a rush of rage come over me, bad enough I want to punch the dashboard and scream the pressure out.

Prester died trying to help me.

Why?

God, *why?*

◆　◆　◆

Javier wraps me in a warm blanket once I get home, but I can't sit still; I need to get out of these stiff, bloody clothes. I need a shower. He's busy in the kitchen making eggs, so I slip away, strip, and stand in the hot water and cry out my frustration and grief. *I need you, partner.*

I never got to say goodbye.

When I get out of the shower at last, dry off, get dressed, I see that I have a text message on my phone. When I open it up, it's a video. In the still shot, I see that it's Prester. Prester, in his car.

I sit down on the toilet, fast, and I breathe through the panic and pain.

Then I hit play.

Prester. Having a heart attack. And someone standing there filming him. I force myself to watch, tearing apart my heart in big, wet pieces, and then . . . then he closes his eyes and goes still.

Gone.

"At least he wasn't alone," a woman's voice says. "Poor old guy."
Then it goes dark.

Another text comes in. This didn't need to happen. You could have let it go. Let it go this time.

Another video pops up. I hit play. It's Javier getting out of the rental car last night in the hospital parking lot.

Another video after that. Pop, in his cabin, washing dishes. Someone filming through his window.

The storm inside me is so violent I don't know *how* to feel. Terrified. Enraged. Agonized. Horrified. All at the same time, like an explosion under my skin.

And another text. Stay home, Kezia. This isn't about you.

Maybe it wasn't supposed to be. Maybe in his mind, it isn't.

I am not letting go.

I feel my hunter's blood, rushing hot and fast with every heartbeat.

This isn't about you.

Oh, it is, you coldhearted bastard. It is.

20

GWEN

I sleep only because I know I must. My family is here. They're safe. It feels like things are resolving, like our normal lives may be just within reach again.

I'm the only one who knows it's a lie.

Four hours later, I open my eyes and slip out of bed, waking without any transition at all. No sense of peace. I silently get dressed in jeans, a comfortable shirt, sturdy boots. I can't risk unlocking my gun safe next to the bed; it will beep, and Sam will wake up immediately. But that's okay. While he was at the station, I moved my favorite gun, the Sig, to the small living room safe we keep under the couch. Extra mags and another box of ammunition as well.

I pause in the doorway and look back at Sam. He's fast asleep. I convinced him to take a rare over-the-counter sleep aid last night, and he's down for the count. Good. He'll need this. His battle is going to be hard too. In some ways, as hard as mine.

I take in the sight of him and try to etch it on my heart, embed it in my brain. I want to remember this moment of quiet. How he looks. How it feels.

I look in at Lanny, curled on her side, pink-and-purple hair spread out in a colorful fan across her pillow. My beautiful, strong, volatile girl, inches away from being someone the world will have to reckon with on her own terms. I am so proud of her it hurts. Tears roll silently down my cheeks, cool against my hot skin, and I wipe them carefully away before I turn to my son.

Oh, Connor, my complicated, wonderful boy. I love you more than I can ever say. I fear for you most of all, but you always surprise me. Always. I drink in the sight of him tangled in a restless pile of sheets, caught between boy and man, and I think, *You will grow up to be like no one else in this world.* Not his sadistic, hateful father. Not like me either. Unique and beautiful and mended strong. It's all I can do not to go in, wake him up, curl him into my arms, and rock him like the baby he used to be.

Closing that last door feels like cutting off pieces of myself.

I collect my holster, my jacket, the Sig, the magazines, the ammo. I add the small ankle holster and .38 revolver, a cop's emergency gun.

Then I look at the clock.

It's eight forty-five in the morning. Outside the windows, the sun is up and warm, generous on the grass. Leaves flutter. Cars move on the street as neighbors leave for work. Everything is normal, everywhere but here in the small space of hell I am in.

I don't have to go. We can face this together. All of us.

I sit down and put my head in my hands, and as I do, my phone alert goes off. I look at it.

Unknown-number text.

A photo of Sam, leaning over the cowling of an airplane.

One of Lanny, taken through her bedroom window as she's sleeping.

One of Connor, sitting cross-legged on his bed, typing on his computer with his headphones on.

And there's Vee, in her ridiculous house shoes and pajamas, standing in her doorway talking to a neighbor.

A shot of Kezia collapsed and bloody by the wreck of her car.

You can stop all of them from suffering, the next text says. The choice is yours. But you have to leave it all behind and come to me. You have fifteen minutes to decide. If you don't leave your house at nine o'clock, I will assume your choice is to save yourself. If you come, leave your phone and any electronics. If your SUV has a GPS tracker, disable it. I'm monitoring you. I'll know if you try to cheat.

"You son of a bitch," I whisper. "At least let me tell them *why*." But I don't respond. I know he won't care. There's no bargaining here. No mercy.

I call Kez. I'm doing it to say a kind of goodbye, to ask her to look after my family, but the second she picks up the call, I know something is wrong. Very wrong. I've never heard her sound like this. "Kez? What is it?"

"He's dead," Kez says. "Prester's dead. He tried to call me and I was asleep, my phone ran down—" Her voice is shaking. "I got video, they just—they just *let him die*, Gwen. Right there in his car. It's Sheryl and the man in the SUV. I know it is. And I'm fucking going to *get them*."

My lips feel numb. *I* feel numb. I know how much Kezia thought of Detective Prester. This has to be a living nightmare for her. "Don't," I say. I swallow hard. "He doesn't want you, Kez. He wants me. I'm the reason this is happening. Not you. He thinks . . . he thinks I'm like Sheryl. A killer."

"Sheryl's with him," she says. "He didn't hunt her. He's using her."

"For now," I agree. "But whatever story he spun for her, he intends to exact some kind of vengeance. On me too. I can't let him take the people I love, Kez. So I'm going. You stay."

"Motherfucker sent me a video of Prester while he was dying in that car. Sheryl took it. It was her voice on the recording, had to be. So whether they killed him or not, they *let him die*. And I'm not staying. They are *going*. And I don't mean out of town, out of mind. We find them, and we end this."

I feel the numbness subside. What's left is a pure, cold anger. "He told me to leave my house at nine o'clock." It's ten minutes to nine. I stare at my clock until my eyes hurt enough to force me to blink. "Not to tell anybody. That must include you too."

"Hell, he already knows I'll be coming. If he knows me at all—"

"You've got a baby to protect, Kez."

"And you've got kids. You need somebody. I'm going, and he's going to pay. But we need to make sure the boys don't follow."

"How?" I know Javier. I know Sam. They're not going to let us go without a fight. Not just the two of us, alone.

"Up to you how you do Sam," she says. "I can take care of Javi."

She's right. He wants me. Everyone else is just . . . collateral damage.

I just sit. Silent. Thinking about what I'm about to do, and why. About how hard it's going to be. About why it's also going to be the easiest thing I've ever done, in a strange sort of way; I've always known that I needed to protect my kids from whatever threats came at them. I've done it over and over again until it's a well-worn groove in my soul. But they're growing up.

This may be the last thing they need from me. The last protection I can offer them. They may never understand that, and I can't leave a record of why I'm doing it . . . but I have to believe that they'll know. They'll understand.

Sam . . . Sam will take it so hard that, in the end, I left him behind. I wish he could know I'm doing that only because of all the people in the world, I trust him—*only* him—to shelter, love, and protect those precious children we both love so much.

But I can't leave him *not knowing*. I can't. So I turn on the video on my phone, and I take a deep breath, and I tell him. I tell him how much I love him, how much I value him, how much I trust him. I tell him to protect our kids. I tell him that I will come back if I can, and if I don't, if I fail this time, that I did it for all of us.

I don't tell him where I'm going because I just don't know.

I save the video, lock the phone, and leave it on the coffee table.

Then I leave the house. I shut off the built-in GPS. I back out of the garage onto the street and pause there, making sure the garage closes, making sure the house is safe and warm and protected to the best of my ability. I idle in the street, waiting.

It's nine o'clock in the morning on Thursday. I don't know how he's going to contact me until I hear a musical tone. It's coming from the glove compartment, and a million thoughts run through my mind. *He got in, he could have left a bomb, he could have been inside our house.* I swallow my rage and fear and open the glove compartment. There's a small phone inside, screen glowing. I answer it.

"Hello, Gina," the voice on the other end says. "I've sent you a map of where to go. I'll expect you tomorrow. Then we can get started."

It's that short, that calm, and then he ends the call. The number's blocked, no way to call it back. I check, and there's a text message with a link. It leads to a map. To the coast of North Carolina.

He didn't tell me to go straight there. Just that I have to get there by tomorrow.

I go to Kez.

◆ ◆ ◆

I drive to Javier's cabin. It's a long way, and by the time I park outside his gate, next to his rental, I'm not calm but at least I'm not screaming. I see Boot lying on the front steps; he gets up, panting, watching me. Boot knows me; he knows I'm a friend. But I also know that he's not my dog, and he can sense the change in me.

He barks, and Javier opens the front door. He's got his phone in his hand, and he looks exhausted and worried, and he stares at me like I'm a ghost he's conjured up, then blinks and says, "Come on inside."

Boot recognizes that I'm allowed, and sits politely as I open the gate and walk up the path. I pat his warm head but get only an appraising look, no friendly lick, and he's already stretched out again on guard duty when the door closes behind me.

Javier puts his phone down. "You didn't say you were coming."

"I need to talk to Kez."

"She's—"

"Not resting," I say. "Not if I know Kez."

He accepts that without comment, except to ask, "Want some coffee?"

"Sure," I say. Coffee is the last thing I need, but if he offered moonshine, I'd probably drink a jug right now. The old Gwen, the sensible one, is conspicuously absent. He fetches a mug and hands it to me.

He's got his own morning potion, and we sit together and drink for a moment before he says, "She's okay. The baby's okay. Thank God."

I hate this. I hate that I'm about to put all that at risk, but I know Kezia Claremont. I know she won't back off, and at least if she's with me in this terrible, dangerous course, I can try to protect her. But I can't tell him. That's clear. "I'm so glad, Javi," I say. "I'm so glad you're here too. They're not expecting you back?"

"Nah. I can make it up." He gives me a long look. "You heard about Prester?"

"Kez told me," I say. It's hard to swallow the next mouthful of coffee. "I'm so sorry. He was a good man."

"He was," Javi agrees, and it sounds hollowed out with real grief. "His wife passed. They didn't have any kids. I've been helping Kez get in touch with some of his nieces and nephews. Pretty grim. She *told* him to see the doctor. But he just . . . wouldn't. It's really hurting her."

I just nod. I don't know what to say. I can't lie to Javier, I *can't*. I finally put my mug down and say, "I'll go talk to her."

He seems relieved, and I hate the guilt that digs its claws into my guts.

I knock on the master bedroom door; I know this cabin like my own home, I've been in and out of it a hundred times over the past few years. Kez calls out to come in.

She's sitting cross-legged on the bed, propped against pillows. Her laptop is open. She glances up at me, and I'm struck by the bruises, the bandages still in place on her head. "I'm fine," she says, probably because of the look on my face. "Did he contact you?"

"Yes," I say. "He sent me a map. I'm supposed to be there tomorrow." I take the burner phone out and show it to her, and she studies it intently. "Kez. Please stay here. I'm begging you, *please*."

"Can't," she says. It sounds utterly certain. "And don't tell me about why it's smarter. I *know* I can't stay here. For one thing, he's afraid of me. He came after me, Gwen. And whether he killed Prester or not—or had him killed—he used Prester's death to beat me with, again. He wants me *here*. So here is where I can't stay."

"What about Javier? Are you going to tell him?"

"I'm sending him on an errand," Kez says. "We'll be gone when he gets back." She looks absolutely sure about this. And she nails me with a look that sears me like a laser. "Don't you even *think* about leaving me behind. You just showed me the map. You think I can't remember it? You think I won't follow you? It'd be a whole lot easier if you'd just accept that *I'm* going to use *you* to get to him, Gwen. Because he's going to be after you."

"I'm your bait," I say. She nods. Oddly, that feels . . . better. Cleaner. "Then you should come separately."

"No point in that," Kez says, and closes her laptop. She puts it away. "He'll be tracking that phone you have. He'll know you came here, and he'll know by now that I can't let this go. He can't afford me as a loose end. If I stay here, he'll clean up after himself, just like he did that couple up on the road who had video of his car. This bastard's been doing this a long time, that's my guess. He knows how to dead-end a trail."

It was Sam's guess too. MalusNavis, a shark gliding under the surface, coming up only to take his prey. Sheryl was his prey. Now I am. Only I won't vanish without a trace. I'll leave a hell of a mess.

Maybe he's getting sloppy at last.

"We should go if we're going," I say. "Last chance, Kez. Stay."

She just shakes her head, says, "Let me take care of this first."

I stand in that room as she walks out and tells Javier that she's got a bad headache, and the doctor's called in a prescription for her at the pharmacy in Norton; she sounds normal, calm, exactly as I'd expect. She tells him I'm going to stay with her, just in case. I hear them kiss. I hear her tell him she loves him.

And Javier grabs his keys and leaves. I left my husband and kids while they were sleeping, and that was incredibly hard. But at least I didn't have to lie to the ones I love.

When I hear the front door close, I step out. Kez is standing silently, staring at the door, and the expression on her face is so wounded. So raw. Fragile and strong and fierce all at once.

She drags in a breath, and it looks like it hurts. "We need to get moving," she says, and heads for the gun case. She takes out two shotguns and hands them to me, grabs a duffel bag, and fills it with shells. I watch in silence as she packs what we'll need—food, water, more weapons.

"Kez—" I finally say.

She doesn't pause as she puts two hunting knives in the bag. "Let's go kill this son of a bitch before anybody else has to die."

21

SAM

When I wake up that morning at nearly ten, everything feels normal. Peaceful. The house is quiet, and I'm a little hungover from the sleep medication. Gwen's side of the bed is empty, but that isn't unusual.

I yawn, head for the shower, get myself ready for the day.

The first hint I have that something isn't right is that the coffeepot isn't full. Gwen is a creature of habit; she always puts on coffee, but the machine is cold, the pot is empty. I stare at that for a few seconds, then start it up and head straight for the office.

I fully expect to find her there sitting behind her desk, immersed in work.

The office is dark and empty. I turn on the lights, and I go around to look at her laptop. It's closed, and when I put a hand on it, it's ice cold. She hasn't been working here.

I find the phone lying on the living room coffee table on my way to the garage. It's just sitting there, exactly in the middle, as if she wanted me to notice.

That's when I start being afraid. Really afraid.

I know her passcode, and I enter it. I get it wrong twice, force myself to calm the fuck down and do it right one last time.

She's left it open to a video file. I don't want to play it. I don't.

But I press the screen, and Gwen's face fills it. "Sam," she says. "I know you're worried right now. I know you're wondering where I am and what I'm doing, and I wish to God I could tell you. But I'm doing this for you, and for the kids. I have to. It's MalusNavis, the one from the boards. He's going to keep coming after our kids if I don't do this, and . . . Sam, I can't let that happen. He hurt Kez already. I can't let him get to you, or Lanny, or Connor."

I pause it, because I can't get my breath against the fury that's igniting in me. *Don't you dare, Gwen. Don't you goddamn dare.* I'm shaking all over, and I know the anger's just a cover for what I'm *really* feeling.

Fear.

I listen to the rest.

"I love you so much, Sam. You—you've made me whole, after all this time. You've made me realize that I don't have to be afraid, because you're here. Because you care. That's your gift, and I value it so much. I know you want to do this with me, but Sam, please understand . . . there is no one I trust more than you to protect our children. I need you to do that for me. I'm asking you, I'm begging you . . . please keep them safe. For me." She smiles. There are tears in her eyes, and my anger's gone now, drowned in those tears. All I have left is fear. "I'll come back if I can. I love you always."

She glances at something, and I realize she sat just here in the same spot as she made this video. She was looking at the clock. I check the date and time stamp.

She made it just before nine this morning. She did it while I was asleep, while the kids were asleep. *This was a plan.* I remember her suggesting the sleep medication last night. She was going to take it herself. Clearly, she didn't.

She wanted me out of the way because she knew I'd damn well stop her.

I go through the rest of her phone with trembling fingers. I see the texts sent from an unknown number, and it's like being plunged into a lake in winter; no wonder she looked so strained last night. So closed in. The pictures of us are threats, implicit but very real.

I go through her emails. Nothing there. I open her photos. Pictures of the kids, of me, of us.

And then, suddenly, a picture of a driver's license, and the face hits me like a punch. *It's Tyler.* But the name on the license says *Leonard Bay*, and he lives on Beacon Street, here in Knoxville. It takes me a second to recall that Gwen said she ran into and chased down a homeless guy who'd mailed Melvin's letter to her. And had a letter from MalusNavis as well. My stomach clenches even before I put it together.

Leonard Bay is just a false identity. And suddenly I know it's all connected. Tyler played that part so well I never even thought to put it together with the sad, self-destructive young man I talked off the bridge. The kid who'd needed my help when he was drowning in despair.

A *malus navis* is Latin for a navigational beacon. *Beacon Street.* Dr. Dave said that he thought MalusNavis lived on the coast. A navigational beacon on the coast.

A lighthouse.

My mouth's gone so dry that my throat clicks when I swallow. My muscles ache from how hard I'm clutching the phone. I type in *pharos.*

Pharos is Greek for lighthouse.

Tyler Pharos. Leonard Bay. MalusNavis. They're all the same person.

I have fucking been played, and so has Gwen.

The hell of it is, as enraged as I am, I somehow can't direct it against the young man standing on that bridge, pressed against the railing. I'd sensed something real there. Something very dark and terrible.

Maybe the person I ought to be angry at is me. I should have put this together. *Would* have, if I hadn't been focused on projecting my feelings onto the blank slate of Tyler's loss . . . if he even has a dead sister at all. That, too, could have been a lie.

My first impulse is to leap into my truck and tear on out of here, find Gwen, and drag her home where she'll be safe . . . but then I realize that I can't. She trusted me to watch over our children, and with the threats in those photos, I can't leave them alone. I can't.

So I call Javier instead. I'm going to ask him if Gwen is there, but he beats me to the punch. He says, "Please fucking tell me that they're with you."

They.

Gwen, and Kez. I feel my heart sink. "They're not there?"

"Kez left me a goddamn *note*. She says she and Gwen have to go finish this."

"Call the station. Tell them that she's missing and in danger."

He laughs bitterly. "She is going to be *so pissed*."

"Do you care?"

"Not if it saves her life. What is she *thinking*? Did Gwen talk her into this? I never should've left her alone so soon after Prester . . ."

"What happened to Prester?"

"He's dead." There's a long pause on the other end. "Shit. I should have known she wouldn't let it go. Not even with the baby."

Kezia Claremont is not the kind of person who can live with letting other people die, and drop it. She was never going to drop this case, but now, with her partner dead, and the fact this asshole already tried to hurt her, put her unborn child in danger—no power on Earth could have forced her to sit back and relax. Just like nothing could keep Gwen from putting herself between her kids and the danger coming for them.

"Call the station," I tell him.

"We have to go after them."

"Did Kez take her phone?" He doesn't answer. "She left it behind, right? We've got no way to find them, Javi. Putting out an APB is the best we can do. If we can stop them before they're too far out . . ."

"Yeah," he says. "I'll do it."

He hangs up. I think about it for a second, and then I text Dr. Dave. He lives in a lighthouse, I say. Or uses one for what he does. Where is it? Give me the state, at least.

I don't get a response for about ten minutes. I don't know whether he had a patient or he just likes to keep me waiting, but I've already checked the gun safes, and found that at least Gwen's gone armed, wherever she's headed. That eases a little bit of my dread. A grain of sand on a beach of trouble.

Dr. Dave doesn't text. He calls. "Sam," he says. "Delighted to hear from you. How are you? Not arrested, I see."

"Fuck you," I say. Feels good. "What state does MalusNavis call home? It's somewhere with a lighthouse."

"I genuinely do not know," he says. "You finally looked it up, didn't you? Navigational beacon. Hence, lighthouse. Hence, coastline. Very good. You can't say he didn't give you every chance."

"You worked with him," I say tightly. "You son of a bitch, you *helped* him."

"Well, I gave him the wanted-poster template. And he needed help from a capable friend to make that Loserville forum post. You know the one."

He's saying, without admitting, that he either made the post on the message board implicating Connor, or he had it done. I want to wrap my hands around his throat and squeeze until the smugness pops out. But I manage to keep my voice even as I say, "Anything else?"

"I gave him the letter from Melvin Royal. I thought it might be helpful."

"How did you get it?"

"Friend of a friend. One of Melvin's little helpers died—natural causes. The friend found it among his personal effects. A police friend, I might add. I didn't steal anything."

Dr. Dave, covering his tracks. But he gave that letter to MalusNavis *knowing* it would be used against Gwen. Knowing it would make her unsteady, vulnerable, paranoid.

I don't answer. My mind is churning, and so is my stomach. It's not like Dave to talk to me on the phone. He's being careful, but still.

It occurs to me he's talking to me because he's enjoying hearing me flail for answers. He's not listening to my words. He's drinking in my pain.

"Sam?" I can hear the pleasure in his voice. "Still there?" He loves the taste of this. And I know I should hang up. But I can't. Not yet.

"Where is he? Just tell me, Dave."

"In return for what?"

"Money."

"I don't need your pathetic little attempt at payoff. I make *far* more than you do. No, I need something else. Something better."

"Like what?" The taste of death in my mouth. The knowledge that I'm making a deal with the fucking devil.

"You provide the documentation you have on me. We'll be even then. And I'll let it go."

Once I have no hold on Dr. Dave, I have no idea what he'll do. What he's capable of doing. But I don't have a choice. "I give you my word."

"Oh, your word isn't good enough—why would you think it would be? I need you to bring it to me, Sam. In person. And I need to destroy it myself. Do I need to explain the consequences if you keep copies?"

He doesn't, because I'm sure he'll come after the kids. Connor, in particular. He knew exactly how to hit the kid where it hurt, and he'll take great pleasure in doing it again, over and over and over, and seeing my son, *my* son, crumble.

Gwen and I are alike in this: neither one of us will let that happen. So I say, "Tell me where and when, and I'll bring it to you. All of it. But you tell me right now where he is."

"You can't save her." Dave suddenly sounds very serious. Very calm. "You don't know who you're dealing with. She's dangerous, I give her that. But he will rip her to pieces. When I tell you I know that, believe me."

It's incredibly chilling, hearing that. But I can't believe it. I *can't*. "Just tell me."

There's a long pause. I want to shake the answer out of the phone. Then Dave says, "Virginia." He hangs up. I let out a long breath and lower the phone. I stare at it, then I look at maps of the Virginia coastline. There are a lot of possibilities. Nine, at least, and that doesn't count abandoned, nonfunctional lighthouses. If I'm even right about that much.

To make things worse . . . I'm almost sure he's just lied to me. Dave doesn't want me to stop this. Not at all. He wants me pinned and helpless and suffering. Dave always lies. I should have expected that.

But he'll still require me to carry through with the bargain. He did, after all, give me an answer. He'll just claim he was wrong.

I have nothing. Nothing but grief and rage and the very real fear that Gwen and Kez have vanished into the dark. Together, at least. But very, very alone.

I watch Gwen's message again. And again.

But in the end, there's nothing I can do now but wait.

I think that might kill me. I need to think of something. *Anything.*

I hear one of the bedroom doors open. It's Lanny, coming out in her pajamas, yawning and shuffling and squinting against the morning. "Hey, Dad," she says. "Is breakfast ready?"

I didn't think about this moment. About what I was going to say to her, or to Connor. But I don't have any choice.

I say, "Sit down, Lanny. I need to tell you about your mom."

I know full well it's going to be a hellish day, but truth is all I can offer them now.

Truth, and love, and trust.

That's what Gwen gave me.

22

GWEN

The impulse to check on the kids, check on Sam—it's so strong and painful that holding it back is like touching a live wire. But Kez is right: we can't take the risk. This man is a killer, we've seen that. And Sam *can't* be part of this now, not if my kids are going to be safe and have at least one of us left to love and guide and protect them. But I don't intend on dying, and neither does Kez.

We're hunters.

Kez, of course, has thought ahead; she knows that Javier will do something to find us, and probably something like file a missing persons report. So she pulls off the highway an hour into our trip and takes a detour to an area I don't know. It's dark, rural, completely anonymous. There, in a beat-up, half-destroyed barn, we meet a tall, thin African American man in a Che Guevara T-shirt who trades my SUV for a small, hard-used Honda. "Can't stay in your car," she tells me. "They'll put out a BOLO for the plate number. We need something completely different if we're going to pull this off."

No words are exchanged between her and the man in the Che shirt; they just exchange nods, and she hands him an envelope that I can only assume holds cash. I don't know how she knows him, and I don't ask either. Doesn't seem like the time.

The Honda runs smoothly but rides rough, and the mileage on it looks high enough for it to have been to the moon and back, but it holds up through the night as we drive the still-busy highways, pulling over to grab sleep when we can.

"We need to talk about what we're going to do," I say, and she nods silently. "We can't play his game, not completely. Just enough to make him think he's got us. Maybe that will throw him off."

"We play for now, or ours will get hurt," she says. "Gwen. He thinks you're guilty of something."

"Apparently."

I sense rather than see her glance. "Helping Melvin kill those women?" I don't answer that. The road noise grinds up the silence, and she finally says, "He seems to have a type."

"I'm not like Sheryl."

"You *are* somebody people think is a killer. He's wrong, we both know that. But it makes sense in whatever passes for his mind."

"I want to stop and buy a pay-as-you-go phone. We can't use this one. I need to check on Sam and the kids."

"No."

"I need it."

"You know he'll be watching us."

"We're not trackable right now unless he's the freaking NSA."

"And maybe he *is* the freaking NSA, you thought of that? Hell, I don't know what those people get up to in their spare time, and neither do you! You underestimate him, we lose."

I want to argue, but she's not wrong enough for me to be right. It feels like we've launched into space, in this tight little can of a car, driving through the dark. Far from home and shelter and safety.

"You're worried about the kids," she says, and her tone is gentler this time. "I know. But Sam is there, and he's not going to leave them. You know that."

"I know," I say. "But I'm their *mom*."

"And you're doing the best thing you can. You're taking the danger away." Kezia reaches over and tries the radio. It's tinny and full of static, but she finds a country station, and we silently let it play for a while.

I'm not sure when I fall asleep, but when I wake up, we're in a different climate—warmer, more humid. The land's flatter. And the sun's coming up on our left. "Morning," she says, and yawns. Stretches without letting go of the wheel. "I'm pulling off at the next truck stop for gas and coffee and bathroom. Want to take the wheel after?"

"I'll drive," I say. "Where are we?"

"North Carolina, just passed the border. Got another few hours to where we're going," she says.

I check the map on the phone, and we're on target. The marked spot is called Salah Point, and it's barely a dot on the map. *Screw it,* I think. He gave me a phone that has internet access, so I'll use it. I search the area around Salah Point and come up with a little history. The area isn't much . . . rural, depressed, same as a lot of the South, only with more humidity. Fishing failed in the mid-1990s for good. The main industry is—was—a cannery that's been shut ever since, and a couple of glassmaking and pottery factories that are barely hanging on. Like most little downtowns, the snapshots the search function turns up feature antique stores heavy on southern nostalgia, light on actual valuables. A Sonic Drive-In and a Dairy Queen. A regional Wal-Mart. The usual.

The last page has a shot of a lonely-looking lighthouse sitting on the horseshoe-shaped bay, and a brief, dry history about it. Apparently it's a historic site, and also a private residence. The harbor it once guarded—though there's no evidence the beacon still works—is called Cully Bay, but the article notes it has another nickname, for the legend of ship wreckers who used to turn off the lighthouse beacon and let ships founder on the rocks to loot lost cargo.

Heartbreak Bay.

"Why does he want us there?" I ask her. She shrugs. "It can't be his home turf. He's not that stupid."

The burner phone he gave us has a small, eye-straining screen, but I make do. I search for anything with Salah Point, any notable events. I strike gold, and my intake of breath makes Kez give me a quick, concerned look. "What?"

I take a swig of water to moisten my suddenly dry mouth. "The top search result for the place is about an abduction and murder," I say. "About ten years ago. An eleven-year-old girl named Clara Watson was abducted, and her older brother, Jonathan, was badly hurt, almost killed. He suffered severe injuries. Her body was found months after out in the salt marsh."

"Jesus," she whispers. "Did they find him?"

"The killer?" I scroll through entries, then click a link and read results. "Not according to the last update. The brother struggled with the abductor, who hit him with some kind of pipe. All the kid could remember after he woke up was that the man drove a van. Case unsolved."

"That has to mean something," she says. "Is the brother still alive?"

"I think so. The parents aren't. Mother died a year after the girl, and the father committed suicide a year after that. The boy was about seventeen when this happened. There's a mention that he recovered. Nothing else."

But I'm wrong, I realize. Putting in Jonathan Watson plus Salah Point gives me a later article. A profile piece. The mention of his sister's murder is one line, described as a "tragedy." The family owned a large cannery on Heartbreak Bay that shut down in the late 1990s. Losing a child and having another one seriously injured wasn't enough for this family; death and suicide weren't enough. They also lost everything in the fishing industry crash that took down a lot of businesses in this area.

The article, though, uses that as a setup for a miracle, because Jonathan Bruce Watson bought a lottery ticket in 2015, on the anniversary of his sister's death.

"What?" Kez asks. I realize I've been silent too long. "What's that look?"

"He won the Powerball multistate lottery," I say. "He lost everything, Kez, and then he won the goddamn lottery. Seven hundred fifty million dollars." I feel the hair raise on the back of my neck. *What someone could do with that kind of money, if they were single-minded . . .* I can't imagine what Melvin would have done with it.

No, I actually can. He'd have become another Israel Keyes, burying murder kits in strategic locations all over the country, killing at his pleasure and disappearing without a trace. Israel Keyes called them *vacations.* It's impossible to know the ghastly toll he really took; he traveled constantly, and admitted to only a few of the apparently unrelated deaths. A serial killer with massive funds, free time, focus . . . could do *anything.*

And then I blow up the photo that goes with the story as large as the small screen will handle. It's not great. A man of medium height accepting an oversize check, looking not delighted but oddly unemotional. A baseball cap on his head.

I feel the knowledge go through me like a sudden, heart-stopping lightning strike.

Leonard Bay. That's a photo of the man I tackled running from the mailing store. Bay, as in Heartbreak Bay.

The injury that flattened the side of his head.

I frantically google one more thing. *Malus Navis.*

A navigational beacon.

Leonard Bay had an address on Beacon Street, according to his license. Which had looked real enough, but $750 million will buy quality fakes.

Kez is asking me questions, but I'm not listening. I do another search, and I find another article about the abduction of little Clara Watson.

Jonathan Bruce Watson suffered *severe head injuries*. I remember the shocking sight of Len's head as his hat rolled away. It isn't visible in the Powerball photo, but there's no mistake. Len is Jonathan Bruce Watson. Jonathan Bruce Watson is MalusNavis.

I had him. *I had him.* And I let him go. I hear a high, thin buzzing in my ears, and that dreadful weight on me again. Panic attack incoming.

No. I refuse. No.

I close my eyes, lean my head back, and breathe through it, ride the twisting waves of panic and sickness until the flood subsides, and when I finally am able to look again, the car is stopped. Kezia is staring at me. We're in the breakdown lane of the freeway, cars and trucks whizzing past without a thought for the way the world has just changed.

I tell her the truth. All of it. MalusNavis's targeted attacks on me. Jonathan Watson's flattened skull. His unlimited resources to fuck with our lives.

She takes it in silently. I can read her expression by the dashboard lights. Then she says, "If he hadn't wanted you to find out, he wouldn't have given you a smartphone. He wants us to come prepared. Know what we're getting into."

I look up the number for the FBI and start to dial it. Kez takes the phone away.

"If you're thinking about calling in the cavalry, I already thought of that," she says. "Gwen . . . we don't *have* anything. Prester died of a goddamn heart attack. Everything else we have can't be traced to Jonathan

Watson, not fast and not directly. We've got threats, sure. But every one of them is vague. He's made sure of it."

"We've got video of him at the gas station," I say.

"Pumping gas. It's not a smoking gun, even if he's with Sheryl. He could claim she was a hitchhiker and he let her off ten miles down the road, and there's no way to prove otherwise unless Sheryl's alive to tell her side of the story."

I feel sick now. "You don't think she is?"

"This man's got a purpose," she says. "He saw his sister get taken. He *failed her*. You said Sam looked into other cases MalusNavis was into. What do those have in common with Sheryl?"

I don't like where she's going, but it feels right. "They were all suspected of murder at some point. At least on the Lost Angels boards."

"Like I said, he's got a type."

"Like me," I say. "Melvin's little helper."

She reaches over and takes my hand. "Not like you," she says. "Not at all. We need to make a decision, now that we know this. Forward, or back? Your choice, Gwen. But this is higher stakes than we bargained for. If you want to call in the feds, the state police . . . we can do that. I just . . . I feel like he's walled himself off for anything like fast action. He'll have time to deal with us. Hurt us. And if he's still got lottery money left, he can disappear without a trace, fast."

"Nothing's really changed," I say. "The stakes are exactly the same. If I don't go to him, he comes for my family. The only difference is that now we know he can actually destroy them without breaking a sweat." I have to swallow bile to do it, but I say, "Forward. He says he wants to judge me. Let him do that."

"I saw the photo," she says. "His head. That man's got brain damage. You can't put your life in his hands, expecting him to be fair."

My life is already in his hands, in all the ways that matter. I just shake my head. "I don't trust him," I say. "But I trust *us*. If we've got to fight on enemy ground, what do we need?"

"A goddamn army."

"Knowledge," I say. I hold up the phone. "And he's given us the keys to the library."

Kez glances at the clock in the dash. "If we're going, we need to make time," she says. "Miles to cover. A lot of them. And Gwen? If he's as smart as you think he is, he's cloned that phone. He's watching everything you do. And tracking calls. If you do call anyone—TBI, FBI, *anyone*—he could know. And he could be a ghost before we get anybody to move on him for real."

"So it's just us, or nothing."

"I think so," she says. "Until we have proof. Unless you want to bet the lives of your kids that he won't follow through on his threats."

I don't answer that. I just get to work.

◆　◆　◆

When I'm done, I've filled pieces of notepaper with details. A paper version of the online map, just in case. A rough sketch of the map of Salah Point, including the bay.

I find more about the Watson family. The cannery's abandoned and locked up, rusting away. The Watson house looks to be located nearby, and both sit on the bay—Cully Bay, according to the map.

The lighthouse still stands, but it's a grim-looking place, regardless.

I buy a new burner phone from the racks and activate it before getting back on the road. We're going to need something that Jonathan Watson can't control. Some way of summoning help if we need it.

I hope it'll be enough.

I don't ask Kez. I just bury the phone Jonathan gave us in the industrial dumpster on the side of the gas station. He'll know we're headed that way. And I don't intend to give him any more advantage than that.

The drive to Salah Point is relentless after the efficient transport of the freeway. The only signs tell me I'm on the right state road, but if you judged by condition, it's long disused. The trees are thick for a while, gloomy, and once they give way to low, swampy growth, it looks even gloomier. Gators sun themselves in muddy ponds, and I watch out for any crossing the road.

It feels like we're going nowhere, and then there's a turnoff and a weathered, shotgun-pocked sign announcing SALAH POINT. I take the turn down a road that isn't better than the state road, and is arguably worse. The landscape looks wild and dangerous. It's probably a wildlife preserve area, or else developers just took one look and decided that swampy wetlands without a single industry to support it wouldn't work out. The animals won. For once.

We're here.

You need to get ahead of him, Gwen. You're prepared. You have weapons and knowledge of the area now. Think like the hunter you are. If you play defense, you will lose. I expect the whisper in my head to be Melvin; it's *always* Melvin. But that voice just called me Gwen.

The voice in my head, the warm and quiet and loving voice . . . that's Sam. My eyes fill with tears . . . not pain this time. Gratitude that it's Sam who's with me now.

Gratitude that Melvin's gone quiet at last.

Kez wakes up as I slow down. She hasn't slept long, or well, but when she swipes at her eyes and says, "Are we close?" she sounds fully alert. And tense.

"A couple of miles until we get to town."

"Damn. Should have ditched the phone once we got everything we could."

"I did," I tell her. "Gas station about a hundred and fifty miles back. But there's only one way into town. And he'll have eyes on it."

The little town comes up on us suddenly, like a stalker from the shadows. We round a curve on the bumpy, crumbling road, and suddenly there are buildings. Not many of them, though—maybe a dozen clustered around the main road. Two or three intersections with no lights, just rusted stop signs. The first block we cruise through, driving slowly, is deserted; there's an old gas station, long since shuttered, the islands where pumps once stood completely bare. A useless **FOR RENT** sign hangs crookedly in the window. A couple of anonymous square stone buildings look like they could date back to American-style antiquity—1800s, at least. Empty shells, no windows or doors. Waiting to fall.

And then, suddenly, there's a shockingly bright red building, neon, drive-in slots. The Sonic serving tater tots, burgers, shakes . . . but it's deserted too. Closed. I check my watch; it's coming up on nine in the morning, so I suppose they'll open up soon.

The next block has an open diner that looks as if it's been there for generations, and it's—for Salah Point, at least—doing good business, with three tables filled that I can see, and a couple of old pickups parked outside on the street. The antique shop that I saw in website pictures is empty, though the painted name survives on the window with a **PERMANENTLY CLOSED** sign on it.

There's something else, I realize—a fluorescent orange poster taped to the door of that empty store, and there's something printed on it in huge, heavy block letters.

WELCOME GINA

I hit the brakes hard enough to jerk us both, and Kez casts me a look before she spots the sign. "Shit," she says. "Gwen . . . there's something else on it. I think it's an envelope."

I back up and park the Honda at the curb. There's not a soul on these streets. The only life is across the street at the diner, and I don't look that way. I feel very exposed. It would be so easy to hit us right here. Rifle shots from a low rooftop, and our brains are on the walls. I have a powerful urge to jam the car in reverse, pull a U-turn, and get the hell *out*. Because whatever is waiting for us here . . . it's going to be hard.

I take a deep breath and get out of the car.

The rank smell of the place hits me hard. There's something rotten here, sulfurous; maybe it's the distant reek from the old cannery, blowing in from the sea. Humidity clings like wet wool on my skin. I hear Kez open her door, but I don't look back. I walk steadily across to the orange poster and the white envelope taped on there. I rip it off the sign and open it. Bold cursive writing. No mistakes.

It was your choice to come here. Everything that happens from this point on will be your decision, not mine.

You can leave if you want. Just get in your car and drive home. That's a choice too. But all choices will have consequences.

This is your first decision to make. I'll know when you've picked up this message. The clock is running, and you have ten minutes to get to me before I think you're not playing fair. There will be a cost if you delay.

Good luck.

He hasn't signed it, but he didn't need to. There's an underlying strangeness to it that is more of a signature than just a name. It gives me shivers. The writing on the paper is precise, but deeply indented. Written with conviction and force. He's been careful about the words he chose too; there's nothing overtly threatening, though the threat overall is there. He could just as easily play it off as a game, a prank. In a town this small, with a man this rich . . . I can't trust the local police. I'm not sure I can even trust the state police; there's absolutely nothing I can give them to really make them believe me. It's all puzzle pieces, and how you put them together.

The other page in the envelope is a printed map of Heartbreak Bay. All the way out on the far end of the horseshoe shore, the lighthouse. He's put a red X over it.

I hand the note to Kez, and the map. She looks at it in silence, and says, "We're not going there first, if that's where he wants us."

"I don't think it really matters where we go," I say. "I think Jonathan's had a lot of time to think about what we'll do, and he'll have planned for it."

Everything but what I'm about to do, because by this time he must believe that we're caught. Trapped in his spiderweb of a town. Out of good options.

I take the burner phone I bought out of my pocket and dial home.

"Gwen?" Sam answers so fast that it takes my breath away. The sound of his voice. The *reality* of him. I feel him here with me as I squeeze my eyes shut. "Oh Jesus, Gwen?"

"I'm here," I whisper, and then try again, louder. "Sam, I'm okay. Kez is with me. We're okay."

"Where are you? Javier is here. We can be on the road in half a minute."

"You can't," I tell him. "Sam, remember I asked you if you'd—you'd look after the kids? In case anything happened?"

"No." He does remember, he's just rejecting the question. "We're coming to get you out of whatever shit you're in. Listen to me: the man you caught, the homeless man—"

"I know. Leonard Bay is MalusNavis."

"He's—" He takes in a breath so deep it sounds painful. "He's also the kid who came to talk to me at the airfield, Gwen. He called himself Tyler Pharos. I should have put that together, should have told you . . . Pharos is a lighthouse. MalusNavis is a beacon. *Fuck.* I could have stopped this, I could have—"

"It's not your fault, Sam." I feel okay now. Centered. Calm in a way I haven't been on this long, hellish trip. "I screwed up too. Look, I need you to convince the FBI that Kez and I are tracking a killer that they ought to be after. Look at my computer. Put it together. Get them moving, Sam."

"Moving where?"

"Salah Point, North Carolina," I tell him. "The lighthouse on the bay. But we can't wait for them. And you and Javier need to *stay there*. If he decides to come after the kids—" I can't finish that sentence. "Please, Sam. Please do this for me."

He's silent for a long, long minute, and then he says, "I will get people to you, Gwen. If I need to lie, I will. But I will get them there. Damn the consequences." It's killing him not to be in this with me, I can feel that. It would kill me in just the same way.

"I love you," I whisper. It sounds shaky. I don't want to let go, but I know I need to. We're out of time. Jonathan/MalusNavis was very clear about that.

I open my eyes once I've ended the call. I look at the little, anonymous town, the nonexistent traffic, the lack of human faces on the street. It feels . . . empty. This whole town is a spiderweb, and we're caught already. It's a long, long road back to anything like civilization.

"Gwen," Kez says. "Why would he let us find out who he really is? What his real name is?"

I think about that. About the way MalusNavis has closed in on me. Shown his face. Given me *everything*, even if in indirect and slippery methods. And I think about what Sam just told me: that he talked this young man off a bridge. That might have been false, just another ploy.

But what if it wasn't? What if, finally, he's had enough?

This may be his endgame. Either way, it has to be mine.

"Kez," I say. "Look at the map."

"What am I looking for?"

"That shows the bay, the lighthouse, and a house, right?" She nods. I reach into the car and pull out the map I drew from the research I did on Jonathan's cell phone, before I dropped it. "What's missing?"

"The cannery," she says. "Maybe it was torn down."

"Or maybe it wasn't. Maybe he left it off because he wants us coming straight for the lighthouse."

She blows out a frustrated breath. "Jesus. Your mind, Gwen. You scare me sometimes."

"We need to go to the cannery," I say. "Let's not keep him waiting."

Kez grabs me by the arm as I pass her, heading for the driver's seat. "Or—and hear me out—we wait for Sam to get real boots on the ground here to back us up."

"He said ten minutes." I gently pull free. "Ten minutes until there are consequences. Whose pictures did he send you?"

She doesn't answer. She just stands there, fists clenched, and then nods.

We get in the Honda and drive.

23

GWEN

We see not a soul on the way out of town. Not a single person behind a window, not a car, nothing. The town feels artificial now, like a movie set.

The whole day feels wrong. Sweatily humid, but cool. The reek of rot gets worse as we drive with windows open, and the Honda's non-existent suspension bounces on every bump and crack. The sound of seagulls crying rings in the air like bells.

The smell is worse the closer we get to the beach. I wonder if a whale has beached in the area. It's that bad, a rancid, fishy smell that makes me want to gag. I breathe it deep instead in the hopes I'll get used to it. Humans are adaptable, that's our real strength. We can adapt to anything, given enough time and resources. Jonathan—clever, strange Jonathan—isn't going to give us that.

I park the Honda near the back fence of the cannery. Kez looks at me, and I look at her, and neither of us speaks. We finally just get out. Kez opens the trunk and hands me a shotgun; she keeps one for herself. We've each got our usual sidearms, but she gives me a hunting knife, and I snap it on my belt. She's got two police-issue body armor vests, and we put those on too. The weight feels smothering, but comforting too.

"Just so we're clear," she says, "this is the end of both our careers if we do this and it turns out we were wrong. And that could be exactly what he wants too."

"We're not wrong," I tell her. But she's also correct. It probably is the end of her career as a detective, regardless; she's out of her jurisdiction, armed to the teeth, ready to kill. And so am I. I've skated out of a lot of close calls. I'm due for a bad fall.

"Okay. Just wanted to be clear about it. Stay together. We don't split up."

"Agreed. Kez?"

She slams the trunk and gives me her attention.

"You don't have to do this. Please think about the baby."

She shakes her head. "I love you, too, Gwen, but fact is, the next person he comes after could be Javier, since I came this far. I don't want my baby growing up without a dad because I backed off. Besides . . . it might be you he really wants. But I want *him*. Prester deserves that much."

Choices. I'm not sure it's right, if any of this is right. But in one sense, Jonathan's correct: everything is a choice. And everything we do will have consequences.

"You got any bolt cutters?" I ask her, and she shakes her head. "Ladder in your pocket?"

"Shut up and pop that hubcap," she says. "Y'all don't know how to improvise."

I smile and use the knife to get the Honda's hubcap off. She catches it and goes to the fence, kneels down, and starts digging. The soil's soft and sandy, and she scoops out a big pile, then flips on her back and slithers under. "Good thing about body armor," she says. "It also keeps you flat for things like this."

Not that I need a ton of help in that department. Kez and I are otherwise of a size, so the hole she's dug works for me too, with some creative wriggling. I roll up to my hands and knees and take a step onto the bare ground. It's harder packed here, but it was used as some kind of outdoor lunch area; there are still a few rusting metal tables and some yellowed plastic molded chairs scattered around. I can't imagine it would have been too pleasant out here in the summer, but no doubt better than inside the cannery.

There's no door on this side, so we head around to the parking lot, which faces a loading dock with six roll-up doors. The pavement is buckled and cracked like dry mud; we watch our footing and head up the steps at the loading dock. Kez tries the metal back door. Locked. We work our way down the line of dock doors. One moves, but not much. Maybe six inches up before it sticks fast. It's a gap, but it's tight. I don't ask, I just go first, and push myself underneath. My belt catches, and for a second I panic, thinking that the door's coming down, that it's automatic and going to crush me, cut me in half . . . but then I suck in my breath and fumble at my belt buckle and am able to fit through. I roll to my knees, shotgun heavy in my hands, and scan the area.

It's empty. An empty warehouse that once would have held pallets of canned food shipping out to the area, if not the country. Very still, concrete the shade of mist and ghosts. It's been cleaned out completely. I don't even see spiderwebs or broken windows. There *are* windows, up high toward the ceiling, which is a blessing because it's otherwise dark. I have a flashlight, but I'd rather save it.

My heart's pounding. My head's throbbing. The reek of dead fish is stronger in here, an almost tangible odor, like it's radiating from the bare concrete. How did people stand it, day after day? They must have never been able to wash the stench out of their hair, their skin, their clothes.

Kez slips under the door and joins me in silent appraisal for a second. "Well," she says. "This might have been useless."

"This room is," I say. "But let's take a deeper look."

She coughs into her elbow. "Should have brought Vicks. This is as rank as any crime scene I've ever been to."

She's right, but we push on. We cross the bare concrete to the far-left wall, where a broad double door stands, big enough to admit forklifts. It's closed. I try it, and the knob turns easily in my hand. When the door swings open, it doesn't make a sound. I'm ready. Ready to fire on him if he's standing there. I will not hesitate.

I'm so focused on that, it doesn't occur to me to wonder why the door moves so smoothly. And then I'm blinded by a white-hot glare of light and a wall of sound so chaotic, so loud that it stuns me like a physical blow. The noise is crippling, astonishing; it drives me to my knees. I've dropped the shotgun and clapped my hands to my ears and I don't care, *anything* to stop the noise, though even that doesn't stop it, only muffles it the slightest bit. I can't see either. Blinding strobes in my eyes. By that time, I realize I've triggered a trap and drop flat, which I should've done in the first place, and try to roll away. The farther I get from the doorway, the better I feel, but I can't *see*. My ears are bells ringing with incoherent noise. Kez. Where's Kez?

Someone's pulling me away from the chaos, hands under my arms. Taking me farther from the torture. *Thank you. Thank you, Kez.* I try to say it, but I don't know if I'm actually speaking, shouting, screaming. My ears don't work yet.

I can't see anything. Just blindingly white ghosts of strobes that persist and twist and move.

The noise gets fainter. The strobes get less blinding. I feel myself being pulled into a dark, quiet area, and I suddenly need to throw up. I roll on my side and do that, horrified and ashamed and wildly out of control, and I can hear myself sobbing and gagging now, but as soft and distant as a memory.

"Kez," I whisper. Or think I do. "Kez—"

A shadow moves in front of my blurred vision and leans close. I try to focus.

It's not Kez.

It's him.

Empty, bland face, expressionless eyes. One side of his head is crushed in, but healed over. It's been years since the day his sister was taken. Years for him to learn how to pretend to be normal, or some approximation of it.

The fumbling uncertainty of Leonard Bay is gone as he searches me, finding and collecting my weapons. I feel a tug at my pants legs, and then he flips me onto my face. Zip ties tug my hands together behind me. Fast, efficient, merciless. I can't get to the ankle gun, if it's even still there.

"It's for your own protection." I hear the words indistinctly, like they're coming from the surface and I'm far, far underwater. "Trust me."

He flips me over again. I'm trying to get control, but I just manage an uncoordinated flail with my legs before he has the collar of my jacket and is pulling me relentlessly onward. I can't see anything but what we pass, and that's just shapes and shadows that resolve into concrete columns, padded iron supports. The acoustics of the room shift, or my ears do, and I realize that we're passing a silent, still sculpture of a processing line. The smell is horrific here. A physical presence forcing itself down my throat.

But everything is so *clean*.

"I knew you'd choose this," he says. His voice is faint under the constant ringing. "Clever people always do this to themselves. You just can't help it."

"Kez," I say. "Where's Kez?" I try to fishtail, slow him down. It doesn't work. He's strong, and when I manage to hook a foot onto a passing support, it just slides free at his next tug. "What did you do to Kez?"

"She's fine. I didn't want to hurt her, you understand that? She's not the *point*. I admire what she does."

He's pulled me through most of this assembly line, I think, but no, it just keeps going. Conveyor belts and metal bins, snaking off in all directions. The guts of the machine. Millions of fish passed through here. Billions. All bled and gutted and filleted and packed for easy consumption. And now it's me being processed.

"You said there'd be choices!" I manage to shout it, and now, finally, my voice sounds nearly normal to my ears, though there's a constant loud, sizzling hiss I'm not sure I'll ever lose again. "This isn't a choice!"

"We haven't even started," he says. "Do you know how much time it takes to destroy a life? One second." His voice is strangely flat and unaffected, like he doesn't know how to communicate emotion or doesn't care to try. If he had an accent, he's lost it with time and training. "Sometimes it takes longer. It took my sister a lot longer to die. Minutes."

I don't know how to answer. I can't tell if the knife is still on my belt. The shotgun's gone. I don't know if I have anything left to use at all.

"Three," he says. "Two. One. We're here."

He stops pulling me, and I immediately roll right to try to twist his wrist, break free, but he isn't surprised. He lets momentum carry me over to my right side, and I feel myself sliding forward as he *throws* me, like a bowling ball. I try to stop myself, but he steps back, and I feel his foot land firmly in the small of my back. I feel a tug and a small, sharp nick of pain. My hands are free. I try to push myself up.

He kicks me hard, so hard I feel all the air forced out of me, and then I'm sliding forward again.

Into the dark.

I hear the door slam behind me and locks being thrown. I hear my own panicked breathing, the frantic slap of my body flopping against the floor. Tile, I think. Burning cold. It's absolutely black in here, except for the pallid strobe afterimages my eyes are still remembering in chemical traces. I force myself to go still, to relax. He stayed outside. I'm alone in the dark. I just need to breathe and *think*.

My hands and ankles are free. I can stand up. I just need to be careful not to bash my head against something, trip, break bones . . . I've always had a low-key fear of the dark, but this is nightmarish. I don't *want* to move. I just want to curl into a ball and hide. Instead, I force myself to take inventory. I've been cut, just a little. I can feel the wound throbbing on my wrist, but it doesn't seem that deep. I feel for the knife, but the sheath's empty. So is my shoulder holster. I reach for the backup ankle gun that I strapped in place, and remarkably, it's still there. He didn't find it. It's a small .38, lethal at close range. I feel miles better with the light weight of it in my hand.

I look for the burner phone I stuck in my jacket pocket. It's gone too.

It reeks in here, even worse than the last room. So bad I cough and choke and nearly throw up again until I steady myself.

It isn't fish this time. I know this smell, this particular smell that the fish odor covers so well.

I'm in the room with death. Something large.

The lights suddenly blaze on, brighter than hope, and I find myself scooting violently backward until my back hits the metal door behind me, unable to take my eyes off what I'm seeing.

I've found Sheryl Lansdowne.

I scream. I can't help it, it just bursts out of me like a blowtorch's flame, piercing and desperate and horrified. My first thought is that she's been broken like a china doll, only china dolls don't bleed when their arms and legs come off. Her limbs are separated a precise distance from her torso. Her head's still attached. She's still dressed in a flannel shirt and jeans; the cuts to remove her arms and legs were so precise that the fabric was sliced clean.

It takes me a few horrific seconds to realize what *else* I see. Sheryl's fingers and toes have a lifeless, bluish tinge to the flesh, and they're actively decomposing, like they've been severed from her for hours, maybe as much as a day.

But her face and the exposed skin on her neck still look pink. Pale, but alive.

She opens her eyes.

"Hello?" She sounds drugged. Calm. Her pupils are enormous, like black holes. "Tyler?"

She's alive. Somehow. Impossibly alive. And then I force myself to look at her body, at the places where the limbs were severed. The wounds are covered with some kind of plastic bandages. She's still bleeding at the edges in a steady flow. There's an IV hooked up to her body, line embedded in her neck. She's getting plasma and some kind of clear liquid in a bag.

It's painkiller. It has to be. Because she's not screaming.

She smiles, like she's been told a joke. Then her face twists, and her eyes fill with tears, and she says, "I didn't want to." As if she's having a conversation with someone who isn't there. I slowly, slowly work my way out of my paralysis and push myself up to a crouch, then to a standing position. I make myself look away from Sheryl and toward the rest of the room. It's just a small, white room—tiled on all four walls, on the floor, even on the ceiling. There's a drain in the floor. Her blood is dripping down into it.

The only way in or out of the room, other than the small drain, is the door I came through.

There's a small electrical outlet on the far wall, and—weirdly incongruous—a small speaker plugged into it. I catch a glint of glass sitting at the top of it: a camera.

Jonathan is watching.

"You have a choice to make," his voice says. "You can sit in this room and watch Sheryl die. It'll probably take a while. Her painkillers will run out soon, and her blood supply. It'll be an agonizing way to go."

I don't know what to say. The tide of horror runs deep here, and I feel I'm being swept away. I finally manage a response. "You said there was a choice."

"I left you the choice."

I look around. There's nothing, other than the speaker. The cord that connects it to the wall. The power outlet.

"You want me to electrocute her? Strangle her?"

He sighs, like I've missed the point. "No. That would be cruel."

I lift a shaking hand to my mouth to stop another scream, or a wild, mad laugh. *That would be cruel.* He's insane. He's utterly, batshit crazy.

"I left you the gun," he says then. "There's one bullet. You decide what to do with it."

"Why are you *doing this?*"

"I gave Sheryl choices," he says. "She was good at killing people, but you already know that. An old lady here, a husband there. But I needed to know how far she'd *really* go. Not every killer is worthy of my time. I told her about the lottery win. I told her I'd marry her, no prenup agreements. That I'd fly her to Paris in my private plane. But I wasn't going to do any of that if she wasn't free. That's all I said. I didn't tell her what to do. I gave her choices."

I feel the floor falling out from under me, and I have to brace myself against that clean, clean wall. "You . . . you . . ."

"I told her to meet me," he says. "When I got there, she was standing there, alone. No car. No children. She made her choice, Gina." He sounds *disappointed.* "And she kept on making them. I suggested that there might be video of us in the house you visited, and that would be a problem. She took a gun and . . . corrected it. I suggested that Prester might be able to track us down. You know what happened; she was actually disappointed that he had a heart attack before she could kill him. I didn't tell her to do it; she made her choices. Everybody does. And now it's your turn."

"You're a fucking monster," I whisper. "No. *No.*"

"Okay," he says. "I'll let you think about it."

He stops talking. So do I.

I sit down against the door again, staring dry-mouthed, dry-eyed at Sheryl. At a woman who, if I believe that smooth, calm voice on the speaker, deliberately chose to drown her two little girls so she could run away with someone who could make all her greedy dreams come true.

Some people deserve death. I know that. I believe that. Melvin did.

But not even Melvin deserved *this*.

I put the gun down. The weight of it doesn't comfort me anymore. I put my hands over my face like a hiding child.

But there's no hiding. Not from this.

I have to make a binary choice. Let her die horribly, in agony, screaming, or end her suffering quickly.

I let my hands fall away, limp, to my knees, and raise my face toward the ceiling. I can't see the sky. I don't know if God is up there. But I pray.

And then I say, "What happens if I kill her, Jonathan?"

He doesn't answer. Maybe he doesn't do anything at all. Maybe he leaves me locked in here with her rotting corpse to make even more horrible choices. Maybe I can hang myself with that electrical cord, at the last. Or maybe he wants me to believe something even worse: that he'll let me out to live with it.

The speaker finally says, "My dad always used to say that crisis reveals character. You're Gina Royal. You helped murder defenseless young women."

"I didn't," I whisper. I feel so tired. So very tired. "I didn't know what he was doing."

"Crisis reveals character," he says. "So we'll see."

When I call his name, he doesn't answer anymore. I honestly don't know what I'm going to do. Who I am. What he wants.

I just weep and desperately, desperately wish that I'd told Sam I loved him one more time, that I'd kissed my kids and told them that they are my reason for living through the hell of my past. I want to tell Kezia that I'm so, so *sorry*.

Just do it, I think, but the voice in my head isn't right. It isn't mine. And I know that the voice, just a whisper, is Melvin's. A cool, calculating part of my mind that Jonathan wants to access and put in control. It's trying to tell me that shooting her is a mercy, and I don't know, maybe it would be. Or maybe it's just the action of a killer. Melvin wants me to do it.

That's exactly why I can't.

Jonathan lost something huge when his skull was crushed. I don't know what it was—what precise brain function should be there and isn't—but what's left is an emotionlessly logical decision-making process. He wins because he's taken emotion out of the equation. Because he's got the unique ability to *endure*.

I take a deep breath, and when I stand up, I waver for a second. The gun is such an easy choice. So easy. It would spare her. It would spare me, too, in a sense.

I sit down next to Sheryl, looking down at her. I put my hand on her cheek and I say, "I'm here, Penny Carlson. I see you. I'm right here. Everything is okay. I know you hurt. I know you're confused. But I'm right here with you."

This is so cruel. So cruel I can barely look at what I'm doing. But her blood supply is low, almost gone, and so is her bag of pain medication. I sit and talk to her. She answers me in low, disjointed sentences, and then she starts to make sense as the meds lose effectiveness. We talk about her folks. She cries. We talk about being out in the sunlight and flowers and grass, and how the wind moves through the trees. I sing to her, low and quiet. Toward the end, when the bag is almost dry, she looks at me and her eyes focus and she says, "Are you here to kill me? 'Cause I did that to my kids?" Her eyes fill with tears. "I did. I did that. Why did he make me do that?"

He didn't. I know that, not because he told me but because he prides himself on control. He makes other people do terrible things. He baits them with whatever they want. What's the old saying? You can't cheat an honest man. But all of us, to some level or other, are dishonest.

Even saints fail.

I can't take her hand, but I keep my palm pressed against her forehead. Just letting her feel the contact. "Penny, did he ask you to do anything else since that night?"

"It hurts," she says, with a strange sort of surprise. She takes in a sharp breath. Her voice trembles as she says, "It's hurting, can you make it stop? Please?"

"I will," I tell her. It hurts to say it. "Did he ask you to do anything else, sweetheart?"

She's crying. Her breath is coming raggedly now. Faster. "I can't feel my arms. I can't move them."

"You're okay," I whisper, and stroke her forehead. "Can you answer my question?"

She blinks, gulps, and says, "I had to. There were two people that saw us on the road. Had to do it." That's the man and woman Kezia found dead. "I was just protecting us."

"Did he ask you to do it?"

"He said—he just said it was a problem. *It hurts, oh God—*" Her voice is thin now. She's breathing faster, more shallowly. Her skin is turning pale. The blood supply that was keeping her brain and organs oxygenated is leaving her fast. She's bleeding out. "I didn't want to. I *needed* to. Or I'd lose everything."

I don't have the heart to ask her about Prester. About anyone or anything else. I feel nothing but horror and revulsion and a strange, awful compassion for her right now, a naked connection of human to human, when all I can do is stay and bear witness.

"Hold me," she whispers. "Mommy—" She starts screaming uncontrollably. She's trembling all over. It's horrible, but I don't hesitate; I rest her head on my lap, and I let my tears fall. I kiss her forehead and tell her it'll be okay, okay, okay, until she's no longer screaming, until it's just ragged, convulsive whimpering. Until it slows to a whisper. Until she's just . . . gone.

It takes an eternity for her labored, wet breathing to finally hitch to a stop.

I sit there. Unmoving. There isn't a sound except for the last of her blood dripping into the drain.

Jonathan's voice says, "Crisis reveals character." I hear locks unfastening at the door. "All choices have consequences."

I find my voice, because I have to. I have no wish to speak to him ever again. "That wasn't justice. That was cruelty. Do you even know the difference?"

No answer. I leave the body of a child-killer, a murderer—in the end, just a desperate, sad, frightened woman—and turn the doorknob. Maybe I'll die when I walk out. Maybe I won't.

I can't really bring myself to care.

He's laid bare horrors to me: The horror of a mother killing her children for personal gain. The horror of her own death. The horror of how relentlessly hollow and easy it is to say *she deserved it*. Maybe someone else can make that decision. I can't.

There's a hallway beyond. No traps. Nothing waiting.

Above me, an intercom engages, and I look up at the black metal screen. "We played a game in the car," he says. "After she killed her children. It's called *Would You Rather*, do you know it?"

"No."

"It starts out small. Would you rather have a nickel or a dime? Would you rather have a salad or an ice cream? But every question has to get bigger. So I asked, at the end, would you rather get shot in the head and die, or lose all your arms and legs and stay alive? And this is what she chose, Gwen. I didn't choose it. She did."

I swallow a sick, horrible surge of bile. "It was a *game*."

"Not really. There's a pattern. Bad people will choose greed and personal gratification. If you do it right, when you ask them, *Would you rather push a button and kill someone else, or say no and lose a million dollars*, guess what they choose? People are things they sacrifice to their needs. I wasn't surprised at how Sheryl chose. She was only surprised I was serious."

It's the logic of a child. The decision tree of a machine. I feel ill, hot, disconnected. I have to brace myself against the wall. The smell of blood and rot suddenly overwhelms me, and I nearly fall. *I can't do this. I can't.*

"There are more rooms if you want to see the choices they made," he says. "Every one of them was a murderer, not just once but many times over. I thought you were one of them. But it's all right, Gina. You surprised me. No one else ever has. It took real courage to do that. Or real sadism. I'm not really sure which you showed me."

"I'm going to find you," I tell him. "And you should be afraid of that."

He says, "I haven't been afraid since that day."

I don't ask which one. I know. At seventeen years old—the same age as my daughter, my God—he stopped being a person and started inhabiting a body on the day his sister died. This has been a long time coming.

"Maybe you will be," I say. "Before this is done."

"I hope so," he says. He sounds wistful. "I really do."

"Where's Kez?" He doesn't answer. I turn in a circle in the hallway, and I shout it with all the rage boiling inside me. *"Where's Kez?"*

He doesn't answer.

I will have to look.

24

KEZIA

When the trap triggers, I'm a step behind Gwen, and it doesn't help. I go down like a sack of sand, stunned by the strobes and the sound, and while I'm completely bashed into shock, I feel someone zip-tying my hands and ankles. A gag goes over my mouth. I try to get myself together, to struggle. I can't. I curl into a whimpering ball, eyes squeezed shut and still burning from the lights that are beating into me, the sound so heavy it's crushing me. I think of my child, begging him, her, the delicate life that's just a fragile collection of cells right now, to *fight*. To *live*.

I don't know how long that goes on. I only know that it's an overwhelming relief when I feel my body moving away from the assault of noise and lights, and then it's suddenly, intensely *gone*. Like someone flipped a switch.

Because someone did.

I'm terrified for my child. I don't know if the baby's okay. *You have to believe,* I tell myself. *And you have to survive.*

I can't see, but I feel the changes. From smooth concrete to sudden warmth. Sun on my skin, humidity close. Fresh sea air, and the reek of the cannery subsides. *Where's Gwen?* I try to blink away the glare, but all I can see are confusing, fragmented ghosts. My ears are ringing, and I can't tell if I'm actually hearing anything or just imagining it.

I'm lifted up and tossed inside something. I feel it give underneath me. *Car, I'm in a car.* I'm lying on a plush velour seat, I can feel the fabric. Someone's talking. I can hear a voice. I don't know what it's saying. I'm scared down to my bones. I don't know where I am, what's happening, and until I can see and hear, I can't *act.*

The car starts to move. I know this isn't the Honda; it doesn't smell the same. Doesn't feel the same. I'm in another vehicle, and I have the awful feeling that it's not Gwen who has me.

My eyes come back first, slowly painting in the world in grainy smears of color ghosted by white rings when I blink. I see the back of a seat, and the rough outline of a head. Not Gwen. The head is misshapen, disturbingly wrong on one side. *Jonathan Watson.*

I try to breathe slowly, steadily, and take inventory. My head aches. My ears are barely working, still buried under high-pitched noise. The gag's tight, expertly applied; when I try to scrape my face against the seat, it doesn't move at all. The bonds on my wrists are tight enough to hurt, and my ankles ache too. I'm in trouble.

He's talking, I realize. But he's not talking to me. He's got a phone, and he's talking into it as he drives. I hear only the sound of it, not the meaning.

Then I hear the *other* voice. He's talking to Gwen.

I try to scream. The gag muffles it. I feel the car slow down and stop, and the driver's side door opens, closes. A second later, the back door by my head opens, and light floods in on me. I blink, trying to really *see* him. I struggle.

He pulls me out of the car and across a long, clean concrete surface. I'm in some kind of building, and when I manage to blink and focus enough, it disorients me. Just . . . space, going up into shadows above me, with a winding steel staircase vanishing into the distance.

Lighthouse. I'm in the lighthouse.

He doesn't pause. Next thing I know, we're in an elevator, a large freight-size thing that moves jerkily and stops with a jolt. By this time, I can see better. Hear more clearly. And none of it helps.

I try to focus on Jonathan Watson. He seems utterly disinterested in me, other than moving me like a piece of furniture where he wants me to be. He pulls me into a corner and props me against the wall like a discarded mop, then walks away to the elevator. He slides a door shut and enters a code into the keypad beside it. I can't focus enough to see what it is.

There's another way down, I tell myself. *Stairs.*

Yeah, if I can cut myself loose. I look around. This is some kind of control center, maybe for the lighthouse itself; the consoles look new, shiny, fitted out with all kinds of touch-screen displays. I don't see any sharp corners that I can rub these damn restraints against. There's a single rolling office chair. On the other side from the rounded console, there's a bank of monitors, and once I glance toward them, I can't stop looking.

There are nine monitors. Gwen is on one of them. She's sitting in a room with a body, a mutilated body, and though I can't see it in detail, I can feel the horror of it. I start to squirm forward, trying to find something, *anything* to use.

Jonathan Watson walks back toward me and stands there, watching me. Then he shakes his head and says, "I'm not going to hurt you. You aren't guilty of anything. But I can't let you interfere either. This is important. You need to be quiet now."

I want to tell him about the baby. Maybe it will make a difference. But he doesn't seem to care when I try to talk through the gag as he takes out a pair of handcuffs. He flips me on my side, cuts off the zip ties on my wrists, and I feel one set of the cuffs going on my right wrist. He pulls me over to a standpipe that's against one of the walls, and then the second cuff clicks on. When I lunge forward, I nearly jerk my arms out of my sockets, and have to pause to pull in painful breaths through my nose.

He's locked me to the pipe. I'm not going anywhere.

He forgets about me almost immediately. He walks over to the chair, spins it around to face the monitors, and leans forward, watching. I look too. I can't help it. My vision is getting clearer and clearer, and the horrible thing I'm seeing sharpens along with it.

"She chose this," he tells me. "Sheryl Lansdowne. You understand, I didn't do it out of cruelty. I let her make all the choices. I always do."

I can't answer him. I blink, and I see Sheryl is *moving*. Just her torso and head. Arms and legs pallid and still around her like some kind of horrific art installation. And even knowing what I know—or at least suspect—I feel a surge of sickness.

"Gwen can stop her suffering, if she chooses," he continues. "I think she will. That's the easy choice."

Gwen has *never* taken an easy path. I don't know what this man is thinking. Or why. Maybe I never will. I try to stay calm, but I'm scared. I don't know if what happened to me back there at the cannery would have hurt my baby. I'm afraid that my nose will stop up and I won't be able to breathe, and that would be a shitty, stupid way to die.

I'm afraid that help isn't coming. That Gwen and I will just vanish off the map like magic, alive or dead.

I just want to go back to sanity. Safety. Javier and the baby and *life*.

Jonathan keeps watching Gwen. He leans forward. Sometimes he talks to her, but mostly he just . . . watches. When Sheryl starts to scream, it's horrible. I shut my eyes and try not to hear it, try not to hear Gwen offering what little she can in the way of comfort. It takes *forever* to stop. *Don't cry,* I tell myself. *You can't cry. You need to breathe. Keep breathing.*

When I open my eyes again, it's silent. Jonathan is sitting back in his chair. I think he's surprised.

He hits a button. He's just unlocked the room, I realize. And Gwen—bloody, distraught, bone-pale Gwen—stands up and leaves.

I listen to their exchange, not because I want to but because I have no other choice. I'm scrabbling with my fingertips against the pipe. It's smooth. No rough surfaces. The floor is too. I can't find anything, *anything* to work with.

Jonathan presses another button, then swivels his chair to face me. He leans forward and studies me like I'm a damn museum exhibit. No feeling at all. "Does the gag bother you?"

I nod. He scoots the chair over and undoes it, and I grab in a deep, whooping breath of relief. Then another one. Then I say, "You need to let us go. Right now."

"I'm not going to hurt you," he says. "You're safe here."

I don't feel safe. I feel handcuffed to a damn pipe. "I'm pregnant."

He freezes for a second. Processing the information. Then he says, "Then I'm sorry for the way I treated you. And the car crash. But you'll be okay. I promise I won't hurt you."

"Then you can let me go. Right now."

He smiles, but there's nothing behind it. It's just muscles moving. An imitation of feeling. "I'd like to," he says. "But I respect you more than that, Kezia Claremont. You could have let this go, and you didn't. You wanted justice for those girls. I did too."

"We're nothing alike," I say, and I mean it down to my last drop of blood. "You let Prester die."

"Not me," he says. "Sheryl. She could have called an ambulance. Maybe saved him. But she didn't."

I feel a real surge of bitter, electric rage. "You're not just some god hovering overhead. You were there, or you were close. *You could have stopped her.* You could have saved him. And you didn't."

He tilts his head, and it looks like a praying mantis taking in its prey. "You should understand what I'm doing."

On-screen, Gwen's outline is moving. I note that in my peripheral vision, but I don't focus on it. I want him to focus on me right now. If he's telling me the truth, if he doesn't intend me any harm . . . keeping him fixed on me will let Gwen move more freely.

"Your sister died," I say. "I know that. You tried to save her." He doesn't answer. Doesn't blink. "You never found the man who did that. I understand how that can make somebody—"

"Crazy?" he says. Too calmly.

"Desperate," I say. Behind my back, I'm sliding my fingers up and down the pipe, trying to find *anything* to work with. I could have dealt with the zip ties, I've had training on precisely how to break them, but now I have the handcuffs to contend with. And I don't know what I'm going to do about that. "Desperate to get justice."

"You think you understand me," he says. "But you don't. You really don't." He pauses for a second, and slowly blinks. "Sam did. A little. He was one of the only people who ever came close to the truth."

What truth? I don't know what he's saying. I can't work it out. And then it doesn't matter, because something's happening on the screens.

"If you make another sound," he says, "I'll kill your baby." It's such a calm, quiet threat. I feel it shudder through me, and it leaves behind a horrible conviction that he *means it.*

Jonathan turns away from me. I hear a slight metallic jingle, and when I look down, I see he's got a small metal carabiner clipped to the belt loop on his blue jeans.

Keys. That's a ring of keys, and even from here I can see a handcuff key on it.

Get him over here, I think.

But not yet. He's completely absorbed in what's happening on the screen . . . and as I focus on it, too, I feel the same magnetic force draw me in.

Oh God, Gwen. Oh my God.

We should never have come here.

25

Gwen

There are more rooms, he said. I think about the implications of that as I walk through the processing room. There are other exits from this room, seven of them. I ignore the big doors he dragged me through before; those lead to the warehouse, to the trap where I last saw Kez.

I have blood on my hands. On my clothes. And I am not really rational.

It feels oddly fine.

"Which door?" I ask Jonathan. I know he can hear me. He's played this game before, with many people. How many, I can't really know.

"You choose."

I do. I pick one at random, and I move past the silent, stinking fish conveyors. This door is smaller. It leads to a hallway running right and left. More choices. I go right. "You going to give me any clues?" I ask Jonathan. "It's not much of a game if I don't know what I'm doing."

"You know," he says. "You'll know when you get there."

I'm not surprised to find that lights are working now. He's kept the power on, of course he has. He controls the building, probably from whatever room he's hiding in.

We're playing hide-and-seek.

"Would you rather be rich or poor?" he asks.

"Neither," I tell him. "Just not afraid."

"That's not how it works. There are only two choices."

"That's why the game is wrong," I tell him. "Because humans aren't binary creatures. We're confusing. We're flawed. We're—"

I stop talking because there are three doors in the hallway, all on my left. The doors are shut. All have glass windows, but when I stand in the middle, I realize all the blinds are closed. No way to tell what's inside.

"Three doors," he says. "Three choices. Two are empty."

"What's in the third one?"

"A tiger who hasn't eaten for months."

I know this one. It's a logic puzzle. *A tiger who hasn't eaten in months is dead.* It doesn't matter which door I open.

So I do it methodically.

The first door is an office with an empty desk, two filing cabinets, and a vacant office chair. It's eerily tidy, like it's waiting for a new employee to arrive.

The second door is the same.

The third door holds the monster, but as he promised in the riddle, the monster isn't a problem anymore. I stare at the old, desiccated corpse. I can't tell race, sex, anything; it's just old skin, hair, and the outlines of bones now. The place reeks. The carpet's absorbed decomposition like a bloated sponge. It isn't immediately obvious how this person died—no severing of arms and legs, like Sheryl suffered. The corpse is handcuffed to a thick U-bolt driven into the floor.

I don't speak. I just step back and shut the door. Jonathan's disembodied voice says, "Do you want to know?"

"Just tell me where you are. Let's get it over with."

"That man abducted young women, some of them barely into their teens. He raped and killed them and made harassing phone calls to their loved ones," Jonathan says. "I gave him a choice of dying of starvation or gnawing off his hand like an animal in a trap. He chose to starve."

I lift my head and see the small, beady eye of a camera tucked in the corner of the hall. "I don't care about your justifications."

"These people weren't unknown," he says. "If the police had worked harder, they could have put the pieces together. They could have stopped him. But they didn't. He *did* have a judge and a jury once. They arrested him for an attempted abduction. The case was dismissed."

"You're not omniscient. You can be wrong."

"I let them tell me who they are. What they've done. What they're capable of doing next." He sounds calm, of course. Certain. "What you've done tells me who you are, Gina. If you want to find me, go to your left now."

"Are you going to keep telling me your stories? Because I'd rather just die."

"Go to your left."

I take the other end of the hall. More offices. More blank, blinded windows. Three of them.

"Did you ever find him?" I ask.

"Who?"

"The man who killed your sister."

There's a very long pause. I wish I could see him, the way he can see me. I wish I could understand him better, because then I'd know how to stop him.

"Three doors," he says. "Pick one. I'll give you a clue. I'm in one of them."

I feel my stance shift, getting ready for battle. A fierce, cold wind blows through me. *He'll be armed*, I think. I still have the ankle gun, and I bend down and get it. There's one bullet, and I need to make it fucking count.

I start at the far left. It's empty.

So is the middle one.

I kick the last door open, smashing glass, blinds flailing wildly at the air, and leap forward in a flat-footed hop while the glass is still falling like sharp ice from the frame. My aim is steady.

I fire at his face. Right in his forehead.

He doesn't blink. Glass cracks. He picks up a mug and drinks from it, and I realize through a sick, bewildered sense of disorientation that I've just shot a huge, flat television screen. It's still working, despite the bullet that I've put through it. Jonathan sips again, staring at me with cool, empty eyes. "I didn't lie," he says. "I'm right here. It's the only place you'll find me in the building, Gina. There are twenty-one more rooms I've used. You can look in all of them. As you do, I'll tell you why. And you'll agree with me. They all deserved it. Every one of them."

I scream at the monitor. I can't help it; I feel a savage upwelling of rage, so deep that it tears something inside me. I can't put words on it. I can't reach him. I can't *stop him*.

He's a ghost. And this is just his graveyard.

That's when I hear Kez's voice. Not here, with me. From the screen. "Gwen, *get out*, he's fucking crazy, he took me to the—"

Jonathan's head swivels to his left, and then the picture and sound both die before she can finish that sentence.

He's got Kez.

I don't go to the other rooms. I don't want to see more of Jonathan's brand of justice. I'm barely holding on to myself as it is.

I need to get to Kez.

And this needs to end.

I shove myself under the still-stuck loading dock door and run across the broken, pitted parking lot. The Honda is still on the other side of the fence, and I wriggle under the chain link, earning bloody scratches on my face I barely feel. I pop the trunk and grab another gun—one of Kezia's, a Smith & Wesson semiauto, loaded and ready—and I see another knife at the bottom of the pile. I take it, and an extra clip, and I slam the trunk.

There are only two choices: his family home, or the lighthouse. I choose the house because it's closer.

The place must have been beautiful once. Now it's warped, weathered, half-burned, and left to ruin. The front door gapes open on a blackened, charred entryway. I step inside and go down the hallway that leads left to the part that hasn't been destroyed.

It's what I suppose in the 1970s would have been called a sunken living room; there's a step down, then another, then an octagonal carpeted pit in the middle. Matted shag, filthy and rotten. Animals have nested here. When I look up, I see jagged holes in the roof where rain has poured down.

Apart from that, it's still intact. Books rotting on warped shelves. A silver artificial Christmas tree leans in the corner, loaded with dirty, still-vivid ornaments. Presents scattered like stones, all still wrapped but misshapen from water and time.

The octagonal pit in the middle of the room is full of sludge. Pillows float on top, bleached pale like dead fish.

I move past it, past the dull, dirty white piano in the corner. Something rustles in the strings, and I flinch, but whatever it is, it stays hidden.

The next room is a kitchen. It's weirdly neat, like the cannery: counters clean and empty, floor shining. Off-green appliances have been polished. I open the refrigerator, afraid that I'll find another body, and gag at the stench of rotten food. I will my heartbeat to slow down, my ears to stop the incessant ringing that hasn't faded yet from that stunning sonic assault at the cannery. I can hear. Just not as clearly as I should.

At least my pulse obeys, coming down to a slightly less painful pace. The kitchen is wrong, but it isn't dangerous. I move on.

The hall is filthy, streaked with mold. Drywall bulges and leaks. There are still framed photos on the wall, but rot has obscured what used to be a loving family, cute children. *This house,* I think, *is a map of Jonathan's destroyed brain. Pieces partly there. Pieces rotting. Some weirdly perfect.*

His room is destroyed. Not by the elements, though the window's broken out and the carpet has wrinkled and molded. This seems . . . deliberate. Someone's taken what looks like an ax to the furniture, left it in silently screaming pieces. Books ripped apart. Bedsheets and clothing shredded.

He hates himself. Or someone else hates him this much. I could weep for the boy he used to be, the one who lost his little sister, but the monster that he is now has to be treated differently.

You held a mother who killed her children, I tell myself. But it's different. Somehow . . . somehow, it's different. I can't define why; unlike Jonathan, I don't really want to understand.

I just want it to stop.

The next room is his sister's, and it's heartbreakingly perfect, a shrine, clean and neat and waiting for a dead child to walk in the door, sleep in the frilly pink bed, wear the neat white nightgown that's laid out on the covers. I look at the boy band posters on the wall, at the stuffed animals, the games. My heart aches for her, not just because she'll never see this but because so much harm has been done in her name.

He isn't here. Kez isn't here. I check every place she could be kept, but there's no trace of her, or Jonathan.

That just leaves the lighthouse.

I go.

26

SAM

Gwen's right about the lack of real, solid evidence, but I try anyway; I call the TBI and get the investigator Javier saw at the hospital, Heidt. I lay it all out for him. I tell him that the man he's looking for is in Salah Point, North Carolina. That he's a serial killer, a predator who took Sheryl Lansdowne and now has Gwen and Kezia too. I make it as urgent as I can, and . . . he says he'll look into it.

He thinks I'm bullshitting him. And I am, but only a little. The facts are there. He's just not looking. Or, at least, not moving fast enough if he is.

I call my friend at the FBI, but I'm told he's on a case and unavailable. Can't be reached. I leave him a long message, and then I ask to talk to someone else.

I know what I have to do. *Exactly* what I have to do. And there will be consequences.

So I tell them that there's a terrorist cell in Salah Point, that I have personal knowledge of a plot involving multiple individuals, and the threat is imminent. I know the language to use; military training embeds that deep. And the agent I'm talking to pays attention. Close attention. I give him Tyler Pharos's description, tell him the alias of Leonard Bay. I link Tyler to all kinds of things, including the abduction of Sheryl

Lansdowne and the disappearance of my wife and Kezia Claremont. I throw everything that might stick at the wall, true or not. I know I'll be in the shit for it. I don't care. By the end of it, I'm practically begging them to get there, *just get there.*

I have no idea if it will work.

I call the North Carolina state police and try the same thing. I can tell they write me down as a crank. There's going to be no help coming from that direction. The FBI, *maybe.* But they'll call North Carolina, and North Carolina will take their sweet time checking anything out. I'm just some nut from out of state.

The only thing that holds me back from just *going* is the knowledge that I need to stay here for the kids. That Gwen trusted me with that, and I have to treat that as what it is: a sacred responsibility. A level of letting go that I never imagined she could manage.

I have to be worthy of that trust, even if it hurts. Even if it's agony sitting here and waiting.

I've told the kids everything. Vee's here, too, huddled on the couch with Lanny and Connor. Nobody's saying much. Every once in a while, Vee tries to lighten the mood, but none of us are having it. Javier's stormed out; I'm sure he's going to be burning rubber to North Carolina, and I don't try to stop him. He won't get there in time, but at least he'll get there to pick up the pieces. Man, that hurts.

I wait with the kids, and it's sheer torture.

It's two long, tense hours later when my cell phone rings. "Mr. Cade? I'd like you to go to your computer, please. I need you to be a witness."

I feel like I recognize the voice, but at the same time I don't. Something's familiar and different at the same time. "Who is this?"

"My name is Jonathan Bruce Watson," he says. "Go to your computer. Do it now. I sent you a link. Please click it."

I go to the office, and as I come around my desk, I see that my laptop's awake, and there's a text message alert. I click it, and the link appears.

"Don't do it," Connor says. He's come out of nowhere, and he looks angry. Anxious. Afraid. "Dad, *don't*."

The voice on the phone says, "You know who I am, Sam. You know you need to click that link."

It hits, then. The voice. Tyler. MalusNavis. The puppet master. He sounds different, though. Maybe this is the real voice at last.

"Where's Gwen?" I ask him. "I know you're behind all this, Tyler."

"You can see her if you click the link," he says. "We're going to play a game. It's called *Would You Rather*. Do you know it?"

"I'm not playing." I cover the speaker on the phone and whisper to Connor, "Go. Now. Get Lanny. *Go.*"

He doesn't want to, but he obeys. I'm alone with the voice on the phone, the link steady and waiting on the laptop screen.

"You don't have to play," Tyler agrees. "That's a choice. Everybody makes choices."

"So tell me what happens if I don't click the link. I can't play if I don't understand the stakes."

"If you don't, Gwen won't come home alive to her children."

I knew that was coming. My muscles tense until my pulse throbs in my temples. "And what if I click it? What then?"

"Then you're participating in the game, Sam," he says. "Everything has consequences. Gwen's guilty of killing people, after all. She killed her ex-husband."

"She had to."

"She helped him kill others."

"She didn't."

"I've seen that she can do terrible things, Sam. When I gave her the option of killing someone kindly, or leaving them dying in pain, can you guess which one she chose?"

I can't answer. My skin crawls. My right hand clenches the mouse, and the cursor is hanging right over the link. All I have to do is click.

"She'd rather think of herself as a hero," the voice says. "So let's find out if she really is. Are you playing, Sam? For her life?"

Lanny and Connor are at the door, breathless and scared. I put the cell phone on mute and say, "Lanny, go call TBI Detective Randall Heidt and tell him that I have a man on the phone who says he has your mother, and he's threatening her life. Tell him to trace the call. I'm going to keep him talking. *Go.*"

She gapes at me for a second, then spins and runs down the hall. Connor is left standing alone, paler than ever. "Connor. Go call J. B. Hall. Tell her the same thing." I unmute the phone when I feel like I'm ready to keep going. "Tyler, we talked. I believe we really, really talked. *I helped you.* I believed you. Come on, man, I thought we connected. When you were on that bridge . . . I know you really felt something. Something real."

He's silent for a long few seconds. Good. *Keep thinking, keep the line open . . .* "Everything I said to you was true. I didn't want to lie to you. You're not guilty of anything."

"If you didn't lie, that means you called me because you thought about jumping."

"I think about it a lot. It's hard, doing this work. Do you understand that?"

"No, Tyler. I don't. But I do know one thing . . . You're not like this. Or at least, you don't have to be like this. You can change."

"Someone has to find them," he says. "These people need to be stopped. They need to be punished. And if the rest of you won't do it, then I have to."

I'm losing him. He's looped back to his crusade again. "Tyler, *please* think for a second about your sister. I said we'd talk about her. Tell me about her. Tell me what she was like."

"I don't want to talk about her. You told me you felt like this once. That someone had to pay. You do understand, Sam, it isn't a *choice.* I have to do this to make things right."

302

I don't know how to save Gwen. I don't know how to stop an obsession like his; I couldn't stop mine, not without time and real work and understanding. And Tyler . . . Tyler isn't like me. I thought he was. That was my mistake.

My mistake could kill the woman I love.

"Please, Tyler," I say. My voice is shaking now. "Come on, man, *please* don't do this. She doesn't deserve this. I'm telling you, she doesn't."

"It's not my choice anymore," he says. "It's hers. And yours. Are you going to play, Sam? Because if you don't, and you could have saved her—I know how that will feel for you. Next time it'll be you on that bridge."

He's right. Oh God, he's right. I don't know if the kids are getting through, if anyone is working on this. But I have to try to keep him on the phone. Gwen told me he was at Salah Point, but if she was wrong, if he's somewhere else . . . the phone trace can pinpoint him exactly. Save her life.

I swallow a terrible mix of despair and bitter rage, and say, "I'm clicking now."

I tap the mouse button.

And I see Gwen. She's standing, swaying, looking up at something I can't see. I can't tell where she is, just a room with shelving. And I can't look at the details. She fills my world. "Oh God," I whisper. "Oh God, baby." She looks desperate, beaten, in pain. Afraid. I'm afraid that he's brought me here to watch her die, and I can't, I *can't let that happen*.

"I'm going to ask you a very important question," Tyler says. "Do you want her to live? No matter what?"

I say, "Yes. *Yes*." There is no other possible choice.

"I thought so." He sounds vaguely disappointed. "That was very predictable."

I stare at the screen, unable to look away. Afraid to blink.

I've never wanted anything more in my life than to be standing with her right now.

27

GWEN

The lighthouse's beacon, I realize now, is working, after all. It's blinking steadily. Calling me right toward him.

I climb the steep hill, sweating, filthy with dried blood and mud and mold. Heartsick but resolute.

There's only a single door on the bottom level, large enough that—like in the cannery—a forklift could be driven inside, if necessary. I reach for the doorknob. Hesitate. I look up, and the camera looks down.

"You asked if I ever found the man who took my sister," Jonathan says through a speaker near the top of the door. "He never did it again. It took her four minutes to die, Gina. Four minutes."

I don't want to feel sympathy for him. I can't. "Did you kill him?" I ask.

"I don't kill people," he says. He means it. "I've never killed anyone directly. Could you die in here? Yes, but it's possible I could too. That seems fair."

"Is Kezia here? Is she still alive?"

"Yes, and yes," he says. "Come in. There's nothing that will hurt you on the other side of the door."

I take him at his word. In his own weird way, I think he's trying to be completely honest with me. I can't—won't—do him the same favor.

The doorknob turns. I step into what I suppose would be a storage room—large, perfectly round, with fixed shelving on all sides that is stocked with cans and boxes. Not a soul in sight.

I look up. The tower's staircase curls up in a dizzying, narrowing spiral. Off to the side is an elevator, and I head for it, but when I press the button, it's locked down. No power to it at all.

I make for the stairs. And something occurs to me. Something important that just . . . doesn't fit.

And then it does fit. The missing piece in a horrible, horrible puzzle.

"Would you rather die, or see someone you love die?" he asks me. I freeze with my foot on the first step. "It's a simple question, Gina. I answered it when I was seventeen years old."

"I'd rather die," I say. And it's true. Utterly true. "But you're not going to make me kill myself. If someone I love dies, it's because *you* killed them, Jonathan. Just like someone killed your sister." I take a step up, then another. I don't know when something will happen, but I know it's coming. The air feels alive with it. It's time to use what I just worked out. The little clue he gave me. "You know what I wonder, though?"

"What?" he says. I've been moving slowly, testing for traps, but there doesn't seem to be anything except stairs to climb. No rooms, no traps, nothing. I move faster.

"How you know it took her four minutes to die?"

The silence is profound.

"You told me you never found your sister's killer," I say. I'm moving up, steadily, carefully, and as quickly as I dare. "Tragic Jonathan, with his kidnapped sister and his dead parents and his house half-burned. Poor little Jonathan, always the victim." I hear footsteps above. I jerk my focus up to the top level. The staircase ends there. "Let's play a new game. Truth or dare. Because I dare you to tell me the truth."

Second curl of the spiral. I'm moving fast now. I need to, I know that. I can feel it. He isn't answering me.

"You want someone else to know," I say. My breathing's fast, ragged, and my whole body aches. "To see you for who you are. Where's Kezia? Is she up there with you?"

"Yes, she is. I had to put her gag back on, I'm afraid; she was being too noisy. But she's alive and well. In fact, I think she's starting to understand me. But do you? You think you're smart. Tell me. Go ahead, Gina Royal. Tell me my story."

"There was no van," I say. "There was no man who grabbed your sister and took her away. No abductor who hit you in the head."

"How could you possibly know that?" He sounds interested. Not offended. Not yet.

"Four minutes. You said it took four minutes, and you couldn't have known that unless you were *there*. So here's what I think: You killed your sister. You took her out to the salt marsh that day, and *you* killed her. Then you had an accident on the way back—maybe a bad fall, I don't know. But when you came to, you knew you had to have some kind of story. You made up the abductor and the van. You just made it up, and they all believed it because you were so *hurt*."

He doesn't answer, and that's how I know I'm right.

"But your mother knew, didn't she? She lasted a year, knowing her son killed her daughter. The papers said it was accidental death, but is that what happened?"

"She died in the fire at our house," Jonathan says.

"Did you kill her?"

"No." He's quiet for a second or two. "She started the fire. She tried to kill me."

There's still no emotion in it. Just an observation, a flat fact with no impact to him. Though I wonder. I wonder if locked inside that damaged brain there isn't a howling, screaming monster made of guilt and pain and horror.

"And your father drowned in the bay," I say. "Suicide. Because he knew, and couldn't live with it either."

"You knew about what Melvin was doing. You helped him do it. Admit it."

"I didn't know. I didn't help. But you killed your sister, Jonathan. Admit *that*."

He's never said it, I think. Never had to. But after a moment of silence, he says, "She was being a brat. I just wanted to teach her a lesson. So I took her to the marsh."

"There wasn't a van. Or a man with a pipe."

"She hit me with a rock," he says. "While I was holding her head under the water. I just wanted her to *stop talking*. She almost got away. I didn't think I was hurt that bad until later. When they found me, I was passed out on the side of the road. I couldn't talk for a long time. I don't know why I told them that story, but everybody believed it."

I swallow hard. "Jonathan, you lied when you said you never killed anyone."

"I didn't," he says. "I was only holding Clara under the water to make her stop talking. Then she hit me. But she slipped in the mud, and she was already . . . confused. She went deeper into the water. She couldn't get out. It was her choice. It took four minutes for her to go under and not come up."

There's so much wrong with him. I can't fix him. I can't fix any of it.

"That part wasn't your fault," I tell him. "You were hurt. Your skull was crushed. You couldn't have saved her."

When he speaks again, I finally hear emotion in his voice. Anger. "I don't need your forgiveness."

"You loved her."

"Love is selfishness. Greed. That's all it is. I asked Sam a question earlier," he says then. "I asked if he wants you to live. He does. Just so you know. And that's greedy too."

I hear something powering up, and I don't understand what it is. Some kind of engine.

"I have one last question to ask you, Gina Royal. Would you rather die falling," he asks me, "or frying?"

I'm on metal stairs.

Oh God. He's going to electrocute me.

28

KEZIA

I stay quiet, partly because I believe him when he says he'll hurt my baby, and partly because I need to wait, to let him get comfortable. I need to act when he's in the middle of something else, when he doesn't have time to think.

Jonathan has Gwen to focus on now. Gwen, who's come to the lighthouse to find me. And him. And I am *helpless*, and I have never hated myself more than I do right at this moment.

I'm sweating buckets. I listen silently to him as he talks to Gwen. As she hits him right in the tenderest spots. Gwen has only words, and she uses them like bullets. I see them hit home.

She's right, I think. This bastard isn't an avenging angel. He's a broken devil, guilty to his bones, and she's just ripped his mask right off.

Would you rather die falling, or frying? He's already hitting a button when he asks it, and I don't think, I don't plan. I try to yell, "Jump, Gwen! Jump!" It comes out as a confused, muffled mumble from the gag.

She's already in motion. She figured it out.

But she's so *high*.

The camera that was on her loses her as she falls. Jonathan's attention swings to another monitor, and I see the blur.

I see her hit the concrete floor, and it is *brutal*. I yell something, I don't even know what it is, more of a denial than anything else. *Gwen, make it, you have to make it . . .*

Jonathan spins his chair toward me and lunges to his feet, and I realize I'm out of time. "I warned you," he says. "You chose this."

I choose the moment that he bends toward me, and I pull my knees in, lever myself up with all the power I can, and *twist*. My bound legs sweep in a fast arc across the floor and hit him midcalf, knocking him sideways. He's crouching, off balance, and it dumps him hard on his side. He lets out a surprised yell, and I twist back and pull my legs in and slam my boots into his face. I hear bone crunch. He screams this time and tries to roll away. I don't let him. I throw my legs over him and pull him in toward me and slam my heels down on his crotch with all the force I have.

He doesn't even scream this time. He gags, mouth open like a dark hole. I use my legs to pull him closer, and then I heave myself up to a standing position over him. He's fumbling for something. I don't have time, I have to *try*.

I brace myself, and I pull forward with everything I have. Weight, strength, *everything*. I feel that broken rib stab hard, and it takes my breath away, but I try again. Again. I feel the pipe joint give near the top, just where it disappears from view. It hurts, oh *God* it hurts, and I think I might break something, but that's better than dying here, helpless.

I lunge one more time, and it snaps free.

Momentum sends me falling forward on top of the man, who's still panting for breath. I have enough control to land knees-first on his chest, and I feel his bones snap. He stares into my face, and even now, *even now*, there's nothing in his expression except a mild, strange frown.

"Stop," he says.

I wonder how many people have said that to him—dozens, at least. I don't stop. I roll off him and pull my knees into my chest as I do, tight as I can despite the white agony that lances through me, and force my handcuffed hands under my ass, press harder to get them around my feet, and then my hands are in front. I do it fast, but he's starting to move with purpose again. I have to be faster.

I lunge for the knife at his belt before he can get to it and cut my feet free, then drop onto his chest again, knees first, and pin him flat. He cries out and flails, nearly throws me off. I grab the key ring and slide it off his belt loop. I've practiced this move before, trying to get out of handcuffs. I know how to bend my fingers, twist the key. I'm free in three seconds, and he's bucking hard, trying to throw me off.

I lunge forward. I put the knife to Jonathan's throat, and I think real hard about cutting. He stops moving and stares at me with wide, glassy eyes. "You could," he says. "Or you could save your friend. She's hurt."

It's a breathless, hot second of wanting to do it, but somehow, *somehow* I don't. I snap the cuff on his right wrist, lever myself off, and drag him to the big, round lighthouse console. It has legs bolted into the concrete. I fasten the other end around one, and I check him for weapons. He's clean. And he's hurt, curled in on himself like a dead bug. Gasping against the pain I've inflicted.

Good.

I look at the monitors as I straighten up.

Gwen's alive. My friend's alive.

And I need to get to her. Fast.

29

GWEN

I don't have a choice, not really. I leap over the railing.

I jump.

I fall.

I land hard and wrong on the concrete, hard enough I feel my lower left leg snap with a searing crack. Something in my side too. I scream, and the sound rings in echoes, funneled to the top. I can *hear* the electricity in the air; I'd have been dead if I hadn't jumped.

I've lost the gun I had in my hand, and I roll and crawl to grab it, and scoot myself backward until I feel a cool concrete wall. God, it hurts so much I'm weeping, shaking, barely able to catch my breath against the pressure of welling screams.

I hear the silence when the generator stops.

I hear Kez screaming. It echoes from the top of the tower like a slap from God, and then she stops. *She stops.*

Oh no no Kez no.

I get up. My left leg is badly shattered. I can't put my weight on it. I make it to the stairs. I jump. Step after step after step, jump after jump. Let him fry me, because if he doesn't, I'm going to finish this. Not for

Sheryl, not for the other rooms full of murderers. Not for little Clara, the first innocent victim in this chain of death.

I have to do this for Kezia.

I'm seven grim, agonizing steps up the spiral when I hear steps coming down to meet me. My ears are ringing again; my head is full of flashes of strange light. I stop, brace myself, and take aim. I see a shadow slide across the railing. My hands are shaking, and I'm not sure I can hit him at this distance, but I have to stop him, *I have to*. I take a breath. I wait. He comes closer, another turn down the spiral.

I see a shot and I take it. I miss, gouging a chunk of concrete out of the wall, and I immediately aim again. Fire again, a continuous spread. He's stopped. Crouching. He's shouting something. I can't hear him, the ringing in my ears is worse than ever, but it doesn't matter, I'm done listening.

I aim. I hold. I'm ready.

Center mass shot.

I pull the trigger. Nothing happens. The slide is locked back.

Empty.

And then I realize that the voice lost in the gunshots and the ringing isn't Jonathan's.

It's Kezia's. "Gwen, stop! Stop!" She's leaning over the railing, face stark with shock.

"Oh God," I say. I nearly did it. I nearly killed her.

Your choice, I can hear Jonathan whisper.

I drop the gun. I'm all wrong and I feel like I'm dying and I just want . . . I just want . . .

The white walls blur. Spin.

Kezia hurtles down the spiral toward me. She grabs me as I start to fall, and then we're both on the floor, and she picks up the gun.

"I'll be back," she says, and I see the intensity, the blind *focus* in her eyes. "I need to make sure he's—"

There's a noise. A loud, rumbling noise. Mechanical. Kez stands up. I'm trying to get my breath. There's something I need to remember, something I need to tell Kez. It's important. But I feel like everything is watery now. Slippery. I can't hold on to the thought.

"It's the elevator," she says. "Try to stand up."

She tries to help me, but I can't make it. I collapse, concrete cool against my face. She's still talking, but I can't make sense of it. Then I'm moving. She rolls me on my back, and drags me across the concrete floor toward the double doors. They're still open, and with weird clarity, I hear the restless rush of the sea beating against the hard rock of the cliff this lighthouse stands upon.

Kez stops. She's breathless, and she's in pain too. I see it flash in her face, along with the sudden despair she feels. She eases me up and braces me against the wall. "No," I try to tell her. "Don't." I can't remember why I say that, but it's important.

But she turns away from me, stands up, and faces the man who limps out of the elevator. Jonathan looks as damaged as I do.

He's got a shotgun. He raises it toward us. "You should have checked," he says. "I always keep a spare handcuff key in my pocket, Kezia."

Kez steps forward, gun in hand.

Oh God. I remember now. I was trying to tell her the gun was empty. I drag the backup magazine from my pocket, but when I try to slide it to her, I miss. It skids into the shadows. Too far for her to reach.

She drops the gun and pulls the knife from her belt.

I can't let her die for me.

"Just go, Kez," I hear myself say. "Please. Go and live for your baby."

The noise in my head is quieting. Everything is quieting except the steady promise of my pulsebeat. I'm still hurting, but something gives me strength.

In that silence, I hear my children whispering, *You can do this, Mom. You can.*

I stand up. I balance myself on one leg, drag the other. I move to stand with Kezia.

Shoulder to shoulder.

Jonathan stands there staring at me. He doesn't scare me anymore. I'm not frightened of anything. I don't even feel the pain so much.

"Do you know who I am now?" I ask. "And do you know who *you* are?" I sound steady. I am steady.

He tilts his head. Shadows fill the hollow on the side of his head. "I do," he says. "I finally do."

He reverses the shotgun in one smooth motion, sticks the barrel in his mouth, and pulls the trigger. The explosion fills the lighthouse. Echoes up as the blood sprays, and what's left of Jonathan Bruce Watson slides boneless to the floor.

Kez grabs me when I start to topple, and eases me down. She puts her arms around me and holds my back to her chest, and then we're both sitting down. Nothing but the sound of the sea, and a faint, distant whine.

Sirens. Those are sirens.

I say, "I tried to kill you."

"You're a bad shot," she says. "Thank God. Help's coming, Gwen. Sam did it."

I can't take my eyes off the pitiful ruin of a man. A shell. A monster animated by hate. *Love is selfishness. Greed,* he said. Maybe he really believed that. Maybe he wasn't sane enough to believe anything at all.

"He made his choice," I whisper.

We've made ours.

We're going to live.

EPILOGUE

The cavalry, when it finally arrives, seems a hundred strong. State and federal agents, paramedics, swarming like a kicked colony of fire ants. I'm taken away in an ambulance, while Kezia stays to answer questions; it doesn't escape my notice that I'm handcuffed to the gurney, but I don't care about that. I just want to sleep, especially once they shoot me up for the pain.

It takes days to unwind the story to absolutely no one's satisfaction except the cold case departments across the country who are finally able to put their open cases to bed with a firm, final SOLVED stamped on the front. There are twenty-three bodies in the cannery. Every one of them has a file neatly labeled in a cabinet at the top level of the lighthouse, where Jonathan kept meticulous records. He wasn't lying about any of it . . . not about the fact that his victims were guilty, at least. Penny Carlson had killed at least ten people. She'd killed her children, the man and woman at the remote house, and arguably Detective Prester, plus left five more in her wake of destruction over the years.

She was one of the *least* guilty of those he'd forced to play his game.

When the news breaks, some clever duck at the Wilmington *Star-News* labels him The Fisherman, and it sticks. I don't know if Jonathan would be happy he has a serial killer nickname, or appalled. I'd rather not try to work it out.

Jonathan left a video accounting of every single one of his *cases*; I'm sure it'll be fodder for psychologists and profilers for years to come. In my case, he'd applied his usual methods. The Lost Angels had been hideously easy to leverage against us. Dr. Dave, the man Sam turned to for information, had been the one to provide Melvin's letter to Jonathan, as well as the posters. MalusNavis's posts had never *asked* anyone to put up those posters. Had never *asked* people to stalk Vee or threaten my children. But hate has a life of its own. He didn't need to do much to kindle the fire and let it smoke us out.

Sheryl had been easy to manipulate too. She could have turned away. Said no. Loved her children more than the millions of dollars he dangled as bait. Everything after that one crucial night was collateral damage, her making the same choice again and again to chase her reward.

But Jonathan chose *first*.

What haunts me now isn't Penny's horrific, pathetic death. Or the innocent eleven-year-old whose death—accidental or deliberate—started this deadly avalanche.

It's the shots I fired in a blind panic, in pain. The shots that I only barely missed. In a way I think that, too, was Jonathan's plan, to make me blindly kill my friend, and it's only luck that saved me.

But I'm alive. Kez is alive. Her baby is a new and beautiful future for her and Javier. And in the end . . . Jonathan chose how to lose his own game.

I have to try to be content with that.

◆　◆　◆

Coming home on crutches feels strange. Like I've left something important behind. I tell Sam I love him, and I mean it; there's nothing but joy in my heart when I see him, and joy when I greet my children again. I should feel better.

I *will* feel better. Therapy isn't fast. But it does work. Step by step, I'm coming back. Step by limping step, I will walk out of this darkness and back into the light, where love is waiting for me.

Because Jonathan was absolutely wrong. Love isn't greed. Greed always wants more. Love is rich enough in itself, by itself. It doesn't need more.

I have enough, with Sam and my children. Enough of everything. Jonathan would never understand that at all.

ACKNOWLEDGMENTS

My first readers (always), Sarah Weiss-Simpson and Lucienne Diver.

My amazing editors Tiffany Yates Martin and Liz Pearsons.

So grateful for the assistance from Candria Slamin, Corlyn Key, Erica Johnson (a girl from Saint Louis who loves to read), and Todd Caldwell!

PLAYLIST

If you've read my stories before, you know that music is a huge inspiration for me during the creation of a story . . . and *Heartbreak Bay* has some tremendous songs that helped fuel my process this time out. Musicians struggle like all artists, so if you can afford it, please buy the music!

- "God's Country," Blake Shelton
- "Rearview Town," Jason Aldean
- "Give Me One Reason," Tracy Chapman
- "Miss Me More," Kelsea Ballerini
- "Mother's Daughter," Miley Cyrus
- "Nightmare," Halsey
- "Still Feel," Half-Alive
- "99," Elliot Moss
- "The Tarantella," Honeyblood
- "Hunter," RIAYA (feat. John Mark McMillan)
- "July," Noah Cyrus
- "Smokin the Boys," Audra Mae & The Almighty Sound
- "Bruises," Lewis Capaldi
- "Hurt," Oliver Tree
- "Lo/Hi," The Black Keys
- "Ilomilo," Billie Eilish
- "Boom," X Ambassadors

- "Take the Wheel," Honeyblood
- "Blue on Blue," Just Loud
- "Tell Me," Diamond Thug
- "Stay," The Score
- "Face the Sky," Diamond Thug
- "Maria," Grandson
- "They Own This Town," Flora Cash
- "Saw Lightning," Beck
- "Dancing with Your Ghost," Sasha Sloan
- "Tell Me When It's Over," Sheryl Crow (feat. Chris Stapleton)
- "Crowbar," Frank Carter & The Rattlesnakes
- "Way Down We Go," Kaleo
- "Cringe," Mark Maeson
- "The Daughters," Little Big Town
- "The Chain," The Highwomen
- "Change," The Revivalists
- "Love Crimes," Hayden Thorpe
- "It Doesn't Matter Why," Silversun Pickups
- "The One I Need," Amber Benson and James Saez
- "Paper Gown," Caroline Herring
- "O Death," Gangstagrass (feat. Brandi Hart, R-Son, and Liquid)
- "Country Girl," Carolina Chocolate Drops
- "Long Hard Times to Come," Gangstagrass
- "Throw It Back," Missy Elliott
- "Killing Strangers," Marilyn Manson
- "Joke's On You," Charlotte Lawrence
- "Bad Memory," K. Flay
- "Haunted Heart," Tyminski

AUTHOR'S NOTE

It's a strange place, 2020, when I'm writing this book. We're in the grip of a pandemic. Death tolls are rising. People are frightened, and wanting answers and hope and an end to fear.

I'm in a strange place too. My own personal tunnel is very long, and I'm walking toward the light. I have soft tissue sarcoma, a rare, aggressive, and fast-moving cancer. I'm starting clinical trials with a research center in hopes of finding a way through.

I don't know if this is my last book. I don't know if I'll make it to the light.

But like Gwen, I am on the path. I am walking.

Like Gwen, I have enough love because of people like *you*, who've made it possible for me to be here to tell this story.

If this is the last of Gwen's story, then I hope you feel it was worthwhile. I do.

I wish you well with all my heart.

Choose kindness.

Rachel Caine

ABOUT THE AUTHOR

Photo © 2014 Robert Hart

Rachel Caine is the *New York Times*, *USA Today*, *Wall Street Journal*, and Amazon Charts bestselling author of more than fifty novels, including *Bitter Falls*, *Wolfhunter River*, *Killman Creek*, and *Stillhouse Lake* in the Stillhouse Lake series; the *New York Times* bestselling Morganville Vampires series; the Weather Warden novels; and the Great Library young adult series. She has written suspense, mystery, urban fantasy, science fiction, and paranormal fiction for adults and young adults alike. Rachel lives and works in Fort Worth, Texas, with her husband, artist/actor/comic historian R. Cat Conrad, in a gently creepy house full of books. For more information, visit www.rachelcaine.com.